Avicenna and I: The Journey of Spirits

Avicenna and I:
The Journey of Spirits

A Novel
by
Manoucher Parvin

IBEX Publishers
Bethesda, Maryland

Avicenna and I: The Journey of Spirits
A Novel by Manoucher Parvin

Copyright © 1996, 2006 Manoucher Parvin

ISBN: 1-58814-048-2

All rights reserved. No part of this book may be reproduced or retransmitted in any manner whatsoever except in the form of a review, without permission from the publisher.

Manufactured in the United States of America

First published by Mazda Publishers, Inc.

The paper used in this book meets the minimum requirements of the American National Standard for Infor-mation Services – Permanence of Paper for Printed Library Materials, ANSI Z39.48 1984

Ibex Publishers, Inc.
Post Office Box 30087
Bethesda, Maryland 20824 USA
Telephone: 301-718-8188
Facsimile: 301-907-8707
www.ibexpublishers.com

I dedicate this novel to the immortal path finders who have offered us their mind, labor, and even their blood to make us freer, more enlightened, and more understanding of each other and nature.

Table of Contents

Chapter One: Death in New York 9
Chapter Two: Sitareh 14
Chapter Three: Who is Me? 23
Chapter Four: Love, In Life After Life 32
Chapter Five: The Butterfly Beckons 43
Chapter Six: The Mausoleum 53
Chapter Seven: Forgetting the Memory 60
Chapter Eight: God Is Great 67
Chapter Nine: Immortal Souls in Mortal Bodies 76
Chapter Ten: The Subject is Love 83
Chapter Eleven: Ibn Sina and Us 89
Chapter Twelve: Ala El-Dowleh 100
Chapter Thirteen: The Mind of Love 109
Chapter Fourteen: History in Hypnosis 119
Chapter Fifteen: The Malady 131
Chapter Sixteen: By Candlelight 139
Chapter Seventeen: Delirium 151
Chapter Eighteen: The Prisoner 163
Chapter Nineteen: Joining the Beloved 174
Chapter Twenty: Being and Nothingness 186
Chapter Twenty-One: Reincarnation 200
Chapter Twenty-Two: Upbringing 209
Chapter Twenty-Three: Death Is Beautiful 223
Chapter Twenty-Four: Another Flight 239
Chapter Twenty-Five: Happy Transcendence 255
Appreciation 268
Acknowledgments 269

Chapter One: Death in New York

What must be done must be done. Procrastination is the heritage of the living from the dead, I remind myself. Fear grips me as I drag my laundry to a basement spookier than any medieval dungeon; the residents call it the "mugging room." New York City locks and chains are useless here—there is no door. Like a ruinous castle haunted by vengeful ghosts, the place silently threatens: peeling paint, water-stained wood, stagnant puddles, trapped smoke, echoes of foul language. The yellow light from bulbs too dim to reach into dark corners worries me. The washer and dryer sit like condemned prisoners, each with one gray, glassy eye staring at me. Why must I descend into this dirty hole just to have clean clothes?

"Oh, Pirooz, why are you here? How could you leave a sunny Persian mountainside for New York's sooty walls, the fragrant flower gardens for the garbage heaps? Who, if not you, brought you to this place, to these chaotic times?"

A sock, like a wagging tongue, sticks out of the laundry bag and laughs at me.

My own breathing is the only sound in the room. As I try to load the washer, it seems to beg, "Not on a holiday! I'm tired of work!" Machines have no voices and no rights; even I, a longtime rights activist, know that, as I know that it is hazardous to side with victims. The martyrs and saints would agree.

Suddenly, in the stillness, a knife cutting the thick air—something meant to be unheard, a sneak attack—alarms me. I twist around instinctively, fearing a mugger. Nothing but a giant cockroach gazes up at me, its antennae slashing the fetid air. Provoked by a vicious, primal loathing, I stamp on it, cracking it like a nutshell. The roach oozes brown slime onto the floor.

Hearing ominous steps, I raise my head. Words strike me like bullets: "Dr. Pirooz, did you have to kill it?"

Sitareh Poonia, my Indian neighbor, disapprovingly examines the evidence of my deed. I have often seen plump roaches swaggering securely from her apartment into mine. "This is my choice, not yours, madam," I want to say, but remain as silent as the blob on the floor. Something about her is compelling. Her silky black hair sternly pulled back, her innocent yet knowing eyes, her enigmatic smile, the fire blazing from her bare shoulder attract, agitate, and transfix me. She is young, yet she seems gracefully aged by some mystical experience.

Her British-accented voice rises: "That cockroach may have held the soul of a poet, a scientist, a worker, a Brahmin or Brahman. Now his soul is homeless."

"A Brahman? A poet? In a roach?"

"Yes, yes. It is possible—quite entirely possible, Dr. Pirooz. You must know of the transmigration of souls from body to body. More is expected from a learned person like yourself."

Something beckons me to her, something alluring, even as I remember her indignant frown directed at a can of pesticide in my grocery cart the other day. To allay my uneasiness, I turn to finish loading the washer. With a handkerchief, she picks up the blob, perhaps for cremation or burial. The eye of the machine reflects her, as I think, "What a fury over a cockroach!"

As though reading my mind, she shakes her head and replies, "A life is a life—God's gift!" She hesitates before softly concluding, "Good day, Dr. Pirooz." She reminds me of my mother showering me with kisses after having scolded me for some wrongdoing.

Later, loading the dryer, I hear the soundlessness of another huge cockroach. The insect is looking me straight in the eye. My foot freezes in midair. Apprehensive of Sitareh's return, I bring my foot down gently, careful not to disturb the roach. Kneeling beside it, I notice that it is a female—it lacks the second pair of wings males have. Roaches nurse their young, so she must be looking for food. Her body is a flattened oval, her vestigial brown wings shine, her head and mouth parts bend backward, the threadlike antennae grope. The roach, inches from my nose, seems to taunt me, "You killed my mate." I flee upstairs. I can bring up my laundry later.

That night, the unspoken words, "You killed my mate," rankle as I fall asleep into a nightmare.

I find myself in the center of an enormous dusty arena surrounded by huge swaying trees with grotesque faces printed on their bark. A writhing snake is the rope binding my hands to a lone sunbeam that pierces the clouds. Giant, red-eyed cockroaches march past. A flock of brilliantly colored, tropical cocks-of-the-rock dance in flight. Surrounding me, cocks fight around cocklebur weeds. My skin broils. A capricious wind sweeps the arena without touching me. The roaches chant, "This life is a remnant of many deaths, as each death is a remnant of many lives."

Sitareh, her white silk sari glistening against a turquoise sky, emerges from an orb of light to untie my hands. She flips the twisting snake aside. The roaches disappear. Running her delicate fingers over my moist forehead, she whispers, "Are you all right, my love?"

Instantly I am illuminated within an enormous source of light, like a candle in a chandelier. For a moment my soul is freed of the impediments of my upbringing. Sitareh withdraws her hands and turns to depart.

"Please stay longer," I plead with her, but she just smiles.

"I must go to a world whose inhabitants listen to one another with care."

I wake up distressed and sweating, with the sheets wrapped tightly around me. The hum of New York persists, like the mechanical gasps of a dying man whose agony is prolonged by a respirator. I imagine the roach's corpse stuck to the opposite wall, still steaming. Fearful of the nightmare and ashamed of the mutilation, I stay awake with my eyes tightly shut. Gradually, Sitareh's reassuring presence in my dream relaxes me.

The next day, Dr. Poonia and I talk briefly in the lobby while digging into our mailboxes. We learn we are colleagues at Columbia University. She teaches Indian civilization and history at the South Asian Institute and I teach economics at the Middle East Institute. I tell her that my mother and two brothers, self-exiles like me, live on Long Island and that my father is deceased, and I learn that Sitareh has no family in the U.S. She tells me matter-of-factly, "Every life is an almost impossible occurrence, but mine is more so, since it's the result of a Hindu and a Muslim love."

A couple of days later, wishing to recapture that sense of illumination from my dream, I call Sitareh.

"I wish to have a visit with you, Professor Poonia."

"Certainly, Dr. Pirooz. I have been hoping you would call."

I wonder why, but instead ask, "After dinner?"

"Fine." Then melodiously she adds, "I wish you a good day."

I get ready to go to work. It is difficult to perform even the simplest task for a pretentious job. Like a minister who has lost his faith but preaches the Gospel for a living, or a spouse who makes love from a sense of duty, I teach what I no longer believe, and so am a discontented tiger caged by my expertise. I have an urge to fuse intellectual and moral issues and confirm their inseparability, but morality is an academic taboo. "Whose morality?" the skeptic objects. Life is bewitching, since truth arrives with difficulty and falsehood comes easily, while the necessary compromises corrode my integrity. Society divides and marginalizes us; I am an alien who has apparently succeeded, but the intense effort to make it in a stylized Anglo-Saxon world has worn down my spontaneity and damped my passion. I am becoming a bore, even to myself.

I now want to retrieve the mischievousness stolen from me when, unguarded, I turned my eye away from myself toward success. I struggle not to let my sensations, perceptions and emotions replace thought and intuition, or to let appearances overwhelm me. I now know that the happiness which requires the cooperation of everyone is nearly impossible, and that the easily available unhappiness could be used for self-realization, instead of being wasted in self-pity. But the world is what it is; it is I who must change. My dilemma makes me deliberate about Avicenna, the Sage of All Sages, his wisdom still undiminished after a millennium. Maybe I can learn from him how to overcome imponderable obstacles and to ascend from what I am to what I can be, and want to be. To journey to where I have never been before I must cross the boundaries of doubt and apprehension. The voyage is difficult since man has become a master border-maker and border keeper in his mind, and out of his mind.

Lately, a premonition, like seeing the invisible or hearing what is not yet said, has come over me. I imagine witnessing a bygone era, when only birds could fly, when rivers chose their own paths, when electricity sparkled only in the skies and machines did not rule souls and rape Nature, and when time was not captured, deformed and squeezed into the misguiding history texts.

As you can see, I am opening my heart to you. There is a story behind every heartache. Literary persons may know how to write stories, but only those they know about. Thus, some worthy stories remain untold. I have an urge to tell you my unbelievable saga. I shall be frank with you and, by doing so, risk rejection, or chance acceptance into your heart. I think each one of us is an story that talks, creates, pretends, sticks its tongue out when no one is looking, keeps, or squeals secrets, finds its own wisdom, swings from steady sadness to moments of happiness, and wishes to go where there is more laughter.

I will never forget my teacher's final answer to my pestering, "What is the origin and destiny of all things?"

"God created all things but not all answers, Pirooz. So no one can discover the answers that God never created. That is your answer, Pirooz!"

Disappointed in books and grownups, but not giving up my search, I asked the same question of a thoughtful-looking ostrich fenced in a zoo. It replied, "How should I know, but I die to know how I forgot to fly."

"This is a big question for you, why?"

"I want to go away boy. The zoo is no home. Have you ever tried to lay an egg in public?"

"No." I looked aside, trying to swallow my laughter.

"I am not so dumb a bird that I don't know where I don't want to be," it told me.

"No ostrich is." I never thought then that in exile I would be an ostrich longing to soar beyond the fence but earthbound by weak wings.

Having given up my youthful inquiries, even the search for life's meaning—a mid-life concern—I wish now to ferry myself from knowing what I am not (the rest of the universe) to knowing who I am.

Something stirs in me today. Why am I attracted to Sitareh, whose sanctimony on insects masks her charm? Her eyes hold the wisdom, the secrets and the melancholy of India, and seem to hold me, too. Is love inexplicable because it is everything (and everything can never be explained), or because God simply didn't create the answer for us to discover? There is no one who would refuse love, or who has not thought of killing someone at some time. Anyway, mankind can discover only what exists or create only what is possible. The rest is either sheer fantasy or just mundane stuff. Life consists mostly of doing the mundane and imagining the fantastic. Do I make sense?

Reminding myself that there is a real life besides my imagined one, which demands chores and compromises, I am resigned to reality's intrusions. However, I wish to live an imagined one, even though I am not certain what life is. I am the fenced-in ostrich who doesn't know how to fly, suffers from being fenced in, and is apprehensive of flying into the unknown. I want to ascend, but I don't know how or to where. It is more and more painful for me to pretend and dissimulate, but it is also frightening to withdraw any further from reality. How far can I dream or isolate myself and still be a social being? Feeling my attraction to Sitareh, I wonder how she deals with such dilemmas?

Playing the melancholic tone poem from Turina's Piano Quartet on the stereo and hearing the cello speak of heartache, a declaration inspired by the free-singing gypsies, I wonder, "What happened to the gypsy in each one of us? I could have been a gypsy, or will be someday, who knows?

From my window, I look at Riverside Park and the Hudson River beyond. Autumn is dazzling the world with a magnificent celebration of colors; the foliage is outrageously sensual. There is a thin layer of happiness on everyone's face like in a wedding. The park and the river are bride and groom. The sun showers them with gold dust and I muse: Whose hands embroidered the vivid gown of fall for the bride and the shimmering, flowing gray for the groom? When did they take their vows, and what was the blessing for these eternal mates? Did mankind hear it? I see the river going into the ground, the couple mating, the semen flowing, spring being conceived.

Now there is a puff of wind. Leaves of the same color take flight together, flutter about, then perch on the river's waves or banks. Perhaps they will fly again in different hues and shapes, from different trees into different winds, giddying someone else standing here in my place. Seeing the dimension of time in everything through the window, I realize that I have paid with my youth for the salt and pepper moustache I wear. And yes, this spectacular season in and out of my mind must be called "ascent," not "fall." My wish to ascend flaps its wings inside my mind and takes flight toward mystery.

Chapter Two: Sitareh

I knock at Sitareh's door, which is next to mine on the fifth floor. Smiling, she opens it. We eye one another with curiosity and warmth. I hand her a bouquet of bird of paradise flowers. She thanks me silently. Sitareh wears a yellow sari and holds a rose the same color as the transparent silk burgundy shawl draped over her bare, solid shoulders. Her lips are supple, her pitch black hair long, soft and loose. She invites me in graciously, while glancing at my shoes. I take them off, reminded of the custom at home. A shiver runs through me as she holds my hand briefly to guide me through a dim foyer into a spacious room, sparsely furnished. She places the bouquet in a bronze vase next to a bowl of fruit on the coffee table. The smoky aroma of incense emanates tranquility. Books lie scattered everywhere, but seem to be where they belong. An antique Bukhara *klim* of geometric designs and pale colors covers the floor. From a framed poster a man with incisive eyes gazes through the window into the infinite unknown. He seems deep in thought, or meditation, with a book in his hands, the title barely readable, *The Canon of Medicine.* I stand flabbergasted. Is Sitareh also enchanted with Avicenna, as I am? She seems to note my bewilderment but lets her curiosity pass.

She points to cushions against the wall and a futon on the floor but gently asks, "Do you prefer a chair?" I shake my head no. We sit on the futon at the table and exchange sympathy with our glances. She hands me the rose.

"I like roses, too." I bring the rose to my lips and get a whiff of it.

"I know that. You buy them in bundles," she replies.

"You seem to know everything."

"I wish this were true."

We lose eye contact for a moment and let silence come between us. My inquisitiveness pricks me. What does Avicenna mean to her?

"Sitareh is a Persian name. It means star," I say, breaking the silence.

"Nothing special! There are numerous stars between India and Persia." Then with a twinkle in her eyes she finishes her thought. "A name is a mystery, like the self it represents."

"Right," I agree. "Who knows where the two come from and how they fuse into one personality."

"I enjoy listening to your records, even through the wall," Sitareh changes the subject.

"Thank you," I reply.

"What brings you to me, Pirooz?" she whispers joyfully.

I savor her words 'to me' as I respond, "You must know why I am here."

"I want to know, not just guess," she replies.

"Hopefully time will unveil my intention to you, and to me!"

Smiling, she offers the bowl of fruit, and I take a persimmon, while the golden fruits on our tree back home glitter in my memory. I place the persimmon on a plate.

Her voice softens, "Dr. Pirooz, I do apologize for my outburst in the laundry room. I abhor killing even an unknown roach since in my very bones I feel the truth of reincarnation. Who knows who or what the roach may have been." She takes a deep breath and continues, "Reincarnation conserves spirits, as nature conserves energy, and just as a person casts off a worn garment to put on a new one, the soul casts off a battered body for a fresh one. It is said that in rebirth, the righteous and the wicked receive their just due."

"You mean, one gets what one gives, life after life?"

"Possibly."

"Then the roach may have got the smashing it deserved."

"Maybe, but why do you want to be the executioner?" Her gaze repeats her comment emphatically and makes me both think and doubt.

I visualize my curiosity reflected in an imaginary mirror, egging me on. "Is there any proof of reincarnation?"

"Yes of course. Child prodigies with vast knowledge or wisdom are proof of learning in their previous lives. Ibn Sina, who is known here by his Latinized name, Avicenna, knew the Koran by heart, was court physician, and master of all sciences and philosophy before growing whiskers."

"How do you know about him?" I ask, prying.

"My parents, both physicians, admired Ibn Sina's medical philosophy and practice. They encouraged me to pursue medicine and learn about his life and ideas. His Persian name, Sina, has a Sanskrit root. It refers to a wise, healing phoenix who nests on a mountain peak in the tree of life, whose seeds can cure any disease. The mythical bird is also mentioned in the *Avesta*, the sacred book of Zoroaster."

"The coincidence of the Sina, the name, and the wise healer, the person, is startling; a mystery, just as you said, Sitareh."

"Maybe the man was the bird," she declares enigmatically.

"You mean Ibn Sina was the reincarnation of a myth—a mythical bird?"

"Why not?" A dimple appears in her mysterious smile. Pointing to the poster, she continues, "I love healers. To him, healing was humane, but self-realization was life's reward and mission."

"Why didn't you follow your parents' advice to become a physician?"

"Frankly, Pirooz, I am unable to witness pain and death day after day."

"You wish then to heal wounded souls like mine?" I grin from thought to thought.

"Oh, my suffering Pirooz!" We break into laughter. Finally she answers, "I wish for a voyage to beyond healing for all of us." She hands me two books from the shelf, *The Philosophy and Medicine of Avicenna* and *The Eastern Foundation of Western Civilization*.

"You wrote these books while still so young!" I exclaim.

She looks downward modestly and says, "I was a schoolgirl ages ago."

After a long pause, she finally confides, "I have a reason to show you my work. Lately, a voice has been urging me to visit Ibn Sina's grave in Hamadan. I want to place my chest against his burial place and feel the earth with my heart." She falls silent, as though already gone to Hamadan.

Visualizing her listening to the heartbeat of Hamadan, I suddenly feel a longing for home, too. I had spent several summers in Hamadan as a child.

"You have been in Hamadan before?" She reads my mind; she is amazing.

"Yes." She waits for me to speak. "Ibn Sina's accomplishments were nearly impossible," I comment with renewed wonder.

"Not nearly, *simply* impossible without reincarnation! Some of his learning must have been just a review of what he already knew from another life."

"But did he know that he knew?"

"Most probably he did not."

"Does the reincarnated soul know its former lives?"

"Not usually."

"Why not?"

"Possibly to forestall bitterness flowing from one life to another."

"Are there any exceptions?"

"Certainly! Exceptions do appear as substantiated claims by some reincarnated individuals."

"You are so certain of your beliefs," I protest mildly

"If I am not, who will be?" Her mysterious dimple reappears.

"Do Hindus believe in God?" A moment transpires, like when souls transmigrate from one body to another.

"We have no specific prophets, holy book, universal dogma, or god. Our myriad gods and goddesses are reflections of a creative light." Sitareh glances at the poster and recites a poem:

> But after all, who knows, and who can say
> Whence it all came, and how creation happened?
> The gods themselves are later than creation;
> So who knows truly whence it has arisen?

"Gods after, not before, creation?" I inquire.

"I mentioned gods, not the God who created reincarnation and evolution to perfect his creatures over time. Evolution is the gene's response to natural challenges, while reincarnation is the spiritual response to life's many difficulties. Perfection is the goal of both processes."

"Ibn Sina maintained that man is capable of becoming a perfect being," I add. Sitareh nods in agreement, but my skepticism awakens. "Still, the existence of the soul is not proven."

"Science will never explain everything," she asserts.

Persisting, I ask, "If evolution and reincarnation together determine the here and the hereafter, then what is left of free will for humankind?"

"As far as I know," she declares in measured words, "only humans decide for humans on earth. Anyway, all things in life are constrained—so is freedom. We are condemned, or perhaps blessed, to choose from what is possible. I imagine that the anguish of unbounded freedom is similar to the anguish of death."

"One confronting us with the agony of infinite choices and the other with infinite nothingness," I interrupt.

"They surely appear that way."

"So what is possible—different and finite for each person—is his or her fate," I conclude.

"True." She returns to her thoughts. "A choice opens some opportunities and closes others. Each minute can be spent only one way. Every human action embodies this dilemma, this trade-off—the essence of the free will."

Silence stretches the space between our thoughts. "Music! I forgot music!" She stands and glides to the record player. Instantly the magical sound of a sarod mixes with the aroma of incense.

My doubts returning I comment, "So the exercise of free will constricts free will!"

"Yes." She crosses her legs, as though enraptured by the mystery of the evening raga, and recites a prayer like a poem:

> From the unreal lead me to the real
> From darkness lead me to light
> From death lead me to eternal life.

"What is the ultimate goal of rebirth?" I ask, feeling like a student.

"Another chance to become perfect, to promote unity with love. I hope that in a future life I shall embrace all of humanity in one hug."

A long pause offers me a chance to observe Sitareh's lush lemon and avocado plants. "Embracing everyone in one big hug?" I ask teasingly.

"Yes," she replies with solemn finality.

I decide to open up myself a bit more. "Sitareh. . ."

"Yes, Pirooz."

"Like a wind with a broken wing, I want to go everywhere, but I am not going anywhere. Who would care to hug me—an exile—who doesn't know why he is where he is."

"Me, Pirooz, me! I care to hug you. I have already done that in my imagination." She beams lovingly at me while the sound of her "me's" hug my name in my unbelieving and dancing ears. I feel a cosmic warmth within me. I hold her hands in mine over the coffee table and then kiss them one by one.

Withdrawing her hand gently, and smiling mischievously, she asks, "Any more questions? Heartaches, Pirooz?"

"You seem to be more interested in the question 'Who am I?' than 'What is humanity?'" I tell her. "The journey of the self, not that of mankind, or womankind."

"Womankind and all! A feminist-conscious Eastern male! Let me check my senses, Pirooz! You are a dream, or perhaps the beginning of a new species." Sitareh breaks into hearty laughter.

"It is my next reincarnation that speaks." I say, playing along.

"You may not be serious, but I take you seriously, Pirooz. I choose to unite my inner self and outer self into a selfhood, to forestall identity crises and self-deception." She hesitates and asks, "Am I boring you?"

"No, no, not at all. I asked the questions. I am learning, but my selfhood is still allergic to roaches," I grin.

Sitareh grins, too. "I have allergies, too, even to people, but killing is not the only answer."

I pick up my persimmon and bite into it. "How does a poet's soul in a roach's body prove ascendance, Sitareh?"

"Progress, even of the soul, meets setbacks in reincarnations. You have misgivings, but that is natural. Remember," she assures me calmly, "belief in reincarnation bestows hope to existing decimated lives."

"If the Day of Judgment is the end, then I think God will absolve our wrongdoing, and we will forgive Him for the miseries He caused and we suffer from. Then, God and man, the creator and the creature, who were separated at the moment of creation, will rejoin each other and live in unity happily ever after."

"A wonderful story, Pirooz."

"Life is a story." Our smiles seem to hug each other. I change the subject. "What do you do with your leisure time?"

"I help at a home for children."

"And I know you are a feminist."

"Humanist is a better term. What more, Pirooz?"

"But what of fun?"

"That is fun! I also do yoga, play the sitar, sing, visit friends, go to the theater and movies, and dream of love."

"Dream of love?" I ask.

"Yes, love is worth dreaming about, isn't it?"

"Yes."

"And what do you do, Pirooz?"

"I am trying to learn who I am and what I must do, and to discover how Ibn Sina achieved self-realization."

"What else, Pirooz?"

I keep silent. Sitareh accepts it.

Soon she serves tea and biscuits and we talk about life in New York City, where I think people are links in a chain of weirdness. Neither of us is sure why we are here. Sitareh points to the poster and whispers, "Who knows? Maybe just for the three of us, you and I and Ibn Sina, to come together. Every effect has infinite causes. You know that, Pirooz."

Sitareh's intensity and freedom from tedium, apathy, and fear are refreshing. Her words, "the three of us," dropped like a stone in a pond, to sink deeper and deeper in me. I shudder, for they seem more than mere words.

"Anyway," she continues, "one's attachment to home or anything worldly is crippling. We must try to waft through space and time like free spirits. Adventure is a risk for growth. Real danger lies not in the risk but in the fear of it. Clinging to illusion is more perilous than facing the fact. Home is only an illusion of security. As you know, Ibn Sina wandered about, too."

"He had to, Sitareh."

"Why do you say that?"

I shrug my shoulders. "I'm not sure."

We talk late into the night. At last I confess to her, "I am a misunderstood exile who dreams of an island where understanding rules and the roots of everything are known. Thoughts of death heighten my consciousness of another world. I have been reading up on Ibn Sina."

"Me, too. What a synchronicity."

"At the moment I wish I were not an intellectual," I complain.

"Why?"

"Because I get so lost in ideas that my feelings lose me."

"They cry out for help and company, don't they?" Sitareh stretches her exquisite hands to me as a smile dances over her glowing face. Something wonderful spreads through me.

"New York imposes loneliness, especially on new arrivals like me," she confesses.

"Tell me more," I respond.

"After years in medical practice in London, my parents returned to their birth town. I wrote those two books at Oxford, and then I wandered here. Hearing your Indian music, I wondered if you would ever try to get acquainted with your Indian neighbor, Pirooz."

"I wanted to, but I wasn't sure if my aloof neighbor wished the same, and . . ."

"And you were thwarted by the reputation of Indian women, too."

"What is that?" I inquire.

"A lifelong forbearance and resoluteness for the little girls who have survived infanticide. Women of India link the old and the new like patient bridges. Our history walks over us Indian women ever so slowly, ever so carelessly, and ever so heavily."

"Yes, Sitareh, Indian women are more patient than stone bridges."

"I doubt you mean that, Pirooz," she says with an infectious grin.

"No, no! I do! I have been in India. I've seen and know enough. But what shores do you span, Sitareh?" I ask joyfully.

"Don't get me started again, Pirooz!" She hesitates before adding, "Have you been pulling my leg?"

"No, certainly not intentionally."

She casts a curious glance at me. "What is in your heart, Pirooz?"

"You!"

Sitareh murmurs, "At first our meeting was only darkness wrapped in darkness, and now it is a light among lights." Her ideas make me glow like a candle in a chandelier. I notice that she notices a longing for intimacy in my eyes.

Glancing down shyly, she pursues her inquiry. "Then what is on your mind?"

"The whereabouts of the spirits you speak of so assuredly."

"What do you mean?" she asks.

Now I show the teeth of my apparently hibernating skepticism. "I believe man is made of matter only and is sustained by matter exclusively; science is the key, and spirit is a wonderful hope, a fantasy, or just a delightful word."

A bit shocked, Sitareh looks deeper into me. "Let us try to get to know the spirit, with no preconceptions, as though we were children; shall we?"

"Let's," I reply almost competitively.

"Do you agree that over eons stardust evolved into organic matter, into living matter, into the brain and the mind?"

"Yes, that is evolution. But what do you conclude from it?"

"Since the mind performs miracles beyond the necessities of mere survival, then evolution must have journeyed beyond biology. So the spirit is the evolution of the mind," Sitareh says. "This final ascendance is no more unbelievable than the stardust evolving into you and me, and into the feelings in this room, and our recounting the story of the stardust itself! Thus man is both matter and spirit, just like sunlight, which is both particle and wave. Photosynthesis creates nutrients, and digestion transforms them into us, into our willpower and emotions and creativity—the human spirit. Thus does the inanimate become animate, and creation is repeated every day."

"You acknowledge matter existing before spirit, then." I cling to something I cannot abandon, but I feel a bit rattled.

"Sure! If you will accept the spirit, I will accept the primacy of matter, even though massless particles do exist." She smiles joyfully, having entrapped me by her logic and holism.

"Oh, my mind!" I mumble.

"You mean, oh, my spirit," she nails the point lovingly.

For a moment, everything appears unrealistic to me, like when I had a high fever in childhood. The bouquet of bird-of-paradise flowers seems to grow out of the coffee table like an oak dressed in colorful autumn leaves. I rub my eyes, concentrate, and resume our intoxicating conversation.

"Ibn Sina also tried to unify matter and spirit," I declare, as though trying to awaken myself.

He will unite us, too. I hear her unspoken thought. A long silence prevails, as though we have climbed separate mountains. I feel alone.

"Any objections?" she asks.

"You are quite a professor, Sitareh!"

"You mean I lectured you."

"All thought-provoking."

"I see." She covers her eyes with both hands and continues, "Forgive me, Pirooz. Unaware, I must have tried to impress you."

"Look, Sitareh, look at my happiness. You are the cause of it. I am more than impressed, and there is nothing to forgive."

Her tiny smiles appear and disappear, attempting to hide themselves from me as I await her response. "Anyway, Pirooz, it is time for me to ask questions and listen to you, but we must do that another time."

Like a flock of birds that instantly depopulates a tree, we rise together. At the door, she offers her cheek to me and I kiss both cheeks and then her lips. She is mildly surprised, but does not pull away.

In my apartment, half asleep on the couch, I realize that Sitareh's sensuality, intellect and spirit have sparked a fire in me. Even her handshake. My lips on her lips, the idea, the reality make me thirst for her even more. Happiness flows through me. I feel like an exile who is finally understood and embraced by strangers.

I imagine the cockroach pleading before being crushed. What did Sitareh do with the corpse? Will I ever know its true identity? Did I free its soul from an encasement ordained by its past lives? The human nervous system bears a detailed resemblance to that of a cockroach, who has existed for over two hundred million years, while the prototype for man was still being designed. To whom does the earth belong, to us who poison it?

Such thoughts are no longer silly, since they are keeping me awake tonight. Curiosity thrusts me toward distant speculations, where a grim stirring awaits. What has gotten into me, anyhow? For a revealing moment I realize that the *perceived* universe and the mind have evolved together interdependently. Is the mind just an observer, or a mirror that the universe fashioned to examine itself? All of a sudden, life as the descent of stardust from the heavens, and its metamorphosis into spirit on earth, and death as the ascendance of the same spirit to the heavens, seem plausible. From stardust to stardust, down and back up.

Sitareh speaks to me of love and light, and what is good and what is not. Thank God someone I know in New York is not value-free. I am ready for a big celebration, thirsty for all the alcohol in the Milky Way.

I feel drawn to Sitareh, as a voyager is drawn to the North Star for guidance, to home, to the beloved. But who is she to me: friend, guru, lover, fellow spiritual journeyer? Would we journey to the city of understanding together? Wrapped within my apprehension, hope flickers like a flame encased in a block of ice. Her confidence and purposefulness are quite unusual. She seems to know me, to have known me before we met. I did indeed hear her unsaid words, "Ibn Sina will unite us." Was this my wishful thinking? Is the physics I learned with dedication and faith invalid, or just a part of truth? Where, I wonder, do science and spirituality intersect? Am I going insane or ascending to a higher level of sanity? Is the first case a prerequisite for the second? Did I find the North Star in a decaying laundry room?

Another question leaps forward like a ballerina: if knowledge can flow from one life into another, can love do the same? Is instant love just the rediscovery of a pre-existing one? Does reincarnation conserve love as it conserves cause, effect and soul? Can love be less enduring than a rose's fragrance, which will live forever? Does love live or die with the lovers? Have Sitareh and I met before?

Chapter Three: Who is Me?

The next day I call my mother. She lives with my brother at the tip of Long Island, and mocks Manhattan as the center of Western civilization. We became self-exiles from monarchy and remain so because of theocracy. After some sweet and sour talk, I fish for sympathy, flinging out my frustration. "Beggars, psychotics and criminals rule the streets! The noise is stifling, the air chokes, the tension rises, brains boil, politicians campaign for everything but fair campaigns, and the Salvation Army tries to jingle problems away. New York is taking its revenge on the residents for being grossly neglected."

"Is this the voice of a stranger?" my brother interrupts from an extension.

"No," I respond. "A beggar, with lice streaming from his ears, sores all over his lips, and encrusted eyes that crack when closed, froze to death in public."

I hear a chilled silence, and I know what it means. "Can't you live at the periphery of New York, my son?" my mother pleads.

I answer, "It may be hell, but it is my hell. Besides, I like being invisible without having to hide. And I am old enough . . ."

"My children are always children to me. Also, be careful with that Indian lady you met."

"You mean I should fear my neighbor?"

"You could be swallowed whole before being tasted."

"You are talking about a shark, Mother."

"I am speaking of reality, Son. I have never known an Indian who didn't want something from me."

"I'll pretend I didn't hear that, Mother," I protest mildly.

"Pretend to your heart's desire, my dear son," she replies softly.

An old anger emerges to sour my throat, but I suppress it, never doubting that she loves me and that her uncanny sense of danger is often on the mark. I say my good-byes before she can suggest what fruit and vegetable juices I need most.

The avoided juice lecture reminds me of my broken refrigerator—a reality. I call the building super. He will be up to fix the machine in a couple of hours. I get busy cleaning up the place, as I would for my mother's arrival. I succumb to what I protest and resist—projecting an image. Quickly I pick up the scattered papers and books, vacuum the floor, dust the brass and glass coffee table, and remove the dead roses from their crystal vase. I think of our old rose bushes back home in Teheran, and of the roses that have journeyed to this vase for their last, brief show. In Persia, rose water is used in ice cream, cookies, weddings, funerals, religious ceremonies and more. And in immortal Persian poems, the rose and canary are lovers. My old canary, a dear friend, died recently. I am too sad to just replace her with another canary. I miss her perching on my index finger to chirp her thoughts, joys and heartaches, and I miss her claws on my bare shoulder.

I breathe easier under the high ceilings of this old building now that the apartment is tidy. The big window is a trusted friend. Through it I watch the world without the world watching me. My apartment is caught between sky and river; I can see life below and infinity above. Life on earth is just a grain of dust, with eyes and ears and minds asking unanswerable questions of an eternally tongue-tied infinity. The cosmos' persistent hum is the moan of the primordial atom, the oneness of all things, at being shattered into this world. Or maybe we are deaf to the cosmos or to ourselves. How long, I wonder, will we remain blind to our own deafness?

I wish that evolution and reincarnation would hurry and perfect all the imperfections. My mother once said, "Pirooz, the world must spin the opposite way to right any wrongs, and all you can do is to spin yourself. One must live the best possible life in a crooked world one is born into. There is little time to straighten the world out, and great odds against it." So for my peace of mind now I dismiss the question, why do I exist, because the answer could expose my insignificance in this world. If it does not matter if I ever existed then I'm already dead, while still breathing.

I look around. Prints by Dali, Chagall, Gauguin, and Picasso cover my walls. My sparse furniture appears as lonely as ever. I see my future in my old, sagging, creaky rocking chair, and notice that, with their withered leaves, my plants are telling me of their needs. I whisper my love to the plants as I water them and then scan the tidied-up room with satisfaction. The blue-eyed super will not think ill of me now; my mother would approve, too.

After buzzing, the door opens on its own. It is the super. He replaces a fuse and leaves with a strange smile; he knows I cannot fix anything. I imagine him wondering, "What can Pirooz teach? How can he help anyone, when he is so helpless himself?" He doesn't suspect my secret: I was born to be a teacher. My students' course evaluation gives me a rave review, although I seem to know nothing and doubt everything.

I have run out of cash, but resent standing in a long line to get my own money back. I collect some change from various pockets and forget about the bank for one more day.

With no classes today, I go for a jog, and later, after a hearty meal of vegetables, fruits, cheese and bread, head out for cappuccino and daydreams at a nearby cafe. I daydream every day, for I find it therapeutic. My imagined world, my own heaven, accepts me without reservation. Heaven exists only in one's imagination, since God's heaven cannot please everyone. He didn't give us the same tastes on earth, and presumably He won't in heaven, either.

Ignoring my surroundings on my way to the cafe, unless I am forced to sidestep something, I hear only Sitareh's British accent in my mind: "We feel things we cannot see. Like souls. If we mourn when the living die, then we must celebrate when what has died comes alive."

That is the reason Persians celebrate spring's first day with the *Now-Ruz* [New Day], since what had died has come alive," I think to myself.

The dance-like movements of Sitareh's hands, the purity of her convictions, and the intensity of her resolve rejuvenate my spirit. With her mysterious smile in mind, I imagine climbing the mountain of hope and letting her tend to my longings at the peak. Up in the clouds, her sari seems woven by her truth. It covers her except for slivers of flesh. Then the gusts of my desire billow her sari away. Who is it that her skin, the object of my desire, covers? What about mine? I wonder about our skins together, mine light brown and hers darker brown, side by side. Do they match? Do we match?

Compulsively, I gulp down my cappuccino and rush home to the full-length mirror on the back of the door. I have not looked in it for some time. I am still tall and fit, but my eyes, elongated and weary, match in weariness my drooping moustache. My black hair is graying at the edges and receding, and my slightly big nose shines with a new happiness and anticipation of more. My face has no wrinkles, not yet, although there are wrinkles in my heart. Will Sitareh like me? Does she care about appearances? Is there anyone who does not?

More questions bother me. Why did my foot stop in midair and let the second cockroach live? Is it a new soul of mine that holds my old sole at bay? What about the pesticide Sitareh saw me buy? Can I ever use it? The spoken words, "Now a soul is homeless," and the unspoken ones, "You killed my mate," unnerve me. If a roach is not just a roach, then what is it? The question keeps returning. Meanwhile, without much deliberation, I begin shying away from meat.

To whom—in a world overwhelmed by immorality—can I confide my new cockroachian moral crisis without being laughed at? My silly obsession takes root. Setting aside urgent chores to seek the shores of history and reincarnation, I head toward my cubicle in the massive Butler Library.

I collect an armload of books, and, like intellectual quicksand, swallow words and ideas insatiably. I learn that reincarnation is not a flower, but a garden, perceived and nurtured differently by different minds. "A Rose blooms, withers, and dies, but it leaves a fragrance alive forever, and so does a person; his soul will not wither away," I read. I still doubt it, but Sitareh's version is more appealing: reincarnation is a spiritual school and court of justice; learning from justice and justice by learning; man and God uniting through the soul's attainment of perfection. Even the Koran alludes to reincarnation: "God creates beings and sends them back over and over again, till they find Him."

I tentatively approach the comforting but perhaps false notion that the end of one's life is not the end of everything. After all, what is the next world, and who is there? Why do I keep pondering, if reincarnation is a mere word and not a re-creative force of the universe? Since my being was not impossible once, then I may come into existence again.

I abandon my daily affairs for long hours of reading and reflection in my library cubicle, returning home only to sleep.

One Friday, as the sun sets colorfully and gracefully. I lug an armload of books to my cubicle and turn on the light to read about Ibn Sina's great scholarly feats. His titles were *Shaykh al-Rais* (Leading Wise Man) and *Hojat al-Hagh* (Reason of God) in the East, and Prince of Medicine and Philosopher of Being in the West. Roger Bacon and Descartes expressed their deep admiration and indebtedness to Ibn Sina, and called him the Prince of Philosophers. Ibn Sina warned of the limitations of logic or experiments, in contrast to leaps of intuition, since the analysis of a single fact in isolation may yield misleading conclusions about the whole. He wanted to expose universal truths, a theory of everything, since all things are interrelated, but he couldn't—he ran out of time, though not before seeding modern medicine with his ideas.

Exhausted from my ruminations, I rest my head on an unopened biography of Ibn Sina written in his own time and fall asleep.

Dreaming, I find myself in a valley at the foot of a mountain that wears snow like a glittering silk gown; billowing clouds crown the cool peak. The mountain is blue granite on granite slashed by veins of white quartz. Mount Alvand overlooks the ancient city of Hamadan, where my mother was born and married. My family vacationed there when we lived in Teheran, before time exiled me to adulthood and fate exiled me to New York. In the foreground a placid pond and a tortuous path worn smooth by horses' hooves lie silent. Stories abound of ancient travelers who lost their way in snowstorms and perished on such passages.

I remember a pond of my boyhood, frowning, disturbed, when I skipped stones on its face. Once, in a tall oak nearby, a crow attacked me, to defend her nest in the treetop. I never again climbed that tree so high. I look around. The trees of summer flaunt their yellow blush of nectarines or the orange and red of peaches and apples. The warm, clear air suddenly turns dark and cold. A snowfall swallows the summer in one gulp. My surroundings begin to disappear into the whiteness. What can I do? I am not afraid, exactly, but I am alone. Sometimes that amounts to the same thing.

Mountains of dark clouds are about to clash. A thunderbolt cracks. A sky-gate opens to a deeper vastness. I hear a clear voice approaching.

"Gorgani, Gorgani."

I look around but can see no one, no one at all. Who is calling, and to whom? Fear of the invisible, the unknown, brings a quiver to my heart. Peering into the depth of the blizzard, I notice an impressive man emerge from the swirling wind. He is bearded, with the clear face of an Irish saint, he wears a burgundy robe and his white hair falls to his shoulders. He smiles mischievously. His gentle eyes under thick, graying eyebrows sparkle with vitality.

He halts a few steps from me, gazes skyward, and murmurs, "Whoever turns from your path, my God, will never find glory." Then he sweeps his hands in a wide arc, dispersing the clouds. In a flash, his now ringing, joyful voice returns. "Gorgani, it is me. Me, Ibn Sina! It has been over a thousand years since we last met."

I am stunned but manage to mutter, "Ibn Sina?"

"Yes, Gorgani. Here. Now."

"But I am Pirooz, not Gorgani," I protest, as if that would quell my anxiety.

"Don't you recognize me, Gorgani?" he asks disappointedly as he steps toward me.

I back away cautiously. Why does he keep calling me by this strange name? I finally recognize him as the man in the poster. I reply eagerly, "Yes, yes, I know about you, Ibn Sina, but who is Gorgani?"

Smiling, he produces from the folds of his robe a painting of himself standing beside a bearded man in a cloak who holds gray prayer beads. I rub my eyes in disbelief, but the man who stares back at me from the picture is me. Me, wearing a clergyman's robe, bearded and holding beads. A "me" that I never knew existed.

"This is you, isn't it—my dear friend and biographer?" Ibn Sina declares triumphantly.

"Yes, it looks like me, but I am not your biographer."

"You certainly were. Remember? We worked together for twenty-five years. First you were my student, then my colleague." A delightful laugh fills the valley, reverberating off Mount Alvand. His eyes brimming with a brilliance that I recall seeing before, he declares, "I see, I see. My God, I missed the obvious, the human condition. You recognize me and everything around you, but not yourself. Ha! 'To know thyself' challenges all of us."

I shudder. "Recognition, recognition . . ." a call grows vociferously in me. "I must recognize the past. I must recognize myself!" But who was I before I was born? The idea cuts through my beliefs like a sword.

Ibn Sina's voice rises. "Nevertheless, Gorgani, I am pleased you recognize me after a thousand years."

Numerous questions crowd my mind, but I can only nod.

"Do you remember our surprise, Gorgani, that your birthday, inscribed in your family Koran, was the very day of the death of my father?"

More relaxed, I protest, "Call me Pirooz, please."

"Very well, Pirooz. But who knows who you were before Gorgani, or who you will be in the next life. As Lady Sitareh told you, 'One may be reincarnated as oneself or someone else, or as a butterfly, a whale or a notion lost in an ocean.'"

Shocked, I ask, "How do you know about Sitareh?"

"I cannot reveal it now, but I will in the future, *En-shaw-Allah* [God willing]."

There is finality in his tone, so I do not insist. The past, the olden times, stream into me like the first shaft of light to penetrate a tunnel being dug inside a mountain, and places and times focus into a unity. I ask, "Are you reincarnated like me?"

"Not that I know of," Ibn Sina says dejectedly. "Before His Grand Meditation, God constituted a Supreme Angelic Council and bestowed upon it His power of life and death and reincarnation, but angelic disputes have torn the council apart; factions have commissioned contradictory prophets and holy books, causing confusion and wars on earth, while adversaries foolishly appeal to the same God for victory. So the angels cannot agree on my reincarnation."

"Why is that?" I respond mechanically.

"Since I denied reincarnation while I lived, some angels wish to deny me reincarnation now that I am dead."

"What is wrong with being wrong?"

"Everything! The angels consider ignorance from someone so generously endowed as myself an insult. The problems in Heaven are alarming. The angels are copying souls to stuff into bodies."

"So the world contains more humans and less humanity!" I mutter in disbelief.

"Exactly, Gorgani. An unfolding tragedy," he responds.

"Why do they copy souls?"

"Because only God can create new souls, and, as I said, He is meditating."

"Perhaps She," I interrupt.

"She! Good God! Him a female! Perhaps so, though I never suspected it. This proves the power of one's upbringing. God, a She, could have conceived the universe and given it birth. Perhaps God, the Father and the Mother simultaneously!" he says to himself.

After a long pause I ask, "What is hell?"

"Infinite conflict and zero understanding, I have heard."

Earth is halfway there, I think to myself, and ask, "And heaven?"

"The opposite of hell."

"I wish I knew what was happening up there."

"And I wish I knew all that is happening down here."

I must try to warn him, "Listen, Avicenna—"

"Call me Ibn Sina. It is my real name."

"I am sorry. It was a slip of the tongue. But now I can recall your full name and title: the Shaykh al-Rais Abu Ali Husain ibn Abd-Allah ibn Hasan ibn Ali ibn Sina."

Ibn Sina lifts his brow. "And I can recall yours: the Shaykh Abu Ubayd Abdul Wahid Gorgani." He returns to my unfinished comment. "Gorgani, you were about to disagree."

"Yes. Science and philosophy have made great strides since ancient times, and, even though you were a prodigy among prodigies in history, I now know more about certain sciences than you. Facts are facts, as you used to say."

"Give me an example," he demands.

"Well, you were wrong about the angels moving the planets in orbit."

"Who does it, then?"

"No one. Gravity is a terrestrial attraction that draws them together."

"How does a physical body know that it itself or the other exists before attracting it?"

"I am afraid I don't know the answer," I reply.

"Has anyone seen, heard, touched, smelled, tasted gravity?"

"Well, no, but no one has seen, smelled or tasted archangels, either."

His hearty laughter fills the space around us. Finally he resumes, "Then gravity, or 'angel-avity,' is the angelic pull of celestial bodies on invisible strings." He grins.

"Gravity as 'angel-avity.' Someone ought to know the difference," I think.

Ibn Sina whispers, "You know, I was wrong to think and teach that death frees the soul to complete and perfect itself. In death one crystallizes until rebirth."

Ibn Sina seems a bit disturbed. "What is wrong?" I ask.

"Nothing." He hugs me, and whispers in my ear, "I shall see you again in Hamadan, the omniscient city where our souls last parted."

"Why do you call it the omniscient city?"

"*Hama* means all and *dan* means knowing—the city of all-knowing."

"Ibn Sina, just a moment, please," I beg.

"Yes, what is it, Gorgani?"

"I have two questions."

"Yes?"

"A few days ago I killed a cockroach in the laundry room. Is it possible to know its identity?"

"Possibly."

"And how do I get in touch with you?"

"Construct a road of awareness and journey on it to me."

"Please be specific!" I implore him.

"'God is great' are the key words, and my tomb in Hamadan is the key place. And remember to forget you have seen me; not a word of this to anyone." Suddenly he disappears, spiraling into the skies and entering a gate far above the mountaintop.

My dream ends. I wake groggy, lost in a sea of unfamiliar thoughts. I begin to consider the impossible. Perhaps I do share the same soul, and, by coincidence, nearly the same appearance as Gorgani. I pick up the biography that I presumably wrote a thousand years ago. Now I find it in English. How amazing. Distracted, I leave the library for home, walking with contradictory thoughts bubbling in my head. I talk to myself: "No! This was just a dream, a movie I created in my mind, and nothing more."

Gradually I sense the street's vibration, the crowd's counter-purposes clashing around me, smell the laundry's ammonia, hear scream-like honking, see the chaotic rushing, and sidestep a speaker who shouts, "Atheists are the loneliest!" Inserting a quarter into the outstretched hand of a young man in rags, I sense dying dreams, detect greedy thoughts, and hear a fragment of a conversation of passersby: "You must insure everything nowadays." "But you can't insure sanity!" I ignore the happenings but remember my mother's plea, "Leave Manhattan, the center of Western civilization, and live on Long Island, the periphery, my son."

I enter my building imagining Sitareh freeing me from the snakes in my cockroach dream. Were the snakes a symbol of false notions pinning down my soul? The programming of my brain by my upbringing? Should I cling to my old beliefs or trust what I have just seen in my dream of Ibn Sina? My dilemma could be anyone's: believe in what I see, or adhere to what I am taught. The anguish of illusion—what is real and what is not—flares in me. I look around the lobby. For a desolate moment it seems that I am canoeing up a worn river to an unknown city, where fates are in turmoil, and metamorphoses are ordinary events. I imagine my friends on shore waving good-bye.

To whom have I pledged silence? To Ibn Sina, to angels, to whom? I am apprehensive of the gravity of my predicament.

I manage to reach the elevator, and sense I am in the real world. Elevators are like places of worship: almost everyone holds a solemn posture and grave silence as the cabin ascends or descends. I feel a prayer welling up. Why does an atheist think of worship?

Sitareh steps into the elevator behind me. She wears a spectacular blue sari with yellow border, and she looks serene. Her smile is charming and more mysterious yet, as though she knows what I also know. I feel somewhat relieved. She absorbs me with a more than approving smile, sensuous like an old wine served on a special occasion. I smile back, my heart quivering with joy.

Mysteriously, the question dawns on me, "Have we been in love before?"

The ice between us quickly melts under a rainbow of mystery and love. The elevator hoists us high, higher, beyond the clouds, beyond gravity, where a mere glance makes one float in the desired direction in the skies, into the beginnings, into eternity. I feel lost in ecstasy. She sees that; she seems to see everything.

We step out of the elevator. She holds me with her eyes for a moment and asks, "Will you come for dinner this Saturday night?"

"Yes, with pleasure. Thank you."

"And will you join me for a sarod recital this Wednesday?"

"How could I refuse this offer."

"That settles it, then."

Feeling elevated even higher, I barely hear her say goodnight.

In my apartment I think, We have so much to talk about, so much to learn about each other. Then I remember my own rationale for reincarnation: whatever happens once is not impossible, so it can happen again and could have happened before.

The next morning I muse, "I will try to know Sitareh and find Ibn Sina, but who knows whom I will know and what I will find. But I am certain that love and not anguish will be my guide."

Chapter Four: Love, In Life After Life

On Wednesday, at the sarod recital, I become lost between two ecstasies: Ali Akbar's heavenly music, and Sitareh's profound beauty. I wonder what I have done to deserve the bliss. What must I do to preserve it? When will I be released from my pledge of silence to Ibn Sina? I want to tell her everything. Am I fashioning a world out of a mere dream?

My dream of Ibn Sina signals the momentous awakening of history within me. I realize that, while my life will be tossed around as in a whirlwind, I must keep my pledge of silence to Ibn Sina for as long as he wishes it, lest he lose his confidence in me. Unable to sleep, I get up to watch Saturday's arrival through the window. The morning flaunts an exuberant sun and a pale moon on its lapels, gloriously heightening my bewilderment.

Later, at dusk, the sun bends over backwards to recover its playful beams, but they cling to the golden hair of schoolgirls, the treetops, the wings of seagulls, and the masts rising above sailboats. This sun is too permissive, I think. Waiting to see Sitareh tonight, my impatience welcomes the stern shadows that hurriedly rake up the stubborn sun's rays and pile them in the sun's backpack. The sun, the gilded journeyer, kisses the horizon good-bye and leaves a crimson smudge on its cheek.

I savor the inspiring view as I await the evening with Sitareh. But somehow I distrust my new good fortune.

As I turn on the light, inner voices of curiosity and uncertainty turn to nagging and gnawing at my new happiness. Read the road signs, Pirooz! Observe the rules of the pilgrim's path and beware the chasm between dream and reality.

After glancing at my watch, I leave for Sitareh's apartment with a bouquet of roses. She guides me in as my hand trembles in hers. The living room is touched with a wondrous scent.

"I hope you are in good spirits, Pirooz." She breaks her graceful silence, while placing the flowers in a turquoise ceramic vase. On the shelf, a Koran sits comfortably beside the four sacred books of the *Vedas*. She notes my observation and smiles. "You are such a spirit.".

"A heavy one!" I answer, as she grins.

"Spirits are not heavy, just estranged. They are exiles in this world, as we are exiles in New York," she says; her words bringing me instant comfort.

As the night deepens, a pair of huge candles burn themselves down for us. Then late, late in the evening, Sitareh leaves briefly, to return with a sitar in her arms. She sits cross-legged on a mat against some cushions. I sit opposite her beside a big-bellied brass urn holding a lush lemon tree. A jug of wine, the blue and orange candlelight and our mutual enchantment are all reflected across the belly of the urn. We gaze into each other's souls.

"I love the sitar and the mind that gives it music," I say.

She smiles at me, "Don't discount the hands, Pirooz."

She offers me a liqueur. I drink to all adorers of roses. I feel that Sitareh and I are the immortal lovers, Sheerin and Farhad, who have momentarily stepped out of a Persian miniature. There is a sense of rebirth, a pardon for all our sins.

Sitareh plays the sitar for a long time, and now and then sings the Indian songs whose meanings I can imagine only in the richness of their sound. The rhythm speaks of unity and eternity.

Suddenly she stops and declares, "I know you so well. I wish you knew me as well."

"How do you know me," I ask, "when I am still trying to know myself?"

"I know you not by worldly evidence. Sometimes it is possible to see most clearly in the dark." Then, with a slow movement, she raises her hand and holds the back of my neck, her delicate fingers meshing into my hair. I remain still, curious, at ease. Gently she moves my head toward her and brings herself closer to me until my face rests on her chest, my eyes touching her heartbeat. As though receiving some exotic nourishment from her breast, I sense an ancient light, a luminous wisdom, flashing through me. Like the fragrance of a lilac caught in the swirl of a breeze, I feel weightless and free and loved. Unexpectedly I find my soul, which I did not know I had ever lost.

Then I hear Sitareh's musical voice, "Rest serenely, dear Pirooz. You are with me once more. Suckle the love in me." I am exhilarated and sweetened like a ripe persimmon on the tallest tree. I press my eyes against her heartbeat to hear more. Suddenly an illumination engulfs me and I glow within it as a light in a chandelier.

Just like fireworks that soar up, up, and up but find no sky in which to explode, I soar higher and higher as her words lead me. "I love only you, dear Pirooz, only you. Stay with me, now and forever. We have been separated for too long."

"For too long?" I respond.

"Yes. Ask no more questions now, Pirooz."

I imagine the sitar playing faster and faster, the notes now fleeing the strings, each one a ruby flying out of an open pouch swinging at the end of a cord. Free of chores and dissimulations, I am my true self. I believe Sitareh. I know she knows something I don't, just as I know something she doesn't.

I hear her voice again. "Convergence, convergence. We must all converge in Hamadan."

I whisper, "Who are we all?"

"You and me and Ibn Sina, our beloved."

Ibn Sina. Us. Convergence. Single words return doubts and reality to me.

"Yes, he has been waiting for us for too long. We must not keep him longer."

"You are sure—absolutely certain?"

"Yes. I don't know how, Pirooz, but I know that I know."

Urgently needing to know what is to be known, I ask, "Why Hamadan?"

"Because something tells me we must find him there."

"Something?"

"No, everything!"

I know that Ibn Sina is buried there, and then, remembering his words in my dream, I stop questioning her.

"He is buried there," she says, echoing my thought.

Inexplicably, a new question emerges. "Why is your name Sitareh?" I ask.

Her mysterious smile returns. "My mother said that her great-grandfather had told her that firstborn females in our family are always named Sitareh. That is all I know."

"They must have known you would become my star, the sitar player in my life."

"Who knows how fate chooses names? Sitareh is for me, and sitar for the instrument I love."

Early in the morning, I lay on the carpet, my head in her lap. She bends over me, and our burning lips meet. My passion soars. But gently she stops me.

"I am on fire, Sitareh."

"Good! Then I will wait until you are cooked and I am hungry."

She grins and whispers in my ear, "Goodnight to you, my love, and greetings to the miracle of our meeting. Before long you and I will sleep and awaken together."

I accept her resolve and kiss her fingers one by one: "Every note you played tonight was a jewel. If I could I would kiss them all."

"And they would kiss you back, one by one, dear Pirooz, for inspiring me to bring them to life."

"May I have a translation of your last song?"

"It is Tagore's. I have it in English." She disappears and returns with a book, marking a page for me.

She offers a last smile as I leave her.

In my apartment I look at the full moon veiled thinly in the city's dust and gloom. I wonder if the same forces still govern the world as before I met Sitareh, heard her sitar, and dreamed of Ibn Sina. I feel happy as I fall asleep.

The next day, as I am preparing breakfast for Sitareh and me, I hear a tumult in the building, but I ignore it. In New York indifference is a necessity; it can prevent insanity. Momentarily I think of my former lover, Elizabeth, who has gone to Egypt to search for truth in history, to study Arabic calligraphy, the Nile, the pyramids, and the pharaohs. And immediately I feel Sitareh filling the void of my loneliness.

Having set a colorful breakfast for us, I wait for Sitareh's arrival. I put on a record of Ali Akbar Khan, the greatest sarod player alive. The notes of a sarod are sonorous and fluid; it is a female instrument, as opposed to the male sitar. A duet between them is a love affair of wonderful counterpoint. Ali Akbar Khan's father began to teach him at four and implored his son to sow the seed of Indian music in the hearts of mankind.

The source of Indian classical music is an ancient Vedic hymn that is not written down but passed from master to disciple. The exotic sounds are improvised and flow from heart to heart, generation to generation. Persian music has enriched Indian music with melody, flexibility, and lightness, Sitareh told me. The tempos vary from the languorous movement of a caravan at the end of a long trip, to the allegro of a bamboo grove dancing in the wind, to the boisterous leaps of a winged horse galloping skyward. Its rhythm of oneness illuminates the soul for a deeper understanding of itself, liberates the mind to love nature, awakens dead hearts and liquidates obstacles to the unity of all spirits. The music bestows wings on me. I starhop over time and reach for the beginning and end of everything.

The sarod's beat picks up speed. A handful of notes heaves about. Space trembles in ecstasy as the exotic sounds pierce it. I let the melodies take me on their journey.

Inexplicably, the music and Sitareh's remarks about Ibn Sina remind me of the words, "God is great." How can this crucial Islamic phrase locate Ibn Sina? "His will is not asleep," I remember him telling me. Ibn Sina denied reincarnation when alive; and I doubt everything, including the existence of the absent God. I am a heretic who doubts even heresy. Maybe the dream contained just the words and pictures from a book I once read. Yet the dream apparently opened the gate of history and let my conscious mind see what I never knew that I knew.

I realize that Sitareh is late. Why? Where is she? An insistent knock at the door stirs me. That cannot be her. Behind the door, I find an Indian lady bent over with age and sadness, her face wet with tears. She is Sitareh's friend. She offers her wrinkled, trembling hands to me. I grasp them instinctively.

Through her tears, I hear: "A murder in the laundry room. God has kept me too long in this world of dark thoughts!"

"Who was murdered? Who?" I demand.

"Sitareh. Her body was found in the big dryer."

I scream, feeling a knife twist in my heart. I close the door as the old woman disappears, stop the music, shut the windows, cover the food with paper, turn off the lights, and ignore the furious ringing of the phone. I pace wildly; I am afraid to stop. What would I do, could I do, if I stop? Finally, I drop face down onto my bed and shake like a seedling caught in a storm. Screams die in my throat, but my tears flow and flow. I am appalled, numbed, and dead in spirit. But the dead have no tears; I must be alive. My new love, the love of my life, is dead. My hope, like my heart, is torn apart. I feel like the last sane man chained to an insane world. Is this world not insane? Am I not chained to it?

My confusion and numbness distort the passage of time. Time slows down, hurries, grumbles, and kicks me in the face, but it keeps ticking, taking away my love. Minutes and seconds march like an invading army, their heavy boots pounding over me, but I feel no pain, think no thoughts, deny her death, long for my own death, and believe in nothing.

My soul divorces itself from my body and screams: "I am ashamed to belong to the human race!" More time passes by like a poisoned river. I feel no hunger, no thirst, no desire to live. Hours later, feeling like the lone survivor of a catastrophe who must live in solitude, I wish to disappear to where Sitareh has gone.

I begin to think, oh, my God! All we did was talk, talk and talk. I burdened her with my numerous questions. Her death is also the death of a mystery, a history, and my fondest dreams. I remember her words, "Dr. Pirooz, one discovers the meaning of life if one understands the meaning of death or actually experiences it."

She is among the stars, but with whom am I left? Who is actually left? Am I me without her? I know no words can describe my world without her and how much I miss her.

I find myself somehow at her funeral two days later. Her body lies in a casket at the end of a hall filled with mourners and incense. She wears her gray sari with the feathery burgundy shawl on her shoulder, a rose in her hand, and a mysterious smile on her lips. She looks alive. She knew the meaning of life before she experienced death.

Friends and colleagues stand before the casket and take turns recalling Sitareh's life into a microphone. An American professor pronounces her a distinguished scholar for bridging Western and Eastern thought. I learn that she published her first book when only twenty-five, in which she uncovered many of the Indian roots of the great religions of Southwest Asia that influenced Western civilization. Her book on Ibn Sina and his contribution to Western thought has been widely acclaimed.

A Brahmin sage in white cotton faces the mourners and declares, "The Veda says, 'The wife is the home.' Sitareh was not yet a wife, but she was a home to so many hearts. She practiced:

> Rouse thyself by thyself,
> Examine thyself by thyself,
> Thus self-protected, and
> Attentive will thou live happily.
> Go unto all lands and tell
> The poor and the rich, to unite . . .
> As all rivers in the sea.

She enlightened the path to unity of all faiths and mankind."

Then the old Indian lady friend addresses the mourners. "Sitareh wrote, 'Men and women, though physiologically dissimilar, have the same roots and are equally vital for the survival and happiness of one another and mankind. For the sake of human ascendance, women and men must have equal opportunity for self-realization and equal rights at home and in society.'" The old lady takes a deep breath, then finishes: "Sitareh wrote uncompromisingly against female infanticide in India, cared for abandoned children, and struggled for nonviolence toward animals, too. She was a tireless protector of all defenseless beings. She possessed the heart of a saint, the reason of a logician, the wisdom of a sage, and the knowledge of the most learned. She was a wonderful sitar artist."

In a moment of anger, I think, "She was also stubborn—very stubborn! I had warned her several times not to go to the laundry room alone."

I hear the lady again: "Sitareh's heart glows and her soul goes forth through the eye—just as a caterpillar when it reaches the edges of a leaf moves on to another, so her soul has left her torn body to move on to a new home."

My name is announced: "Now Dr. Feraydoon Pirooz, a close friend, will say a few words." I must give a eulogy . . . no one warned me of this obligation. My footsteps protest as I walk to the podium. Bewildered, I glance about and see ears waiting row by row. I notice the microphone's commanding presence and hesitate. "Sitareh was a star that shone love. I was fortunate to reach for that star and touch it briefly. Her illumination still flickers in my heart even though she is . . ." I stop. My throat is dry and squeezed, and my voice is dead. The throbbing of my heart reminds me that I am not speaking, that I am a mere statue on a podium. I hear a hush. Instantly, my eyes speak by breaking into tears. They speak loudly as a tear flows down my cheek. I feel distraught, helpless and isolated before people who expect words, not tears. I sense their eyes scrutinizing me. My head spins. I struggle once again, thumping the podium gently to coax some words from the dead wood, but none appear.

Suddenly I find my hands enclosed in the old woman's. I hear my own muted voice: "I love Sitareh." She guides me to my seat gently and reassures me, "She wanted truth, not praise. Your tears were truth. You were eloquent.

Truth always is." For another moment, everyone's anxious eyes remain on me as though I am the one who is to be laid to rest. At last unobserved, I glance at the coffin once more as I begin to regain my composure.

Unable to see Sitareh stilled or listen to the forthcoming expressions of sympathy, I rush out into a cold rain that makes my face ache. The rain is steady, an enduring painful weeping. No tears are as cold as this rain or my feelings for the world. I keep walking to nowhere, grief stalking me everywhere.

Soon I see nothing, I hear nothing, I feel nothing, I am absolutely numb and my legs carry me without my volition. I wish the rain would gather into a flood and wash away my mind. A bitter memory is a burden; it acquires a life of its own. My mind will not obey my will to forget, so the anguish of emptiness prevails and grows in me and knocks at my soul, saying, Wake up to your loneliness. For a brief moment it is not her death I mourn but my sweet memories of her, now buried beneath her bitter fate. I hear the sitar of my Sitareh. The music, a true expression of her humanity, is supremely eloquent and melancholy. I keep playing it in my head, as if on a record player.

Sitareh will be cremated in New York, and her ashes strewn over the Ganges near the city of Sangam, where she was born. Each ash will fly afar to feed all forms of life. Who or what will she become? Reincarnation, is it possible?

"Why, but why?" I ask repeatedly. I would have given the killer all the change in the world if he had only asked. She would have done the same; she would have given anything to preserve any life. Perhaps the killer just wanted to kill, as hunters do.

Sitareh knew the law of karma. The killer is destined to become the victim of an equally violent act himself. So, ironically, Sitareh would grieve for her own murderer. I know she would!

I want to scream at my fate, "There is ice in my eyes and fire in my heart; tell me which I must give! Why must good people like Sitareh suffer most?"

I hear an answer from within, "Now you know that the sadness of death surpasses the joy of life, and that God has not created answers to the questions that really matter, as your schoolteacher once told you." You cannot discover what has not been created, I remind myself.

Nevertheless, I ask myself, "Why must your happiness be so brief? What have you done?"

A few days later the old Indian lady knocks at my door again. She looks lifeless. I invite her in. She waves her head "no" the way Indians do—a fatal no, side to side. I see teardrops dried on her wrinkles. She hands me Sitareh's poster of Ibn Sina and leaves saying, "I loved her, too."

I talk to myself and to Sitareh: "You were my soul! How can you be gone so suddenly, leaving me alone with unsatisfied longings for us?"

As I look at the man in the poster, he is looking at me, too, and we seem to know each other. He appears to be grieving for the loss of Sitareh. I can tell this, but how, I cannot tell. He seems to say, "That is life! You may hold your lover no longer than a sleeper clinging to a sweet dream."

"One can make wishes," I reply, "but one needs others to realize them; only the wishing is solitary."

Sitareh's words come back to me: "He has been waiting too long. We must not keep him longer." But there is no "we" anymore. And I wasn't even allowed to tell Sitareh of Ibn Sina's appearance to me. Haunting questions emerge. Why did she love me or say she loved me? What had I done to deserve it, except to admire her? Why did she say we have been separated for too long? Why? Why? Why?

I see a mountain of grief and one of bewilderment rising around me. I am alone in a valley between Sitareh and Ibn Sina, overwhelmed by both their presence and their absence in my life. Why is the world suddenly so empty?

Who and what are Ibn Sina and Sitareh to me? Why did Sitareh think that the three of us must converge in Hamadan? How did Ibn Sina know of Lady Sitareh? Why did he wish me to keep his appearance secret even from Sitareh? How did I know his full name, and how did he know Gorgani's full name in my dream, since I did not know it myself? Will I ever know the answers?

My grief and my curiosity struggling in my mind, I feel the excruciating cycles of denial, anger, protest, sadness, and resignation. I loved Sitareh without knowing her.

Later, finally calm, I contemplate rebirth and begin to accept the notion, doubting it and then accepting it again. I invite my doubts in; but like considerate guests, they never overstay their welcome.

I open the book Sitareh gave me to the page she had marked and hear her sitar and voice in my heart again:

> **Unending Love**
> I seem to have loved you in numberless forms, numberless times,
> In life after life, in age after age forever.
> My spell-bound heart has made and re-made the necklace of songs
> That you take as a gift, wear round your neck in your many forms
> In life after life, in age after age forever.
>
> . . .

> Clad in the light of a pole-star piercing the darkness of time:
> You become an image of what is remembered forever.
> . . .
> We have . . . shared in the same
> Shy sweetness of meeting, the same distressful tears of farewell—
> Old love, but in shapes that renew and renew forever.
>
> Today it is heaped at your feet, it has found its end in you,
> The love of all man's days both past and forever:
> Universal joy, universal sorrow, universal life,
> The memories of all loves merging with this one love of ours—
> And the songs of every poet past and forever.
>
> —Rabindranath Tagore

A difficult and lonely week ends with a call from my mother. I can tell she is in distress. Suddenly she breaks into sobs but manages to tell me that an Iraqi missile has killed my favorite old Uncle Mehdi in Teheran.

I feel my soul wracked with pain, pain on top of pain. Then I remember when as a boy I used to ride on my uncle's shoulders. He was the one who taught me how to swim, play chess, and pass a soccer ball in delicate ways. He took me to movies when my father was on his frequent business trips. He introduced me to a Persian translation of Thomas Jefferson's writings: I'll never forget him repeating Jefferson's great statement that the only justified war is the one for freedom. What are Iraq and Iran fighting for? Whose freedom?

I feel new tears and wonder, "For whom am I crying?" Maybe I cry for each one of us who must subdue a murderer within ourselves. I think I know where the world must go and what humanity must become, but I don't know where I must go and what I must become. Maybe I am crying for myself, because I am lost, I am alone. I miss Sitareh so much. Now I am exiled from everywhere except my own consciousness.

In the evening I glance resignedly at the darkening clouds and whisper to the nonexistent deity, "God, look on me, be with me. I am so lonely."

I imagine hearing His reply, "Oh, poor Pirooz, everyone must die. That is My rule. You will manage to overcome Sitareh's death. You must do what you must without Me."

I fall asleep feeling isolated in a congested world. People of the world, naked, masked and lost among ice mountains at the North Pole, chant:

> God, come to us
> And smile.
> Stay with us and
> Hold us tight.
> Kiss us once, even twice.
> We are so lonely,
> Lost in crowds and ice,
> One by one, alone.

The next day, I leave the crown of Western civilization for a weekend visit with my family, to heal my wounds and those of my mother. She misses the Friday sermons of the mullah who draws a flood of tears recounting the martyrs' deaths, and the sight of the Alborz Mountains rising behind our old house, and the magic of the Persian language, too. She is thrice exiled: from her fig trees at home, from the ground she believes angels fly over, and from my father's burial site under the shadow of a minaret in the city of Ray, near Teheran. She has demanded to be buried beside her husband.

My father, on a business trip to Hamadan, met my Uncle Mehdi, liked him and befriended him. Soon he asked if Mehdi had a sister, and sooner yet he was married to a girl of thirteen—my mother. The consummation of the marriage had to wait a couple of years for the bride to grow up. I was the first of three sons of that marriage.

Now, driving over a lonely road near my brother's house, I murmur, "God, come home, hug me, kiss me on the cheek. I am Your child. Tell me that You love me, that all will end well for me and for all exiles—your lost flock."

My visit is a complicated one. In my brother's yard I find a stray cat trapped in a wire cage. It has bitten their pussycat, so "it must be put to sleep," as my brother put it. The words "it" and "sleep" are meant to sound benign, a cover-up for an execution.

I protest, "A murder is a murder! Animals think and feel. What sets us apart from animals is our genius for self-deception: through words, religions, myths, false ideologies and sciences. Animals deceive others to survive, but man deceives himself for nearly nothing."

"Is Professor Pirooz done lecturing?" my brother interjects, not very seriously.

"'Put it to sleep!' What a gem of self-deception, to kill without killing," I insist with some irritation.

I see my mother's worried eyes beg for harmony. "We haven't seen each other for some time. Please! I demand a cease-fire this second!" Then she calmly asks, "What shall we do, then?"

"I will release the cat in the forest."

"This will just shift the burden to someone else," my brother argues.

"It may or may not, since the cat can survive in the wild."

Before my brother can respond, my mother intervenes, "You two never cease being brothers. Give yourselves and me relief and behave like mere acquaintances."

We fall silent as I think of Sitareh's influence on me.

Later in the evening, Persian music, Persian food, Persian conversation, and the exchange of heartaches soothe our hurt feelings. All my family express their deep sorrow for the loss of Sitareh, whom they never met. My mother advises us, "Let us understand that bonds of affection and irritation hold us together like every other family. In America, people treat their pets better than each other. We need not copy this Western attitude." I recognize her allusion to the dispute over the cat.

We finally reconcile, knowing we must while uprooted and estranged from our surroundings. Unqualified trust glues us together, thanks to our mother.

Two days later, as she kisses me good-bye, my mother asks, "How is your ulcer?"

"In good hands."

I am sent back to New York with some of my favorite date pastries.

On the way home, my heartache assails me again. Doubts and uncertainty cloud everything. I must remind myself to concentrate on driving. New York looks empty to me, and my uncle's death is yet another bitter memory that will stick to my future.

In my apartment, I wonder what does make sense. The senselessness of everything grips me like a heart seizure. Struggling, I ask, "Almighty God, make it comprehensible for me. Please!"

A voice, seemingly as real as reality, sounding like Ibn Sina's, reminds me, "God has a universe to look after, Pirooz. You are a detail, and He is not concerned with details. Use your mind. Figure it out for yourself, Pirooz."

Chapter Five: The Butterfly Beckons

The mournful weeks struggle by. Often in my dreams Sitareh sings and plays the sitar for me. Her love is a seedling that grows in me, even though she is dead. I feel that Sitareh and I were a secret oneness that no dawn will reveal. I should have been more sympathetic to her views, but guilt cannot give me solace or guidance. Sitareh was special; she meant what she said. "One can learn from everything, even from horrors," she told me, and I must now do just that.

I read Sufi lyrics of the Persian poet, Rumi, who, like Ibn Sina, understood mysticism deeply to produce this verse:

> Love sweetens bitter things,
> Love turns copper into gold,
> Love makes medicine out of pain,
> Love resurrects the dead.

"Love resurrects the dead. Love resurrects the dead." That is my impossible wish. I moan, glowing and burning down like a candle.

To keep my mind from tragedies, I jog in the park. It is calming, like viewing an art exhibit. But paintings are still and with each brush stroke the painter must have died a little, while the greening park is alive and its painter is immortal. I try to enjoy spring's arrival, the warming days, as the trees, birds and fish do, to accept the world as it is, without Sitareh, and to keep my fantasies of what might have been from overshadowing what is. "To see things as they are is also to see God, since He created them as they are," Sitareh once said. I replay the chess games of masters, read Rumi's poems, listen to Mahler's *Resurrection* Symphony and remind myself that what is must pass, and what has passed will return.

Awakening to my soul's prerogatives, I feel guilty for having abandoned it to neglect. I confess before the universe to true humility, even nothingness, conscious that any being may teach me what I have neglected to learn. I recall lines from the *Mathnawii* of Rumi:

> Without love there would be no life, or else,
> How is the soil transformed to plants?
> Why are the plants sacrificed to be gifted with the spirit of man?

Inexplicably, a bothersome question returns to me: Was the crushed cockroach just an intruding insect? But plants and animals have souls, too, Ibn Sina declared. So whom did I kill? Though it is soothing to believe in reincarnation, I still cannot accept it. I am not the converting type. My heartbeat may announce belief, but my mind entertains doubt.

I search for a brighter light, even when I feel somewhat enlightened. I wonder about my dream; am I Gorgani resurrected? If so from what and where? These puzzles whirl in my mind endlessly. I would be more hopeful if I believed that only death is dead.

I wish I could talk to Sitareh or Ibn Sina once more. Why did Ibn Sina demand that I keep his appearance a secret? Who or what was he protecting? Did he only think of saving me from ridicule? Is he protecting himself by dissimulating? Would God create some answers anytime soon to free man from the tyranny of curiosity?

To survive, Ibn Sina practiced dissimulation, warded off accusations, and took flight from ruler to ruler to outlast the dangers of jealousy, bigotry, intrigue, conformity and boredom. I read his poetic protest:

> It is not easy and trifling to call me a heretic, since
> No faith in God is firmer than my own.
> Being the unique person I am if heretic I am
> Then there is not a single true believer in this world.

In my dream Ibn Sina kept from me how he knew Sitareh. Must the dead keep secrets or dissimulate? This reminds me that I, the living, must also dissimulate. Only the times and what is being dissimulated have changed, that is all. I teach what is expected of me, but now and then I warn my students of the disease of the sacred system, "Your textbooks are hazardous to your mind, since they discuss mostly appearances. For instance, how can we tolerate hunger and disease in our midst despite our wealth and lofty claims of humanitarianism? What power thwarts the majority's demand for gun control or national health care? Who gave the bosses the power to homeless people? These micro-dictators induce self-censorship not by the threat of arrest, but the fear of joblessness. Why do a few profiteers control TV and turn our children into junk-food and junk-culture addicts? If churches compete for our dollars why are they tax exempt? Why are the masses programmed to act against their own ultimate interest? Why is America nearly heaven for some citizens and almost hell for others? Shouldn't America be beautiful for everyone?"

An educator, I consider it a duty to diagnose ignorance and enhance knowledge, as a physician must diagnose disease and enhance health. However, if I raise uncomfortable questions, indoctrinated students, colleagues, administrators and journal editors, to whom dissent is heresy, would make my life stressful, making dissimulation a survival instinct just as in ancient times. How free am I, anyhow? One must change willingly or be changed unwontedly, I realize. I long for relief from pretending, and from pretending to believe the pretensions of others. I open up my heart to the world and to history, to confess that I wish to escape from this apparently good life, this golden cage.

I desire ever more strongly to find the higher reality of which science is a low level, and religion and ideology perhaps lower yet. How can I experience reality and become enlightened by it? My guide must be Ibn Sina, the only soul I know of who was free of greed and ascended to the zenith of humanity. I immerse myself in the life and work of Ibn Sina to learn how he overcame the obstacles to self-realization.

Sitareh's mysterious smile accompanies me all the while. She lifted me to a new understanding, like a windstorm that catches a snail and carries it to a distant tree for a new life. But where am I now and what is the new tree I must fasten myself to?

I must look for what is behind appearances, behind whatever covers everything else. I must seek the spirit that unites everything—what is seen and what is unseen. Sitareh's death impels me to bid farewell to what I was and greet what I will be, through the endless journey of self-discovery and self-realization. I sense her spirit encouraging me to voyage beyond healing, beyond reason. I hear the mysterious voice. "If you love God, you will discover Him in your heart." God revealed to the Prophet Mohammed, "The only means for My creature to approach Me is through deeds I have prescribed. Then I will be the Ear with which he hears, the Eye with which he sees, the Tongue with which he speaks, and the Hand with which he holds." It is a mysterious love that propels me back to the source of my being. But why do I think of God, when He never seems to think of me? Am I condemned to God's indifference? Is humanity condemned to His silence, to His absolute separation until the Day of Judgment?

I must lift myself up by myself, like Ibn Sina. I isolate myself from mundane distractions. My volition acquires a will of its own. Attuning myself to my new goal, I absorb new knowledge, experiences and understandings with cold efficiency and strive to ascend beyond what I have been or am. I feel Sitareh holding my hand and I hear my own footsteps on the path to salvation in this life.

After much reading, reflection and meditation, I can clarify my initial ambiguities about God, the soul, life, death and rebirth, but new concerns emerge at the edge of my new consciousness. My rejecting God, the soul and the idea of rebirth has been intellectual, not emotional or total. Since God is not an emotional emptiness, then faith must have deeper roots than just rationality.

Reason and science, artifacts of civilization, arose from the curiosity deposited in the core of humanity, well beyond what is necessary for survival. While reason and science hold human confidence—because they work—we must not allow them to subdue emotions and instincts, which are also basic ingredients of humanity. I must not reject the call of my instincts without understanding their message; and I must let wisdom to be both the cause and the effect of my reason and emotion harmonizing as in happy matrimony. Societal norms will not be my ultimate guide—they have changed from epoch to epoch, like everything else including the concept of God itself. I identify with the future.

I gaze into reality and observe the invisible harmony of form and function, of sameness and variation that define life, and unite one's unique self to this diverse world. Multiplicity disappears if one can perceive the wholeness of time, space, things and life. But still I must accept that life must be lived, even though it may be a futile search for illusions like truth, happiness, heaven.

One day, skimming through a scholarly journal, I find a letter of mine to the editor, in which I object that an article about music as therapy made no reference to Ibn Sina, the originator of the subject. Anger conquers me, even though I strive to conquer it. How many times will scholars here claim an unjustified originality for themselves? A couple of weeks later, I receive a letter from Teheran:

> Dear Dr. Pirooz,
>
> I commend you on your letter about music as therapy. I am a psychiatrist interested in the history of medicine, especially in Ibn Sina's medical theory, practice and ethics.
>
> By observation and keen intuition, Ibn Sina established a crucial link between psychology and physiology. He theorized that music, by relaxing the mind and lifting the spirit, enhances the body's intrinsic healing power. Ibn Sina himself practiced meditation, with similar results. He also introduced the concepts of identity crisis and self-realization into psychology and education.
>
> He promoted an empirical approach to medicine and pharmacology. Moreover, by using autopsy as a research method, by discovering the contagious nature of tuberculosis and water and soil as contaminants, by detecting microbes without benefit of microscope for observation, and by the systematic use of alcohol as an antiseptic, he established the foundation of modern medicine.
>
> A professor of the history of science recently speculated that, armed with a microscope, Pasteur may have been inspired to

look for bacteria by Ibn Sina's insight about the invisible tiny beings that carry and cause infection.

This tale is long, and a brief letter will not do it justice. If you ever visit Iran, please get in touch with me, and we can further discuss Ibn Sina.

With respects,
S. Bastan

The name Bastan, meaning "ancient," intrigues me. Is my mind a repository of an ancient culture with a modern Western veneer? Don't the ideas and spirit of Ibn Sina, Attar, Rumi, Omar Khayyam and Hafiz live in my mind? Aren't their spirits alive in the Persian soul?

I write a long reply:

Dear Dr. Bastan,

Your letter was a surprise, both for itself and its contents. It impelled me to conclude that Ibn Sina's golden age in Persia contained the seeds of the Italian, that is European, Renaissance, since his works and those of many of his contemporaries spanned the gulf between ancient knowledge and modern science.

Ibn Sina founded workshops and directed group research, indeed a modern endeavor. The *Shifa*, his vast philosophical and scientific encyclopedia, is the most comprehensive ever written by a single person to this date, and was a primary source of learning in Europe for centuries. It explores and extends all classical fields, except for politics.

I wish to add to your comments that, in physics, Ibn Sina correctly explained the formation of winds and cyclones, and proposed that the red and black coronas surrounding certain celestial bodies were gases that caught fire from their constant motion. Ibn Sina's discoveries of the properties of light and his anticipation of the wave theory of light helped Roemer, centuries later, to measure the speed of light. In biology, he declared that consciousness evolved from mineral to plant, to animal, and finally to human. Rumi elucidated Ibn Sina's idea about evolution in his ode:

> At the moment you entered this world,
> A ladder was placed in front of you to allow you to escape.
> First you were a mineral, then you became a plant,

> Then you became an animal: how could you ignore it?
> Then you were made into a man gifted with knowledge, reason and faith;
> Observe this body, drawn from dust: what perfection it has acquired!

Darwin also characterized evolution as nature's progress toward perfection. Ibn Sina used dialectical logic to study processes such as psychosomatics, self-understanding and self-realization. To Ibn Sina, spirituality appeared to be the next stage in human ascendance.

Ibn Sina's scrutiny of Aristotle for inconsistencies and errors of fact, while not abandoning Aristotelian logic, was later adopted in Europe and considered a foundation of the Renaissance. He bequeathed to human thought the concept of the *intellectually intelligible*, which distinguished what is thinkable and expressible from what is not, a profound influence on all subsequent philosophy. Ibn Sina's *thought experiments* became centuries later a favorite intuitive tool of Einstein.

In linguistics, Ibn Sina anticipated the current school of textual deconstruction through his analysis of the structure of Arabic, the language of scholarship in his time.

Your letter prompted me to rethink various strands of my thought. I commiserate with your comments.

Historians in the West have conjured diverse images of the ill-defined notion of the Italian Renaissance. The images add up to a rebirth or revival of Western civilization that separates the Middle Ages from the modern era. But the Middle Ages are not as dark, or as un-classical, as myth would have it, so the beginnings of the Renaissance are fuzzy, pushed back by some scholars to roughly the period when Ibn Sina's major works first appeared in Latin. Nevertheless, the central features of the Renaissance are the rediscovery of antiquity, humanism, the triumph of the scientific method, the growth of universities, the discovery of the world and of man, and the resurrection of individual will.

Ibn Sina's ideas of the centrality of the self and the inherent dignity of the individual were a catalyst to Renaissance humanism. The core of these transformations occurred in Ibn Sina's time and spread to Europe through translations, trade and the Crusades. For example, Ibn Sina's colleague, Biruni, one of the great scientists of all time, precisely measured the specific weight of many materials for the first time, accurately calculated latitudes and longitudes on earth, and explained the earth's rotation on its axis. Biruni also wrote the first secular world history and geography, boldly affirming, for instance, that the Indus Valley had been a sea basin in the remote past.

Historians write what pleases the powerful, so, if the Mongols had not crippled Persia, the facts and the historians' stories about them would have been different. The West's recent and continuing economic and military dominance of the East has also created historical and informational imperialism.

The West has appropriated an authentic Persian and Islamic renaissance of Ibn Sina's time with insignificant acknowledgment. The colonialists expropriated not only wealth and cultural artifacts (witness major museums), but also ideas and History itself. For example, the non-historian Bertrand Russell described Ibn Sina's medical work as merely a repetition of Galen! He fails to explain why it was Ibn Sina's text that was taught and practiced universally and almost exclusively, and why physicians who knew better saved the greatest praise for him.

If I sound frustrated, it is because I am! Until what is known is fairly acknowledged, the West will never consider the East as equal, and the East will never forgive the West for colonialism. And there will be no peace.

Another nuisance is how some writers call Ibn Sina just a Muslim, or even an Arab, because most of his scholarly work was in Arabic, the scientific language of his time. I think he belongs to the family of man, but if his nationality must be specified, then his birthplace and abode were Persia, and his mother tongue and his patrons were Persian. He wrote books and poetry in Persian, too, which no Arab poet would do, then or now. Ibn Sina never lived a day in an Arab land.

However, if scientific language is the criterion of nationality, then Arab scholars writing in English today must all be British, and European writers until modern times were all Romans, since they wrote in Latin. This list includes the Polish Copernicus, the German Kepler, the Italian Galileo, the French Descartes and Pascal, and the English Newton, *et al.* And if religion is the acid test of identity, then these same learned men are to be lumped together as merely Christian thinkers. But neither

Arab nor other scholars ever call them Romans or just Christians. So, to call Ibn Sina an Arab or just a Muslim scholar is to placate authority and not to adhere to the truth.

The extent of politics in science and history is scandalous and sickening. A truly human self-realization implies defanging nationalism from human consciousness, or else disputes would arise not just over boundaries but also over the nationality of deceased thinkers.

The Italian Renaissance—which I define as the revival of the future—was seeded in the Golden Age of Ibn Sina, who, as a symbol of his era, speculated about or invented many elements of what we consider modernity. Therefore, history should bestow upon him a new title: the Grandfather of Modernity! Ibn Sina was modern even in his private life. Marriage and family were to be a choice, not an obligation, since family responsibilities might inhibit self-realization.

I also hope to meet you. Meanwhile, our exchange is informative as well as therapeutic for me.

With best regards,
F. Pirooz

Sitareh's spirit seems to guide me to probe deeper into my soul. Gradually I devote myself to the idea of a journey to an old world, like a prisoner trying to escape a life sentence. I listen to a call from far away, "Return home, Pirooz. Come to me."

I think of Ibn Sina's wish and of Sitareh's theme of convergence. I am drawn to Hamadan, to Iran, to Ibn Sina who is lost at the bottom of piles and piles of history and the abuse of his detractors. Convinced that science and reason will struggle with faith and passion forever, I begin to feel the same anguish Ibn Sina must have felt, and wish to see the beginning and end of everything in one glance.

Spring is now in full bloom. Finally, Ibn Sina's call and Sitareh's wish win me over. I listen to a recording of a Persian *tar*, a three-string instrument, and gaze at the tree of life, woven in silk on the woolen Persian rug hanging on my living room wall. It reminds me of the tree where Sina, the wise healer bird, nested, as declared by Zoroaster and recounted by Sitareh to me. The tree rises from its bed to spread upward and outward. Roses, geraniums, tulips, lilies, carnations, and even a big sunflower blossom in its limbs. Nightingales and other birds in colorful silk rest on its lush branches. I imagine exotic scents wafting from the tree. On the ground below, around its trunk, a couple of rabbits, a deer, a lamb, a squirrel and a big ostrich seem lost in a wondrous trance. I concentrate on a Monarch butterfly that is woven in its flight around the tree.

Her golden wings with black outlines are open and delightful. Unlike the birds resting in the branches, she has never rested, not even for a second in one hundred and fifty years of the carpet's life. This is not a rug, I think, but a book of life. The silken tree is hurting, its threads degrading knot by knot in the fumes of the city, just as nature is debased. Both the rug and I are uprooted from our place of birth, but the rug, unlike me, never complains; it dies without a whisper.

I imagine a slight shiver in the rug and behold the fluttering wings of the Monarch. Flying out from the rug as though from its cocoon, the silk Monarch alights on my knee, and without hesitation or fear she asks, "Why have you been so sad?"

It does not seem strange to be talking to the butterfly; nothing is anymore. "I miss Sitareh," I answer.

"I know," she says. I shudder at something familiar in her voice. "What else?" she asks.

"I miss my home."

"All of a sudden?"

"No, but more now than ever."

"Why don't you go home?"

"Then I would miss what little freedom I have here."

"But you may find new freedoms—even freedom in a prison—free of everything worldly except walls. Look at me. I am free, although imprisoned in a rug. Free yourself from yourself, and all will be free."

I glimpse freedom in a new way and glow like a spark curling among the twigs in a fireplace. "Oh, my mind!" I mutter to myself.

"You gaze at me often. Why?" the butterfly asks.

"Because you are beautiful and in flight."

"But mine is a flight without motion," the Monarch says.

"So is the human flight to happiness."

A tear from the Monarch falls in my lap. "I used to be trapped in silk, but my soul can roam free."

"People are also trapped in wishes, ideas and things, even unexamined virtues," I answer. "Look, despite all physical motion, the human spirit sags, grounded and entangled in worldly concerns. Boundaries! Self-erected barriers confine us in numerous ways."

After a long pause the Monarch speaks again. "As a silk butterfly, I will live long, longer than my designer and my weaver. I watched your grandfather and father grow old and die, and I am watching you grow old, and I will watch your unborn children grow old, too. But you are the first to search for your soul and the soul of life, all lives. I hope you succeed."

The butterfly flutters back to her fixed place on the rug, as I flutter from doubts to a fixed resolution: I must go to Hamadan. I know there is a war between Iraq and Iran, with people being slaughtered in the skies, in the seas and on the ground, all in the name of God. Oh, God! Announce that these are all lies.

God, if you exist and are awake, please stop the carnage! Then, looking at the tree of life on the carpet, I declare, "I apologize for the wounds that man inflicts on everything, and I beg mighty Nature's forgiveness in not destroying man in revenge." I hear Nature cry within me, for I am Nature, too.

If only Ibn Sina would return and use his wisdom like a thread to close these wounds, to heal life on earth. Was he not a surgeon, a healer, a sage?

Now, to diminish my isolation, I try to expand my generosity, to become closer to others, and to curtail my selfishness; I resume my human rights activities. I recall a thought of Rumi's, "He who is distanced from love is a bird that misses her wing," and tell myself I will grow wings and fly. I decide to leave for Hamadan as soon as the semester is over. I know my journey may follow the same path as Rumi's:

> A few words sum up my life.
> I was raw, I was cooked, I was burned.

Chapter Six: The Mausoleum

The first time I visited Hamadan, I was a boy with questions bubbling in my head. My father would respond patiently and spark my curiosity. He told me that Hamadan, called Ecbatana in ancient times, was designed to unite the microcosm of the city with the macrocosm of the universe. The citadel had seven concentric walls, like the orbits of the visible planets. The innermost ring was gold, the color of the sun, for Sunday; the second a glowing silver for the moon and Monday; the third nearly scarlet for Mars and Tuesday; the fourth a sparkling blue for Mercury and Wednesday; the fifth amber for Jupiter and Thursday; the sixth near-black for Venus and Friday; and the seventh ring was white for Saturn and Saturday. This design symbolized the sacred number seven in the star-cult of the Iranian Medes, and pointed them to a vast vision of the unity of all things, which Ibn Sina and other great Persian Sufis inherited.

"But, Baba, is the moon a planet?" I asked him.

"The moon is the satellite of Earth, itself the sun's planet. It proclaims its existence in the sun's illumination on its face, my son. And as it burns down, the sun offers its body to sustain lives, thoughts and feelings on earth. It even energizes a monkey's kiss. Man and the sun and moon are one." Years later, I wondered if Persian astronomy inspired the Greek Aristarchus of Samos to propose the sun as the center of the solar system, for which some authorities charged him with impiety.

The architects of Ecbatana suspected that the sun's apparent rotation around the earth was an illusion. My father warned me, "Appearances can mislead one to act against his own interest. Look deeply into all matters of learning, and, once you are satisfied then look deeper. Journey in search of the roots of nature, history, society and yourself." I am now journeying to the depths of the past to discover a path to the depths of the future.

Then, with pride in his eyes, my father said, "Some exquisite pottery and artworks, the crown of human creations of six thousand years ago, were excavated nearby. A wise phoenix hatched one of the early eggs of civilization in Hamadan, perhaps, and our ancestors nourished it. It grew into a magnificent bird that is still soaring to new heights." (And now I remember Sitareh's mythical bird, Sina.) "Know and take pride in our heritage, my son, but observe, humanity is a flock journeying alone in the universe. And in the stormy seas of history, Zoroastrians, Jews, Christians, and Muslims have survived together on the ship of Iran since ancient times. Hamadan symbolized the unity of everything, including the faiths and the faithful." I can still see my father's big and satisfied smile. When I asked him where the city's name came from, to my surprise he said, "I really don't know, but it first appeared as 'Hamadana' in an inscription of the Assyrian king Tiglath Pileser I, from the eleventh century BC."

He took me to the old grave of Ibn Sina and described his accomplishments in terms a boy could understand. My father also told me that I was lucky to be born in Iran, into a rich heritage that nourishes men like Ibn Sina, and that I must try to preserve the tradition, make my own contributions, and pass it on to my children and enlighten the people of the world. Once he said, "Iran must honor the mothers who can fulfill themselves only through their sons." At the time I didn't understand what he meant. Then he said, "I was very proud, my son, when you told your mother, 'If it is difficult to be as good as you wish me to be, I think of your love for me, and then it becomes easy for me to listen to you.'"

Hours, continents and oceans pass as a roaring 747 carries my reveries back to their nest. Just before leaving for Hamadan, I managed to sublet my apartment for the summer. Renewing my expired passport proved to be a hassle, calming my mother's nerves an effort, and crossing a picket line at the airport a dilemma. I fly over the Atlantic thinking. Why do I feel wound up by the death of a roach, the mysterious smile of a deceased Hindu, the brilliance of Ibn Sina, and a silk butterfly that flew just once?

Relaxed after a glass of wine, I savor the warmth of my family's farewell and wish that for my mother's sake I had accepted the tiny Koran she had wanted me to carry for protection. Sitareh's smile accompanies me to Hamadan, as I wonder: Where is my home, in the past or future, in the U.S. or Iran, in this world or the next? Why does my heart tremble at the mere thought of return?

My heartbeat picks up, then pounds violently as the aircraft approaches the runway in Teheran. I have not been home in a long time.

A cousin of mine, now grown into a bearded, heavyset official of the Islamic Republic, must intervene to save me from the customs office's scrutiny. Still, I spend a good part of the day waiting, explaining and paying bribes. My trouble is that I wear a tie and no beard, carry a Newsweek with a picture of a couple in bathing suits, but no Koran, and apparently have no respect for the revolution. I dare not say, "Revolution for what, and for whom?" I have come from the house of Satan to the realm of angels, so I must now suffer the painful purgatory of transition. I throw my tie in a wastebasket to please the officials, but to no avail. They confiscate my books, even a dictionary, and hand me pamphlets instead. A contaminated alien, I must be sanitized before entering Iran. My mother's prophetic advice comes to me, "Who knows how the Holy Book, the Koran, can help you!" I bear the homecoming harassment patiently. Now I am an alien both in my birthplace and in my adopted home. If I don't submit to their norms I will be alien to them, and if I do I will be alien to myself.

In the car my cousin warns me, "The authorities are very edgy, edgy and arbitrary. Be very cautious about what you say, what you do and what you think. We are in chains. These are harrowing, suffocating, and violent times. The Islamic Guards are angels of death, who will murder even a little joy when they find it."

I grumble, "Even innocence is a sin, then?"

He grumbles back, "Anything may be considered a sin now."

"Are the horror stories about human rights violations true?"

After some thought my cousin replies, "The words 'human' and 'rights' have little significance or relevance anymore. Add to them the word 'life,' too."

"But they promised justice and freedom," I protest. To this my cousin responds with a knowing smile. I remember my mother's old reminder to me, "Good Muslims keep their promises, my son."

"Why do you work for the regime?" I ask my cousin.

"I pretend to care for them as they pretend to care for me and the nation." He looks around as though worried about eavesdroppers. Then, in a hushed voice, he says, "Agha Pirooz, what choice do I or other cynical officials have?"

"You are not the only one who has to pretend. I dissimulate in the U.S."

He is shocked that I have a hotel reservation and plan to leave Teheran the next day. He begs me to stay with him for old time's sake, "the time we were free of fear," he declares. Wishing to present souvenirs to his wife and children, I joyfully accept his invitation. Everyone welcomes me with excitement and showers me with questions during and after a colorful dinner. The enthusiasm of these strangers, who are my relatives, is infectious. We compare life in America and Iran and avoid talking about the war. I sleep well that night.

The next day, as my cousin drives me to the bus terminal, we encounter the tangle of a traffic jam. A mullah has driven the wrong way on a one-way street. "To them, their way is always the right way, God's way," my cousin quips. "Nothing is the same anymore. Rocket attacks on the innocent are ferocious. Modern war turns man into a beast, with claws stretching over mountains and devouring people with one pounce. Men return from work to homes in ruins, to their families torn apart, part buried, part in hospitals. War veterans search their memories for their lost limbs. The good has become bad and the bad has become worse and the worst has become hell. I wish I could leave home, too." Then, in parting, he gives me a bear hug. I will miss my cousin, even though I had never missed him before.

The bus takes me across Teheran. Slogans splashed across walls and radios overwhelm my senses. I read a wall, "This war is a holy war. Ours is a holy regime. The Imam will guide us to victory." Dilapidated cars groan and take revenge on people with their toxic fumes. Anxious eyes peer out of veils to weave among bearded men with turbans and guns. War panic runs quietly through wrinkles extended from face to face like cracks in a baked wasteland; people are prematurely aged. Waiting lines linger even after the goods are gone.

Women are severed from their aspirations, as non-whites are in apartheid. They are walled inside their homes or hidden by black chadors, buried under chores at home or menial tasks in government or business—all in the name of Islam. Revolutionary women look strange, even ridiculous, marching around with guns sticking from their chadors. I ask a passenger, "How can they make war while holding onto the chador?" He shakes his head as if to say, Where have you been? The two words, 'black' and 'apartheid,' stick to one another, in Iran as well as in South Africa.

The bus is delayed when an army convoy blocks traffic, but the people are patient, having become expert in waiting and imagining, it seems. Spirits sag deeper and deeper into abysmal despair. Numerous physicians, artists, scientists and managers are being forced to abandon the home they love. They know too much. I hope they leave to live and come back. The reminders of these self-exiles hover over the ancient land, like a feather shed by a bird that has flown far away. I feel a pounding ache in my eyes. I cover them with both hands to block out the painful scenes.

The old bus climbs through mountain passes and past barren fields and small villages. Passengers chant "God is great" on dangerous heights, and the trees flap their leaves, shedding big tears from last night's rain. Suddenly the bus lurches to a halt while a bomb crater in the road is filled.

At a lunch stop I glance about, noticing flowers and birds dancing in colored costumes so similar to each other. The thirsty rocks, the busy butterflies, the scared lizards, a stream with a turtle on its bank, are all points in a vast pointillist landscape. If I can't live in my homeland, then at least I can be buried here; death lasts longer than life, I think.

I remember Sitareh's admission to me and mine to her that we really didn't know why we were in New York. Oh, yes, this was one doubtful moment in Sitareh's life that she let me observe. Is doubt essential to the soul's integrity? Wouldn't free will, even history, be strangled if doubters were suppressed? But to a friend who first planted the idea why are we here, in my head, I replied, "Why are we anywhere?" Were we pulled to New York for some reason, or just pushed out of our home?

At the Hotel Ibn Sina in Hamadan, the same question bares its teeth at me: Are you here at the invitation of a ghost? I pass the walled hotel grounds bursting with flowers. The peeling stucco discloses its wounds to me, as though asking for help. Granite pillars, aged like faces in a worn painting, lift up the low-rise structure. Colorful rugs decorate the lobby. My room looks out onto the garden. The clanking of the hot water pipes reminds me of the clerk's inquisitive questioning when I checked in.

A glance at an old map of Hamadan shows the huge central square, like a fountain, that feeds six radiating boulevards, each nearly one hundred feet wide. A nearby north-south artery, Ibn Sina Avenue, runs past the mausoleum and my hotel to end at Ibn Sina Square, which is decorated with statues of him. Darius and Shahpur Avenues, run nearly east-west; Cyrus and Baba Tahir Avenues run southwest-northeast, and Ecbatana Avenue runs north-south. I refuse to accept the new Islamic names for them. The creator must name what is created.

The boulevards of Hamadan pass many historical sites, some old and humble, some new and magnificent, such as the modern mausoleum of the Sufi poet Baba Tahir Oryan. Numerous artifacts excavated from the city, including large gold and silver plates commemorating historic events, repose in museums or in private hands around the world.

My heart asks me, "Why does Hamadan cause me to pound so furiously? Am I a drum? Is Hamadan the drummer?" Am I marching to a mystery or to sudden death? I am free of longing to be at home, free from immigrancy. This is home. I feel free here where I should not, just as I did not feel free in New York where I should have. I feel free to imagine, to journey in history, to wander in my expectations, and to touch my roots in Hamadan and find myself. It doesn't seem to matter now if I cannot protest the regime's repression. But is this all? Couldn't I have found my self elsewhere? I speak about the soul, but do souls really exist? My doubts surface coldly like unwelcome early winters. Relieved that at least I am where I want to be and not where I have to be, I sleep soundly that night.

The morning air is so fresh, as though it has been kissed like a child and sent off to school. The sun looks brighter, too. After breakfast I walk a mile to visit Ibn Sina's mausoleum. Ibn Sina's bones were transferred from an old grave to this site, designed by Houshang Seyhoun, a painter-architect with an acute sense of history.

I mount a few steps to a large patio with a hexagonal fishpond and a fountain in the center. I pass by large columns and enter through a majestic wooden gate into a corridor. A plaque on the left wall misspells the architect's name. Later on, I learn that it may be a deliberate mistake, the only imperfection in the complex. "Only God can make perfect things,"—and He obviously preferred not to, I complete the saying.

I pass Ibn Sina's old gravestone and that of a friend who provided him shelter in a time of crisis in Hamadan, and arrive at the center of the mausoleum. An iron chamber surrounds a large, new marble tomb, adorned with inscriptions, including a verse from the Koran, the same eternal book that lived in Ibn Sina's heart:

> "In the name of God, the merciful, the compassionate, . . . Who bestowed upon him knowledge and wisdom, . . . This is the tomb of the Shaykh Al-Rais, the Reason of God Abu Ali al-Husain ibn Abd-Allah ibn Sina. As reported by his biographer, Al-Shaykh Abu Ubayd 'Abdul-Wahid Al-Juzjani [Gorgani], Ibn Sina was born 370 and deceased 428 [lunar calendar of the Hijra Era, equivalent to b. 980 AD and d. 1037 AD]."

A poem praises Ibn Sina for his wisdom, a sunbeam from the East, and his soul, illuminating like Moses'. Ibn Sina's own poem, about the soul's ascending towards God like a bird, is inscribed in marble on the interior walls.

A gray tower, like a huge, twelve-sided pencil with open sides to let light in through the glass ceiling of the crypt, rises above the marble tomb, which is the focal point of the mausoleum. Sunlight adorns it in daytime, and moonlight glorifies it at night. When I glance up, I see reflected the long names of Ibn Sina and Gorgani on the ceiling. "My old name beside his!" I wonder, am I already accepting that I was Gorgani? I feel no doubt, but I think doubtfully. Again my feelings and thoughts wage war. I smile at my predicament: this is not just an identity crisis, but a crisis of history in one soul. Questions bubble in me as they did when I was a boy, though my father is no longer here to answer them. Like mankind, I must find my own answers.

I crane my neck to look to the very top of the tower. About ninety-five feet high, the tower is made of steel, concrete, and huge slabs of granite cut from the side of Mount Gangnameh of the Alvand Range. Darius the Great and his son Xerxes engraved their glorious deeds on the breast of the same mountain. Their inscriptions are called Gangnameh, meaning treasured documents. They praise Ahura Mazda, the God of Light and Goodness, and ask Him to keep misfortune from the royal dynasty.

The pavilions surrounding the mausoleum tower contain a library and a spacious lecture and reception room. The furniture is embellished with magnificent ancient designs. Throughout the complex gifts from around the globe are on display. The entrance gate opens onto an elevated patio. Although the new mausoleum was constructed a millennium after Ibn Sina, the tower is in the architectural style of an old memorial in Iran, the Konbad-e Ghaboos, the tallest brick structure to survive from the ancient world. Ten columns with Hellenic motifs, each representing a century, rise at the entrance facade. They are reminders of Ibn Sina's initial devotion to Greek thought. Mount Alvand stands guard with a white cap. The universe of Ibn Sina, brimming with stars, with love, with angels, and with God, completes the scene in my mind.

The mausoleum embodies Ibn Sina's life, work and soul. The holy words on his gravestone represent his mastery of the Koran as a child; the columns symbolize his command of Greek knowledge as a young man. Finally, the tower, depicting the bursting of a new continent of Eastern thought from the seabed of history, reaches for the heavens, as if Ibn Sina's soul, arms, mind, were stretching skyward toward the heavens, struggling to ascend to the mind of the Creator, Whose self-intellection created the universe. Truth-seeking and healing took Ibn Sina ever closer to the ultimate source of knowledge, faith and love, his God. I see the tower piercing a mysterious luminosity. Oh, my mind! Could Ibn Sina's soul be the reincarnation of the wise healing bird, Sina?

I finally come down to earth. I seek out the custodian to tell him, "Agha Akbar-o-allah, I wish to visit the grave privately."

"Why, Agha?"

"It is a secret I cannot reveal."

"Where do you come from?" he asks me.

"New York. I arrived yesterday."

Akbar grins widely and knowingly. "In my dream last night, the Master told me to trust and oblige the new visitor." I shiver inside but keep silent. "I will leave the door unlocked tomorrow evening, after the closing hour. I will break the law and risk imprisonment or death for the Master's wish," he assures me. "But I want you to know that you will risk more, not less than me."

"How is that?" I inquire in alarm.

"Well," he explains, "they will torture you to reveal your real purpose for unlawful entry at midnight. And no one would believe your truth."

Chapter Seven: Forgetting the Memory

Lying in bed in the Hotel Ibn Sina, I gaze at a speck on the ceiling and know I must endure tomorrow's dawn and dusk to visit the tomb alone. Not knowing what else to do, I examine the case: The future must be malleable—putty, not stone—or else why should I ponder my alternatives. But, even so, can I mold events? Instead of answers, I hear the fear of the unknown trickle into my heart, filling it drop by drop. Can I cross death's gate, meet a ghost, return and still be me? Yes, I answer myself. Happiness and truth are ghosts, too, Pirooz, and you have been chasing them all your life.

The tomb will be empty and pitch black, with Islamic Revolutionary Guards lurking in the shadows, perhaps. I have never trusted darkness, ghosts, arbitrary rule or the next world. If the Guards find me, would they believe that I have come to visit a ghost? A court will ridicule my true mission and throw me in a dungeon.

Trying to expunge my fears and loneliness, I whisper, "I need counsel. Will any help come?" Hearing no answer, I pretend to phone the universal operator.

"Yes?"

"I want His phone number."

"Him, the Divine Being?"

"Yes, God."

"The number is an irrational one, the pi, an infinitely long number."

"Then it will take an eternity to dial it!"

"Yes, forever."

"Thank you."

Having convinced myself that I alone am in charge of my destiny, I wish all of us knew that there is no emergency number to heaven. I will blame no one for my being here or being alone in my adventure to meet Ibn Sina.

When I asked Sitareh what she wished to be, she replied, "I would like my body to be a needle, my soul a string, and my life the sewing of an embroidery uniting mankind. Just like Ibn Sina, the Prince of Love, who cared for life, all lives, and who respected kings and paupers, savants and the untaught alike."

"How do you know this?"

"Do you, Pirooz, know how you learned to speak, think or imagine?"

When I asked why she wanted to go to Hamadan, she had answered, "I have longed for a spiritual journey to the sage I feel I know intimately."

"Intimately?"

"Yes, intimately." Her reply echoed reassurance, but vanished, as echoes do, though now I can hear it again.

Through the window I see the sun and moon together. A rainbow arching over the fountain springing from a bed of tulips welcomes me with a smile. The vision is soothing and healing. I feel rested, having slept soundly.

After a breakfast of lentils, bread and tea, I hire a cab for the day and take off for a village near Mount Alvand I knew in my youth. The friendly driver wears a huge moustache, his smile showing big white teeth, one of which is chipped.

The morning is as fresh as the dawn of time. We arrive in a valley that separates Mount Alvand from its western ridge. The majestic peak holds up the tent of the sky, where the sun, moon, and stars are printed. Its upper elevations are outlined in snow, like the white hair, eyebrows, and moustache of a proud old man. Even the summer sun respects the whiteness on top. The valley, perfumed by sweet-scented flowers, lies about me as it did in my childhood. Nothing seems changed except me. I look around. Springs fill gurgling streams that feed the orchards. Certain Dervish brotherhoods believe Alvand contains the philosopher's stone, in which one can behold the answer to any question. Many peasants think that the grass that glistens under the rays of the sun embodies the alchemists' goal—the ingredients that transform base metals into gold. Some whisper that Ibn Sina mixed pollen with powdered fruit seeds and herbs to treat broken hearts. Can I be my own alchemist and transmute myself from base metal into gold, from the worldly into the spiritual?

Old Alvand has a memory; it has known homeless paupers, restless travelers, and monarchs in their palaces at the ancient capital, Ecbatana. Mount Alvand witnessed Queen Esther in the embrace of King Ahasuerus, or Xerxes, more than two millennia ago, pleading with him not to heed evil counsel in exterminating the Jews. The scroll of Esther records the salvation of the Jews, who celebrate on the eve and morning of Purim in joyous drinking, feasting and hospitality. Since the Jewish faith declares that God creates the cure before the pain, then Esther must have been God's remedy for unjust rulers.

Now Esther lies off Darius Avenue, near Ibn Sina's old grave, in a humble tomb topped by a small dome, with a fish pool but no fish, and a rabbi who comes but seldom. The souls of Esther and Ibn Sina must have spoken together of peace and love. The dead may speak, but only the living can act. The dead do not choose to be dead, but the living can so choose. The dead have no fear of homelessness or arrest, for death is the dissident's home, the exile's cure for rejection, and it ends the flogging of the psyche of the immigrants who are also dissidents—like me. Ibn Sina and Gorgani as dissidents migrated from city to city, seeking safety to do their work.

I walk through the village that clings to Mount Alvand's skirts like a thirsty child asking for water. Stones round and smooth, the breasts of the earth, bulge from the narrow, winding paths. The villagers' curious glances follow me, for I am a stranger to them, as I am to myself. Nothing has changed, even though man has already walked on the moon. The breeze that has caressed Alvand's snow and picked up the fragrance of a thousand flowers mixed with nectarines and animal dung revives my memories. I am awestruck that memory can be resurrected by a single scent, a musical note, even another memory. I have memories of memories, some of them as sweet as the sweetest nectarines or bitter as a life unfulfilled.

Unfulfilled. The word rings in my head. Am I insane, breaking the law to meet a ghost? I push my doubts away and instead reminisce about the past. If a memory is painful, shall I then forget it? But how can I forget Sitareh? What of my dreams; are they nothing, or am I nothing, because they are unattained? Unrealized dreams can crystallize into remembrances, too. Man is condemned to dream beyond his possibilities, to remember what is best forgotten and understand more than what is necessary to survive. I should no longer ask, "What is the beginning and destiny of everything?" but merely, "What will happen tonight?"

I smell the scent of earth freshly plowed and watered for summer vegetables and spices, the scent of things that have ripened or are ripening or will ripen. Man selects a bouquet of smells through numerous olfactory cells, each recognizing one odor. I remember my father telling me, "Nothing exists without a reason." I see the relevance of his words in each cell in my nose. I see his face as clearly as I see the mud and stone huts around me.

A washed klim hangs folded on a tree to dry, like Dali's soft watches, except that the passage of time is so slow here, maybe because of the age of the place. The carpet reveals to me its weavers' lives, folded by their fate. I remember a visit long ago to a carpet workshop. My mother wanted me to learn how hundreds of knots per square inch were made into exquisite rugs. She wanted me to see the children's toil and realize "how lucky I was" to play carefree. But I saw more than just my good fortune. I saw the cold, dusty, gloomy and impersonal factory. I saw the children's hollow eyes, pallid faces and aching fingers, and I heard their sad songs as they knotted colorful woolen threads around the cords that ran up and down wooden frames. They wove their lives and bodies, even their pain, into the knots, and, whenever I step on a rug, I can hear a stilled scream, the articulation of the inarticulate.

When my family spent summer vacations in Hamadan, I would go looking for the remotest ponds, for the tree with the sweetest mulberries, for the horse that galloped faster than the others. But now I look for the soul of a man dead a long time past. Perhaps the years, my years, prod me to contemplate my soul—the immortal soul. Memory and reality unite with what is neither remembered nor real, but imagined. I pour out my dreams, memories, and thoughts, the entire burden of my mind, into the world of perception. I see, hear, and touch their vividness, concreteness, and also their sadness. I wish to cry, but my eyes are drier than a desert and no tears come. I wish God, having created a difficult world, would make tears easy.

With just a cryptic hint from a dream, I want to find Ibn Sina, touch his wisdom and ascend beyond the disappointing self I am stuck with. I want to ask every "intellectually intelligible" question I can of Ibn Sina, who seems to understand both worlds. Like a ghost I want to cross all barriers and become a pilgrim to the citadel of understanding, where I cease being a dissident exile, and every kiss will make one wiser, and everywhere is home to everyone. I refuse not to understand the other or to be misunderstood. How long can we be strangers to ourselves, to one another, and to our own humanity?

Ibn Sina believed in the centrality of the self and human dignity. To him, neither uniqueness and multiplicity, nor spirituality and materialism, were contradictory. He worked intensely, played wholeheartedly, helped generously, and loved unboundedly. To Ibn Sina *freedom* of choice meant *autonomy* of choice, and *autonomy* of choice meant *sovereignty* of the soul. The anguish of the unattainable often submerged him in despair, but he emerged from it again and again. He denied that the price of existence is alienation from nature, society and God, for the Sufi way could overcome alienation and dissolve the anguish of change and death. His innovative spirit aroused the hostility of traditionalists, but he never ceased to innovate. He conquered forces that tended to mold him against his will. By making history Ibn Sina proved the power of his soul to expand the consciousness of the self and others. I want to learn his secret and liberate myself and others from being molded for unworthy causes.

What about my consciousness? Me? Am I the one who is talking to you, or the one who is lost trying to find himself, or the one who perished in my upbringing, or even in ancient times as Gorgani? Am I the one who is longing, or the one I long to become? Am I just some historical sediment that can speak? Is there more to me than what will lie in a grave someday? Does it matter? If it does, do the answers to such questions exist? Are they discoverable? I know that things like mountains, continents, established sciences, strong beliefs and personalities, or even galaxies are not as permanent as they appear. Death may not be permanent either, so why should I fear it? In search of my soul I will break the law and enter the tomb tonight.

I hear the bark of a stray dog, the meow of a frightened cat, the crow of a cock confusing dusk with dawn. I watch the last peasants leaving their fields for home. I know that peasants live simply and die simply here, but with a keen awareness of all the plants and animals. They keep their unhappiness to themselves, resigned to a future as difficult as the past they have survived. I can imagine the suppers' ends, the stories told while tea is served with cubes of sugar. I have been in their huts and want to believe that nothing changes there except some names. History, even its varnish, seems to remain fixed in those little huts next to the graveyard. But, alas, I know better, I know nothing is constant, not even in the graves or the skies. I walk with these thoughts, feeling momentarily liberated from time's authority. In New York, the weight of time pressed on my back, but now I see the joyful stars in full bloom in the clearest sky; I have yearned for that sky for so long. I see moonlight falling onto the gravestones and reflecting up from them, connecting the buried bones with their floating souls.

Why is Sitareh not with me now? My last words to her, "Good night," should have been, "Good ever." Fate kept its secret from me, even as Sitareh appeared to know it. But there was no first admission of my love, no last kiss, no last cry, no fuss, nothing, nothing, not even a prolonged embrace to indicate this was our last moment together. So many days are between us already, but it seems only last night that I put my face on her chest and felt her heartbeat with my eyes. "Soon we will sleep in the same bed and wake up in the same bed," she said. Her promise revealed her feelings. Every word! I think of Sitareh, who built a bridge to an old world for me and then left me to cross it alone. But am I alone? My love for Sitareh seems to grow in me day by day, as though she is with me in Hamadan and we climb Alvand together hand in hand. Is she here with me now?

It is late in the fateful night. The cabdriver puts his *nay*, a reed flute, to his lips. I am lost in the past and in the wondrous presence of wise Alvand, of the Persian stars, of the air that tastes as though it had never been breathed before. The music of the *nay*, enigmatic like moonlight, carries to me in a crisp wind. Seeing birds dance, I am convinced it is instinctive, a primeval form of communication. The music implores me to dance, and I happily oblige. I move as if buoyant. I feel life should be a lasting dance. But with whom am I dancing or communicating tonight? With my fears? The driver sings the *nay*'s story told by Rumi.

"Hearken to this Reed forlorn
Breathing, ever since 'twas torn
From its rushy bed, a strain
Of impassioned love and pain.

'The secret of my song, though near,
None can see and none can hear.
Oh, for a friend to know the sign
And mingle all his soul with mine!

> 'Tis the flame of love that fired me,
> 'Tis the wine of love inspired me.
> Wouldst thou learn how lovers bleed,
> Hearken, hearken to the Reed!"

But the *nay*'s doleful tale compels me to dance ever so slowly and gently, so as not to wake up the moonlight or the dead. Finally the music stops, and I stop dancing. Maybe the cabdriver wants to go home.

Suddenly a voice outside my imagination summons me to Ibn Sina. I remember my agreement with the guard, his promise to leave the door unlocked. I must not lose this opportunity. I impel myself to overcome my fear and rush to the road and into the cab. "Take me to Ibn Sina's mausoleum. Then you are free for the night."

The driver is shocked. "The tomb is not open at this time of night."

"I know the danger and more," I say. I just want to touch the ground there."

He shrugs in bewilderment. "Visitors always know something I don't!"

"What do you mean?"

"You seem free of the fear of arrest and torture. Everything is a mystery to me, Agha. Life is a mystery, you are a mystery, and I am a mystery to myself. I stick my head up to see better, but all I find is more mystery." He shakes his head, "The well I am in, better said, the hole, is too deep, and no one hears my cry for help."

"You are in a well?"

"The well of fate. Dry for some, rich for others."

For a while he drives silently, and I ponder his confession. Then he asks, "You have been in this village before, Agha?"

"Yes, when I was a child. My great-aunt owned a cherry and apricot orchard with a big pond on it."

"The pond with the little island?"

"Yes, how did you know?"

"My father worked in that orchard until he dropped dead."

"I remember Mashdi Jaafar. He was kind and fun," I say.

"I know," the driver agrees. "See, Agha, you could never have guessed this. There is no end to mysteries."

I say to myself, "I guess so. I guess. One mystery after another. The sun shines on a new world every day, like a new consciousness seeing things differently. I wonder if what I see defines me, or if what I am defines what I see."

"What do you mean, Agha?"

"Nothing, just pondering another mystery."

"Oh," he replies.

"By the way, what is your name?"

"Heyroun Gholi."
"Heyroun, meaning perplexed!" I exclaim.
"I didn't make me, but I did rename myself Heyroun. And your name?"
"Pirooz. You are a great artist. You made me dance in a fateful night."
"I just blow the air, Agha. It is my soul that plays and sings."
Driving toward the tomb he says, "You must have liked the fruits here."
"I loved them."
"Do you still like Hamadan?"
"Yes." Then I ask, "You must love it, too?"
He laughs, "Love, love with passion? Just for your ears, I have passion only for my neighbor's daughter! Oh, she is really something! Those tiger eyes, sumptuous lips, giggling breasts, the smile, the walk. Oh, that walk! It hurts me to talk about her walk! She is a torture. Beauty as a torture, Agha. Have you ever heard this mystery?"
"Beauty as a torture," I repeat with a new understanding. "What is her name?"
"Zahra," he replies, and I mumble, "Zahra. Sarah in the Bible, maybe."
Then he sighs and reluctantly continues, "I do like Hamadan. My wife and kids seem to like it, too. But how can we tell, Agha? We haven't been anywhere else. The winter is cold and tough and fuel is dear, but spring is such a beauty—you may want to lift up her skirt and peek underneath. Isn't this true, Agha?"
"Every word," I egg him on.
He pauses, then declares, "Summer is passion fulfilled."
"What about fall?"
"A beauty in the arms of the wind."
"Are you a poet?"
"No. Poets have had to hold many jobs, but I know of no poets driving a taxi. It is the poet's mind that should wander around, not his body in a used car."

For a long moment I feel that the taxi is at a standstill and Hamadan is marching by, exhibiting its robustness, adventures, and generosity in accepting me, a soul in search of something, perhaps itself, perhaps a resting ground. Is Hamadan the *all-knowing* sage, the *Hama-dan,* as it sounds in Persian?

I recall my father's words: "Hamadan is the nest in which history hatched one of the eggs of civilization." If Hamadan has lasted so long, I will last one night in it. I catch my inner voice in the whirlwind of doubt and dread within. I will enter the tomb! At midnight I shall cross over between the two worlds.

The taxi is soon at the tomb. I pay the driver, who waves as he speeds away. I can walk back to the hotel. His worried look reminds me of my own anxiety.

Chapter Eight: God Is Great

The midnight is full of moonlight. I look around, wishing as never before to be solitary. I am resigned to my pilgrimage; in fact, I feel condemned to it. Not yet ready to enter the tomb, I sit beside a rose bush and try to allay my apprehension. Have I come here to risk arrest for a visit with a ghost who invited me to his grave in a flimsy dream of mine? I wait for new courage while feeling a prayer upwelling in my heart. I refuse to pray, but now prayer will not refuse me. Ibn Sina prayed for inspiration when tackling stubborn problems in science or philosophy and claimed that God often guided him to the solution. But he drank wine, too, which violated dogma, and he subtly challenged Islamic orthodoxy, thus antagonizing the Mullahs. "God did not create matter, He gave form to existing matter," claimed Ibn Sina. "But only in God do *what* He is and *that* He is coincide," meaning that all beings owe their existence to causes outside themselves, except God.

My thoughts swirl and clash. What am I doing here with these thoughts? I ask the moon, whose light, Ibn Sina wrote, originates beyond all earthly lights. Can my mind—can any mind—make sense of the fantasy that has drawn me here tonight? I try to apply his great philosophical insight, "intellectually intelligible," to my predicament. Are God, the soul, rebirth, and my dream intellectually intelligible? Are they or are they not? Why does my heart pound? Is a pounding heart comprehensible? What does it say? I thought I had resolved my doubts, but doubts are deceptive; they resurface when least expected. Is my volition sound? I peer at the tower illuminated in the moonlight and realize that, to Ibn Sina, God and the soul were intellectually intelligible. Is the concept understandable, relevant, applicable, here, tonight?

These questions stick in my mind like the multiplication table. I look south at Mount Alvand, but I hear no answers. Finally I resolve not to let doubt and fear of the unknown or of self-ridicule stop me. Reason cannot explain what is beyond its reach.

I look at my watch. It is exactly midnight and the city seems sound asleep. Together, the moonlight and a sudden glow within me dissolve my dwindling doubts. I accept my dread, even my horror. My intuition subdues my reason, my belief in the primacy of matter shrinks first to an alternative hypothesis, then to a mere curiosity.

I trust the leading wise man, and I will defy the law and the fear of this world and the next to try to reach him. I will enter the mausoleum, come what may. I imagine Ibn Sina's soul wrapping mine like the sari that was Sitareh's shroud. She was drawn to the great physician because he prolonged many lives, and I was drawn to Sitareh because she opened my mind to the heavens, to the possibility of what had seemed nonexistent. She opened my mind to the beauty and vitality in all forms of life and to the sensibleness of death for all beings. "It is between birth and death that one must ascend beyond worldly desires," she had said. This was the perfecting of the soul, the purification necessary for its reunion with God.

Her knowing smile later nudged me to a Persian spiritual pasture, Sufism. In *The Book of Directives and Remarks*, a testament of his final thoughts, Ibn Sina described the Sufi's spiritual journey from the very beginnings of faith to the highest stage of a direct and uninterrupted vision of God. To follow the Sufi way is to obey the commands and prohibitions of God as exemplified in the words and deeds of His Prophet. The Prophet declared, "The search for knowledge is incumbent upon every Muslim," and "Knowledge without practice is a tree without fruit." For the Sufi, truth is his path and love is his attainment of God, because the greatest attributes of God are truth and love. The mystic, led by spiritual masters, reaches many virtues along the Sufi way, acquiring wakefulness, repentance, self-examination, humility, sincerity, charity and courage on the ladder of spiritual perfection that the Sufi must climb.

Ibn Sina knew he must be disciplined and relentless in overcoming all obstacles on the Way to God, but he also delighted in the pleasure of worldly existence. He wore silk garments, accepted high office, and enjoyed the admiration flowing to him as a wise man. He sought the external glow but didn't neglect his soul. His body was a human body, his mind a god's, and his spirit a saint's. He couldn't help it; he was what he was and he tried to be what he could become by self-realization.

My hand trembles and my thoughts tremble with them. Fate is a big gate that swings open on a little hinge at the push of a finger or a gentle breeze, or by a key word or an incident like stepping on a cockroach. If the incident was insignificant, then why do I fancy that I may one day know the identity of the deceased roach? And why has an insect's death become so momentous in my life? Now I sense that my fate is just a few steps ahead of me as I walk to the building. Cautiously I stop to look around one last time. Is a Guard hiding behind the bushes or one of the mausoleum's Greek columns or the walls? I check and check again, like a cat in new surroundings that can smell dogs lurking nearby.

Patches of clouds holding hands move about as though dancing to the cosmic hum, the Big Bang's fallout. I step over the moon shadows cast by the silent columns watching me. I push open the unlocked wooden door. Its eerie moan penetrates the stillness like the screeching of a swarm of locusts. I look around in fright to see if anyone heard it. I quake at the thought that the custodian who left the door unlocked for me could be an informer. Yes, I admit to myself, I am afraid, even though only yesterday I had convinced myself that I wouldn't be.

Suddenly a clatter breaks the still night. For a moment I freeze. In horror I pull the door almost shut and seem to stop breathing. Footsteps rush up the stairs behind me. I am caught! the thought rumbles through my mind. A voice calls out, "Stop, Agha! Stop!" I twist around to find a hand outstretched towards me. Handcuffs. Arrest. The thought hammers me and the prolonged moment of anguish seems endless.

"You erred, you gave me too much, Agha." His hand holds some cash.

I take a deep breath, as though awakened from anesthesia, and manage to reply to Heyroun Gholi, the cabdriver, "No. I made no mistake. It is all yours."

He mumbles, "Another mystery!" and walks away. I try to calm down.

The moonlight sweeps away darkness and sets aside my dark thoughts. I recover my wits and push the door open again. Walking towards the tomb chamber, I hear my own footsteps and heartbeat. The hall seems too long. The words collected in the mausoleum library are all mute, even though they have a lot to say. I am mute, too.

I look up to see the tower rising above the skylight. Tense, I lean my head against the structure, as if to ground my remaining fear through its granite base. I sense the tower's forbearance, my aloneness, and the privacy of all things in the tomb's dimness. I remove my shoes, push open the iron gate and step up to the marble headstone covered in the silk blue satin of moonlight. I am pulled slowly to my knees, as though by gravity, while a stirring passes through me. Kneeling, I place my forehead against the stone in the posture of a praying Muslim and whisper the key words of my dream, "God is great." Always doubtful of God's existence, I've never pronounced these words with such solemnity.

A gentle force stretches me chest-down on the gravestone. I cast reason and skepticism aside, suppress fear, resign myself to what will be.

"God is great! God is great!" My voice echoes in the tomb and the words journey perhaps from this world to the next. A slight ripple in the ground vibrates against my chest. Is it the earth or my own heartbeat?

A crisp voice rings out: "Salaam, Gorgani. Welcome to Hamadan. Your visit is the Divine will, even though at times you doubted His wisdom."

My hair rises like nervous needles; I shiver and feel on fire. I clutch the gravestone, holding on to the voice, to the glow.

"Set aside your fears and focus on the immaterial to find me, Gorgani."

"I have," I barely manage to pull the words out of my throat. "I will do as you say." I tremble with joy and apprehension at touching the two worlds. I am alone, yet he is with me. Exalted and uncertain, I reassure myself: the great healer would not let me come to harm. My fear is routed. I feel safe!

Knowing my thoughts, he declares, "If you must have fear, Gorgani, fear the living, not the dead." His warning resurrects my dread of immanent arrest and torture.

Suddenly, the moon hides behind the clouds, and a still, pitch blackness surrounds me as I lay prone. I hear a flapping, like that of a wounded bat, a crackling, and then an ominous echo. Terrified in the darkness, I notice that the dead man is silent and may be gone. "Ibn Sina, Ibn Sina," I whisper, so that only he will hear me.

From nowhere, assertive steps advance towards me. The ground moans under their weight. An excruciating breathlessness and a burning in my throat presage death. Instantly, a hand weighs on my shoulder. "Oh, my God!" I wheeze as fear stabs me in the heart. I bear a long, shivering moment of terror and dread.

"Help!" I scream, while tightening my hold on the stone. "Help, Ibn Sina!" I beg the dead man. The torture mounts, but nothing happens. Fatally trapped, I dare not turn to look up, for fear of facing a hellish monster or men with guns.

The hand withdraws, but I dread its return. The threat is more bloodcurdling than the reality. Paralyzed, I sweat with chills; evil may be standing over me. I wait for the lethal moment, expecting nothingness to swallow me whole, but the jaws of annihilation do not shut, and I continue to exist lifelessly.

"Who is there?" a shrill voice ricochets in the dark. This is not the voice of the cabdriver, my battered mind resolves instantly. The deadly hand returns, horror overwhelms me, a shooting pain strikes me, and my mind shuts down. I pass out in a frozen darkness that dissolves memory. Time continues to expire while I am gone, but, like the dead, I cannot tell its duration.

I seem to awake to a nausea and into a new world. Time is halting; it sticks drop by drop to my returning fears. "Agha, Agha!" I hear again. My eyes remain shut from anguish of what they may see, as two hands lift me up. "Agha, Agha! You passed out." I open my eyes to the sounds. Under the faint moonlight, a specter disrupts my blurred vision. Nothing is steady or clear, everything shimmers. I squint, trying to focus. A face emerges, floating in space. It ties my tongue, shuts off my voice, and stillness agonizes me. "Oh!" I finally screech with astonishment as I fight another fainting spell. "God! Almighty God!" Seeing the face, my tongue turns numb again.

The face! This face. The suspended face appears and disappears in the tomb's light and shadows. I know this face. It is not threatening, but I am threatened. With eyes shut I mumble, "Sitareh, Sitareh! Is it you?" There is no response; silence is crushing. Is she a specter? Are new ghosts deaf? Have I been shot and killed already? Where are we? Questions hammer me. "Speak!" I demand of the silent ghost. "Am I dead, too?" I ask, remembering the blackened period I awoke from. "Speak to me, Sitareh!" There is no answer. Is she dead or not? Am I alive? The specter is mute, and my body is glued to the gravestone. Death rules my inquiry.

She stares at me, puzzled, as though I have intruded into her coffin. Suddenly with agitated footsteps, the specter's vague outline backs off into darkened space, but her penetrating eyes still bear heavily on me. Do ghosts make sounds? My anxious mind searches for an answer to ward off the threat to its own sanity and existence. My fright subsides a little as she examines me with curiosity and alarm. I have frightened her, but I don't know why. I must not approach her, even if I may be dead myself.

"Who are you? How do you know me?" the ghost finally speaks.

I want to answer but cannot. Believe your eyes, believe your ears, Pirooz, I admonish myself. This is really real. The ghost stares at me, waiting, waiting inquisitively for answers. But who is supposed to give answers to whom? I wonder. Why doesn't she recognize me, if she exists? But she seems less unreal now. Are the memories of the dead dead, too? A resurrection without memory, perhaps.

"How do you know me?" she demands. "How?"

"Of course I know you! But I thought you were . . . and . . ." I mumble.

"I was what?" she insists.

"But I thought . . . I thought you would recognize me," I manage to respond.

Suddenly it dawns on me that we are talking in Persian, and Sitareh could not speak the language. The new shock alarms me once more. Who am I talking to, if not to Sitareh? Maybe death is the gate to all tongues, too. I step back. I must conquer fear and look harmless to her, I tell myself. Don't ruin this opportunity to know both worlds, Pirooz. Persisting in my hopes, I beg her: "Sitareh, it is me!"

More secure, she demands, "Who are you?"

"Pirooz. Pirooz, of course. Your Pirooz."

"Dr. Pirooz?"

"Yes, yes, yes!" I feel unburdened. She is regaining her memory. "But if you don't recognize me, how do you know of my doctorate?" I demand.

"I am Sitareh Bastan. I sent you a letter to New York regarding Ibn Sina."

"What letter?" My agitated thoughts and memories crash into one another.

"To New York. About Ibn Sina's work on music as therapy," she raises her voice slightly, trying to wake me up. "And you answered me, a long, thoughtful reply."

"Oh, yes. I remember. Music as therapy. Ibn Sina, the Grandfather of Modernity. And your initial 'S' stood for Sitareh?"

"Yes."

Two Sitarehs who look uncannily alike. The impossible is possible.

We fall silent as the moon reemerges from under the clouds and floods the tomb with fresh, reassuring light. Seeing her face clearly makes me feel secure. She focuses her gaze, bursting with questions, even objections, on me.

I gaze back at her and try to comprehend everything with my eyes. Why is she here? An intense curiosity inflames my mind. What is this woman doing at the tomb at midnight? She may also be asking herself, why is he lying on the gravestone? Is any of this intellectually intelligible?

Daringly, she approaches, until our shadows nearly overlap. A sudden joy sweeps away my remaining reservations. I see a Sitareh, her mysterious smile with a dimple on her chin and her melancholy eyes. Love resurrects the dead. I want to put my face on her chest and hear her heartbeat with my eyes again. The reappearance of wonder in me, after a dreadful period of darkness, is delightful. What use is a wonderless life, I muse for a moment in the midst of the waning turmoil.

"Now I understand. You were in touch with Ibn Sina," she remarks with awe. "I shouldn't have intervened. But you were shaking and seemed to be in agony, even in danger. I feared the worst. I am a physician and have a physician's instinct."

Disappointed that Ibn Sina's voice has disappeared and bewildered that Sitareh has appeared, I reply, "I am all right. It is done." Then to reassure myself of the unbelievable, I ask, "Are you really real?"

"As real as you."

She grasps my hands in hers to prove her realness. They are soft and warm, yet firm. We stare at each other. I feel something vital flow from her to me. I open my arms and gently embrace Sitareh. She accepts me like a mother who finds a lost child. I touch my own teardrops on her neck. She holds me tightly as her warm, reassuring words flow, "We two love the same soul."

I let go of her. "We love . . ." I stop myself, seeing myself in her eyes.

"We love what? Whom?"

"You will know." I am evasive.

Again she tolerates my reluctance to reveal my thoughts. Having lost the opportunity to speak to Ibn Sina, suddenly I sense danger again. "Let us leave now. It is fatal to be caught in the tomb."

"Fine," she replies. "But tell me, how did you recognize me, Dr. Pirooz?"

"Not here. Later, perhaps." I keep my promise of silence to Ibn Sina. "We have broken in illegally, Dr. Bastan. Let us leave immediately." My own words add to my alarm. Without a word, she hands me my shoes. I close the chamber's gate, then shut the main door behind us.

Outside under the moonlight, I observe that Dr. Sitareh Bastan is about the same age as Sitareh Poonia, though fair of face. She wears a white silk blouse with a long, blue skirt, and a scarf covers her hair—a bit casual by Islamic standards.

"We have a lot to talk about," I suggest and wait patiently.

She sizes me up before she makes up her mind. "You are staying at a hotel?"

"Yes, the Hotel Ibn Sina."

"I am staying at my deceased grandparents' house. May I offer you a snack, perhaps?" Her simple invitation pours ecstasy and apprehension into my heart.

I glance at her. I feel my hunger. "Thank you, yes, I would like that."

We walk to her car. The monument seems to shrink as she drives slowly south along Ibn Sina Boulevard. She appears unfazed by our adventure. I try to accept the impossible, to put the past and the future aside and explore the moment. Ibn Sina's statue watches us as we pass the square named for him. Dr. Bastan's house is on *Farmandary* (Authority) Street in the southeast of Hamadan.

Suddenly the flashing lights of a police vehicle are with us. Sitareh's face turns pale. "It's the Islamic Guards," her anxious voice whispers as she pulls to the curb.

A young man rushes to our car. He points a blinding flashlight in her face and then in mine. "Are you married?" he asks.

"No, but. . .," Sitareh replies, covering her eyes.

"Are you brother and sister?"

"No."

"Then you have no business being together. I must take you in."

"He is—" Sitareh begins.

"It doesn't matter who he is anymore," the guard interrupts, "or where you're coming from or going to." I keep silent, thinking that Sitareh knows best what to do.

"What is your name?" The Guard's accusatory tone rises in volume.

"Sitareh Bastan."

The Guard trains the torturing light right in her face again. "Dr. Bastan?"

Sitareh covers her eyes once more. "Yes. Turn off that light, please."

He switches it off. "You once treated my mother and my sister, and you refused payment, figuring we couldn't afford it. Do you remember?"

"I'm sorry," Sitareh replies. "Not specifically. I have done it not infrequently."

The Guard smiles. "Well, Dr. Bastan, remember, you should not be seen alone with that man again. This is the Islamic Republic, not Hollywood." He turns around and shouts to the other Guards in the police car, "They are family."

Sitareh draws a deep breath. The two cars run in opposite directions.

For a while we avoid speaking of the Guards' intrusion or our graveside experience. Sitareh and I keep silent as if to digest our anxiety and extinguish our curiosity. At last we glance at each other again. I don't want to press or be pressed for vital information right now. Instead, we talk of our work. I learn that Sitareh studied medicine in Teheran after finishing high school in France, where her father was a diplomat. She did her residency in psychiatry at Johns Hopkins University. She works in a Teheran city hospital and has a small private practice. She is interested in memory and hypnosis and the problems of gifted individuals.

She relates her work to Ibn Sina: "His memory was phenomenal and his creativity nearly unmatched in the history of the mind. It seems that the loss of an object, like a home, a friend, a lover, a manuscript, or freedom sparked his creativity. Psychoanalytic theory explains the creative process as a healing."

"Interesting! Creative work transforms loss to gain, pain to joy, and darkness to light, the ultimate alchemy! Is this a new theory?" I ask.

Sitareh's eyes glitter. "No. Some classical Persian poets hint at it. A rose blossoms as the lovesick nightingale bleeds on its thorns and sings love songs, in one poem. Blood is shed, the rose blossoms, and the bird sings creatively."

"The creative seed germinates on the grave of what is lost," I conclude.

"Yes," she says. "God bless God for creating man creative."

"I dare not say it, but a curious idea just lit up in me." I feel very relaxed now.

"What is it?" Sitareh asks.

"God's joy of creation was a compensation for His loss of privacy—in the world that didn't exist—when He created the universe."

"That is a cosmological psychoanalysis of the Creator!"

"I wish the Creator would break His silence and speak to us. God creates and destroys stars and worlds while we humans talk and talk and talk."

"You are right, Dr. Pirooz. Quietly He embodies all powers and wisdom—even death may be an act of love by God."

"Call me Pirooz," I say.

"Fine. Call me Sitareh," she says as she turns onto a narrow side street. We fall silent, like the old gods who could speak but remained always silent.

Finally I tell Sitareh about my childhood visits to Hamadan, my self-exile to the U.S., my work as a disenchanted political economist and Middle East expert. I divulge my doubts about the significance, or even validity of what I write. "I don't feel free to tell the whole truth."

"Why do you write, then?" she asks.

"I am trapped professionally. Like a parakeet who returns to its opened cage for food and safety, I must return to my obligations for sustenance. My writing about authority is silent about what I call the 'parakeet complex,' the author's dependence on the keeper of his cage—authority. I cannot seriously challenge authority and still maintain authority's approval. This is worse than complaining to God about God, since you may lose what you have. We are priests bound by discipline. The high priests, such as administrators or editors, tolerate only minor infractions of the main paradigm, and colleagues even less. They demand that students learn what to think, not how to think. Repeatedly we are told how free we are, but I don't feel it. Dissimulation is second nature for me. I an not sure if submissive scholars have no conscience or are just intimidated." I wonder why I am pouring my heart out to her.

"Maybe a little of both, plus indoctrination, as you said. How did Ibn Sina react to alienation?"

"By recognizing and overcoming the anguish of an identity crisis," I tell her. "Let his poem speak for him:

> How I wish I could know who I am,
> What it is in this world that I seek."

Sensing that I am withholding something, Sitareh smiles mischievously as she brings the car to a halt. "We have more to talk about, Dr. Pirooz. Don't you agree?"

I agree and reflect that Sitareh Poonia didn't know how to drive, though she seemed to be in touch with another world. Sitareh Bastan seems more in touch with reality, caring for the ailing. She speaks Persian, but not Hindi, she wears a skirt and blouse, not a sari, and she is a psychiatrist, not a cultural anthropologist. Are the two women somehow the same except for upbringing and culture? But if different, why are they both drawn to Ibn Sina and me? Both are confident, intelligent, sensitive, and look similar, though Bastan's skin is a shade lighter and she is a little taller and thinner than Poonia. Even so, they could have been twins. Thoughts and questions besiege me as I leave the car. Who am I to be entangled in this bizarre affair?

Horror and love and fate's capriciousness all clamor for the attention of my tired mind. Nevertheless, I am exhilarated with fear and anticipation. Is this a replay of events in New York? Which are more dreadful, muggers or Islamic Guards who make arrests and ruin lives arbitrarily? What have I learned from Poonia's death and from my suffering? Have I recovered the irretrievable? What should I expect from her reincarnation in my life? Dr. Sitareh Bastan opens the door to the courtyard and turns on a number of lights with a single switch. I feel something turned on within me, too.

Chapter Nine: Immortal Souls in Mortal Bodies

A chorus of neighing from the stable greets us. The horses object to the car's noise. My host tells me that the stable abuts an abandoned carpet workshop on the property. Sitareh and I walk to an old house with stone walls at the city's outskirts, not far from the orchards and farms of Hamadan. We climb the stairs and tour the house. More lights blink on. Rooms are spacious, ceilings are high, windows are expansive. The entire second floor opens onto a huge balcony overlooking a courtyard of fish pools, flowerbeds, and fruit trees. Rose bushes in all colors abound, and honeysuckle vines wrap oaks lovingly, breathing out their perfume.

Sitareh's grandfather was a landlord who marketed *roghan*, a Persian cooking fat made from butter. He sold the business just before he and the grandmother passed away. "With them gone, the house revealed all its deterioration to me. There were termite-nibbled floorboards, rotten beams and some old, skewed, malfunctioning fixtures. I persuaded my parents to keep the house and helped to revive it. A restless urge compels me to revive things," she confesses.

We enter a reception room with an exquisite beige carpet, a chandelier with lights sparkling among its crystal earrings, and cherrywood couches covered in green velvet circling an antique coffee table with carved human figures for legs. A pair of silver candleholders and a large silver-framed mirror sit on a ledge that is draped with a hand-stitched Persian embroidery. A familiar face reflected in the mirror transfixes me. I turn my head to find a framed poster of Ibn Sina on the opposite wall. It is no spirit, and I breathe easier, before becoming alarmed that it is a copy of the same poster that hung in Sitareh Poonia's living room.

"Please take a seat."

I do. On the other wall, a picture of 'Ali ibn Abi Talib, the first Shiite Imam, stares at me with pensive eyes. His graceful presence reminds me of my long-forgotten reverence for this saint, scholar and courageous man. I feel I have been here before a long, long time ago. How do I remember this house? Why have I returned to it?

I remember my grandfather in Hamadan, with his huge, white moustache and twinkling eyes. He would hold the bowl of a long-stemmed pipe, taking big puffs, and coughing world-shattering coughs. As his smoke rings expanded while rising, he kidded me, "Tell me, my *naveh* (grandson), why does the smoke rise? Why do the leaves fall? And who holds the stars up?"

"You tell me, Baba Bozorg (Grandfather)," I would retort, and then instantly cover my ears in jest, to damp his coarse, ear-shattering laughter.

"If only I knew."

On the occasion of my first day in grade school, he gave me my first watch and said, "Don't you ever be late for school!" Oh, how much I loved him. That day he could have walked on my eyes, as Persians say.

Now I visualize him after he fell from his galloping horse, a little blood at the corner of his mouth, and the physician shaking his head. I hear the screams of the mourners and taste the bitter coffee served at his funeral, the only occasion at which most Persians drink coffee. He proved that a youthful spirit can defeat time's invasion, and his loss taught me that death cannot annihilate love. I still love him, and I see his big smile and hear his thunderlaughs now and then.

Sitareh interrupts my reminiscence. "Would you care for some wine?"

"Isn't it illegal?"

"Yes, Pirooz! But so is your looking at me when my scarf is off. The earliest wine in history, vintage 5500 years ago, was found in Sumerian jars at Godin Tepe (Godin Hill), not far from here. The grape grower, the winemaker and the drinker were most probably our ancestors. Anyhow, I believe God is the judge of what is sinful, and no ruler should usurp this Divine right."

"It is the arrest that worries me," I reply, still bothered by the policeman's blinding flashlight in my face. Sitareh frowns as if suffering from the same memory.

"We are safe here. Would you like some?" she insists.

"No, not this late. Thank you." Wishing not to awaken my ulcer, I dissimulate.

"Espresso, then?"

"Here in Hamadan?"

"Yes, in Hamadan," she teases me with a smile. "I always bring my brewing paraphernalia with me. I can't live without it."

"It will keep us awake," I resist.

"Don't we have much to talk about tonight?"

She leaves the room to prepare a snack. I look around, wondering how such bizarre events as occurred tonight arise. What is the intelligence behind them? Will Ibn Sina come back? What was Sitareh Bastan doing at Ibn Sina's grave at midnight? This is not just atypical, but mysterious. Do I feel for her as the one I loved? What am I to do? What am I to tell her, and what withhold?

Returning with a tray, Sitareh places bread, cheese, pastries and espresso on the table and announces, "Please help yourself."

I notice that the plates and utensils are placed in exact symmetry. I fill my plate while she brings in a bowl of fruit that reminds me of the one in Poonia's apartment. She sits opposite me. "I think Ibn Sina is luring us to him, but I don't know why. Maybe you are wondering what I was doing in the tomb at midnight. I wonder the same about you and am still curious how you recognized me," she says, practically in one breath.

"Well . . .," I begin.

"I am not done, Pirooz," she says softly. "I could not sleep tonight or wait till morning to visit the tomb. This tempestuous urge to find him is relentless."

"Well . . .," I hesitate, before I tell her about my trip, without mentioning Poonia or my dream of Ibn Sina, while wondering what she is withholding from me.

"Is that all?" she asks.

Still shocked by her sudden appearance from nonexistence, I am now in Sitareh's gaze as I was in New York. I find little difference between the two Sitarehs, nor do I feel differently toward them. Poonia's murder was a nightmare that ended at the tomb. I watch this Sitareh's pearl earrings swing as she bends to pour espresso for me and I note that she has braided her hair meticulously.

Inexplicably, Ibn Sina's poster signals to me, "You may tell her everything."

"Pirooz, I asked you if you have told me everything." She breaks my reverie, as though in touch with my thoughts.

I hold my forehead in my hands, trying to hold on to Ibn Sina's presence in my imagination. I feel swept away by something ineffable.

"Pirooz, what just happened to you?"

"He just told me to tell you everything."

"Him, Ibn Sina? How?"

"Somehow, through your poster."

To her questioning stare I almost plead, "Do you believe me?"

"Yes, yes, I do believe you—as a matter of fact, I do. I felt something, too."

We stare at one another, puzzled. I tell her about Poonia and my dream. She rises and raises her voice. "Our meeting is not a coincidence, then! It is all orchestrated." She tosses her braid back, swings about, sits down and calmly announces, "So, you are the reincarnation of Gorgani."

"Perhaps."

"Not perhaps! There is nothing more real than your dream!"

"You sound so sure, like Sitareh Poonia," I say.

"Yes. Let me see, did you know the name Gorgani before your dream?"

"I don't think so."

"But you were reading up on Ibn Sina just before the dream?" she asks.

"Yes, his mystic philosophy, the *Book of Directives and Remarks*, to be exact. But not his biography, which I had also borrowed."

"So you are absolutely sure you never . . ."

"Absolutely sure."

"And in your dream you didn't recognize the name Gorgani at first?"

"No," I reply. "I cannot recite the full names of Ibn Sina or Gorgani even now."

"This is consistent with your not knowing his full name. But you dreamed the whole thing. You knew the names but didn't know that you knew them."

"That is why I am here," I say, "but I have no clue what Ibn Sina wants."

"And why are there identical Sitarehs?"

"Do you believe you and Poonia have the same souls?"

"I am perplexed," she says. "We cannot have the same soul if we coexisted."

"In my dream, Ibn Sina mentioned that angels do copy souls."

"So both our souls are copies of another soul, but whose soul?" We stare at each other in awe, as unanswered questions pile up like an anthill.

"By the way, what did Ibn Sina tell you tonight at the tomb?" she asks.

"He said, 'Free yourself from worldly concerns and concentrate on the immaterial to find me.' He wants me to be as I was before I came to be—a soul."

"He wishes you to discard the past, your ego, even your free will. He has enticed you across nine time zones into the heart of danger. Why?"

We fall silent. I grind these disturbing thoughts beneath my wisdom teeth.

"Pirooz, let's not withhold anything. Is that possible?" she almost begs me.

"You, the psychiatrist, ought to know."

"Openness, even to oneself, is difficult, but let's try it."

"I admit, I have longed for intimacy, a potential blocked by fear," I say.

"One must be intimate with oneself first, Pirooz. And, as a Sufi would say, real unity is possible through a motion towards God. If you desire everlasting form, you must find it in formlessness, and if you wish for self-knowledge—an escape from the ordinary to reach the extraordinary—you must die to yourself and see yourself not as you are, but as God Himself or a creation of His. Even me!" she says with a smile.

"You sound so sure."

"Do we have a better choice than to be positive?"

"Has Ibn Sina ever appeared to you, Sitareh?" I ask abruptly.

She hesitates before responding, "Yes. He asked me to come to Hamadan."

"That is all?"

"Yes, but I don't know why, Pirooz."

"Well, why don't we use Ibn Sina's own syllogisms to discover his intentions?" I say and proceed to answer my own question. "According to him, syllogistic is the science of utilizing what is known to learn about what is unknown, what exists and is true, and what exists and is near the truth, and what exists and is false; a journey from matters understood to matters yet to be understood."

Sitareh thinks out loud. "All right, how would he have tried if he wanted to know what we want to know now?"

"Well," I begin, "he would start with a series of questions. Firstly, what is the thing, the object of inquiry? And if it is, that is, if it exists, where is it? When is it? How is it? And lastly, why is it?"

"Let me try them intuitively, Pirooz," Sitareh answers. "The *thing* is his soul. It does exist. The *where* seems to be everywhere, including in our dreams. The *when*, the time of his appearances, is unspecified, at least to us. The *how* depends on our following his instructions, or on his inspirations. But the question of *why* is a problem. What does he want from us? Why are we drawn to him?"

"Or why is he drawn to us?" I add. "Ibn Sina uses the senses to observe, and reason to draw conclusions about the earthly things he calls 'sublunary.'"

"But are all our experiences sublunary?"

I keep silent, since I don't know what is what—matter or non-matter.

"Forget the question, Pirooz. Continue what you were saying."

"Reasoning must start from the first principles of understanding."

"Sorry, but what did he mean that?" Sitareh asks.

"Whatever is self-evident, like the whole not being the sum of its parts."

"For example, man is more than the sum of his organs?"

"Yes," I reply. "Then syllogisms will reveal the unknown from what is known. Because one's upbringing indoctrinates without the mind recognizing it, Ibn Sina cautions against opinion, bias and memory entering reasoning surreptitiously."

"How sad! For most individuals, upbringing is everything. It is fate."

"It is language, religion, culture, ideology, taste and consciousness."

"Let's get back to what you were saying about his logic," Sitareh reminds me.

"Certainly. Syllogisms can only extend what is already known, as geometry uses self-evident axioms to prove complex theorems."

"So there is more in our experiences than we know," Sitareh interjects. "Let's go back to the question, why is it? Why are we entangled in this web?" she demands.

"Is it a web or an opportunity?" I ask.

"Both! Maybe we become more entangled now to become freer later."

"Ibn Sina said that only a struggle divides ignorance from the truth—God willing."

"Tell me, Pirooz, what do you think of God?"

"I am bewildered now, but normally I think that when idols, the moon or the sun or the Nile River, were named god and worshipped, the word God projected a clear image or meaning for the worshipers. But close our eyes and imagine the invisible God: what is pictured in our mind?"

"Nothing. No form, no substance. Nothing specific," she replies.

"Then God is just a word, but an exceptional one, since, unlike other words, it corresponds to no object or clue of one in the mind. The word 'God' had already been invented before the great world religions assigned it to an invisible, immutable, omniscient and thus unimaginable and incomprehensible being."

"But fear and love of God does exist in the mind," Sitareh says.

"Of course. Like the fear of a dark, empty space or the love of happiness."

"Didn't you mention the Creator before?"

"Only as a figure of speech."

She casts the strangest glance at me. Smiling, I shrug.

"Then what about religions?" she asks.

"They are words with moral content, good, bad or indifferent. Many have come and gone, some survived, but each claims to be the true one, though they are equally true and equally false, since they are equally unsubstantiated."

"What about your experience tonight?"

"Like the existence of matter, it suggests the existence of spirits. Instead of one mystery, we now face two." I think of the cabdriver's mysteries.

"It is nice to believe in God," Sitareh says.

Despite the turmoil of the night, we seem collected and thoughtful. As though guided by an invisible light, I talk to myself, and Sitareh listens as she would professionally. "Remember, Sitareh, that reason alone is insufficient to find the truth. Meditation may let us experience what is beyond reason and science and our preconceptions. Instincts and indoctrination could hold us back or cut us off from deeper understanding."

"I agree. Meditation may let us see things as God made them, not as someone in the past told us what they were. It is time to be daring, Pirooz, daring to believe and to love the invisible!" she suggests softly. "What do you think, Pirooz?"

"Worldly addictions, even imagined virtues, are an idolatry that separates one from the true self. The self, the one that the world sees and shapes, and the subjective self must regain their unity and integrity in order to transcend themselves."

"We must prepare our souls for the arrival of Ibn Sina in our lives," Sitareh replies.

"Arrival" reverberates in my mind. Arrival of what or whom and from where? You speak of him as a savior."

She flings her braid to one side. "I believe him a savior."

We stare at each other, knowing we share a great secret. Sitareh takes a sip of espresso as I whisper, "Thank God you are alive, Sitareh."

"Thank God, Pirooz! I've been alive since I was born," she grins.

"And I have lived before, before I was conceived for this life, perhaps," I reply.

Sitareh sighs. "And the coffee is getting cold."

We seem to have climbed to Alvand's peak, where the snow sleeps in peace forever, but other unknown peaks await us. We keep silent and look out over the vast space and eternal time surrounding us. In New York I was submerged in future anxiety or imagined glories, or else buried in the disappointments of the past. I never stood on the bridge connecting past and future, gazed down and experienced the flow of time around and through me, never seized the vitality of the moment I inhaled and exhaled.

But now I feel the now, the present, in fullness. How wonderful to feel the present unsullied by past or future. I had vacillated between solitude and society, but now, with Sitareh resurrected, I don't feel disjointed from reality. But if she leaves me, would this feeling be gone, too? I wonder. Suddenly, for a long moment, I feel like a single light illuminating everything around me. Oh, my mind! I exclaim to myself.

Finally I say, "It is late. I should return to the hotel."

"There are extra bedrooms here. Wouldn't you like the moon to be your night light and Alvand your guardian angel?"

"Yes, that would be perfect."

"Then come with me."

"Thank you."

I ponder things for a long while before I fall asleep. The city, Ibn Sina, Sitareh, Gorgani, me! I think of things close to me yet beyond my comprehension.

Chapter Ten: The Subject is Love

I sleep long and deeply. Sitareh Bastan awakens me with a knock at my door at noon. Soon she and I sit across a colorful breakfast table set on the balcony overlooking the garden. There are bread, honey, butter, nuts, feta cheese, yoghurt, and fruit, all fresh and pure, all free of bulk processing and chemicals. A cage hangs from a nearby fig tree, and a pair of vigorous nightingales set it quavering, the suspended mirror within sparkling for joy.

Sitareh wears a long blue velvet robe and her face glows like a star left behind by the night. Her elbows rest on the table and her long fingers cradle her chin. She is serene, beautiful and confident. The warmth of her alluring eyes and her charm set brush fires in me, while her eyelashes sweep away my longings.

A housemaid glances inquisitively at me as she places a samovar on the table. Sitareh thanks Firoozeh and introduces me. "Agha Pirooz," says Firoozeh, "my father told us about your grandfather's adventures." Her comment amazes us. As Firoozeh tells her story, Sitareh and I learn that our grandparents knew each other.

"The men loudly cursed their own luck when they played backgammon," Firoozeh reminds us with a twinkle in her eyes.

"My grandfather was a horseman, a free spirit and a poet of sorts," I say.

"This is all news to me," Sitareh adds.

Unbidden, the cabdriver's sparkling eyes, his drooping moustache and his words appear to me. "Life is a mystery. There is no end to mysteries, Agha."

Sitareh waits for me to resume. "If we search widely over the earth and deeply into the past, eventually everyone is linked to everyone else," I remark.

"True, mankind is one, forever," Sitareh says.

Firoozeh leaves, and Sitareh pours tea for us. The roses' perfume urges the nightingales to serenade us and the sun to reach its zenith for a better view of our togetherness. Hearing the nightingales, I can imagine my limitations as a cage, and my conscience the suspended mirror that reflects light. I don't sing, but I do speak and dissimulate. I barely resist the urge to cover my eyes and shout insanely, "There is no sun, there is no moon, and the stars have fallen into the pond at night and drowned." But still, I am pursuing a soul—the impossible; or maybe I am pursuing my own true self—the possible. Would I find a lost soul or myself remolded as someone else in exile?

"Please help yourself, Pirooz." Sitareh brings me back to the real world.

I enjoy the breakfast, especially the bread freshly baked in a brick oven.

"How long will you be in Hamadan?" she asks.

"Till the end of summer, perhaps, or until I find what I am looking for."

"I thought so," she confirms. "But what about your teaching?"

"I will have to take a leave of absence if I stay beyond the summer. It will be difficult. What about you, Sitareh?"

"I am on leave for a few weeks. The hospital director realized that I could lose my own mind treating war casualties uninterruptedly for two years. I have to return to Teheran a couple of times meanwhile. I feel guilty for abandoning my patients, especially the young war widows."

"Then we are in this together to seek Ibn Sina."

"It looks like it," she says. Our eye contact cements our resolve.

Firoozeh returns with a bundle of my mail forwarded from New York. As I leaf through it, some letters from my colleagues in Arabia catch my eye. They bear postage stamps depicting Persian thinkers as Arabs. My frustration loosens its own tongue. "Why did these presumably Arab scholars like Ibn Sina, Biruni and Al-Razi prefer to be born in Iran, speak Persian, work in Iran, have Persian patrons and die in Iran, and never miss Arab lands or make a journey there? I don't understand how these oil sheikhs can make such absurd claims and revise history on their stamps and books. This false nationalism frustrates even thoughtful Arabs. A dear Lebanese friend of mine is furious at the practice. Doesn't Islam consider the truth to be a supreme value? After all, Persia produced many great scientists and artists before its conversion to Islam."

"Pirooz," Sitareh chides me, "for a humanist, how can you become such an instant nationalist? Our Muslim brothers and sisters are complimenting us by calling Persians Arabs. They used to call us *Ajam*, which was not at all complimentary."

"How can you call a lie a compliment?" I ask her.

"Most compliments are lies," Sitareh says with a grin before continuing. "Now that we know our purpose, let me ask you something . . ."

I playfully interrupt her, "You may, as long as the subject is love—what Ibn Sina cared most about. Look at the fish, the birds, the squirrels courting, pollen seeking pistils, the bees matchmaking for flowers. Look at the summer born from the womb of winter. Look! Look, Sitareh! Love is everywhere."

An enigmatic smile spreads over her face. "Fine, I see love bursting everywhere, Pirooz." She glances down at her tea for a moment of reflection and then up at me. "Did you love Sitareh Poonia?" she demands.

I hesitate, surprised at the question, "Yes, I loved her. It was out of the ordinary, like a predestined love. I wished neither to possess her nor to be possessed by her, but for us to be illumined together."

After a pause, she asks quietly, "And me?"

"Excuse me?" I exclaim, feeling a tremor within.

"I said, 'And me?' Do you love me?" Her voice is soft but solid, like silk wrapping granite.

Caught in my own net, I am tongue-tied. True, I raised the issue, but still, she is audacious to ask if I love her—her question crisscrosses my mind like a frightened bee.

"Just like that?" I finally blurt out, responding more to my own surprise, even ecstasy, than to her question.

She sips her tea, as though she had asked about the weather, lifts her eyes from me as a psychiatrist would and lets me sink into my innermost self. I struggle to capture the moment and find an answer free of regrets and expectations, free of everything except truth. But what is the truth? I don't wish to betray either of us, even inadvertently. I alone could know the answer, but I don't. Is this woman the Sitareh whom I lost and mourned, the one who packed spiritual nourishment and sent me off alone on this journey, only to appear again at the end, knowing a new language and wearing a new skin? Certainly this is the Sitareh who lifted me up from Ibn Sina's grave, embraced me, and helped me regain my being after moments of nothingness. Are these Sitarehs the same or not? If they are, why am I doubtful, and if they are not, why am I not certain? The curiosity sparkles in my mind like a blue diamond.

Finally, seeing what seemed invisible before, I answer, "Dear Sitareh, I hesitate because I want to experience the truth, if possible. Ibn Sina believed that truth can only be experienced, except what is self-evident, like the laws of arithmetic. Despite a nightmare in New York, I am still on the same journey to know you. I have longed for you, whoever you are. But now that you, a dream come true, speak to me, I am thunderstruck." I take a long pause to hear my own words echo in my mind before resuming. "But I cannot deny that you are also she, my beloved, who seems to have been resurrected for me. You and Sitareh Poonia may have the same soul, but you were molded differently somehow. I need time to sort out what is what and who is who, and whether I love one person or two, one alive and one dead."

"You are not certain?" she asks.

"This is not real to me yet. Nothing is certain in a dream that appears real."

Her eyes focused on me, she declares, "In time, you will find differences and similarities between us. Identical souls can evolve into different persons."

"Poonia and I met already in love, which may unbelievably be the case for us, too. It all is astonishing, I need time to believe that the impossible has happened."

"I hope I am more than a look-alike," Sitareh says solemnly.

"Of course you are," I reassure her. "But did you know you would meet someone last night, Sitareh?"

"Yes, I had a notion. That is why I embraced you, a stranger, in a tomb."

"How? How?"

"I have no idea where notions come from, Pirooz."

We fall silent, tasting the sweetness of the honey and the bitterness of our inability to pierce the mystery enshrouding us. I want to ask her if she loves me, but I dissimulate it. If her question was strange, mine would be a sign of madness.

"What are you thinking, Pirooz?" she demands.

"That you are right. I must know you for yourself, and it will be a pleasure, not the tough struggle for truth that Ibn Sina envisaged."

"I am pleased to hear that, not just for me, but for us." Her smile of reassurance carries me to a seductive darkness, full of magical expectations and the scent of honeysuckle, where lovers play hide-and-seek. Wishing to find the source of the fragrance and love, I look into her eyes and ask, "And you?"

"We met when you were lost in a trance, except . . ."

"Except for what?"

"Reason slips through my fingers like a fish. I do feel a mysterious bond between us, and I accept it, even welcome it, as inevitable." She sounds like Poonia, and I shiver inside. We stare at each other for long moments.

I point to the nightingale singing without a score, a wordless song of joyful love tinged with the sadness of captivity. The nightingale watches the rose through the bars, just as a soul, captive in the body, tries to see the God it loves from a distance. Love, not philosophy, fills my heart now, so, to divert Sitareh's attention from the subject of love between us, I recite the words of Attar, the nightingale of Sufism:

> My love is for the rose, I bow to her;
> From her dear presence I could never stir.
> And though my grief is one that no bird knows,
> One being understands my heart—the rose.
> I am so drowned in love that I can find
> No thought of my existence in my mind.
> Her worship is sufficient life for me;
> The quest for her is my reality.
> Her buds are mine; she blossoms in my sight—
> How could I leave her for a single night?

Sitareh stares at me lovingly.

I continue, "Ibn Sina wrote that the indivisible soul, non-extant prior to the body, can perfect itself by using bodily senses, acquiring knowledge and disciplining the passions. When alive, he denied reincarnation, but, according to my dream, death has changed his mind. Death kills stubbornness, making it easier for the dead to change their minds. He told me that the dead can retain the thoughts they bequeathed to this world, but those are all they take with them to the next world."

"How interesting!" Sitareh exclaims. "The soul must seek truth and love to perfect itself, and truth and love are the only things the soul is allowed to keep on its journey between the two worlds. Now, going back to the body and soul, if I say 'I,' this 'I' does not refer to my body but to my soul." She sighs and waits.

Inexplicably the possessive pronoun "my" used with "body" and "soul" shifts the ground under me and sends tremors to my body and to my soul, so I barely manage to say, "Yes."

The nightingales grow quiet, the breeze hesitates, and we stop eating. There is a lull all around.

"I don't recall Ibn Sina's proof of the soul, Pirooz."

"You are taking me back to the classroom, Sitareh."

"Do you mind, if it is for me?"

I resign myself and begin, "He demonstrated the existence and chief attribute of the soul with a thought experiment. Imagine being suspended in space with no physical awareness or perception of three-dimensional physical. Still, you would be conscious of one thing, Ibn Sina proclaims . . ."

"The 'I,' the individual self, the soul!" Sitareh finishes.

"Right. That is why, no matter if an individual loses his sight or limbs, the 'I' or soul remains intact. Ibn Sina denied bodily resurrection but insisted on the soul's immortality."

"Of course," Sitareh says, "if the past and present conditions for two births were identical, then the same body could be reproduced. For instance, if coincidentally identical sperm and eggs meet." She hesitates, looks warmly into my eyes and finishes her comment. "Perhaps souls that lead pure lives and achieve their potential continue in immortal bliss, but failed souls seek reincarnation for another chance."

To hear Bastan voice the ideas of Poonia shocks me. I barely manage to follow through. "To exist is good, to perfect existence is better."

"What impact would the copying of souls have?" Sitareh inquires.

"Well, the perpetuation of war and mendacity, the two curses of man, I imagine."

"Did God foresee the consequences?"

"I don't think so, because He deprived Himself of omniscience by creating human free will, the only true random variable to an external observer. Otherwise, our lives would be as predictable as an eclipse, and God could stage the Day of Judgment even before the day of Creation, and no one could be held responsible for anything. But God would not deceive Himself and wait for history to unfold just to know at the end what He already knew all along."

"Islam denies this, you know," she reminds me.

I shrug. "Apparently Islam is contradictory on this issue. Either the first cause determines all subsequent effects or not. One cannot have it both ways. That is why interpretations and reinterpretations and interpretations of reinterpretations of the Koran abound in history, on this issue and others. For instance, the holy government, brimming with clerical authorities, is unable to clarify Islam's position on private property today. Is God on the side of capitalism or socialism?"

After a pause she resumes her questions. "Why has God embarked on His Grand Meditation?"

"Who knows? Maybe to overcome the temptation of curiosity."

"Curiosity for what?"

"For human action, the unpredictable. Remember, God created curiosity."

"So, man is the only curious and creative being, next to God."

"Yes, yes." I feel lost in the realm of my own speculations.

"What did Ibn Sina want? Did he really mean what he said in his poem?

> How I wish I could know who I am,
> What it is in this world that I seek."

I reply, "For a man in flight from city to city, and fighting to reconcile reason and faith, he accomplished a great deal, pushing himself and history forward." I lower my voice. "His soul stood between the spring water of purposefulness and the salty sea of doubt. The love of truth and truth in love gave him hope, but his inability to reach the ultimate in truth or love brought him despair. He believed that only intelligence and love make man worthy of the creative effort of God, so he dedicated his life to the two essences of creation: love and truth, healing and knowing. As Rumi said, 'Love is our mother. We are born of love.'"

"Who wound you up, Pirooz?" she smiles at my zeal.

"No one but you, Sitareh!" Now I think I am ready for a walk with this lovely, inquisitive woman.

Sitareh stands up. "After our walk we should visit the mausoleum library."

"Fine. I agree. Thank you for a magnificent breakfast."

"Thank Firoozeh, Pirooz. She made it."

"Thank you, Firoozeh," I tell her as she starts clearing the table.

"I enjoyed preparing it for you, Agha," Firoozeh says and casts her beautiful brown eyes embellished with long lashes on me as Sitareh and I depart.

Chapter Eleven: Ibn Sina and Us

As we walk along a neighborhood street, I say to Sitareh, "Ibn Sina's spirit is turning my non-beliefs into beliefs. I am now a materialist who suspects that there is more to the matter than meets the eye, or the mind. I wonder what he knew in the past and what he knows now about the next world."

"I've studied his medicine."

"And I philosophy," I admit.

"Ideal!" she exclaims. "Specialization and the division of labor. We can share what we know to know his mind, the key to what he may want now. I feel in my bones that we must learn everything about him and us, in both worlds."

"Exactly," I agree, unaware of what I am getting into.

We walk in the outskirts of Hamadan, toward a fountain Sitareh admires. Hamadan bestows another sparkling day on Sitareh and me. Orchards grow behind low walls that encircle the yards, some trees still bearing flowers, some sweetening fruits. The sun's rays hold us gently. I bask in my good fortune for being at home and in love. Sitareh's resurrection—a miracle or just an improbable coincidence?—overwhelms even Ibn Sina's call to me, for I am more interested in the living than the dead. I want new memories, not old ones regurgitated. I glance at Sitareh; she is real, her searching willpower showing in her pensive face.

"What did God create?" she asks.

"Let's start with the uncreated."

"All right, Pirooz."

"Ibn Sina considered God, possibility, matter and time co-eternal—none created."

"What does possibility mean? How is it eternal?"

"Possibility is not a substance, but the potential for a being, like an invention before it is made. The possibility for all things existing now must have always existed."

"So God did not create matter, according to Ibn Sina?"

Sitareh's question whirls in my head, reflects from a kite skittering overhead, and disappears in the laughter of the boy who holds the string. "God formed the world from matter that already existed, as a craftsman fashions a doll out of the available clay. To create matter from nothing is impossible, and what is impossible is impossible even for God. Ibn Sina said in effect that nothing is always nothing, matter is always matter, and the two never transmute, not even for God."

"How about time which has no beginning or end? Who made it?" she resumes.

"Ibn Sina reasoned that if time had a temporal beginning—a birthdate, so to speak—then its creation must have taken place after a duration of non-existence. But then, a period must have preceded a non-existing time, which is not possible. And if there were an end to time, then what would be the duration after the end?"

She stares at me, then asks, "And space?"

"If a void existed, it could not be pure nothingness, because any enclosure has dimension and position and is divisible. Empty space does not exist, or, in the words of Aristotle, it is an empty thought. Ibn Sina agreed with that, insofar as I know."

"Is space infinite, Pirooz?"

"No, what actually exists cannot be infinite."

"It has boundaries then?"

"No, not necessarily," I say. "Unboundedness and finiteness are not contradictory. For a two-dimensional being who sees only its surface, a smooth globe has no boundary, even though it isn't infinite. Imagine a blind ant on the globe."

"I am glad to be three-dimensional." A mischievous smile glows in Sitareh's face.

"I am glad you are, too! What do you think of space, Sitareh?"

"Space is generous. It embraces everything, our feelings, too. What would we do without space? I love space, and a lot of it, and emotional space, too." Her glance snuggles up to mine as she finishes.

"Consider me space now," I say to provoke her.

"Some day, Pirooz. There will be time and space for everything!" She grins triumphantly, just like Poonia, who told me, "I will wait until you are cooked and I am hungry." Is Sitareh Bastan cooking me now, for when she is hungry?

"And your thoughts about time and space together?" she asks.

"Time grinds my cells to death, and space will swallow the powder left of me."

After a silence, as if to digest Ibn Sina's ideas, she says, "So his God could not exist outside of the time or space. He was then less than the Abrahamic God."

"Indeed. In the business of creating possibility, matter and time out of nothing, He is less of a God. But remember, reason is as much God's gift to man as is faith. How much greater is God that He made man capable of understanding His beautiful and functioning Creation. That is what Ibn Sina believed and how he reasoned."

"How strange. What did God actually create, then?"

"The idea of this world," I reply. "Among all possible worlds God could have made, He forged this one, his ideas molding existing matter into this universe."

"I don't wish to blaspheme, but was this the best world God could have created?"

"Who is to say? God consulted no one; this very existence is His choice."

"Isn't it a sin to imply that God is such an absolutist?" Sitareh objects.

"God did it alone. The world is His case, not ours or the angels'."

"The theologians must not have been happy with Ibn Sina's cosmology."

"That is why the mullahs never forgave him," I reply.

"Then who created matter, according to Ibn Sina?" she persists.

"Matter, matter, where do you come from? He must have pondered that hopelessly. I believe no one knows the answer, not even Ibn Sina, who tried to formulate the theory of everything," I say, grinning in puzzlement.

"And so much matter, too." She flings open her arms as if to hold the world.

"Yes, and all supposedly packed into a single atom in the beginning."

"Where were we then, Pirooz?" She breaks into a broad grin.

"All united. Nothing separated. God still held the ideas for everything in His mind, Sitareh." I interlock my fingers to show how close we were then.

"Does God know where matter comes from?" she resumes.

"Ask God!" I reflect for a moment, then resume. "Some consider Ibn Sina a materialist and others an idealist, since he was a Sufi."

"What do you think, Pirooz? Is Ibn Sina a materialist or an idealist?"

"Let me think," I respond, but wonder why she awaits my every word as if it were the Prophet's. Does she want to know me, Ibn Sina, or just share ideas?

We walk into open country, where we climb a narrow path through swaying wildflowers and colorful thoughts. A breeze from Alvand wraps us gently, and each wildflower proves its existence with a fragrance. There is no car in sight, only an occasional person on foot or a horseman. The dirt road makes me feel close to the earth, and the stones under my feet remind me of the ups and downs of existence.

"Come on, Pirooz. What is the answer?" she demands.

"Wait, Sitareh. Let me tell you a tale my grandfather told me. It may help."

"Please do." She is enthusiastic.

"At the gate of Heaven an angel asked Ibn Sina, 'What is your name?' Ibn Sina purposefully gurgled a few made-up words, curious to see what would happen. When the angel reported this to God, the Almighty broke into laughter. 'That must be Ibn Sina. He surprises Me, too, especially with his position on Me, even though I gave him the potential to think what he thinks. Let him in!'"

Sitareh's smile is full of joy, yet she commands, "Continue!"

"Ibn Sina did not believe in a God who transformed nothingness into somethingness, and if he had denied God's existence altogether, he would have jeopardized his own existence. That much is clear."

Sitareh shakes her head in disappointment. "Nothing has changed. It is the same now, even worse. The rulers condemn curiosity—the very creation of God—to death. God created silence also, but one must remain silent when one has nothing to say or is about to repeat something, not when one fears saying what is in one's heart."

"How true, Sitareh," I reply. "This presumably Holy Government imposes silence on us but not on itself, thus abusing God's will."

"All right, Pirooz, enough of philosophic politics."

On a hillside covered in vegetation, we reach a little fountain and drink from it. Her thirst quenched, Sitareh breathes deeply, stares into my eyes, and says, "Let's drink from Ibn Sina's thoughts until we are intoxicated! Let's be patient." I nod my approval. We return home, lost in our thoughts.

Later as we are driving to the mausoleum, I spot a patrol car full of Islamic Guards. Instantly my terror of arbitrary terror returns. My incaution has put us in danger. "Look out, Sitareh," I shout. "The Guards have spotted us."

"Don't be paranoid, Pirooz," she replies calmly. "They won't bother us in daylight, and I am Islamically dressed. This black chador is my shield, or my shell." She returns to her thoughts. "He was enchanted with the idea of unity."

"Yes," I reply as she swings sharply into a broad avenue, pulling me toward her. "We talk about nothing but Ibn Sina's work."

"Don't you like that?"

"Yes, but . . ."

"Aren't we here for his sake?" she says with soft assertiveness.

"I hope we are in this for us, too."

"Certainly. But he is the cause of our togetherness. Let us explore it to the end. Or perhaps our togetherness is the cause of him."

"Is that all?" I say disappointedly, still seeing the two Sitarehs as one.

"For now. For a start. Let time do its work. Let's find new light and grow like a tree into new space with new branches."

"And search for roots, too." I protest.

"What is the purpose of creation?" Sitareh asks casually, ignoring my remark.

"How should I know?" I reply with a grin.

"Just Ibn Sina's answer, please. As I said, you are my only expert around."

The word "my" sticks in my ear while I try to concentrate on an answer. "Ibn Sina considered love the essence and purpose of existence."

"Let me see," Sitareh says teasingly. "I love, therefore I exist!"

"Yes. Or I exist because of love. God Himself is lovable, a lover, and beloved, according to Ibn Sina. He also said, I prove my existence by my action."

We glance at each other and both smile, her enigmatically, me desirously. Traffic becomes thicker and horns blow now and then. We are approaching the square. Seeing Guards march by, I say, "Ibn Sina worked under the watchful eye of clerics and rulers. He must have dissimulated, perhaps even from history."

"He would have to do it again, if he lived here now." Reminded of my own dissimulation, I am saddened. "Tell me what is in your heart," she demands.

"Spirits like Ibn Sina form the Persian spirit," I say. "To know ourselves, we must know them. But that is not enough. We must revitalize the future by ascending from the past, and not treat modern thinkers indifferently or harshly, as Ferdowsi, Attar or Hafiz were treated in their time. Also, the brilliance of a Hafiz should not blind us to new stars, whom we must love and support before, not only after, their deaths. Persians are ancestor worshipers, like the ancient Chinese and Egyptians."

"Love of the dead or love in death is Persian," Sitareh responds.

I put my hand on hers. "We exist not only in the past but also in the present, hopefully with new illuminators."

She stares at my hand, surprised and pleased. "It refuses to move!" I protest.

"Fine!" she charmingly replies. "Your hand may know something we don't." With her eyes fixed on mine, she lifts it and touches my palm to her lips. Walled in by nightmares until I discovered Sitareh Bastan, I sense my hope awakening. Again happiness looks at me, so I look it straight in the eye, to make sure it is there and I am not imagining it. Right away a green light thrusts us towards our destination.

As if her dimple were a font of holy water, I submerge myself in it, and there I find thoughtfulness, curiosity, beauty, humility and strength, but also a mystery. She was extraordinarily meticulous placing plates on the coffee table our first night. In America she counted the days away from home. She is in awe of a healer whose soul has acquired substance in our lives, and she wrings me for every bit of information. She is exacting, yet her interest in me is not built on friendship or courtship, but is spontaneous, as with Poonia. I sense a convergence of our fates, our unity with history, with Hamadan, with the cosmos, with the very soul whose invisibility breeds doubts about its existence. Seeing is no longer the acid test of being or non-being for me. How could I deny to myself my recent experiences?

Sitareh glances at me. "A penny for your thoughts, Pirooz."

"How generous! No one would pay even that much."

Sitareh points to a ruined building. "A missile hit it last week," she says.

Now, besides Guards looking to arrest me, I must worry that missiles are pointed at me, at us, at the people of Iran. What am I doing here? Several identities do possess me, even haunt me, pulling and pushing me here and there. I am ancient and modern, Eastern and Western, believer and nonbeliever. I speak English and then Persian, I am political and yet wish to get away from it all. I am an immigrant in my own home. I am in love with a dead woman who is also alive. With these different identities, I must be schizophrenic, but I am not. Not now, not yet. Love heals a shattered mind, and hope holds all of my selves together.

At the mausoleum, Sitareh parks the car in the sunshine. I wink my thanks to the guard, and he winks back, knowing that my wish was fulfilled with no harm to anyone. We pass through the gate that now stands wide open. The interior looks more spacious in the daylight. I feel bright. A few visitors, most of them somber, are entering or leaving. Women are well covered in chadors, except for their brown eyes. Children pull their mothers forward, for they are in a hurry. Men look up at the tower in amazement, as though it holds up the universe. Ibn Sina, Philosopher of Being and Prince of Medicine, is treated almost as a saint, and his mausoleum is a shrine.

I glance at Sitareh walking at my side. Even under cover of the chador she emanates grace and seriousness. A thin strand of hair emerges from under her chador, revolting against the Islamic dress code, but it seems to pose no danger here.

In the library, Sitareh asks for Ibn Sina's *Canon of Medicine*. The librarian stares at us one at a time, as if surprised to find someone borrowing the great book. Sitareh holds it up to the sunlight streaming in, and, in a low voice, announces, "No single book in medicine has been as influential or useful for such a long time as this one."

I feel I am on a journey, not an outing, but I don't mind, since Sitareh is with me.

Gazing at the book admiringly she says, "I love it. It is still healing in India, China and vast regions of the Orient."

"How is that?"

"Physicians in the East have established statistically that some of Ibn Sina's prescriptions are more effective than modern drugs. As a pharmacologist, Ibn Sina studied seven hundred and sixty different drugs and their proper uses."

"Did someone count them?" I ask half seriously.

"Yes! And some find it difficult to accept that a thousand-year-old healing voice is still alive."

This is new to me. "Tell me more about the basic ideas of the *Canon*."

"That's my part of the bargain, Pirooz, so I must quench your curiosity. Ibn Sina considered medicine a branch of knowledge, not dogma or superstition. This approach banishes quackery and the supernatural from medicine. Medicine must derive its knowledge from clinical observation and experiment and from the natural sciences, since man is a part of nature. The physician must use analysis and synthesis to find the prevention and cure of a disease. Ibn Sina drank at the fountain of Greek philosophy and medicine, mastered the works of Hippocrates, Aristotle, Galen, as well as later Muslim, Christian and Jewish scientists and scholars, and made many original and fundamental contributions of his own. He illuminated the path of progress for others. He knew intuitively some of what we now know objectively."

Sitareh pauses as though fatigued by repeating the obvious.

"More?" she asks.

I had been waiting for more. "Yes, please."

"What about?"

"What is the heart of his medical contribution?" I inquire.

"Aristotle said that complete knowledge of a thing is possible if we learn four things. First, the material at hand; second, the molding force that holds it together; third, the cause that gives it form and quality; and fourth, the purpose and function for which the thing was made. Ibn Sina introduced a theory of interaction among these causes and investigated their ultimate synthesis."

"Like Hegel's dialectic." I interrupt.

"Really? Still, in medicine Ibn Sina proposed the unity of human organs and their functions in the body and then the unity of the body with the environment. His work sounds as fresh as a new song, since the interaction of man with nature is a modern concern. The psyche expresses itself in two ways: as the mind through cognition and as the heart through emotion, and both thought and feeling affect health. Ibn Sina not only recognized psychosomatics, he articulated it profoundly."

Enlightened by Sitareh's explanation, I become more interested. "How did he apply this to diagnosis, healing, and disease prevention?" I ask.

"Finally your curiosity is fully awake!" she teases me.

"You are my only Ibn Sina medical expert."

She smiles at my mimicry and continues, "His theory and practice rest on four foundations, which determine every illness. First, 'inheritance,' or what one is endowed with at birth. Second, 'temperament,' or the state of well-being one achieves. Third, the external factors, and fourth, the inherent natural endowment of self-preservation, or, as we call it today, the immune system. Ibn Sina studied the interactions between energies within the body and external forces." She sounds like the physician that she is.

"Do you think his medicine and philosophy dovetail?" I ask.

"Roughly speaking. I am not as familiar with his philosophy as I should be. He tried to combine intuition and experimentation to reach the truth in medicine, just as he tried to reconcile idealism and materialism in philosophy. For Ibn Sina, body and mind interact to cope with nature."

"How did he deal with psychological maladies?"

"Some of his works on psychology, for instance, *The Relationship of the Body and the Mind* or *The Origin of Grief* or *The Interpretation of Dreams*, are still of interest to students of psychosomatic medicine. He was the first to describe trigeminal neuralgia, differentiating facial paralysis into central and peripheral types. His book on drugs for the heart seems to be the first on the subject of psycho-pharmacology. Also, he gave a precise clinical description of meningitis and its various diagnoses. Also, his work on medical definitions brought order to the chaos of medical terminology . . ."

"This is most fascinating," I interrupt Sitareh.

"What part or aspect of his work?" she asks me.

"He also classified philosophical and scientific terminology, both in Arabic and Persian. He was a great philologist, and his contributions remain valid today."

"You and I have turned into Ibn Sina's admiration society."

"So it seems. Did he have any shortcomings in medicine?"

"As you know, he was a controversial figure in life, and he remained so in death. William Harvey, the Englishman who first described the circulation of the blood, knowing the *Canon*'s silence on the subject, still announced, 'Go to the fountainhead and read Aristotle, Cicero, and Avicenna.' But the scientist Ibn Zuhr criticized the *Canon*. These are two extremes. Some criticism is due to the progress of science, but some comes from the envy of would-be iconoclasts." Sitareh finishes with a sigh of relief.

"Like all great men, he is studied, learned from, praised, and also cursed."

"It is unbelievable how modern Ibn Sina's ideas are, like the use of music as therapy. He was a Pasteur without a microscope, who could discuss microbes without seeing them. What a mind's eye!"

"Any more miracles?"

"Yes. He once cured a young man in Bukhara of digestive irregularities and headaches. When the ordinary remedies failed, Ibn Sina diagnosed an emotional disorder. He mentioned neighborhood streets while he took the man's pulse. The pulse rate increased suddenly when he named a narrow alley. Ibn Sina soon found that the secretive boy was in love with a girl living there. The parents consented and the lovers married, and all his symptoms disappeared."

"Geomedicine," I whisper as I notice a teacher and a few students entering the room. Sitareh seems oblivious to such events now.

"Yes, but genius-medicine is more apt. This is part of the folklore about him."

"But let's not forget that Ibn Sina was part of a Persian renaissance with a great many scientists and scholars contributing to it."

I see fatigue in Sitareh's eyes, so I stop questioning her, even though questions parade across my mind in colorful costumes, all demanding attention.

"How about lunch?" she says, breaking the silence.
"Where?"
"A picnic in the fields, in the bosom of Mount Alvand."
"Sucking granite milk and collecting berries?" I ask.
"I have packed a vegetarian lunch. If you need meat, you must hunt for it."
"What with?"
"Your bare hands." She tries to stifle her smile.
"What am I supposed to catch?"
"Rabbits."
"I am not that fast."
"Then eat the vegetables that won't run away. Maybe there is a good reason why rabbits run away from you and potatoes don't." Our joys and smiles intermingle.

Would Poonia's soul be jealous of Bastan, whose logic and charm I find such a delightful contrast? What other extremes has she? I notice that a touch of shock and anxiety are glued to me since her reemergence.

We return to the car. Sitareh plays a tape with a soothing violin and piano duet. She travels south past the hotel, and swings around Ibn Sina Square, pointing out the American Hospital as we approach the city outskirts. Then she turns southeast, heading for Mount Alvand. The car begins to climb the slope like an ant on a hill.

Out of the city, Sitareh whispers as if to make sure no one hears, "Thank God there are no Guards here." She removes her chador, baring her face, like the moon emerging from behind dark clouds.

Gradually the breeze picks up, and soon strong winds buffet the car. "Ibn Sina, following Aristotle, wrongly believed that winds cause earthquakes," I say.

She winks at me. "Please note it is not me but you who wishes to carry on."

I continue. "Anyhow, Ibn Sina wrote, 'We are a grain of dust floating in a wind called fate. At most we can think of our path and perhaps reflect a bit of light, but the wind will carry us where its mind is set and where its will must.'"

"Nevertheless, Ibn Sina did not bend to the winds of his time," she adds.

"No, he courageously flew above them."

Mount Alvand's snowy summit looms ever closer. The car climbs beside a mountain stream, one of hundreds of spring-fed waters that cascade down Alvand's flanks. The car turns sharply to skirt a granite outcrop, and before us is a lovely, secluded pond set in a meadow carpeted in wildflowers. A grove of huge old walnut trees grows on the pond's bank.

We are at the edge of the meadow when, suddenly, from the cloudless sky, an earth-shattering thunderbolt strikes the car. Immediately the vehicle shudders to a halt and the music stops. A long, dreadful moment expires and our stares at each other freeze in alarm. An unearthly voice, carried on a warped wind, floats down to us. "Greetings to you both. Hope be with you. We shall meet again when it is possible."

Instantly everything returns to what it was. The engine hums and the music returns. Sitareh's face flushes, and her voice shatters into singular words: "Did-you-hear-him? Did you?"

"Yes, yes, I heard him," I whisper. "Now he has spoken to us together."

Sitareh's hand trembles. I am not panicked, having had some experience with the spirit. Inexplicably, I scream skyward through the open window, "Stay with us longer, Ibn Sina. We need you!" I hold Sitareh's hands. "He won't harm us," I say.

Later, sitting by the pond's bank in the shade of a walnut tree, we eat our lunch silently. Nothing tastes as it should; everything is spiced with expectations. We remain silent in case the spirit should speak to us again. The spirit exists beyond a doubt. We could not possibly have imagined the same voice at the same time.

On the way home Sitareh whispers to me, "We heard Ibn Sina speak. Why does he visit the earth, and choose to follow us around? Doesn't he like it where he is?"

"Maybe he is bored with heavenly order or disorder. But who's following who? We are also searching for him, Sitareh," I say, trying to cheer her up.

"But why is he following us?" she repeats hopelessly but relentlessly.

We stop at the hotel to get my shaving kit, and, as I am about to leave the car, she suggests, "Isn't it more practical if you move into the house, Pirooz?"

My heartbeat picks up and drums wildly. I am thunderstruck again, and my face turns red—I can tell by the surge of heat on my skin. My dream, dead with the death of Poonia, rushes to me, smiling with open arms, but I am so numb I can't greet it and hold it as I wish to. Is that all she meant, only more practical? My unspoken question swirls in my head. I am like a lover who struggles to blurt out "I do" at the altar. Ibn Sina's greeting steps up to me with new colors: "Hope be with you."

I get hold of myself. Unable to resist her offer, which might change everything for me, I say, "Yes, Sitareh. It's more than just practical, however. Thank you." As I pay my bill the clerk seems to scrutinize me.

We return to the house and soon are in our own rooms, just to ponder in solitude our reality that is made of dreams and the spirit's words: Hope be with you.

I try to find some sense and order in my life, but understanding refuses to come, as though locked away beyond my reach. It must be my fault. I think that I am not thinking, surely not what could take me from what I already know to what I ought to know. Nevertheless, for me, reality is no longer what it used to be. There is a new reality, with a vocal spirit at its core. Finding the case even more fuzzy and confounding than before, I linger mysteriously at the edge of the unreal, even of doubt, like a nameless creature despairingly seeking its identity. A soundless voice calls my name through the deaf wall separating me from Sitareh. I am in love with her—with her memory in New York, and with her reality in Hamadan—and I see my face in her eyes just as on the night we met at the tomb.

In the evening we have a quiet supper before retreating to our rooms to sleep. We agree to postpone discussing our new encounter with Ibn Sina's spirit and draw conclusions later. I tell her, "We must find a way to find whatever we are not sure of."

"Why such a brief appearance?" Sitareh wonders. "Doesn't Ibn Sina know how much we love him?"

Chapter Twelve: Ala El-Dowleh

Late in the afternoon, I am alone in my room. A chorus of singing birds accompanies the pirouette of the ballerina earth for the royal sun. The globe, dressed in a multicolored tutu, bows to the sun at dusk. The earth worships the sun eternally, thanking it for every sunbeam and for holding at bay the devil's night-without-dawn. I imagine Sitareh putting on her nightgown.

Guided by the spirit's suggestion, I distance my mind from my body and close my eyes and cast out sounds, desires, and thoughts, to float in space, stripped of everything except the "I," my soul. Immaterial and solitary, I chant, "Love is the mother of life," until a flicker rises within me like the sun hesitating to emerge from the sea at dawn. I float in the void, with no sense but existence and intellect. I journey on invisible wings from wakefulness to sleep and beyond to a deeper wakefulness. A storm of history whips me into a bygone era. I pass from now to then, and from here to there, from the dark into brilliant light.

A muezzin's call beckons me and a carved stone lion wakes with a long, slow growl. Emerging into a late summer afternoon, I find myself in a long, white cotton shirt and black, airy pants walking beside Ibn Sina in a flower garden. Even at fifty, Ibn Sina is handsome and charismatic, his white beard and hair imparting the aura of a prophet, and an embroidered phoenix takes flight from his silk tunic.

We round a pond in which fish dance courtship. The sun glitters like a diamond on the heads and necks of a double row of majestic cypresses, immortalized by Persian poets. With color, scent, and a dance in a breeze, flowers compete for the attention of bees. The gravel yields with a whisper to our sandals, proving its existence.

I am puzzled and disoriented. "Where are we?" I ask Ibn Sina.

"At the Amir's palace, Gorgani. You have been here before."

"Oh, yes. True." Somehow I remember: every Friday the learned of the city gather here to read poetry and discuss ideas under Ibn Sina's direction. The Amir Ala el-Dowleh of Isfahan, a great patron of learning, presides.

Ibn Sina quickens his step, whispering, "We are late. I wish to arrive before the Amir, but without uttering a word Esther prevented me from leaving earlier. She is irresistible."

"You made yourself late, then. You love her so much."

"Yes, I cherish every moment with her. To me, the mingling spirits and bodies of lovers are the greatest joy, the best therapy for a low spirit. Loving is God's will, and it is my duty to obey Him."

"But Esther is Jewish."

"No, Gorgani. Her soul is universal, though her heritage is Jewish. I loathe dogmatism and conformity. Children are born free only to be branded like cattle by ethnicity, religion, nationality and race, all instruments for the authorities to divide souls and exploit bodies. We must keep our relationship a secret; dissimulation is man's curse on man. My Esther, like the ancient Queen of Persia, is a peacemaker. She keeps a majestic silence until I ask her to open her heart, and then she opens the heart of her people to me as well. Conflicts between Jews and Muslims worry her. She wishes for a just resolution, but, alas, human souls are susceptible to bigotry. She offered to change her faith, saying, 'To protect you and my people, I would change my religion a thousand times. Is not love the essence of faith, humanity, and God?'"

"She is young and beautiful and yet so wise, like Queen Esther," I add.

"Yes. Another star in my life: Sitareh, my dear mother, and Esther, both named after the fixed stars of the heavens. But I want you to know, Gorgani, that I am more in love with her spirit than her beauty."

"Good! At your age, you should be moderate in your indulgences."

"I want to be free, at least in private, and I want my years to be in breadth, not just in length. God, not any ruler, may judge you on love or wine or beliefs."

A deep loneliness covers his face, despite the admiration of the people of Isfahan for him. He is weary but still sparkles like a diamond lost in a stream of time—a muddy time. "I am in love with truth," he once said, "but I know the clergy will never allow me to court her freely and she will never marry me, pretentious suitor that I am."

He winks, "How fares your lady, Gorgani?"

I blush internally. "She is well, thank you, Leading Wise Man."

After being recognized by a guard, we enter the palace and walk through a foyer into a large salon. The windows fill with light and I tremble with expectation. Men sit with folded knees on exquisite carpets or recline on cushions against the walls. I recognize many faces: a distinguished theologian and his colleagues from the Friday Mosque, a rich silk merchant who is a patron of the arts, a court official who is a historian, a tribal chief visiting Isfahan, members of the Amir's family, an astrologer, poets and scholars—no women. Most wear cotton and some wear silk. They hold prayer beads, speak in whispers, and drink sherbet. As we enter the hall, Ibn Sina acknowledges greetings with his sparkling eyes beneath thick brows. We sit at the head of the room on a richly carpeted dais. A servant places a silk upholstered divan on the dais for the Amir, who wants Ibn Sina near him. A commotion erupts in the foyer, servants bustle about the hall, everyone grows silent, and a herald proclaims, "His

Excellency, the Amir, has arrived! Praise be unto him! God grant him a long life!"

Everyone rises. The Amir walks briskly to the divan—with his vizier and entourage following—and sits, signaling for all to be seated. The sun's rays reflect with deference from the Amir's white silk robes and glistening rings. He twirls his moustache and beckons to Ibn Sina. The court poet rises to recite a new poem praising the Amir's wisdom, as the Amir beams with the confidence of a just ruler.

We wait for the Amir to announce his wish. Immediately he says, "We have heard that you bring important questions for the Leading Wise Man. Let us hear them!" All eyes shift to Ibn Sina, energizing him no matter how exhausted he is.

An old, white-bearded man slowly raises himself up. "Leading Wise Man, what is the purpose of studying nature, man, and the cosmos, when one knows in advance that human limitations will constrict and distort the seeker's comprehension?"

Ibn Sina knits his brows and replies, "Learning just for curiosity or reward lacks an essential purpose. Science is not morally indifferent; it must serve all creatures and obtain knowledge about God, Whose wisdom is manifest in His Creation. So the closer one comes to truth, the closer one approaches God."

There is a pause. The Amir wears a wide smile; Ibn Sina is a genius in his eyes, a jewel in his crown, and a source of wisdom in his kingdom.

Ibn Sina continues, "My respected brethren, the world is the unity of manifold things, but Divine Independence is the unity of the unique, the first cause and the first effect, together at once." He sighs and waits for a rebuttal or another question.

At length a young man asks, "Leading Wise Man, you have stated the purpose of acquiring knowledge, but how should we seek truth, and what is the path?"

Ibn Sina hesitates, perhaps seeking inspiration for a precise response. "There are many paths. One may use analysis to understand the components of things, and synthesis to comprehend the whole. In medicine, the organs, the body, the mind, and nature must all be investigated singly and then jointly. Observation, experimentation, and reasoning are all useful but still insufficient to know the totality. One must then link the medical results to the metaphysical purpose of life. Only contemplation and intuition can transcend the limitations of science and reason. Furthermore, ethics and faith cannot be satisfactorily expressed in a language evolved primarily for objects and earthly affairs. A profoundly rich language must develop to express their essence."

"In any case, one must use both exoteric and esoteric principles to understand how actuals create potentials, how potentials become actuals, how particulars merge into universals, and how universals give birth to particulars..." He halts to clear his throat. "... but we must keep in mind the unity of Creation and the dependence and insignificance of everything before God."

"Leading Wise Man, what is man?" a hesitant voice requests.

He replies, "I have proposed that the mineral soul and then the vegetative soul can ascend to the animal soul, and the animal soul to the human soul, which in turn may ascend to the divine spirit. In such a way, man embodies the essence of minerals, plants, animals, and potentially the nature of angels. Man, a microcosm, possesses all the levels of existence, and the intellect is the inner foundation of his being. He is endowed with the gifts of self-evaluation, self-discipline and self-realization, so man the knower can understand all things, since he has undergone, and emerged from, inanimate, vegetative and animal states, and man the lover can cherish all things because he is a part of all, and man the doer can transcend all things because he is more than all he has been, is, and will be. Man is a process towards a perfect being."

The Amir signals his wish to speak. The hall becomes still. In such gatherings, his remarks usually come at the end. "Define the Creator you have just spoken of, and prove His existence as though for non-believers."

"I shall do my best, Your Majesty," Ibn Sina replies. "I start with an abbreviated proof. Existing beings, like pearls, roses, honeybees, people, and stars, are not self-created; therefore their cause must be outside of themselves. One may thus imagine a long causal chain, which must end in God, since it is impossible for an actual chain to be indefinitely long. So the cause of God's existence must be within Himself, making Him the Necessary Being for all possible beings, such as us. In my view God is not a body, nor the form of one, nor intelligible matter for an intelligible form, nor an intelligible form of intelligible matter. God is an essence—indivisible into form or substance. He is intelligible to us because He exists."

The Amir smiles. "So it is that logic shall support faith. Proceed."

I wonder where I am, if this is a dream or history repeating itself in my mind. My wondering ends when a scientist speaks. "Leading Wise Man, how should we approach a problem that seems insoluble?"

"Heave the problem into the air," Ibn Sina replies with a gesture, "let it shatter on the ground, and examine the pieces. Then reassemble it, inspect it forwards, backwards, inside out, outside in, find examples and counter-examples, formulate a solution and test it. Divide the problem and conquer! If you are still unsuccessful, tighten your assumptions or widen them. Never tire, never give up, unless you can prove the problem insoluble or trivial. Be patient, come to know the problem as a friend, attack it like an enemy. Think, sleep, and pray over it! Go back and repeat everything again. Consult others without shame. Always recollect the sweetness of the solution, to motivate yourself for new efforts."

A scholar says, "This involves logic, experimentation, imagination, speculation, struggle, patience, hard work, and faith. Every human resource!"

"Yes, but a small sum to pay for the discovery of a priceless truth! And we must recognize that science is an instrument of knowing as well as what is known of nature."

A silence full of admiration fills the great hall and a smile grows on the Amir's face.

"How is it that things come to be what they are in our minds?" someone asks.

"All things are in God's mind first," Ibn Sina replies. "For example, the idea of a cat is before all particular cats. When cats are created, felinity comes into being in each one of them. We notice cats' likeness to each other and perceive the general concept, 'cat.' Accordingly, thought demonstrates generality in form after Creation."

Now an old man, wrinkled and folded over with age yet still dignified, says, "Leading Wise Man, praise be to your intellect! You have stated the supreme reason for and the methods of research, but what should be the goal of education?"

Ibn Sina's eyes light up. The hall also lights up as the sun emerges from a bank of clouds. The Amir turns toward him and Ibn Sina pauses for a long moment.

"My respected elder, man's dignity is rooted in his essence as a potentially perfect being. To learn is 'to lead out' rather than 'to stuff in.' Rote learning must not replace the imaginative use of one's mind. We all need to acquire facts and skills, but we should journey from what we are to what we ought to be through cognitive, emotional and spiritual ascendance. Learning is not jewelry to be worn, but a way to achieve one's true potential. I appeal to all nations, to old and young, and to masters and slaves, to accept and practice the holy words: 'God will not change the condition of men and women until they change what is in themselves.'"

"Leading Wise Man, in the process of learning, how must a good Muslim practice the verses of the Holy Koran if they appear inconsistent?"

"Respected colleague, you had asked this question before and I had requested time to reflect upon it. The verses of the Koran, as well as of other Holy Books, are God's response to history through the prophets' minds. After all, history is an artifact of man that shapes man. Some verses of the Koran relate to specific circumstances and some are general principles. It is possible and even necessary that the general appear in conflict with the specific and abrogate it without either one losing its revealed status. Let the Holy Book speak to this question and to us directly: 'If we [God] abrogate a verse or cast it into oblivion, we reveal a better one or one like it . . . [S.2:100]'"

Ibn Sina, hearing no objection, sighs with relief, glances at the Amir and continues, "For example, no physician is able to provide a single cure for a lifetime, since each ailment requires a different treatment. God's revelations are incremental. The Koran is the last of the Holy Books, and within it God's will is revealed."

Suddenly a messenger enters the hall. His anxious eyes, jerky motions and halting breath indicate his urgency. The Amir acknowledges him, whereupon he rushes to the throne, bows, hands the Amir a letter, and as suddenly disappears. The Amir opens the letter and frowns. Then, a big smile crossing his face spreads security in every heart in the room. It must be good news. "Proceed!" The Amir's joyful and assertive voice fills the hall.

"Leading Wise Man, how does your philosophy differ from that of the ancients, Plato and Aristotle?"

"It differs primarily in the subject I have chosen to study. I expound the question of being and nothingness, Plato the theory of Ideas, and Aristotle the doctrine of Potentiality and Actuality. God bless their souls for opening my mind to profound ideas when I was a young man. They are great teachers for all ages. But remember, we must scrutinize all ancient knowledge as closely as possible. Nothing should be accepted because of its author's reputation."

"Leading Wise Man, you have written poetry and studied physics. Please speak to us of the difference between art and science."

Without hesitation Ibn Sina replies, "Man loves beauty and incorporates it into art; he also discovers and uses the secrets of nature to invent. There is no conflict between science and art, since both stem from the same origin—the will to understand and to create. Proportionality is not only mathematical but also aesthetic—it holds the same essence in calligraphy as in geometry, in poetry as in architecture. Let us be what our Designer foresaw, creators in arts and discoverers in sciences. Brought forth through the interaction of mind and matter, art and science are secondary creations since they are forged by humans—the created."

"How can we believe we are creators, too?" someone asks.

"By creating we prove over and over that man is made in the image of God."

"What of the truth about oneself, man, nature, God? Shall we resign ourselves to not knowing it in full?"

"Aside from the Divine Being all things are limited, and human knowledge is no exception. A spiritual inner journey, however, will take you to the stars within you."

A man says, "Speak to us of the purpose and destination of this journey."

"Its destination is the Divine Being, and the purpose is unity with Him. Assume you accept the invitation of a sage and begin your inner journey and fly like a bird across the universe toward your origin."

The Amir interrupts, "Like the Sina embroidered in silk across your heart."

"Yes, Your Excellency." Ibn Sina resumes, "There are obstacles on the path. If you are trapped by ignorance, envy, selfishness, greed, arrogance and hatred, a flock of birds—sages with a similar mission—will rescue you. You must fly higher until you pass all traps, never heeding the alluring bait of the evil hunters. Then you will ascend to the peak of a mountain from which you may gaze on a limitless vista. From there you will fly higher and higher, past the heaven of the fixed stars, and their light will cleanse your soul of your remaining vices. Then you will be guided to the absolute love, beauty, and wisdom, God, and dissolve in Him like a raindrop in the sea. In union with God, you become eternal like Him."

"In the beginning, when there existed no space, no time and no matter—nothing—where was God?" a doubter asks.

"There never was, is, or will be a beginning with nothingness. Had there been one, what was before the beginning? Nothingness never existed. Our knowledge of the universe is expanding but will remain limited, perhaps forever."

"Where was God? This question is blasphemy!" protests a mullah.

"No!" Ibn Sina replies. "Such questions are not blasphemous; since God wishes man to know. It was God Who created curiosity for man to discover truth."

"Can we question questions even on matters of faith?"

Ibn Sina turns to me. I clear my throat and speak. "Yes, or else man would lack the capacity to ask questions—any question—or would be endowed with answers at birth."

"Where is God now?"

"I know not where, if not everywhere, even in good hearts," Ibn Sina declares.

"If the soul ought to ascend, why is it confined to the body, Leading Wise Man?"

"I shall read a poem of mine, not as a definitive answer, but something to reflect upon." Then his brilliant declamation intoxicates the audience.

> "Why then was the soul cast down from the high peak
> To this degrading depth? God brought her low;
> But for a purpose wise, that is concealed
> Even from the keenest mind and liveliest wit.
> And if the tangled mesh impeded the soul,

> The narrow cage denied her wings to soar
> Freely in heaven's high ranges, after all
> She was a lightning-flash that brightly glowed
> Momently over the tents, and then was hid,
> As though its gleam was never glimpsed below."

An inquiry about Ibn Sina's new terminology results in a long discussion. A philologist responds, "You are a philosopher and a man of great wisdom but not sufficiently versed in linguistics to please us with your answer."

As the Amir frowns and all eyes turn to Ibn Sina, a pensive wave crosses his face, as he tries to overcome his annoyance and maintain his composure. He doesn't let his legendary wit wither his accuser. "My esteemed colleague, I have no claim to philology, but I daresay you may come to see my point in the near future. Please let us hear your own reply. Alternative views bring forth deeper understandings. Let us not trap ourselves in old ideas or in fear of new ones."

The philologist offers a long-winded response rooted in traditional notions. The Amir seems impatient with the envious man. At length, Ibn Sina, hearing no further questions, recites a poem:

> "Within an age become exceedingly strange,
> Cruel, and terrible, wherein we need
> More urgently a statement of our faith
> And intellectual arguments thereto."

Finally the Amir rises, waves farewell and leaves the hall deep in thought. We leave behind him, a small retinue following us out. In the foyer the Amir invites Ibn Sina for a discussion of funds for astronomical research.

Out in the garden, Ibn Sina explains to me, "That learned philologist is an untiring pest. I have no objection to his answering philological questions, but he invariably keeps his silence until I speak, even though it is clear that our views diverge. I must promote philology, since words are crucial in representing the material and the immaterial worlds. To me a sentence is a miracle, since it can resurrect in the mind an actual event that may never happen again, or invoke an image of an event that never happened at all. I want to conduct a thorough study of language, this great creation that recreates humanity, generation after generation. Please help me collect every book written on philology in Persian or in Arabic, Syriac and Greek."

"Of course, Ibn Sina. But do you have the time to tackle a new field?"

"No, but time and effort will come to me when I need them!"

His mind shifting, Ibn Sina mumbles, "Esther tells me that the water supply to the Jewish quarter is being manipulated for extortion. I must report this to the Amir. I hope he won't mind hearing of the concerns of his Jewish subjects." Then he smiles, "The problems grow faster than their solutions. What is this all about, Gorgani?"

"That I don't know," I reply, "but Esther's problem can be solved. Your cause and her cause are just and the Amir is a just ruler. You must have noticed with what admiration he looked at you when you gave your answers."

"But the most worthy causes have caused me the gravest difficulties."

"Yes, man seems to resist self-knowledge. Falsehood has powerful allies, even within us. Alas, unreasonable rulers have cast difficulties upon people in the past, but fortunately, Amir Ala el-Dowleh is an exception."

Ibn Sina seems pleased, nevertheless. He has never felt as secure as he does in Isfahan. All of a sudden, as we skirt the fishpond, I hear the sound of a drum. Ibn Sina adds, "You must be open to all possibilities and to what fate brings you."

"What do you mean?" I ask with sudden anxiety.

"Just that. Accept the unexpected guest."

Then Ibn Sina disappears, as the garden and the ancient time I am in also disappear. I wake up from history and open my eyes to the present, but it is my ears that demand attention as I hear a knock on the door.

Chapter Thirteen: The Mind of Love

The steady knocking at my door awakens me to a new reality. God, is this the future that knocks at my consciousness now? Where have I been, and where am I being taken? I twist like a seedling caught in the first storm of spring. With Ibn Sina still on my mind, I wonder if perhaps behind the door is another world waiting to swallow me whole. Not sure if I am awake or still dreaming, I listen. Past and present cross, one leaving, the other entering my mind. The knock comes again. Sitareh's voice probes the room like a streak of light through a crack under the door. "Pirooz, Pirooz, it is me." To be sure all is real I glance out the window to see the moon beside Mount Alvand. Shadows of trees dance on the opposite wall. A breeze with no name and no face reassures me that all is real, that I am me and no one else.

I think, "Sitareh, now? Here?"

"Pirooz, it is me," she repeats. "May I come in?"

"In my bedroom?"

"Yes. In your bed!"

Her erotic suggestion brings me fully awake. Reality converges into one picture, "bed." I remain suspended; what should I do or say? The dilemma pounds the walls of my heart as I meekly ask, "In my bed?"

"Yes. Ibn Sina suggested it!"

"He did?"

"Yes. I thought you'd be expecting me."

"He only told me to accept the unexpected," I reply.

"That is me!" I hear, and then the door creaks open.

Like a gentle flame, Sitareh enters the room in a golden negligee. Her footsteps over the moonlight are sweet, and her breasts billow in the transparent negligee. My desires blossom; they are not mine—I am theirs. Sitareh approaches me slowly, a luster wrapped in mist. I thirst for the wine that flows toward me and am emblazoned by my own expectations. She wears no shoes, no bra, her braids are untied, and her loose hair flows sensuously over her smooth, bare shoulders. Her gown lets the breeze, the moonlight, and my passion in. Her silent steps approach my bedside temptingly. I look without looking, know without knowing. We are coming together, at last. Poonia, me, and Bastan—all of us together, with history watching. The thought is more powerful than the reality, the future more tangible than the present. It is impossible to wait more, but without waiting nothing is possible.

She pulls back the sheet and lies beside me. I quiver and the bed quivers with me. Our happy glances exchange unvoiced words. My passion flares as I let my fingers slip under her negligee. The softness of her skin intoxicates me, and she shivers like a leaf in the wind.

I hear myself. "I love you. I love you, Sitareh."

Clinging tightly to me she whispers, "I am yours, Pirooz. I have been yours since I was born. My presence here is his wish, but my love for you is all mine." I have no choice but to surrender myself to her. "You are mine, Pirooz! I am yours!" Her voice is such a wondrous melody and poetry.

Her skin is silky, slippery, fiery hot and thirsty for my touch. "I love you, Sitareh. Our love is new, yet I will love you forever."

"I know. I know. Say no more, Pirooz."

I see love reflected everywhere as though inside a house of mirrors. I disrobe her; she disrobes me. Our lips touch, our fingers clench, and our breathing quickens. Suddenly, and for an instant only, a voluptuous calm engulfs me. I want this fervor to spiral slowly and last forever. I want to smolder and feel the sparks all around and within me. I kiss her lips, neck, shoulders, and breasts with the searing tongue of a tiger. I find everything my lips desire. She twists and turns, kisses me back. She moans as dew moistens her soft, light skin. Our faces meet and our legs entwine like her braids. A throbbing warmth beats against my thigh. My rapid breathing tickles her body, which in turn tickles mine. I can feel her heart palpitate like a hungry beast, aroused and in need. We whisper. We explore. We caress. We squeeze. We tremble. We moan. Then I hear her lascivious groan, "Pirooz! Please! Now!" We shrink the space between us. We merge, becoming one and complete. Floating in the timelessness and spacelessness of the dominion of love, she is the breeze and I am the cypress, and then she is the cypress and I am the breeze; we wax and wane. I hear my own screams as my burning candle now upside down squeezes part of its essence and drips it into its complement.

Love creates as creation becomes love. The divine will is realized. We pass the empyrean of fixed stars and enter the pavilion of supreme love, with wine flowing in streams and roses dancing on the arms of olive trees to the music of the *ney*. Intoxicated by the glow in my heart, I hear the poet Rumi's words:

> Love says: There is a way,
> And I have gone it several times.

After a satisfying sleep, I wake to see the sun afire in the windowpane and doubt if anything is still real. My wondering ends abruptly as I find my right hand in Sitareh's grasp. Her breath caresses my shoulder blade with a rhythm of fulfillment. All things appear crystalline and vivid. I know why I am here—all good deeds stem from love. I fall into a deeper tranquility and gaze within, but I am not alone. She is with me, I can touch her inside me, as she touched me inside her last night.

Sitareh's large hazel eyes open. Her hand slides over my forehead as though testing for fever. She whispers, "Did you sleep well, my love?"

"I am lost in an astonishing tale, but wish to remain lost there forever."

Feeling her lips on mine, I sense a resolve in her kiss. As though seeing my thoughts, she asks with a conquering charm, "Will you marry me, Pirooz?"

"Why so soon?"

"I am not sure." She hesitates. "Something is calling me to you and to him."

Has Ibn Sina willed our marriage? I wonder.

At the breakfast table, I sense we have arrived after a long journey. I put my hand over hers and realize that I have never loved so passionately and tenderly. And this is not all. I have always loved her; something in her and me was woven together by the first weaver, before even consciousness was invented.

As we finish our breakfast, I relate my dream of Ibn Sina to her. She listens carefully, taking mental notes, asking for details: "Do you remember the image of a phoenix woven in Ibn Sina's tunic?"

"Yes, it was stunning. The Amir commented on it."

"Did you see any tapestry?"

"Yes, there was one on a short-legged table where the Amir placed his drink."

"What was its design?"

"Leaping deer, grass, flowers. Why?"

"I wanted to make sure your vision was actual history. Centuries later, textile artists and fashion designers in Florence, Italy, adapted these Persian patterns to heavy silk and wool weaves. Sassanian leaping deer appear in early Renaissance textiles. Merchant voyagers from the Middle East to Venice and other ports on the Mediterranean made this diffusion possible."

"How do you know all this?"

"I have been interested in weaving since childhood. In fact, one of my interests in Hamadan is its ancient tradition of carpet weaving. Fabrics made here, even from Ibn Sina's era, are in museums around the world today."

Finishing her tea, she says, "I will go to the mausoleum this morning. I am sorry to spend such a special day away from you, but you need time to yourself. I would be very happy if you give your answer to my proposal tonight. It is your intention, not a marriage vow, that I want now." It seems there is nothing to be said, yet I want to hold her, to kiss her, to tell her I love her a thousand times, but I feel something mysterious pulling her away, a mission stronger than the love of a woman for a man.

She gets up to go. She is naked and I see how perfectly she is carved now. She puts on her negligee casually, as if wishing that I register a clear memory of her beauty.

"Leaving so soon?" I ask and beg.

"Yes. I want an answer to something very special, and I cannot wait."

My morning smile falls to the ground and shatters as if in a fallen mirror. She leaves without explaining her insight to me, even though we had promised to keep no secrets. Why? Is secrecy woven into creation? Is this why both man and beast beguile, bait and bamboozle?

Marriage! Sitareh is the gate of paradise to me, but I must abandon this world to enter the next. I have come to Hamadan to explore the past, to experience the unity of seer and seen, and to grasp what is beyond all veils and appearances, beyond the senses, beyond physics and chemistry and biology. I have not come here to be wedded, even to a Sitareh! I have already been married and divorced; is that not enough for one life?

A furious bombing raid in the distance breaks my thoughts. The vision of Poonia in her casket floods my heart with fear. Might fate snatch another Sitareh from me? Why do I let paranoia cloud this sunny day of love? Can't I trust that I am happy and enjoy it? All this is absurd, I assure myself. I shall not be paranoid. History does not, will not, repeat itself. Sitareh Bastan will be back, back in my arms again. I will be her husband—hers!

I am in the garden when the telephone rings furiously. In a minute Firoozeh's scream fills the world. Rushing upstairs I hear the clunk of a heavy object. I find Firoozeh collapsed on the floor sobbing as if all is lost, her black hair spread around her shoulders over the beige carpet. I lift her head. Her crystalline teardrops run down her porcelain cheeks. They are the only things that are clear to me.

God! My heart pounds the word in protest as my mind demands, Why? I am numb. Firoozeh is numb, too. I cannot ask anything because I am frightened to hear the answer. Waiting engulfs me. I wait with Firoozeh leaning on me, her wet face in my hands. The black telephone receiver lies beside her, thrown from its cradle, the twisted black cord connecting them churning as it churns my guts. Suddenly Firoozeh is transfigured into the old Indian lady who brought me the news of Poonia's death, her wrinkles like a dry riverbed now flooded with fresh tears. Finally I manage, even dare, to ask, "Please, Firoozeh. Tell me, what has happened?"

Firoozeh stares vacantly past me as she struggles to find her voice. "Oh, Agha. She's gone. Finished. Dead." Then she breaks into sobs again. I let her lean against the coffee table, but she falls on the floor face down beside the receiver beeping, beeping, beeping the news of death, making her shiver.

I rise with a blurred mind and step out onto the balcony. I look up at the clear sky and scream, "You! You, the absolute despot. You, the murderer of all things. Wasn't the blood of one Sitareh enough to quench your thirst? Did you have to devour two Sitarehs in one year? Couldn't you have left one for me?

You, my only enemy, go ahead, kill me, too. What else can you do to me?" I don't know if I am addressing, a despotic fate or a despotic God. Is God fate?

I scream, "Sitareh, come back. Come back to me, my love." Inexplicably, a darkness overwhelms me. I stop, glance at everything once more, and shout desperately, as if to a lover sinking in quicksand, "Sitareh, wait for me. I am coming to you." And then, out of control, I walk to the edge of the balcony two tall stories high, impelled to leap over onto the brick path below. I see the bricks shiver.

I step forward but my jacket pulls me back. I turn around. It is Firoozeh. "Agha, Agha Pirooz, please! Please don't do that. Don't, Agha. Sitareh Khanoom is not dead. I have lost my own sister, my only sister. Today, visiting my uncle. It is the bombs. No one is safe, even outside of town. The bombs, Agha, that's all. My sister is dead." I hold Firoozeh for a moment before she frees herself and rushes downstairs.

For the next couple of hours I sit on the balcony and watch the parakeets sing, play and make love, gradually freeing myself from the cage of my fears. My Sitareh is alive; she will soon be back in my arms. I look to the skies, imagine stars and angels, and feel my silent tears speak of my longing for some security in this life.

I rush to Firoozeh, hold her in my arms and express my sympathy, managing to comfort her somehow. She shivers in my arms and gazes at me with her melancholic eyes.

I must find my answer to Sitareh's proposal before she returns. I pace restlessly around the garden, trying to hurry time's passage, as if time were the problem and not my impatience. I try to experience my innermost emotions. Pausing at the fishpond, I look into the water with some curiosity. My lover is not dead, but her sister is.

"What must I do?" I ask the resident goldfish. If butterflies answer me, maybe fish will, too. Their color reminds me of Sitareh's negligee and I shudder.

The fish are lucky; they have all the answers they need at birth, in their genes. I know I must utter a clean "no" or a clean "yes" to Sitareh. I know that what I say will be final and irreversible. I know Sitareh. When an important argument is at a crossroads, she only considers the mutually exclusive paths. To her it is life or death, good or evil, knowing or unknowing, right or wrong. In our case, I suspect she meant marriage or separation now, and nothing in between. I can see that the two Sitarehs are alike; even their seductiveness hides their ironclad seriousness. Are they the same?

The ripples in the fishpond distort my reflected face. My worried frown examines me from the water, and the fish dance through my fears. I take a deep breath and sense last night's memories drowning in the garden scents. A chill breeze descends from Alvand, sharpening my mind as it struggles against my heart: to say yes or no to Sitareh. I open myself to nature and don't resist what it invokes in me.

I know that by saying no I will lose her for a second time. I hardly know her, yet I have known her forever. I dare not say no, yet there is more in this than just not daring. So I will say yes, not because I cannot say no, but because love commands me to say yes. I will enter the gate not knowing what is on the other side.

I lie on the gravel and look in the pond that holds my reflection, the oaks, the butterfly and the fish, the stars and the universe. It is difficult to believe that from the beginning of time whatever has existed above the earth will be reflected in this fishpond, even in my eyes, even in these words. The fish joyfully dance through the history of everything as I just try to find an answer.

The telephone rings again, and I hear Firoozeh answer it. She comes to me to say that Sitareh has called to plan our dinner tonight, and Firoozeh has told her what happened earlier. Soon Firoozeh leaves to be with her family.

The day passes quickly as I wait to tell Sitareh, "Yes! Yes!" I am moonstruck, and for one who is moonstruck a quick vow is normal. Day evaporates into the night sky, and the remaining droplets of light shimmer and soar higher. Night arrives with all the stars hanging on its gown, each in its place, even if I cannot tell them apart. I hear Sitareh's musical words, "Where are you, Pirooz?"

"In the garden." Then I whisper to myself, "lost between my two Sitarehs."

"I have something for you."

Her voice is a summons, though a remoteness hides in her words, "for you." My thoughts and dreams disappear as I rush upstairs to hold her and tell her of my resolve, but I find her angrily circling the coffee table and agitatedly talking to herself. "I have established one link; it is as it should be. But the other link puzzles me."

"Let me in on this, please, Sitareh."

"You see, Pirooz, Ibn Sina's learned mother was named Sitareh."

"Ibn Sina mentioned that in my Isfahan dream. I remember now."

"Maybe I am her reincarnation, but then . . ." She falls dead silent.

Suddenly my elation fades to apprehension. "Then what?"

"If I am his mother, what in the world am I doing making love to Gorgani? Why did he send me to you?" she exclaims, raising her voice.

"I wish I knew," befuddled, I reply mechanically. I recover to add, "Remember, names are not souls. My name is Pirooz, but I am Gorgani, apparently, and you are one Sitareh among many. We need more evidence than just names."

"You mean I am not his mother?"

"I mean we don't know. Just that. I am Pirooz, you are Sitareh, and we have a life to live. And I trust Ibn Sina. Why would he match the wrong people? Love can't be wrong," I assert, deeply hurt.

She only quickens her steps around the coffee table, holding her chin and muttering to herself. Her frown is as rough as the wrinkles on the oak bark. I cannot hear her or guess what she is up to, what she wants, what is the cause of her reversal. As the silence lengthens, I finally manage to blurt out, "So your proposal is off?"

"Yes, for the time being, until we know who is who."

"Don't you love me?"

"Yes, I do. But this is beyond love."

"What is beyond love?"

"My love for you is just the beginning of my love for all. This is not my journey alone. Pirooz, I still love you, no less than last night. I will always love you, but you see, more is at stake. Don't you see, this unfolding drama outweighs our love, even our lives? If our planet happens to hold the only intelligent beings in the universe, then we are chasing the greatest healer ever. This is why ours is no mere story of a man and a woman in love, but a cosmic saga."

"But our love does not conflict with our search!"

"Maybe not, but we must not choose wrongly."

"I see what I see. I conclude that Ibn Sina has brought us together."

"Yes, I know that, Pirooz."

Shifting emotional gears, I look at her and say, "I am the doubter, but I have no doubts now. Why can't we trust him, Sitareh?"

"I do, but not blindly, Pirooz." I keep silent.

Then she charmingly asks, "If you love me, can you give me a simple gift?"

"Yes, Sitareh, but . . ."

"Wrap some patience in your bittersweet smile. I want to taste that smile!"

Her charm sweeps me up like the wind rocking a sailboat. I smile and reply, "All right, you have my patience! But let's be open as we promised."

She nods approvingly. "I also know the rest of your dream last night."

"You do? What do you mean?"

"What you dreamt was a true event. I read about it today. Three years after he asked Gorgani for research material, Ibn Sina, having mastered philology, composed three Arabic poems filled with rare words, and also three essays, each in the style of a different great scholar. He then put them all in an old binding and asked the Amir to give it to the disagreeable philologist. The Amir agreed to claim he found it on a hunting expedition and ask the philologist its authorship and the value of its contents. The scholar was baffled and answered wrongly, and when the facts became known he apologized to Ibn Sina for unjustly criticizing him. The disputation provoked him to create his great linguistic masterpiece in twenty volumes. Ibn Sina, who never lived in an Arabic-speaking region, knew the essence of the language better than any native speaker. Did you know about this before your dream?"

"No."

"Are you sure?"

"Yes, positive."

"Let me think, let me think . . ."

"Let me think," I interrupt her. "Remember, Ibn Sina told me I am Pirooz now, I have been Gorgani before, and perhaps . . ."

"Someone else before that!" I hear joy in her voice and see a wave of comfort cross her face. "There may be more in this, more in you than Pirooz and Gorgani!" A huge silence hangs between us like an empty pond tasting the inflowing stream of understanding.

"Do you have your answer to my proposal?" she asks.

"It is yes, yes!"

"I knew it!" Her disarming smile reappears quickly and almost childishly she says, "I know I hurt you, but can I still sleep beside you tonight?" A sparkle—a celebration for happiness and sadness joining—springs into her eyes. Do I see this, or do I imagine it? She has waited for my answer with a confidence of knowing what it is.

I am frightened by her emotional twitches, all based on improbabilities. Now she sounds like a woman in love who is trying to make up. With some hesitation, I respond, "Yes, but . . ."

"But, what?"

"I am puzzled and hurt by all our ups and downs."

"Is that all? I hope our promise of openness still holds," she says. "Of course. I withhold not what I know but only what I am unsure of. After all, our life should not depend on speculations about speculations."

Then, hearing again her words, "Can I sleep beside you tonight?" my heart dances like a courting crane: hopscotch, swing the wing, splash in a marsh, twist in flight, and land with one wing up and one down while calling my mate to accede to my urgings to love. But I also sense my fear lurking in spacelessness.

Trying to set my doubts aside, I leave her and put a record on the stereo. It is a slow dance tune of the Fifties. I remember it so well: the one the bands used to play for the last dance of the evening. I take her in my arms and we dance slowly and closely. I feel buoyant, enjoying the moment, this very vital moment, immensely. I dance with history, in the city of history, and I will not worry about what comes next.

But I become apprehensive again—what has caused Sitareh's change of heart? Such a sharp swing in her resolve! Why should it matter if I could have been someone else besides Gorgani more than a thousand years ago? Is she not in love with Pirooz? With me? She says she is. Why must we let history come between us?

She sees my puzzled look and asks, "What crossed your mind just now?"

"You and your mood swings, and history coming between lovers."

"Brooding won't help you, . . . you must accept me and history as we are, Pirooz! Anyhow, my great-grandmother was a crane!"

"Oh!" I reply, surprised by the synchronicity of her comment and the courting cranes in my imagination.

We have a wonderful evening, except that I feel a slight gnawing at the core of my existence; Sitareh's swift turnabout and my uncharacteristic submissiveness play havoc in me. I calm myself, remembering that she said, "My great-grandmother was a crane." I know cranes are steadfast in love and loyal to their mates until death sets them apart. That thought brings a smile to my lips.

"What are you thinking, Pirooz?" she asks.

"I think the Archangel Gabriel may have revealed God's message to the wrong species. 'Until death do us part' works better for cranes."

"Maybe!"

What next? I wonder to myself. Inexplicably I feel naked and vulnerable before a tribunal of the future. I think of a friend of Ibn Sina's, Baba Tahir Oryan, the maddest and the wisest man in Hamadan, a delicate poet whose deep sensitivity flowed from his heart, with an angelic humility and an absorption in things beyond sensory perception.

"Pirooz, where are you?"

"In Hamadan, the city found by Jamsheed the wise mythical king!"

"When are you in history, then?"

"A thousand years ago."

"With whom?"

"With Baba Tahir. Let me recite one of his quatrains for you."

"Please do. I need it!"

> How fair is love with blood of two hearts blest.
> One-sided love is ache of soul at best.
> And if Majnoon has burnt in fires of love,
> How scorched with flames was love in Laila's breast!

I fall silent and can hear Sitareh murmuring to herself, "Not even Baba Tahir knows who loves more and longer and purer."

I do not reply. A deep sorrow overcomes me, which only my non-existence can erase, the non-existence that Baba Tahir understood so well that he already assumed it when he was still in existence. Sitareh lets me alone to fully experience my sorrow. Now I see why Baba Tahir is so admired: by showing us the possibility of experiencing non-existence while existing, he frees us of fear and leads us to spiritual ascendance.

In the distance, an explosion recalls me to the here and now. Another Iraqi bomb, a new feature of life in Hamadan, is a keen reminder of the immediacy of death. I wonder if I will meet Ibn Sina's spirit again in this world or the next.

Suddenly snapping me out of my reveries are the alarming words, "Our togetherness is a sin, Pirooz!"

Another of her unpredictable changes of heart stuns me. Nevertheless I manage to say, "For me, love is never sin and sin is never love." Collecting my thoughts further, I add, "Anyhow, sin is no more than hidden subjectivity—different faiths, different times, different sins, different hells, Sitareh."

"To you, is the self, the individual, a prelude to faith—some faith?" she asks.

"To whose faith, if not my own, must I adhere, Sitareh?" I wait expectantly.

"One faith per person, then?" she inquires.

"Yes, if needed, like one soul per person responsible for his own deeds."

Sitareh pauses, looking down at her hands. After a moment she looks up at me. "Listen, Pirooz, what if I have conceived . . ."

I am thunderstruck. "You have conceived?"

"I don't know, but it is possible. A woman's body is like the sea, dominated by the lunar orbit, not her own will. Our timing was perfect," she says with a sigh. "Anyhow, it is a fact that we are living together. For legitimacy's sake, I must become your *seegheh*, your temporary wife. That is for a fixed duration and payment, if you remember. It is voluntary, not for pay, so it is not a case of exploitation." She smiles as her eyes examine mine. Can she still read my thoughts in them?

"But why a lowly *seegheh*?" Even though Islam is willing to sanctify a temporary liaison, nevertheless a *seegheh* retains a certain stigma.

"Because of the dangers if we are caught living together, and the fact that it is noncommittal for each of us." She sounds determined.

I turn to face the window, as my Westernized life flashes before me, intruding the sudden burden of reality into the dream-like atmosphere of this ancient city. My *seegheh*! I never thought I would have a *seegheh*! But our living together must be legitimate. I fear the Almighty less than the Islamic fanatics.

Resigned, I turn back to her and reply, "Fine, Sitareh, but I would prefer a regular marriage. Anyhow, if you are really pregnant, we must do some more thinking and rethinking."

"All right. The first thing tomorrow we will go to the Alavian Mosque, a charming old place I want you to visit, and find a mullah to perform the rite."

Chapter Fourteen: History in Hypnosis

"You should get a driver's license here," Sitareh says before getting into the car to drive to the Alavian Mosque. The psychiatrist, hidden within a black chador, is on a secret mission. She is a secret to me, too.

"You look like the id submerged in darkness, Sitareh."

"I have been an id ever since I met you!" She looks bizarre steering in the chador. "I feel I'm in a kangaroo's pouch—"

"Hot, in motion and carrying me around, too," I interrupt. Our attempts at lightheartedness don't succeed in lifting my heavy heart. I feel caught in several traps, each tugging to possess the whole of me. Why am I joining in a "temporary marriage," something I never thought I would do, and so furtively, with no friends or family around?

The Alavian Mosque, over seven centuries old, lies in the northwest of Hamadan. I am amazed at its simplicity and dignity, with its time-worn walls of bright native brick. There are hundreds of historical sites in Hamadan, some yet to be excavated, so the past is always in sight. I remember my father explaining, "If you go into the cellar of some houses here and dig a few feet down, you will be in Ecbatana in the time of the King of Kings, Darius the Great."

We enter a quiet courtyard to inquire about a mullah who resides nearby. The *mihrab* and the gypsum moldings are intricate, mystical and inexplicable, resembling the wrinkles of a serenely aged Sufi embracing time that wrecks the body but enhances the spirit. The god-like architect invested the structure with a soul that is closer to ultimate reality than the visible bricks. Under the central dome a tomb covered with turquoise blue tiles holds a forgotten member of the Alavian family, descendants of the Shiite Fourth Imam. The Koranic inscriptions on the interior walls are as beautiful as their message. I recognize a verse entitled "Mankind," which calls to mind my mother's advice, "The first command of God to the Prophet was 'Read!' You must read in order to know, my son."

We locate the mullah who will perform the ritual for Sitareh to become my *seegheh*, my wife for a set duration and a payment called *mahr*—a more unpleasant transaction than a wedding. Nevertheless, I submit. The mullah, a small, cautious man with a full beard, takes us across the compound to his humble home. We sit on an old klim in a tiny room under a picture of the Imam 'Ali holding a scroll, his face luminous. After some questions, the mullah asks, "For how long will you be *seegheh*?"

"Three months," Sitareh answers, her eyes avoiding mine.

"What is the *mahr*?"

"A Koran," she replies.

"That is all you are asking from this man as *mahr*?"

"Can there be a more valuable *mahr*?" she replies, startling the poor mullah.

"*Na, na, Zaifeh! Staghferollah!* No, no, the weaker sex! God forbid!" he cries. "Nothing equals the Holy Book in value. Of course not!"

Sitareh's antic smile shows in the corner of her mouth out of the chador.

A few Arabic words from the mullah seal the business at hand. Heavenly authority has approved us as temporary mates, and we are legally safe under earthly holy rule. A boy brings us tea and sugar cubes, and the mullah hands us a document recording our agreement. I pay him a donative with the nagging feeling that I have been taken and sold something I didn't want. Safely in the car, I complain, "A transitory marriage in a historic place. I would have preferred the reverse."

"I would have, too. But now you have rented me for three months, Pirooz!"

"This is no joke, renting people and suppressing people in our country," I reply.

The next day the two of us take an early morning stroll. She appears as contemplative as I am, so I leave her to her thoughts.

Finally I complain, "Your magnificent house should have a warmer shower!"

"You are lucky it has a shower at all, Pirooz. When I was a child we used a commercial bathhouse."

An airplane drones like a lost lamb in the sky. Staring at it, Sitareh says, "Ibn Sina knows something about us we don't. We are in love, but he brought us together, maybe for his sake. Why won't he tell us what he wants of us, Pirooz?"

"Maybe he can't, or maybe he doesn't wish to."

"I think we ought to try hypnosis, Pirooz."

"What do you mean?"

"Since you are Gorgani, I can hypnotize you and, through suggestion, learn about Ibn Sina and you, without waiting for his whimsical visitations. He wants us to take a risk, but he won't take us into his confidence."

"The future is risky anyway, with or without him."

"The difference is that he has an image of our future in mind, and we don't."

"But I must recall history, not just my childhood. Could this be harmful?"

"I think not. But the impossible no longer intimidates me. Maybe we can direct our past and future at the same time." She smiles with confidence.

We sit on a rock under a weeping willow while the moon still hangs in the morning sky. Sitareh suggests, "Please let me hear you give the highlights of the lives of Gorgani and Ibn Sina together."

I recount what I know. Ibn Sina's father, Abdullah, was born and raised in Balkh, in the province of Khorassan. Balkh, with the Persian nickname 'the glittering,' was a commercial, political, intellectual, and religious metropolis where Muslims mingled with Christians, Buddhists, Manichaeans and Zoroastrians. Khorassan was where men like Ferdowsi, Rumi, and Ghazali were born and raised—the cradle of Persian civilization, and so of world civilization, at the time. Pilgrims from India, China, Turkestan and Arabia converged on the city to be enlightened. Ibn Sina's father was a well-educated man, steeped in the intellectual ferment in Balkh. When he was governor of Kharmaithan, the "Land of the Sun," near Bukhara, Ibn Sina was born in August of 980. The family moved to Bukhara, where Ibn Sina achieved fame as a young man. He educated himself mostly, since he outgrew his teachers faster than his clothing. He mastered Euclid's *Geometry* in one night. Bukhara was now the capital of the declining Persian Samanid dynasty and home to many scientists, scholars and Islamic theologians, and to one of the two greatest libraries in the world then. After his father's death and the approaching collapse of the ruling house, Ibn Sina went to Gurganji, a flourishing city on the banks of the great Amu-Darya River.

I stop and glance at Sitareh. At my temporary wife. Now I understand one reason for elaborate religious ceremonies and big wedding parties: they help make becoming a wife or husband believable and memorable.

"Go on, Pirooz," she urges, business-like.

With a sigh, I continue. In Gurganji Ibn Sina met and befriended the great Persian scientist, Biruni, and the distinguished physician, Masihi, and others. Ten happy and productive years followed until Sultan Mahmood of Ghazna, the Turkish conqueror of a vast empire between India, the Persian Gulf, and the Caspian—excluding central Persia—demanded Ibn Sina's residence at his court. Ibn Sina, fearing the Sultan's dogmatism and preferring Persian patrons, refused to comply and, to escape Mahmood's wrath, crossed Khorassan in disguise. Masihi, his dearest friend and colleague, a refugee with him, perished along the way.

"Where did Ibn Sina meet Gorgani?" Sitareh interrupts.

"In Gorgan, his next stop."

"Oh, that city, forever breathing the salt air of the Caspian. I have been there; it is a jewel. I wish I had been there then!" she reminisces.

"But Gorgan has been sacked by Turks or devastated by earthquakes a few times, so it is used to death and rebirth. Misfortune is woven into its history, just as a marvelous climate is woven into its citizens' souls, and lively colors into their carpets."

"Why did Ibn Sina go to Gorgan?" she inquires like a prosecutor.

To find a good patron, Amir Qabus. But those were turbulent times, and unfortunately, when he reached Gorgan, the Amir had already been overthrown and perished in prison. With no patron in sight, Ibn Sina was so distressed that he wrote a poem ending: "And when my value rose, no one cared to buy me."

"He sounds like an economist," Sitareh says.

"The science was not even born yet, but he wrote some political economy."

Upon hearing this poem and learning of Ibn Sina's presence in Gorgan, Shirazi, a supporter of the arts and sciences, took Ibn Sina under his wing and purchased a house for him. Ibn Sina responded by taking flight into new thoughts. Here he met his pupil, lifelong friend and biographer, Gorgani. After a few years sojourn, they left Gorgan. I pause, unsure of exactly what Sitareh is looking for.

"Go on, Pirooz," she urges me, taking mental notes.

I continue. Despite personal hardship and financial and political difficulties, Ibn Sina continued his work while journeying southwest, away from Mahmood's grasp.

"Why did he leave Gorgan?" Sitareh wonders aloud.

"I am not sure what he ran to or ran from."

"Oh, how I would like to know what made him run! But go on, Pirooz."

He went to Ray, a cosmopolitan city near present-day Teheran, where a widowed queen ruled. When invaders threatened Ray, he retreated to Qazvin and then to Hamadan. Here he was the vizier at one time and a prisoner at another. Then in Isfahan he enjoyed the most productive period of his life at the court of Ala El-Dowleh. Fourteen years later Ibn Sina fled when the army of Sultan Mahmood sacked Isfahan. Soon afterwards he died in Hamadan.

"He had difficulty settling down!"

"History had difficulty settling down, too," I reply. "The brutality of the times and the restlessness of his mind turned him into a wanderer."

"But what can have been his motives? Was it only security?" Sitareh insists.

"Why must we become detectives?" I object. "He knows where to find us."

"Yes, but for our own identity and future, we must seek the answers."

We stare at each other. Curiosity, like a lone star, twinkles in my mind. My new wife—unbelievable as that sounds—is right; we must learn all we can, even though I am not certain why or how.

Suddenly Sitareh interrupts my reverie. "I want to take your mind to when Gorgani met Ibn Sina."

"Shall we begin now?" I say as I marvel at her persuasiveness, for in one day she has become my wife, my hypnotist, even my psychoanalyst.

She half-smiles and tells me to relax and breathe deeply. She removes her pearl necklace and swings it in front of my eyes, telling me to count down slowly from one hundred. I obey her. My eyes become heavier as I hear her words, "You, Gorgani, are meeting Ibn Sina for the first time, in Gorgan." I drift into a deep sleep.

An absolutely dark and soundless moment passes. I look at myself. I am about fourteen but look older. My parents are dead. My uncle and I are guests of Shirazi, the generous patron of Ibn Sina. We are in the *biruni*, the part of the house women may not enter when there are male visitors. Ibn Sina himself, a man in his thirties, magnificent in disposition and attire, sits beside Shirazi, and many eminent men of Gorgan have come to hear him. My uncle is interested to know if Ibn Sina will accept me as his pupil. Everyone in the room is in awe of him. His eyes glisten with understanding, curiosity and kindness, interrupted by flashes of great intensity. He seems to touch everything, even the stars, with his gaze. I like him right away and he quickly notices my attraction. Ibn Sina inquires about the progress of my studies, and I reply in detail as he listens carefully. He seems pleased with my attainments. He asks if I can take dictation. My uncle interrupts, "Yes, Leading Wise Man. He can take dictation in both Persian and Arabic. He can also . . . Ah, but that is not relevant."

Ibn Sina responds, "If it is not private, I wish to know."

"It is no secret, I play the flute," I respond. "I began at five with my uncle's reluctant consent, but now, hearing me play, he approves wholeheartedly."

"Music is the food of the psyche, isn't it?" Ibn Sina stares at me for confirmation.

I nod. I feel he has taken a liking to me. He is writing a book, called *The Origin and the Return*, and has begun work on *The Canon of Medicine*. He needs clerical help. I tell him, "It is a great honor if you would accept me as your assistant." I love my uncle, who is my guardian, but I want to choose whether to continue to live with him or to share in Ibn Sina's adventures.

He glances at my uncle and at Shirazi. They smile and consent. Then softly he tells me, "Join me at morning prayer tomorrow and bring what you need for a long sojourn. Much work remains undone, young man!"

The mystical wisdom in his voice crystallizes my wishes. All my training since the age of four will now bear fruit. He wants me!

After dinner someone reads a new poem, and the ensuing discussion of poetry leads to Sultan Mahmood. Now Ibn Sina talks and everyone listens. "It is not love of science and art that excites the Sultan's patronage, but the praise scholars heap on him. No one can rule by sword alone, not even Mahmood. He commands learned men from near and far to come to his court, even against their will. His Sunni orthodoxy hampers creativity, since no one knows how or when they may transgress the threshold of his tolerance. He ordered

Batinis and Mutazilites carried off in chains to Khorassan, imprisoned or stoned to death, and valuable books burned."

A Turkish guest disagrees. "Ruling is a brutal business, no matter who rules, but it is not the Sultan, but his subjects, who kill and plunder. His primary interest is power, I agree, but his propensity for the arts and sciences is sincere."

"The sovereign is more responsible than his subjects," Ibn Sina replies. "Anyhow, I had to flee from Gurganji to avoid being abducted to his court. Ferdowsi fled, too, when Mahmood did not appreciate his great verse epic, the *Shahnameh, The Book of Kings*, and failed to compensate him with the agreed sum. Ferdowsi, an old man, and I met in the city of Harat. He lent me the *Shahnameh*, and I read it in three days, nearly fifty thousand verses. Ferdowsi proposes that knowledge is power; he is more concerned with power than with love. The book contains the history of Iran and civilization from the dawn of time to the Arab conquest. In the *Shahnameh*, Ferdowsi narrates the invention of agriculture, husbandry, tools and textiles, house and road construction, writing and government, and the creation of civilized order. He even explains how esteem for art and science arose. Furthermore, he depicts the conflict between Turkish nomads and the settled Persian civilization from very ancient times. In the book, the Persian hero, Rustam, warring with his Turkish nemesis, Afrasyab, represents the struggle between good and evil, or culture and savagery. The same wars still rage today, as Turkish tribesmen encroach on Iran from beyond the Amu-Darya. The *Shahnameh* begins in myth and ends in history."

Ibn Sina falls into his patent pause while all eyes focus on him.

Shirazi says, "Tell us more, Ibn Sina, about Abul-Qasem Ferdowsi and his work. We are greatly interested in his lofty goals and accomplishments."

Ibn Sina obliges. "Fleeing from the Sultan and facing an uncertain future helped us to speak our minds. I told Ferdowsi that the *Shahnameh*, though in a monotonous meter, is sonorous and majestic and will preserve Persian language and history for the ages. He replied, 'You are right about the style, but remember, life is repetitive—good and evil are relentlessly at war, even in our souls. The *Shahnameh*'s meter conveys the rhythm of the seasons, history, and even our heartbeats. My dear learned man, it was the best I could do.' When I asked how long he took to compose it, he replied, 'Over thirty-seven years—my life's mission.' I asked if I could offer a specific criticism, and he said, 'That is the best anyone with good intentions can do.' So I asked, 'Why do you both praise and curse our tormentor, Sultan Mahmood?' He thought for a long time and said, 'Well, had I known the future, I would have been more cautious. The Sultan is generous to those who glorify him and brutal to those who question him. He scorns the independent existence of any soul but his own. I hope he will mend his ways one day. God has given us all the capacity to learn.'"

Ibn Sina looks around at the faces in the room. "When I asked Ferdowsi his opinion of my compiling a scientific and philosophical Persian vocabulary, his eyes lit up. He said, 'This will complete the resurrection of the Persian language—a great human heritage. Do it, Ibn Sina, by all means. God bless you for your intention and give you strength to realize it.' I wanted to question him more but I refrained. Ferdowsi said, 'Open your heart to me, Ibn Sina. There is nothing to lose and much to gain; stories are for telling, not for keeping in one's heart. Often what remains unsaid is far more important than what is said. This is not Mahmood's court, where true stories drown in a sea of silence or indifference, where falsifiers prowl like sharks and swallow the truthsayers.' Then he smiled and said, 'We are friends and we are free here.' So I asked, 'Why did you depict Zahak, the only king with no royal blood, as the most evil ruler of all time? Did he really have growing from each shoulder a snake that fed on the brains of young men? Did he rule a thousand years? Persian children must learn the truth: what is prideful and what is shameful, equally.

We all waited intently, while Ibn Sina took a sip of sweetened, diluted rosewater. Then he resumed, "Ferdowsi listened to me carefully before he smiled. Could I have tasted his smile, it would have been acid, bitter and burning. He said, 'Of course royal blood has nothing to do with just rule; it is finite and will always end in commonness. But what is done is done. The story is not mine anymore; it belongs to the world. It will show that no one can write a perfect verse according to everyone's taste, just as God could not or would not create a world satisfying to all creatures for all times.'

"Ferdowsi thought for a moment before concluding, "The *Shahnameh*, like all human artifacts, reflects two spirits: one contemporary, the other permanent. I am certain that perceptive readers will not judge all of the *Shahnameh* entirely by the standards of their own time. I composed the tale of Zahak when I was young and equated royalty with nationhood. I still do, but with some qualifications: maturity softens beliefs; in time, grapes become wine. Hindsight is like a cure that reaches the patient too late. Notice that I am now running from the royal court.' He took a deep breath. 'I regret some of my work, just as Rustam the hero mourned when he killed his son, Sohrab, thinking him the enemy commander. Sohrab revealed his identity only after Rustam inflicted the fatal wound, and then the cure from the mythical bird, the Simurgh, reached him too late. To respect my work because it seems perfect is a false respect. Nothing is perfect, but we must strive for perfection. True admiration stems from truth. The *Shahnameh* is now out of my hands and in the heart of history.'

"Then Ferdowsi recited this autobiographical poem:

> Much toil did I suffer, much writing I pondered,
> Books writ in Arabic and Persian of old.
> For sixty-two years many arts did I study;
> What gain do they bring me in glory or gold?
> Save regret for the past and remorse for its failings
> Of the days of my youth every token hath fled.

"I stared at the great and fatigued old man until he spoke again, 'You have at least one more question, Ibn Sina.' Ferdowsi had guessed what was in my heart.

"So I asked, 'You are a Muslim, Ferdowsi, yet you consider the Arab conquest of Iran a catastrophe. Why is that?'

"'My dislike of the invasion is understandable, since Islam could have conquered my heart without the occupation of Iran. Invaders are abhorred, because they never consult the invaded nations or history,' he explained. Inexplicably he became angry, his face turned red and he spoke with agitation. 'Look, my first name is Arabic, as are those of many Persians. Alien words have invaded our language and culture, leaving its integrity in doubt. Worse, our scholars write mostly in Arabic now, a language not accessible to most Persians.'

"'What has happened has happened. Not much can be done about it immediately. I promise I will write in Persian, too,' I promised Ferdowsi.

"He threw me an approving smile and then a puzzled glance. He calmly said, 'I look to the right and I look to the left. Nowhere do I find the beginning or the end.' The next day, before we left Harat, he said, 'I appreciate your questions and remarks. Only the fanatic believes any artifact is sacred or perfect. We must reexamine history because it is us, and hear it from different sources, not just from the mouths of conquerors, who are just glorified pillagers anyhow. If the present is distorted, then what do you expect from history books?'

"I told Ferdowsi, 'You are one of the brightest lights in this world.'

"He looked up and said, 'Beside the sun, all lights sum up to nothing.' We embraced and said our farewells, both escaping from the clutches of the Sultan. A verse of Ferdowsi predicts his own immortality. I believe it shall be so."

Shirazi asks, "What measure of a man is this Ferdowsi?"

"A man of great integrity, one who can carry a nation's history and language on his back, one who was completely convinced that individuals could save history and individuals could make history. He loves Iran more than anything. I say, 'I exist because mankind exists,' but Ferdowsi says, 'If Iran ceased to exist, then I would not be.'"

Ibn Sina falls silent. I, Gorgani, stare at him for a long moment and realize, even at fourteen, that I want to be near this enormous source of light all my life.

The next day I move into Ibn Sina's house, knowing in my heart that my life and Ibn Sina's will be lived together. This will make my uncle both sad and happy, sad because I have been like a son to him, and happy because I will learn from the greatest teacher alive.

I play the flute for Ibn Sina our first evening together. When I finish he looks contemplative. "Your music makes me love life more even than truth."

"What is music, Master?" I ask.

He smiles at me, "You must tell me. You make it, Gorgani!"

"But Master, I want to be enlightened by your insightful thoughts."

"Music unites reality, the self and God. We shall soon explore music theory and music therapy, Gorgani."

Later in the evening Ibn Sina meditates in his room. I can hear him recite the Koran, and chant in a low voice, "I am speaking and I am listening to His world and His words. I am Him, He is me! I am Him, He is me!"

Suddenly, the flute, the man, the scene, and the ancient time squeeze into a vanishing dot. I struggle to lift my leaden eyelids. Sitareh looks at me strangely, as though I have just emerged from a grave, out of nothingness. I am exhausted.

"Did it work?" I ask anxiously.

"Yes. You know it worked!" she cries in triumph. "The past is not dead, and the future is not unreachable. Tenses are interactive, hopes and despairs reinterpret memories, and memories form new hopes and despairs."

"When truth meets people for the first time, only a few embrace it, but gods enter and exit minds as if it were a stage. The fire, sun, idols, even false ideas have been worshiped; and people have killed people over them. The visible gods then merged into the invisible God, and belief in magic turned into belief in religion and then to science, but bestiality continued. Real history is the human sickness and the recorded history is the human vomit." I say in one breath as if talking to myself.

"One's upbringing resides with the self, just as history—good or bad—within a society.," Sitareh replies. I am reminded of Khayyam's quatrain:

> The moving finger writes, and having writ,
> Moves on. Nor all your piety nor wit
> Shall lure it back to cancel half a line,
> Nor all your tears wash out a word of it.

To rid our minds of burdensome thoughts, Sitareh takes me to Ali Samad, a gigantic water-filled cavern in the belly of a mountain north of Hamadan, an unbelievable sight. We take a rowboat deep into the mountain, where stalactite and stalagmite teeth, sharp and icy and elongated, are as threatening as time's sharp teeth on my skin. We whisper to avoid eerie echoes and not to waken the beast that is the mountain. The rock frightens us with sharp cracking noises. Sitareh sees my apprehension and comforts me.

At home, Sitareh puts her arms around my shoulders and lifts herself onto her toes. I bathe in her love. For the moment the me, myselves, and I are transcendent in one whole self who loves Sitareh, who loves himself, and who loves humanity.

Just before turning out the lights, she whispers to me, "Soon we will visit the ancient stone lion and make a wish. It is an old custom in Hamadan."

We hear Iraqi bombs from far away. Sitareh inches closer to me. Trying to get her mind off the danger, I say, "Just as Iranians of all ethnicities are strung together into one nation by time, I wish rivers would weave humanity into one family."

She whispers, "What childish dreams you have, Pirooz!"

"In your arms I am myself, Sitareh, and that makes me happy and optimistic."

"I know, Pirooz-jon. You belong to the future, my beloved, but it is the present we are condemned to live in."

The next day Sitareh in a black dress and chador and I in a black tie attend the funeral of Firoozeh's sister. Sitareh contributes a check towards the rebuilding of her uncle's house. A few days later we set out for the stone lion sculpted during the Parthian dynasty about two thousand years ago. Invaders had overturned it and it lay indifferently for centuries. Recently, it was put on a new pedestal in the east of Hamadan, where once stood an ancient palace from whose gates imperial power poured forth into distant lands. I imagine the Parthian archers that slew numerous Romans marching past the lion's proud smile. The lion has survived plunderers trying to split its belly for treasure. Some believe it makes wishes come true.

Sitareh climbs onto the lion's back and raises her voice. "How do we look?" She looks tiny on the huge beast, who seems determined to depart for some mysterious place. Sitareh pulls her red scarf down to her neck and lets it flare through her jet-black hair that billows in the wind, looking vibrant and sensual, with no fear of the Guards. She winks at me, puts her head on the lion's neck, closes her eyes, and makes her wish.

I snap her picture and help her down. Our lips meet and stay together for a long, memorable moment. Her soft finger touches my neck, my being, and so the present turns sanguine. The silent lion will never inform on lovers.

Then, hearing a car approach, Sitareh withdraws from me, frowns and pulls her scarf up to hide her hair. A pang shoots through my guts. Why must the state come between lovers? Why can't we be what we are, with harm to no one? As if nothing had happened, she calmly insists that I mount the stone lion, too, and make a wish.

So I climb and ask the lion, "Where am I?"

I hear him say, "On my back like the others."

"What do you want, stone lion?"

"I want my bygone glory. What do you want, Pirooz?"

"To know, to love and to be free."

"Really! Here?" The stone lion falls stone silent, perhaps dissimulating.

On our way back, Sitareh comments, "Should we tell our wishes?"

"No! Someone or something may try to stop a revealed wish."

She throws a strange glance at me and I respond with a smile. Maybe she is not used to having her wishes disagreed with. With her scarf in place, we drive to a bazaar off the main square to buy groceries. Sitareh prefers to shop herself usually and select fruits and vegetables one piece at a time. Shopkeepers know her and treat her with great respect, even reverence. The bazaar has not changed for years: dark, quiet, uncrowded at this time. I feel like a child for an instant. At the post office, I purchase some stamps and stationery. Sitareh insists on paying; "In Iran, you are my guest."

At home later in the evening, I glance at Sitareh as she sleeps. I wonder about us. Do I really know why she wanted a temporary marriage? Uneasiness overtakes me and keeps me awake. In their persistence, these questions make faces at me. Then I remind myself I must write my mother, but I must dissimulate everything. A devout Muslim, nevertheless, she has many doubts about the *seegheh* institution, thinking it is sanctified prostitution, a necessary evil, at best. I look at Sitareh for answers. She wears a smile like a happy child. Sitareh Poonia's prediction, "Soon we will sleep in the same bed and wake up in the same bed," makes me shudder inside. I close my eyes and wonder, Who is this new wife of mine?

After breakfast, she disappears and, returning, hands me a package wrapped in a maroon silk. "This will sweeten the bitterness of our temporary marriage."

"What is it?"

"A family treasure, a gift to Pirooz-*jon*. The word '*jon*' in her voice, meaning love and life, sends joyful shivers through me.

I unwrap it. "The *Shifa!*" I exclaim. It is Ibn Sina's great encyclopedic masterpiece, a leather-bound manuscript copy over four hundred years old, a foot long, more than two inches thick and very heavy, as though bearing the great effort embodied within it. I open it with awe as my mother would the Holy Book. The calligraphy is dazzling and precise, as though it were typeset. An exquisite miniature painting heralds each chapter, epitomizing its prodigious ideas. In one section, constellations of thin red lines trace complex geometrical figures in the wide margin. The book is an astonishing creation, like Michelangelo's Sistine Chapel ceiling. For centuries it was the main reference for subjects other than politics. "Are you sure, Sitareh-*jon*?" She does not answer, but steps forward and puts her arms around me. Her lips touch mine as we squeeze the book between our hearts.

Finally I speak. "I have no gift for you."

"Yes, you do. I keep it in my heart. It is your love for me." Sitareh places the book in my hands, steps back, and holds my hands holding the book. She smiles enigmatically. "You will never leave me, Pirooz?"

"Never. Will you, Sitareh?"

"Not of my own volition," she says.

Chapter Fifteen: The Malady

The restaurant is a humble place, with old wooden chairs and tables, no tablecloths or carpets, the only decoration a picture of His Excellency Imam Ali—the fourth Caliph of the Sunnis and the first saint of the Shiites. Sitareh orders a lunch of yoghurt and rice, and I order chicken kebab, the house specialty. Scents of broiled vegetables don't tempt me as usual, since they must compete with the smell of my past and future, as if they were on the broiler, too.

"Ferdowsi is God's gift to all." Sitareh breaks our silence.

"I agree, but this regime says otherwise, belittling Ferdowsi in order to reenact the Arab invasion of Iran and re-export Islam to Arab lands."

"Do you hear how strange you sound?"

"Yes, I do. This is God's country now, we are told, but Iraqi missiles are blasting it, we need not be told. How strange can it get, Sitareh?"

In the background, Iranian State Radio plays martial music in between war propaganda and religious sermons, to fill all ears in the country and leave room for no other sound. Passion plays inflate the heroism of ancient saints beyond belief and embellish them with new episodes. I gently ask the owner if he will turn down the volume.

"Of course, he whispers." If I did not dread the Guards, I'd shut it off. I work, eat, obey and act dumb like everybody else. They have turned us into blind donkeys."

"True, any voice other than the Ayatollah's is the Devil." He glances at me quizzically and leaves. I notice the hotel clerk, who eyes us from a table nearby.

Sitareh frowns and whispers, "Where is your sense of danger, Pirooz? He could be setting us up for the police."

"To me, the radio blares the voice of deception. If the zealots could hear not just what the State sanctions, but other versions, too, they might recognize the roots of their xenophobia. Television is the archangel Gabriel; always demonizing someone else, making people think what are not their own thoughts, and hate what are not their own hatreds. It readies ordinary folk to crucify, crusade or nuke others without a pang of conscience. Yesterday our neighbors killed our children with mustard gas, claiming it was God's will, and some Iraqis must have believed it." I raise my voice above a whisper. "Whose archangel Gabriel is the true one, Sitareh?"

"Some people do doubt television," Sitareh objects.

"They are powerless and will never be on television themselves to accuse television."

Sitareh grins, "Gabriel was inconsistent in antiquity, too."

"And the holy books contradict one another, and the prophets stay silent, like dinosaurs," I interrupt. "Man will conquer the universe someday and subdue the One who runs it."

"Stop it, please, Pirooz," she pleads. "Complain all you want at home."

"I love being in your protection, Sitareh."

"I wish I could protect you, Pirooz." We swallow a few silent minutes, as if mourning to ease the pain of our own words in our own hearts.

I fall into a reverie. If my recent experiences are real, then what was unreal before? If they are unreal, then what is real now? Is this woman I am wedded to also my dead love, Poonia? Even though Sitareh sits opposite me, I must struggle to put away my loneliness. Such questions can isolate someone, but they can also be the result of isolation. I hope that Sitareh's obsession with Ibn Sina and her reservations about me will end, so that I will have a chance to learn more about her. She seems to hold so many stars within her; I want to touch them one by one, and be thrilled by them all. But will she let me?

Inexplicably, a thought about Ibn Sina's wanderings comes to me. "Sitareh?" She looks up. "Ibn Sina swept like a storm from city to city, from one difficulty to the next, perhaps to avoid conformity or seek some security we can't guess at now. But maybe the threat of a secret found out impelled him to move on."

"What secret? A family secret possibly?" she asks.

"Well, Ibn Sina's father was an Ismaili, a heretic who read hidden meanings in the Koran and believed in the succession of seven instead of twelve Imams, as most Shiite Muslims do. The authorities in Bukhara blamed Ibn Sina for a fire in the great library that destroyed many rare and ancient books, claiming that the young scholar had memorized all the books and wanted exclusive knowledge of them. To make their evil accusations worse, they linked them to his disavowed Ismaili beliefs."

"He loved books, and this story was never a secret, anyhow."

"True, but this could be the key to a deeper problem," I say as my taste buds follow the aroma of cooking into the kitchen. Soon my mind shifts. "Ibn Sina couldn't heal the malady of sectarianism that rulers manipulated for their own interests, proving that man's savagery to man is worse than the plague. Ibn Sina agonized over this malady and tried to escape it mentally when he couldn't do so physically."

"Do you mean his refuge in Sufism?"

"Yes, I do." Sitareh stares at me as I continue, "He took flight not only from the Sunnism of Sultan Mahmood's court, but also from Aristotle's materialism. He flew to a mystical world where his spirit was free even when his body was not, figuratively or literally." There is still no sign of food. "Thank God this aroma has no cholesterol."

"Be patient, Pirooz. This is not McDonald's."

We hold hands under the table for an instant like spies passing microfilm. The Islamic Republic forbids any display of affection in public. I shake my head, frustrated by hunger for everything. My imagination works like an appetizer; it makes me hungry for being myself and knowing the world as it is and acting freely to make it better.

"What do you mean, figuratively imprisoned?" she asks, trying to keep me busy.

"His soul was confined like a convict in his body, he believed. He searched for a spiritual haven, but, while he never found one, he did lay the groundwork for a reconstructed Sufism, the spiritual home of Persians . . ."

"Mysticism existed before him, no?" Sitareh interjects.

"Of course. Sufism arose from Buddhist, Jewish, Islamic and Persian roots."

"What does mysticism do for the Sufis?" she inquires. "Your version, Pirooz."

"It releases the soul from the body shackled in the real world."

The waiter arrives with a stained white apron at his waist and a big tray of food. No one utters a word. I am the first to take a bite of the warm bread. The chicken is tender, and the salad of cucumbers, tomatoes, onions, hard boiled eggs, lemon, salt, pepper and olive oil is fresh.

I glance at Sitareh. She smiles at me lovingly. "Are you happy now, Pirooz?"

"Yes, hunger and happiness don't mix. When it comes to food, I am a materialist, having faith in oxygen, calories, vitamins, minerals and protein first and last."

Appreciation twinkles in her eyes, filling me with great joy. My meal becomes a delightful journey with her. I take a sip of *doogh*, a yoghurt drink sprinkled with basil, mint, salt and pepper. For a while we just enjoy our meal.

"I am eager to hear more from my oxygen-driven lover," she says, sipping her drink and basking in my admiration.

"OK. This is how I see it. Ibn Sina did not avoid all the traps—worldly pleasures—on the Sufi way. He enjoyed his silk garments, jewelry, the admiration of kings, colleagues and lovers, the appreciation of those he healed, and his own statesmanship and charisma as he tasted everything, so long as it didn't harm anyone but himself. He realized some of his plans and failed at others."

"How could he be a Sufi and immerse himself in worldly pleasures? Didn't Saadi say, 'Cherish not your body; . . . Wise men cherish virtue only'?"

"True, true, but Ibn Sina practiced the core of Sufism: a fearless search for truth, the primacy of love and the possibility of direct intuitive cognition of and unity with God. He enjoyed possessions rightly earned through his own talents, but he also abandoned them with ease. Ibn Sina was an active Sufi who did not withdraw into more contemplation and resignation to authority. He struggled to become perfect, since he was not born perfect."

As I take a big bite of chicken, she interjects, "It tastes good, doesn't it?"

"Yes. For years I was a vegetarian, but America changed me. Thank you for tolerating my carnivorous ways."

"You are what you are. Pirooz-*jon*, a deer transmogrified into a tiger."

"And when a carnivore is attracted to a herbivore?"

"Then God save me," she replies, grinning widely. We stare at each other, barely hiding our joy. "Continue, Pirooz."

"Sitareh-*jon*, I want us to climb to the pinnacle of self-knowledge, and you wish me to descend to the depths of ideas already melted in the past."

"There will be time for your mountain climbing later, Pirooz-*jon*."

Impelled by her wish, I resume, "Ibn Sina aroused controversy by flaunting his love of wine and music in a puritanical society, but his wit and medical genius helped him survive the dangers. He stretched his mind and body in work and play to extremes, as he did his seeming irreligiousness and prayer. He crossed the boundaries of the unknown and explored thoughts outside his own time, always keeping faith that man is beyond what he appears to be because man is God and God is man. Just visualize what a world we would have and how happy everyone would be if we all realized our potential the way Ibn Sina knew how."

Feeling satisfied, except for an urge for wine, I say, "How would Ibn Sina advise me on health, since I want wine and wine is not good for my sleeping ulcer."

"He said, first, know your body and don't mistreat it. Second, use preventive care to maintain your health, because it is too precious to leave to physicians or prayer alone. Third, once sickness strikes, understand that it is a part of the self that can be healed or, if incurable, develop the discipline to bear it. Fourth, no one knows the true value of health but the unhealthy. Anyhow, wine is God's creation. Even Islam didn't prohibit its moderate use as medicine. And Ibn Sina believed that some maladies of the psyche required wine for healing."

"Ibn Sina cuts his own profession down," I remark.

Suddenly two Guards enter the restaurant and scour the room. Conversation drops to a hush. The owner scowls at me and turns up the radio. Sitareh adjusts her scarf to cover every last strand of hair. The Guards talk to the hotel clerk in hushed tones, glance at us and leave as suddenly as they arrived.

Instantly, a one-legged war veteran sitting two tables away raises his voice. "What do they want from us, poking their noses in our meals?" He raises his voice so everyone can hear. "I miss the war. In battle I had faith in the goodness of the Islamic Republic. Now they have amputated my faith, too, and non-belief will drive me mad."

"Amen," we hear whispers.

Sitareh and I finish our lunch in silence. At length she says, "Let me ask you what I was about to, before the Guards intruded. "What was the social role of the Sufis?"

"At first Sufi leaders took up the cause of the towns and guildspeople against the courts and landlords, but later the mystics preached passivity, and thus rationalized the injustice of the Turkish occupation. The dark side of Sufism is its flight from the real world, its passivity and inertia, and its reliance upon God for everything, since worldly problems are insoluble. Hafiz, the great Sufi poet, who valued freedom no less than love, lampooned pretentious mullahs, greedy police and unjust rulers and preferred the company of beggars to them all, was one of the exceptions."

"Independent thinkers are no better off today. Are you critical of Sufism?"

"Not necessarily. I wish to free myself from unworthy attachments and purify my soul and be a courageous critical thinker, as the Sufis once were. But I don't appreciate Sufis who flee reason and science for gnosticism and obey the old seers unconditionally. I think we should make the world better than we found it, not abandon it. Sour Sufis don't inspire me, that's all!" Now, thirsting for some wine I say, "Thank you for the meal, Sitareh. Now let's go home."

Sitareh replies with a sparkle in her eyes, puts some cash on the table, and we depart. Crowds bustle around us as we walk to the car, and I look at her closely. Her scarf matches the natural pink of her lips. Her hazel eyes are enigmatic. She looks more beautiful to me every day. My world has shrunk to her and Ibn Sina, and become lost in a mystical bubble.

In the car, she says, "What points of Sufism attracted Ibn Sina?"

I look skyward and sigh before answering. "Monotheism and the unity of all existence, despite its apparent diversity; God's invisible presence everywhere; the soul's longing to perfect itself and return to God the beloved. Plus, there is wine and beauty. Intoxication prefigures one's ecstasy when God appears in one's life, and beauty mirrors the contemplation of God's perfection, which may reveal itself in art, knowledge, love or a soul. Ibn Sina, not a traditional Sufi, uplifted humanity with ideas, science, reason and medicine. He struggled against conformity. The real world was as much the object of his attentions as his own soul. Have you studied Sufism?"

"Some. To practice psychiatry I must know all aspects of Iranian culture. I also remember my father and his friends discussing Sufism at home. We will discuss it again." She talks to herself, "I still wonder about the secret you say may have contributed to Ibn Sina's sudden flights. Maybe we can discover it in further hypnosis, or maybe he will volunteer the information. What was important to him is important to us, Pirooz." After a long pause she asks, "By the way, did he keep his promise to Ferdowsi?"

"Yes, he did. Late in his life he wrote *The Book of Knowledge*, a great compendium of Persian philosophical and scientific terms. Since virtually all books at the time, including many of his own, were written in Arabic, he is the Ferdowsi of science and philosophy in Persian. May I ask something personal, Sitareh?"

"Yes."

"You said that your father was a diplomat and presumably rich. How could he be a Sufi, too?"

"Simple. He went into diplomacy because he wished to contribute to peace, but he became disillusioned on discovering that peacemakers are powerless. From then on he said and did what he had to in public, but did what he wanted in private. However, this dual life turned him into a bitter disciplinarian who demanded perfection. My character vacillates between my mother's tenderness and my father's toughness, between the dominance of love and the dominance of reason."

"That is quite a revelation!" I exclaim.

"For you only! Don't you want to know me, who I am, for better or worse?" Somehow our smiles intermingle.

A commotion brings us to an abrupt halt. Dust blows about as on a battlefield. A squad of Guards has rounded up several boys for the front.

"Let me tell my parents!" one begs.

"Get in the truck! All of you draft dodgers!" yells a heavily bearded Guard.

We hear more pleading and more yelling, but the muzzle of a gun silently enforces the holy command. The boys in the truck gasp for air like netted fish thrown into a boat. The truck links the two worlds of life and death for them. They will walk across a minefield to clear it for the tanks. Their flesh will dangle from smoldering trees or burn with Iraq's mustard gas.

Sitareh shakes her head in despair. I blurt out, "Damn it! They are too young to die! Can't we do something?"

"Watch yourself, Pirooz," she cautions. "We will be arrested if you protest. This holy regime presumes to make no mistakes, so any criticism, especially during the so-called holy war, is treasonous."

Sitareh drives cautiously past the Guards and speeds away. It is painful to know that Iraq offered Iran billions in reparations for a cease-fire, and the regime spurned it because they were more intent on punishing Saddam Hussein, the culprit, than on saving Muslim lives on both sides of the front. Revenge overwhelms compassion for the proclaimed holy men.

"The killing is real, but the cause is unreal," Sitareh says with intense frustration.

The dead voice of Poonia, "Learn to suffer in silence," and my cousin's remark, "Soon the Guards will come for my children," echo in my burdened ears.

As she nears home, Sitareh seems troubled again. "Pirooz, I don't know why, but I think our time is running out."

"Why? We have the whole summer. You know, Sitareh, you keep me on the razor's edge."

"Even if we had the whole century, I sense that our timing is crucial, and our opportunity to reach Ibn Sina may be ephemeral."

"Any reasons?"

"Nothing I can put my finger on," she says.

"What must we do, then?"

"More hypnosis. We will choose some critical episodes in his life, when we know Gorgani was present."

"What are our questions?" I ask.

"First, who am I? Second, are there others in you besides Gorgani? Third, why is Ibn Sina attracted to us, and why are we attracted to him? What is his plan, and what is our role in it? Fourth, is this all a dream or is it real? Do we exist and have we witnessed a non-existence come into existence? We must also decide if we wish to do his bidding. I feel that someone is putting ideas in my head. I love you, but I will not be your wife just because he wills it. As you know, love and marriage are not the same. Each can exist without the other."

"And they usually do, unfortunately," I suggest, but Sitareh doesn't seem to hear. Silence settles between us. Sitareh's dispassion is almost frightening. I fall deep into my thoughts, dreams, concerns, curiosities, wonders, desires and sink into the past while staring up at the future, with the present at their intersection. Does Sitareh feel the same? Soon we are home, where we retreat to our rooms to rest.

After an hour pondering, I return to her in the living room. Immediately Sitareh suggests, "Under hypnosis you can recall Ibn Sina's stay in the city of Ray, his journey to and his triumphs and imprisonment in Hamadan, his escape to Isfahan, and his return to and death in Hamadan. Maybe next time you can ask him some questions. Oh, but you cannot! You, Gorgani, can only remember. If we discover why he denied himself the stability of a home, maybe we can find out why he is interested in us."

Her heart brims with curiosity, even apprehension, and seems to skip a beat. I step forward and hold her in my arms. "Do you notice how doubts, fears and hopes wage war within and between us, Sitareh? I am not complaining, only observing. We are more research partners than lovers."

"We are in love, but our goal lies beyond our love. To learn his method of self-realization is good for us and everyone."

Instead of answering, I kiss her lips. She relaxes her face against my chest. "You have a noisy heart, Pirooz!"

"And you are intoxicating it, Sitareh."

She smiles, but it freezes on her face like a frozen rose. Abruptly she becomes serious. "Yes, yes, Pirooz-*jon*. Maybe the next hypnosis will reveal something we want to know, or, if he appears to you or us again, we can tell him that unless he takes us into his confidence we shall return to our previous lives."

"That is a threat to him or to me?"

"No, it's a statement, Pirooz. We will do everything for him, but he must do something for us, that is all."

"But I feel threatened, too, Sitareh."

"Let us handle one problem at a time," she replies. I stare at her, bewildered as she calmly concludes, "I seem to have had the same problem before, with someone else withholding information, a long time ago."

"What do you mean?"

"I don't know what I mean! I would die to know the origin of that thought myself."

"Our unknowing expands as we search and think and try to know more."

"We know that we know more, but we also know that we know less. To know what needs to be known is knowing." As soon as Sitareh says this, the lights go out. "Knowing," her last word, turns into darkness. Blindness becomes universal.

"An air raid!" Sitareh whispers, as though the Iraqi bombers might hear.

Explosions shake the world. Lightning spreads over the ground. Windows reflect fire and tumult. Violent braying from the stables precedes a deadly silence. I wait. We wait. Another nearby raid ends in a lull that seems to lurch towards us. My stomach churns. People bombing people; how senseless and cruel. I fear death and despise my fear. Suddenly I realize that in this journey I have been overly joyful and then overly dreading, one after the other, repeatedly.

I hold Sitareh's hands as if that could bring us peace. She whispers, "The theocracy is unable to protect us or to pray the enemy away."

"The dead will be undercounted; and they won't be able to correct the statistics, or to protest their inaccuracy," I add.

"I must go to the hospital as soon as this is over," she says to herself.

Chapter Sixteen: By Candlelight

I know that life starts with pain and ends with pain, but in between, who knows what it may bring? A huge explosion signals more destruction, and a chorus of screams crawls from the distance. Sitareh and I wait. The basement seems too far away to run to. I probably look scared, and I am. Contemplating my sudden death is brutal. With death creeping toward us, I don't pretend to be courageous or even thoughtful. I have pretended enough. We wait in a blackness that swallows my hopes; Hamadan was supposed to revive me, not kill me. Must I die in some scheme unknown to me? Regrets whip me. Why didn't I listen to my mother and stay in a much safer New York?

Another explosion flashes to reveal our ashen faces. Seeing Sitareh breaks my isolation. I whisper, "I love you," and she squeezes my hand. We wait—it is all we can do. Pitch darkness and stillness fuse into lingering apprehension. I listen, and the blackness also listens. Our ears are our eyes, too. I try to remember how I died in my previous life.

Hurried footsteps, mumbling, and a flickering light enter the room and interrupt my dread. "What is happening, Firoozeh?" Sitareh whispers to the approaching light.

"The bombing is over, I hope," the maid replies, placing candles on the table. I see my face distorted in the polished curves of the bronze candlesticks. Firoozeh is in black, mourning her sister's death for at least forty days. She grumbles as she rushes out, "Bombing is a devil's game, the blackout is his field, and each death is a score."

"She is amazing," Sitareh whispers to me, trying to sound calm.

The clock ticks off our last seconds of foreboding as time passes while everything else stands still, all waiting. The clock's ticking counts our last seconds of foreboding. Inexplicably, I ponder my search for Ibn Sina. Half seriously, I say, "You can't question the spirit's motives, Sitareh!"

"What choice do I have but to question him? I will not follow him blindly."

Her final word "blindly" mocks the candlelight dueling with the darkness. An eerie silence replaces the bombing raid. My heartbeat turns wild. Sitareh huddles by my side, her hands quivering in mine. She senses something that overwhelms even our fear of the bombs. In the unnatural stillness I hear a soundless creak, like the step of an approaching soul.

A voice comes, calm as a reflection in a mirror. "You know, I wish to heal but never to cause anything that needs to be healed. I was praying for your safety. I love you both as you love me. I want to merit your trust and tell you everything I know, but I cannot explain what remains unclear to me. I have doubts, too."

A reply catches in my throat. Sitareh's voice struggles to address our invisible visitor. "Can souls have doubts? Surely death dissolves all uncertainty."

"Doubts flourish in both worlds. As entropy degrades matter, doubt and curiosity, God's gifts to man, promote knowledge. The angels speculate that God Himself had doubts at the moment of creation."

"You know of entropy?" I ask.

"When I was alive I knew that matter degraded, but I overheard the term from a newly dead physicist, who wondered aloud if entropy operates on the soul, too. The angels giggled at that. They are a giggling bunch, I gather."

"Should I doubt you?" Sitareh boldly confronts Ibn Sina.

"Your question implies your doubts. But how can you doubt me, Sitareh?"

"I question not your existence but your intentions."

"My intentions are good!"

"So is our curiosity," Sitareh responds.

Finally I growl, "Explain, please! We all love the truth. Am I only Gorgani?"

"Let us know what we want to know, please, Ibn Sina," she adds.

"I will, my dearest. I will, my mother!" His voice carries the heavy weight of truth. We tremble as if in an earthquake. "My mother . . ." Ibn Sina's words resonate in the flickering light and shadows. Sitareh's son! The clock has stopped ticking. Time, stuck in the clockwork, jolted and warped, suddenly unwinds and spirals back into what was foregone. I recall Sitareh's premonition of being his mother as her voice rises. "Yes . . . yes, but tell us more; tell us what you can, my dear . . . my dear son." She responds alertly but with a touch of anxiety. I am transfixed as a solemn moment stretches, uncertain and incendiary. A wave of silence separates the living and the dead. Our glances turn to resignation. Slowly I become aware of my heartbeat again.

We wait for the spirit to speak again. We wait forever, it seems, until we hear, "It is not possible to tell you everything now. I shall visit you in the mausoleum library six weeks from this Friday at midnight and answer your remaining questions."

Still, Sitareh asks, "Why can't you answer us now?"

"That also I cannot reveal."

Sitareh resumes, "Should we continue hypnosis?"

"Why not? Use every ethical method of learning. Hypnosis might reveal the history of tears and fears and my long-lost correspondence and spoken words, since time is the graveyard of such evidence."

Hypnosis! I reflect that people smoke, overeat, pray, envy, hate, pretend, befoul the earth, exploit and kill, as though hypnotized to conform. I remember my own struggle with academic conformity, all a world away now.

"How did you overcome the pressure to conform?" I ask him.

"I conformed just enough to survive. It wasn't easy to placate the clergy, or the kings or the queens. I suffered more from conformity than from any illness."

"We suffer from it today, too," I add.

"However, in death conformity and gravity are also dead," the spirit says.

Sitareh asks, "How do you know about gravity?"

"Pirooz told me at our first encounter."

"But you ridiculed gravity as 'angelavity,'" I interrupt.

The spirit chuckles before his voice turns serious. "I have thought it through. I suggest gravity binds the body, as conformity confines the spirit."

"But gravity and conformity provide some stability in our lives," Sitareh objects. "One keeps us on the ground and the other keeps us social."

"Nevertheless, both constrict," says the voice. "Defying conformity will never die. The soul fights conformity in the maw of authority, and the body defies gravity inside a metallic bird. This proves that neither conformity nor gravity is invincible."

"What metallic bird is that?" Sitareh asks.

"I think he means an airplane," I answer.

"Why have you brought Pirooz and me together?" Sitareh demands.

"You are bound by love and the will of God, not mine." He reveals nothing, but his words, "My mother," echo like a faraway bell.

"You are being evasive, Ibn Sina," I protest, surprised at my audacity.

"I share your anxiety, Pirooz, but that is all I can say until I next appear."

As Sitareh and I exchange puzzled glances, Ibn Sina declares, "I have some questions. Will you update my knowledge?"

"Why do you have questions?" I intervene. "Is not curiosity dead for the dead?"

"No, not for me! I am a curious soul. I want to know it all, alive or dead."

"Tell us, what is death?" I ask, having pondered suicide once.

"An experience I am bound not to divulge now."

"You question us now, but we can question you only later?" Sitareh protests.

"That is what is possible for now." In the ensuing silence, he waits for his answer to sink in before resuming. "How do you define consciousness at present?"

"The sense and thought processes by which an individual defines himself and his environment and conceives goals is part of consciousness," Sitareh replies.

"You use thought to define consciousness, which includes thought. This is circular, dear Mother," Ibn Sina mumbles.

"Only more thought can explain thought by more words," I retort. "And words must define other words. Everything is circular. No ultimate cause or effect exists; all things are interrelated. Our mind reflects the universe bending on to itself to know itself. If the mind tries to examine itself, then the examiner must also be examined by the examined. The circle has no ends, like pi, God's will, Ibn Sina!"

"Very well. What have you learned about the mind?"

"Mental activity does not depend on a structure called the mind. However, we know more about the brain, the engine of perception, sensation and thought." Sitareh talks of the electrochemical flow of information and command. "Various groups of nerve cells sense, think, communicate or imagine collectively, accomplishing what is impossible for any single cell to achieve, just as specialists collaborate to run a complex enterprise. Self-replication, parasitism, competition and cooperation are not the work of a single commander in the brain."

The ghost interrupts, ". . . because that would require a commander within the commander, *ad infinitum*, until the last cell, even the last atom in the last cell. How wonderful, there is no king inside the brain, just as there should be none outside."

"Exactly," she replies, and then resumes. "Science today can explain many ancient mysteries—magnetism, photosynthesis, rainbows, digestion, and reproduction, questions you investigated or were curious about. But self-examination of the self, *ad infinitum*, causes the consciousness to split and turn incoherent, alienating itself from itself and the world. In this era only the brain can know the brain—to know thyself." No one knows how physical bodies like the brain, sustained by a physical world, give rise to love and hate, or the sense of beauty and ugliness, or justice."

"I wish to solve this mystery!" Ibn Sina whispers. "How the mind—I mean, the brain—smiles when it is happy, frowns when it is sad, why it loves and how it gathers information, makes up theories, stories and religions, and holds our dreams."

"And why it kills or destroys its habitat and yet wishes to survive and prosper and make gadgets to lift itself to the moon and beyond," I complete his wondering.

"Explain, dear Mother! What did history do to the conception of the mind?"

I notice that Sitareh is jolted, so I try to reply and keep the spirit with us longer. "First, astronomy abandoned the Earth as the center of the universe; then evolution dethroned man as the center of life, and finally biology undermined the metaphysical status of the mind. The mind is under siege now that the outer ramparts have collapsed. Tradition does not reign in science, just as you stipulated. But the world has shrunk, and a human identity crisis looms. So our collective mind should search for our true identity and destiny: who we are, and what is our potential. We must also undo God's wrong doings to us—

like eradicating germs—or overcoming constrictions He imposed on us by creating tools to see, to hear, or even to understand further, and to fly away. Immortal man will make a better God! We will become what we have never been."

"But God bestowed upon man the diversity of talents and the possibility for collective thinking and working—the most useful means of ascendance provided man adheres to truth and love," the voice protests. Sitareh nods approvingly. My anxiety has subsided, and now the near darkness seems soothing.

"How does the brain relate to mind?" Ibn Sina inquires.

Sitareh replies, "It is impossible to sort out how the sense organs, the brain, and culture interact and together create the so-called mind, even though we now know that certain parts of the brain are responsible for certain functions. Strangely enough, damage to that part of the brain responsible for emotions could cause the loss of rationality, since emotions are known to contribute to reason and adaptive behavior. Some claim the mind is a computer program for the brain written by our social activity. Left isolated—that is, unprogrammed—a child will become a mute savage, but an animal's brain lacks the hardware to absorb human attributes, irrespective of the programming. Even so, chimpanzees are taught to perform simple addition and communicate by signs."

"I knew that animals had souls," Ibn Sina says. "But what is a computer?"

"An artifact simulating thought, without creativity, ethics or feelings," I reply.

"We had a few of them in my day. They were kings!" His laughter fills the room.

"Computers will be kings again," I intervene. Sitareh smiles.

He pauses and, as though talking to himself, says, "The mind can ascend beyond what exists—including itself. No artifact will ever do that. Without moral scientists, greed will abuse science, as theocracy abuses spirituality."

After a thoughtful moment, my puzzle of how Sitareh could be the spirit's mother returns. Sitareh appears cool, like a hot furnace set outside in the winter cold.

"What about the science or art of rearing children?" he asks.

"Educators today run a maze to a professional reward. There's a mathematics maze, a science maze, a medicine maze, an engineering maze, a law maze, *et cetera*. Professionalism, greed and conformity are the fatal results."

"That is terrible. Education must promote, not stifle, the drive to self-knowledge, self-realization and creativity."

Sitareh returns to upbringing. "Freud linked childhood to personality formation, and self-preservation and sexual instincts to behavior that is constrained by civilization, with the life instinct balancing the death wish. Jung, on the contrary, called life a meaningful adventure continually influenced by all circumstances. Jung complained that human conflicts reflect divine discord. Just as man was once revealed out of God, when the circle closes, God may be revealed out of man—the holy spirit resurrected from the collective human soul."

"Can one speak thus about God without having his tongue cut out?"

"Yes, in many places, but not here in Iran. Besides, the authorities have more subtle techniques than tongue-removing these days," I reply.

"What about upbringing?" I ask. "Isn't it a dead issue for you?"

"Death is not forever, as life is not forever, Pirooz." His surprising answer astonishes us both. "Tell me more about scientific progress."

Momentarily bewildered, Sitareh shakes her head and explains the theory of evolution and advances in medicine.

"Wonderful!" says the spirit. "I had an inkling of evolution; I called it a movement towards perfection. Now I understand that peculiar man in heaven named Darwin. He has never left the banyan tree he lives in. He waves a protest sign and chants, 'Why are there no monkeys in heaven?' He wants to meet his ancestors at last."

"Darwin annoyed authority when he was alive, too," Sitareh says.

"And the clergy made his life miserable," I add.

"That is not news!" Ibn Sina's chuckle echoes in the room. "But tell me, can aging be cured?"

"Potential longevity is unchanged, but medicine can prolong lives, through better nutrition, sanitation, prevention and cure," Sitareh says.

"I am pleased to hear that my recommendations are being implemented. Are there any new barriers today to preserving one's health?" he asks.

"Yes, modern industry is a cancer industry, also bringing forth overpopulation and new war technologies and perhaps the end of life," I report.

"I see, I see," he says. "Ancestors act as the angel of death for their own progeny. Most unfortunate. Evolution may be a bridge from imperfection to perfection. Only an evil, more evil than evil, can kill it." The voice stops before saying with a sigh, "I hope the earth will become a planet of reason and love."

"All hope is not lost." Sitareh adds. "Genetics may guide the path of evolution."

After her explanation, Ibn Sina remarks, "But this intrusion into nature could prove harmful. The use of science is not always benign, even with the best intentions."

"But it is unavoidable," I add. "The self-conscious mind will strive to determine its own and Nature's destiny. So evolution evolves itself to its own fantasy using the human mind!"

"Most amazing, man altering nature, his own mother. I hope this is all for good." The spirit falls silent again. It is remarkable that this ancient sage is so curious and that we can enlighten him. My store of knowledge suddenly seems inadequate. "And what of physics?" Ibn Sina asks relentlessly.

I summarize what I know of Newton and Einstein and the search for a unified field theory. For the first time, I appreciate my undergraduate work in physics and engineering. But no physics can help me understand talking to a ghost or what he meant by calling Sitareh his mother. I become agitated again and focus into space to seek the invisible. I remember gazing into the night sky once with my child's eyes, trying to find a grinning moon hiding behind the silly clouds.

"A search for the unity of physical forces," he wonders. "If brains consist of the very same atoms as all matter, then there must be a unity of mind and matter, too, or else physics collapses. I tried to discover the theory of everything, to unify science and faith, but it was impossible for me. I suspect that God did create a theory of everything, since the universe is clearly a unity. Man must search for it as a conscious step towards unity with God. Man can also seek unity in biological, intellectual, creative, and spiritual forces."

"Is all research a search for Him?" Sitareh asks.

"It is. God is the ultimate truth. My birth bestowed faith on me, and my death confirmed it." Ibn Sina is silent. Is he still with us in the flickering candlelight? I glance at Sitareh's questioning face, for I long to press him on what he meant calling Sitareh his mother, though I dare not ignore his wish. Hoping to keep him with us, I ask, "Do you have any more questions?"

"I have. Do the laws of relativity assert that I am not dead, or not yet born, for some observers in some corners of the universe?"

"Yes, depending on the observer's distance from the earth."

"I wonder why time would wish to be relative, since God, being co-eternal with it, could not have created it so. Furthermore, absolute time would have been easier to understand. But then light must travel at an infinite speed, which is impossible. I also wonder if matter can be divided indefinitely."

"Scientists keep finding smaller and smaller particles within the atom," I answer.

"What about light?" he asks me.

"Your notions about the wave theory of light is synthesized with the corpuscular theory." I imagine the picture of Ibn Sina who smiles from my wall in New York. The ghost speaks to himself. "I wonder about nothingness. If nothing existed once, then it couldn't be nothing, since it existed. That is why I never understood the clergy who claim that once there was nothing but an immaterial God. How could *time* ever not exist?"

The spirit turns silent for a while, then, as an after thought he asks, "And the science in which one cannot touch what one studies, astronomy?"

I tell him that man has touched the moon already. I describe the stars as enormous, fiery and mobile, and black holes as tiny, dark, irresistible and all-devouring.

"Can tiny things devour huge things?"

"Yes, by squeezing them to almost zero size." I tell him of galaxies carrying gigantic baskets of stars to unknown places.

"Tinier and tinier particles in the atom, and larger and larger objects in the skies. Has anyone found the limits?"

"No," I reply. "The unboundedness of being resembles eternity in time. Curiosity makes the human mind the conscious eye of existence. But the eye is myopic, the consciousness is prejudiced, so both sight and thought may fall prey to falsehood. The mind cons itself, then finds itself guilty of conning itself. The perpetrator becomes the judge."

"Oh, God!" Ibn Sina replies. "And we thought the stars were fixed, fastened to the heavens forever. If I had the chance again, I would not let appearances trap me. Has it yet been determined how the universe came to be?"

"Don't you know the answer?" Sitareh responds.

"No more than I did when I was alive."

I summarize the Big Bang and the problem of whether the universe has sufficient mass to halt its own expansion and pull itself toward a final implosion.

"I see. Retracing the path of expansion leads to the origin and the measure of deceleration predicts the destiny. How clever! God! For a clear mind, it is all so simple! Now I wonder if the Almighty is also subject to the constraints of relativity? Can God alter physical laws He Himself created?" He pauses. "Anyhow, without research there is no error, but not to research is the biggest error. Still, I want to know, how did the first particle originate?" the philosopher of existence insists.

"Man will never know," I casually respond.

"But it will take forever to find if your statement holds true forever, Pirooz! Tell me, what is the object of your era's philosophical investigations?"

"Clarity," I declare.

"You must elaborate." I admire the ghost's curiosity.

"Philosophy's main task today is to clarify its own purpose and logically elucidate thought and its relation to reality. First, it acknowledges that a world exists outside of the mind; second, that there must be a correspondence between words and objects, language and reality, or else philosophical discourse would be futile, since it would not be about reality, but only invented words debating invented words."

"Very interesting," the ghost whispers as I pause.

"Third, language corresponds to reality in two ways: word to object, and sentence to fact. Every word, like 'apple,' is the link between the actual thing and its meaning, or an object and its mental image. But sentences, unlike words, make statements of fact that are true, false or meaningless. A fact, such as, 'the earth is round,' is not an object. The earth exists, while its roundness is true or false."

I notice that Sitareh puts her finger to her lips, and I try to finish. "Anyhow, science discovers facts, while philosophy must identify what we know and how we know it. If language does reach out to reality, then the logical structure of propositions in science or mathematics reveals something about the structure of the real world. Philosophy should avoid defining all words. For instance, it is absurd to discuss what the word 'meaning' means. So some basic words, like 'mother,' are to remain undefined but understood. Words are the keys, or the keys are in the words."

"I see," the ghost speaks with a new exuberance. "Words are thoughts, and thoughts become visible only in words. Even God needed words to reveal Himself in the Holy Books. Words link heaven and earth, nature and man, and man and man. Without words, the mind is mute."

"Oh, my mind!" I declare with the flash of insight. "But it was man who invented languages; words came before religions, not after. How do we know if God, heaven and hell are merely words? And since God, through heaven and hell, tries to control man, then the artifact, the word God, controls its creator, the man, much as idols rule their makers."

"Pirooz, God is not just a word!" Ibn Sina's angry voice burst from the darkness.

"Have you seen Him, or Her yet?" I respond instantly.

"No, not yet."

A deep silence prevails. We wait. Ibn Sina coolly follows his own thoughts. "One more question. What is the state of history in your time?"

"What do you mean?" I inquire.

"In my time, history was drunk and crashed into everything. Is it sober now?"

"You heard the explotions; we the living must bury the dead. This is the new history—still drunk, sick and brutal," I reply. "I want to wring history to find what is in it, just as history wrings me to find what is in me."

"Tragic. The whole and the part wring each other for truth," he says.

"Do you want to come back to this world?" Sitareh asks softly, her face glowing like a candle's last flare.

"Why this question now?" his agitated voice demands.

"Because your curiosity is knocking at the gates of life."

"My curiosity determines my wants, not my wants my curiosity. That is all."

"How do spirits visit Earth?" I ask.

"All I know is that it is not impossible."

We fall silent, for we must not ask personal questions tonight. I note a disturbance in the candlelight as his voice descends. "I wonder if it is possible to know the world as it is, to see it undistorted by the mind's filter. There must be a way out of circularity, the enclosed brain and the programmed mind."

"An all-knowing mind emerging from a confined one?" Sitareh asks.

"God made self-improvement a supreme value and possible, but did He put a limit on the mind improving the mind, nudging the evolution forward to love and to transcend itself? I am intrigued by this idea because if there is no limit to this progress then what prevents the immortal man as Pirooz says to become God—the master of himself and the universe!"

I follow his thoughts. "How true. The human mind is the progeny of evolution; but it must care for its progenitor, like a grown child for its aged parents. Immortal instinct must overcome the death instinct."

Suddenly his voice fades. "I love you both. Remember our appointment. I shall see you soon."

"We will hear you soon," I hasten to reply.

The window rattles as if light were walking through it. The electric lights come on, and Sitareh and I blink, speechless. Finally I whisper, "A dead man is more curious than many who live in these times."

Sitareh smiles faintly. She seems to have spent her last drop of energy, courage, vitality. She is frighteningly pale. If she is his mother, who am I? The question returns, freed by the spirit's departure. Sitareh keeps her gaze on me as though on my thoughts.

"What is happening to us? What does he want?" I raise my voice in protest. "How are you his mother?"

She slowly, haltingly whispers, "The spirit asked many questions, just as little Ibn Sina used to. And I couldn't answer most of his questions, just like in the past."

Suddenly her head slumps on my shoulder. She is immobilized with her full weight against my chest. I look at her and see Sitareh Poonia in a casket, wrapped in a gray sari, a silk burgundy shawl over her shoulder, a rose in her fingers and a mysterious smile still living on her stilled lips, like the one on the Sitareh now in my arms. The funeral echoes in my head. I hear words of life, death, love, beauty, truth, dedication, innocence, kindness, intelligence, soul and heaven all around. I hear tears unshed and smell the Indian scents. I see the mourners with heads bowed down, and I feel my own spirit bowed as well. I feel words stuck in my throat and eyes cast on me as I struggle to deliver the eulogy. Has she died again? What have I done? Vertigo is my response. The candlelight vainly battles to overcome the electric lights; I sense Sitareh battling for life, but the future's hellish eyes accuse me of murder. I manage to lay her on the couch. Detecting no pulse, I scream for the maid, but she already stands by, watching us in dismay. Firoozeh holds a mirror to Sitareh's mouth. We wait for truth, for life. Gradually, a trace of steamy shadow darkens the mirror. Firoozeh smiles into the fog on the glass. Soon she sprinkles rosewater on Sitareh and taps her face gently. "Lady Sitareh, there are no bombers coming. The murderers have gone to bed."

Through my constricted throat I manage to shout, "We must call a physician."

"No need for that," Firoozeh replies, pointing to Sitareh's opening eyes. Color returns to her face like greenery to springtime, and her breathing deepens. I feel my own life return as her fingers squeeze mine. Her lively eyes open completely. I sigh in relief, for, without her, I wish not to feel anything. I kiss her forehead.

She smiles widely, "Has he gone?"

"Yes."

"I believe he loves us, and we love each other, and we love him. I believe—"

"Yes?"

"I just want to rest now," she says.

"Very good." I am sure that more than exhaustion stops her from explaining, but I don't insist. Maybe Firoozeh's presence inhibits us. Remembering Ibn Sina's oblique answers, I wonder if the tendency to cover up is inborn, like instinct. Is life a cover-up becoming conscious of itself? Like mine?

Fearing another fainting spell, I keep my thoughts to myself. Questions prick me as I reprimand myself for not knowing how to resuscitate her.

Late in the evening pangs in my abdomen remind me that the stress of events has brought back my dormant ulcer. Suddenly I remember that the spirit refused to tell us what death was. Will I ever know?

When Sitareh has recovered, I wait for her to speak of Ibn Sina's shocking revelation.

"Pirooz-*jon*, what did you mean when you said that we must behave immortally to become immortal?"

"It is the core of my new thoughts." I pause. "The good thoughts, good words and good deeds of the self, tribe, or even nation, are not good enough any more. To save the habitat for all life and all time, and for man to spread into the universe, we need immortal thoughts, immortal words and immortal deeds that consider the welfare of all, now and in the future. We must banish selfishness from the human soul. Global well-being in infinite horizons must be central to all our decisions. Man must behave immortally to become immortal. Like God and the universe."

She kisses me. I am immersed in a happiness I have never experienced before.

"You must tell me more about immortal things." Gaining a second wind, even a second life, Sitareh announces, "I must go to the hospital now. The injured need me."

Surprised I ask, "Are you sure you are all right, Sitareh-*jon*?"

"I am sure, with mind and heart together."

"Then I will come along to do what I can."

"Thank you, Pirooz."

We return from the hospital at dawn, dead ourselves from helping the injured. It has been a night filled with blood and screams.

Chapter Seventeen: Delirium

At our breakfast Hamadan presents a magnificent morning, as it did to the King of Kings in ancient times. Sitareh drinks the last drop of Darjeeling tea and speaks thoughtfully. "I know you want to know more, Pirooz-*jon*, but I am not certain myself why I passed out last night. I am fine now, and thanks for being so caring, and above all for not pressing me to explain. You and I are now living in a world we never knew existed. I think we should accept our story as we find it and keep it to ourselves.

Excited, I respond, "Yes, it is not the wars—victories or defeats—we must remember but the thoughts. We must know our past without letting it shackle us; love our parents without letting them dominate us. We Persians are fixated on past glories. Intellectuals today worship Ferdowsi, Rumi, Hafiz and Saadi, but ignore contemporary artists and scientists. Living in the past alone is a resignation to death."

Sitareh gazes at the sky, "We are not the only tribe fixated on the past." Then a grin sweeps over her face. "Did you swallow a canary for breakfast, Pirooz?"

"No, I am a canary, in love and singing, Sitareh," I answer and ride the winds of passion because she loves me, and I feel I deserve her love. I glance at this beautiful and strong-willed woman and cannot help admiring her.

Sitareh knits her brow and turns serious. "To learn how I am Ibn Sina's mother, or who else you may be, or what his intentions are, we cannot rely solely on a spirit who is restricted or reluctant to tell. And no amount of worry, sleeplessness, or analysis will unlock such mysteries. Hypnosis is the way, even though it only recalls the past, not the future. You agree with this plan, don't you, Pirooz-*jon*?"

"Yes, Sitareh-*jon*," I assure her, but I feel the sting of her cold logic.

"We know that after Sultan Mahmood overthrew Samanid Persian rule at Bukhara, Ibn Sina fled to Gurganji, east of the Caspian Sea, where the Khwarazm-Shah, the local ruler, took him under his wing, and Ibn Sina met and befriended the great scientist Biruni and the physician Masihi. When Sultan Mahmood demanded that the scholars at the Shah's court join his, Ibn Sina and Masihi, disobeyed and escaped westward to Gurgan. Masihi perished on the way, but Ibn Sina survived and found a patron in the wealthy Shirazi. When Shirazi died, Ibn Sina left Gurgan with Gorgani for the city of Ray, where he accepted the patronage of the Queen Saeedeh Shirin, graceful, cunning, and an able administrator. She held power as regent for her son, even after he came of age. Ibn Sina became counselor to her. Now let us recall their time in Ray by hypnosis. But give us juicy details this time, Pirooz! We may be lucky and learn about earlier events, if Ibn Sina speaks of them," she concludes solemnly.

"The missing link," I add, and mentally prepare for hypnosis

Sitareh reassuringly holds my hands and gazes at me gently. I grow relaxed, receptive, and willing to explore. I remember that my previous trance was like climbing a mountain peak twice: changing from Pirooz to Gorgani and then back to Pirooz. I hope this time it will be less arduous. While Sitareh dangles her necklace in front of my eyes, I count down from one hundred. My eyelids feel heavy and heavier . . .

Pitch darkness pours from everywhere, to fill the world with night, before turning into light, to fill the world with daylight.

"What do you do, Gorgani?" I hear Sitareh as if from far away.

I assist Ibn Sina and learn from him, and I play the flute. Ibn Sina practices medicine and continues his research, including sacrilegious secret autopsies. Worried that the men who provide him cadavers may talk, he pays them handsome sums. The need for secrecy prevents Ibn Sina from including his detailed anatomical sketches in *The Canon of Medicine*, a tragic dissimulation. He confides bitterly to me, "The authorities want me to cure them, but they don't want me to know anatomy, not because it is an unethical use of science, but because it may threaten their dogma. What do the clergy know about science, and how can they judge what they don't know?"

Ibn Sina has embarked on a project to summarize the fundamentals of human knowledge in one single, grand book he calls *Shifa*. He prays to God to give him the years he needs to complete it. Meanwhile he complains of life becoming ever more complicated. Queen Saeedeh fancies him. It is not easy to refuse a gracious, generous and powerful queen, but Ibn Sina values his freedom most. Marriage is another shackle that he must run from. He once remarked that a queen's consort is fit only for a harem of men, and that it is difficult to tolerate a woman who talks back, unless she is thoughtful.

"What about men?" I interrupted him.

"The same, Gorgani," he replied. "You can't reason with someone who is emotional, selfish and illogical. They think they know and don't want to know that they don't know. Rich men and women should wear a little doubt and modesty instead of so much jewelry!"

"But Saeedeh is intelligent."

"My sovereignty is not for sale to anything," Ibn Sina retorted.

Saeedeh ingeniously dissuaded the great conqueror, Sultan Mahmood, from waging war against her with the argument, "If you defeat a widow, you will be cursed, and if you lose, you will be laughed at." But she may not be able to thwart Shams el-Dowleh, her older son, from attacking her kingdom.

"What do you think of these times?" the voice questions me.

These are times when Muslims kill Muslims, sons and mothers wage wars, and truth seekers take refuge in exile, times when power and gold vanquish love and truth, times of darkening horizons when intellectual luminaries are unable to lighten the hearts of rulers and must flee their homes, times when even the great Ferdowsi is a refugee inside his beloved Iran.

Ibn Sina soon finds Ray insecure and unsuitable for his work, so we must leave again. He wonders aloud, "How many times must I start anew? How many times can I tear my roots from the soil which has become a part of me? Where are my homes, friends, books and attachments I have had to abandon in the past? These are misplaced times and times of misplacement. Homes pass me by as days pass others; but unlike a nomad, I can never return to the same pasture, it seems."

This is a fateful pattern in his fugitive life. Patrons value his genius, but only on their terms. Ibn Sina needs spontaneity and creativity. Like a flood, his ideas exhaust or threaten fanatics, clerics and leaders alike. In his travels he longs for a sanctuary to seek truth without fear, but autopsies torment him, because the critical research and teaching tool is an abomination punishable by death. He believes that, unlike property, the same knowledge can be possessed by everyone. No one must set limits on curiosity, since that would diminish the God's gift to man—the unlimited curiosity.

Taking flight from the exposure of his autopsies, from Saeedeh's demands, and from impending military onslaughts, we head further west for the city of Qazvin.

In a rush, we leave most of our possessions in Ray. In Qazvin, his income is just enough to make ends meet. The city, seeing him as a great healer, expects miracles every day. He teaches personal hygiene and preventive health care, exhausting himself working day and night. I warn him to slow down. "Pain grows like a weed, and weeds will never stop growing, Ibn Sina."

As autumn comes and the weather turns cool and crisp, Ibn Sina falls ill, with high fever and icy chills. The disease is not diagnosed yet, but 'the healer needs healing himself,' he tells me. Though he rests, drinks water, takes medicine, and applies wet towels to his forehead, his fever worsens. He is like a sturdy tree struck by lightning, fallen and aflame. He twists and turns, mumbling in a delirium. I listen carefully to episodes from his past.

I hear him urging his dear colleague, Biruni, to flee with him from Gurganji. "Biruni, don't submit to the Sultan, escape with me and Masihi. How can our Christian friend, Masihi, live in comfort in Mahmood's court, if even we cannot? This ruler will whip our souls while saying, 'Rejoice, rejoice for being in my court, for praising me! Rejoice at your good fortune!' Oh, Biruni, I am surprised that you, who calculated the diameter of the globe while the learned still believe the earth was flat, could submit to that despot's will. We must take flight in disguise before sunrise; our likenesses will be posted soon for defying the Sultan. We must take nothing but the bare necessities. Biruni, come with us; our Iran is so vast. We will be refugees, but not from the truth. We will seek truth no matter where falsehood forces us to escape to. You tell me no, Biruni, because you wish not to be a refugee from authority. I understand that, too. Then Masihi and I may never see you again. You gave me a new eye to see a new world widely, deeply, clearly and wisely. I will miss our debates and the fraternity between us. So your final answer is no. I will miss you, Biruni."

Ibn Sina feverishly frets, "I have left my mother, Lady Sitareh, alone in Bukhara. Her letters do not arrive. As a fugitive, it will be more difficult to correspond. If she grows sick I will not know and cannot try to heal her as I heal others. I give alms to strangers, but I cannot send her even one gold or silver coin. Oh! I feel guilty for leaving my old mother in Bukhara. She will understand and forgive me, but I will never understand or forgive myself—not even in my grave."

His face and body damp from exertion and fever, he waves his hands and speaks to me again. He is lost in the desert while fleeing the Sultan's conscripts. I hear his delirium: "At high noon the scorching sun is an ally of the Sultan, each ray a sword in a conscript's hand. No water, no greenery, no safe refuge. We are stranded here with nothing but hot sand and the skeletons of perished men and beasts."

Ibn Sina pulls his arms up over his face, as if to shield it. "The desert is endless and vulturous, the sandstorm violent, the pebbles on fire. We are chained by the Nature. I can hardly see. Masihi is consumed. Try harder, Masihi! We will walk slowly. We will reach an oasis soon." Ibn Sina pauses, then talks anxiously: "Oh, Masihi, don't tell me your oasis is in the sky, not yet! You said yesterday that we must try as hard as we can until God saves us, just as we treat our patients the best we can until God cures them. Come on, come on, Masihi. Don't kneel in the sand. Come! I love you! Your prophet, Christ, who is our prophet, too, loves you. He will save us. We will reach Gurgan. The cool waters. Willows. Gentle shadows await us. Yes, yes, we will reach fruit trees, good people. I think. I hope. The salty breeze from the Caspian will cleanse us. We will heal, study and write books. I promise. The storm will die, the sun will set. The night will save us. Wait. Please wait."

Then his words become jumbled until I hear him again: "Don't say this sun may not set, Masihi. I promise! It will set; it always sets. The desert will cool. The gentle moonlight will light the path to our wishes. I know it will. The Sultan has no troops here. Do not let his will conquer our will!"

There are more unintelligible words before he sounds lucid again. "I agree with you, Masihi. Yes. Kings and lords are our friends when they are sick, but, once recovered, they forget who we are. This is true, but what can we do? Stop healing? Remember, once you said, 'Every day a star is killed but no one misses it in the night sky . . .' Don't become my missing star now. Don't leave me, Masihi." He raises his voice. "Masihi, I cannot see you. Oh, my God! You have fallen—your head is nearly lost in the sand. Your mouth, even your eyes, are filled with sand. We have no water to wash them off, no balm for your scars. The wrath of the desert, the sun, the storm, our fate, is worse than the Sultan's. I wish for an eclipse now, a temporary relief from the sun. No, no, you must not, you will not die. So many who need your healing await your arrival. Your mind is one of the keenest, your heart is the kindest I have touched. Oh my God, there is no pulse. . . . Masihi is gone, all gone."

His voice wavers "Masihi, my Christian brother, is free of fear at last."

Broiling with fever, he screams suddenly, "It is a lie! I didn't set fire to the Bukhara library! I almost lost my life trying to save the books. I love books more than my eyes!" He screams and covers his face as if the books on fire are his eyes.

In my short life I, Gorgani, have never seen a man like this; I am terrified and fear for his life. What must I do? If he cannot cure himself, who can? "God, save him for himself, for me, and for the people," I beg the Almighty.

Ibn Sina lies quietly for a while, then explodes, "No, no! I am not an Ismaili; my father was. Religion is adopted, not inherited. He is dead, I am not. Don't blame the living for what a dead man was or was not. Each Muslim is responsible for his own deeds. Let God be our ultimate judge. Let Him judge me! Let Him be God!

"Oh, the library is burned, Masihi is dead in the sand. God forgive me for questioning, but why are power and wealth so often bestowed on the wrong hands? Since You are not impotent, unjust, or misinformed, why is the world what it is? Why is it not what it ought to be? Who is on trial? Who? If I could, I would turn the world upside down and give the free spirits what they want! Oh, my God! Forgive me for blasphemy! I pledge to comprehend what is incomprehensible to me now."

Suddenly, through his fever, Ibn Sina opens his eyes and takes my hand. "Gorgani, is there any water here, any peace, any happy dreams, any relief?" Smiling, I run for water. He is back with me, thank God.

The next day Ibn Sina's fever subsides. He patiently explains to me Biruni's great scientific and scholarly work. "In *The Chronology of Ancient Nations*, Biruni recounted world history from deep in time past and unified it with geography that is wide in scope. His method of measuring the Earth's diameter was truly novel. From a hilltop of known height, Biruni sighted to the horizon at sea, this line being tangent to the Earth's curved surface. From this point on the horizon he drew an imaginary line to the center of the Earth. With these two lines at right angles, the line from the hilltop to the center of the Earth forms the hypotenuse of a right triangle, whose length is the Earth's radius plus the height of the hill. Then Biruni calculated the radius of the globe using the geometric properties of right triangles. Very ingenious, don't you think?"

"Yes, please go on, Master," I say.

"He calculated latitude and longitude and discussed the earth's rotation on its axis as though he held it in his own hands. He tried to see to the end of time and space in his astronomy—a daring feat, even for a visionary. He discovered that the Indus Valley had emerged from the sea in very ancient times, before the Creation according to the Holy Bible. He was worried if he should write about this possible conflict between faith and science. This problem will doubtless spread as science penetrates deeper and deeper into the secrets of nature, while dogma meanwhile remains fixed. Nevertheless, it takes a long time to recount Biruni's work.

"Oh, how I miss walking and talking and debating with my dear friend, Biruni. He didn't mind my disputations, nor did I mind his. What wonderful books he has written; he has made so much known to so many. Nothing escapes him as his mind unveils the secrets of nature. Biruni, more than anyone else, made me aware of the importance of evidence in scientific inquiry. We agreed that intuition may be vital, but one must examine it with evidence whenever and however possible. Is this world just a caravansary? Of late I have only experienced my existence as this relentless feeling of being a refugee. It stalks me everywhere. Maybe God is revealing something to me—I should try my best to understand it." Sipping water, he says, "Masihi, the man who understood so much and so clearly, died dazed by a storm and blinded by sand. What a Christian he was! The only Christian I knew who was a real one, who did love his neighbors and who did turn the other cheek. He was a saint. I have yet to meet a real Muslim, one who is compassionate and tolerant, a true image of God. Gorgani, did you bring with you *The Book of Return* I just finished?"

"Yes, Master. I brought all your notes and some necessities, too. When you are well we will retreat to a mountain village for meditation and rest."

"And away from the Sultan's rage, sandstorms, the undertakers' blackmail, and threats of pillage," Ibn Sina interrupts me. "God, help me to heal and search for truth in the midst of the chaos and brutality I was born into."

"But not all life is suffering, Master. After your full recovery, we will go to Hamadan at the invitation of a new patron. I have heard very good things about her."

"For a young man you have great composure."

"Whoever loses his parents in childhood either matures fast or perishes fast."

"So true, Gorgani. You are the one who grew fast and so well!"

"Thank you, Master, but may I pester you with a question?"

"Yes, of course."

"Did you disapprove of Saeedeh's rule because she is a woman?"

"At first, I thought she usurped her son's right. As it turned out, she is a shrewd administrator. In any case, Gorgani, I care little whether the genitals of rulers bulge out or bow inward, only what is in their mind and spirit, and the quality of justice they secure for their domains. Yes I wish wisdom for the rulers, and patience for the subjects."

The Master's words embarrass me. As I blush, inexplicably I see Ibn Sina shrink to a dot on his bed, which recedes further and further away. Then all is gone and darkness prevails. I wake up from history to Sitareh's smiling face.

We stare at each other. I am utterly exhausted.

After some time she asks, "Have you ever been in Ray, Pirooz?"

"Yes, my mother took me on a century-old huffing and puffing train when I was a boy. She frowned at the boys prancing on the roof and jumping on and off the slow, moaning train. We visited the shrine there. Ray's ancient glories did not survive the Mongols' destruction. It seems as if Persians are condemned to build beautiful things and Mongols to destroy them. The twelve Zoroastrian temples in Ray are gone, and instead we have twelve sacred Imams. It is strange, isn't it?"

"I just realized another strange thing, Pirooz. Ibn Sina drew the first detailed anatomical sketches, not Leonardo da Vinci, but that was a major reason for his flights." Sitareh turns on the light as the sun's rays take flight from the treetops. Once more, Ibn Sina and Sitareh's exchange as mother and son storms my mind, but I bite my tongue, repressing my burning curiosity: How could she be his mother and I be Gorgani? I remember that she said only a ghost could tell us how.

Sitareh, the psychiatrist, has turned pensive. "I wonder if he loved himself?"

"Why do you ask that, Sitareh?"

"I observe self-hatred in my patients. The self is not a unity but a composite of selves, not all striving for the same goal. So the fractured ego may vacillate between extremes of self-love and self-loathing. He may have subconsciously hated himself for choosing a tumultuous life, for abandoning his mother, or for not becoming a father. Maybe he wishes to come back to do what he missed then."

"Come back to where?" I am annoyed by my own confusion.

"I think he has wishes and perhaps plans. He may be in control of us, too."

"If free will exists at all, isn't it dead for the dead?" I think out loud.

She shakes her head and we fall into solid quietude, Sitareh staring at her papers while I watch her. Finally she says to herself, "My feelings about Ibn Sina and you and me provide me a clue, but a mysterious clue I dare not reveal." She runs her hand through her hair and moves on before I can ask any questions. "Where do I fit in this puzzle of motherhood, times, souls, reincarnations, and the law of the conservation of love and hate, Pirooz? I fear that where I fit is where I will meet my fate. We have a choice: to stop now or go further on this journey. In any case, I am very concerned about your well-being in these tumultuous times in Iran, Pirooz."

"Are we in the present or in the past?" I shudder at my own unearthly question. My life in New York seems light years away. Is this really happening? "Ibn Sina is not the only object of my love or search anymore. Whoever we may have been, we are now flesh and blood on our own account, reaching for each other." The psychiatrist listens to me as I open up. "Pregnant or not, will you marry me, Sitareh?"

She casts an enigmatic glance at me but keeps her thoughts to herself.

"I want an answer, Sitareh!" I insist.

"I don't know what to say or even if I am pregnant. Besides, there are numerous practical problems. For example, where shall we make a home? I cannot give you an answer now, even though I want to." I stop, fearing a confrontation.

A quiet evening follows, both of us deep in thought—although, I suspect, not entirely similar thoughts. Agonizingly, she details the Iranian state's intervention in research, teaching, and medical practice. "Just as in the past, faith is in control of science; the clergy claims to know the truth without providing any proof," she concludes.

"Some things don't change. In the U.S. free expression may also prove hazardous to one's career. In despair, we avoid discussing politics and war."

I wait for the nights, since I know she will then be in my arms or I will be in hers. Tonight, just as Sitareh and I kiss goodnight, there is a knock at our door.

"Firoozeh, what is it?" Sitareh inquires.

"The *pasdaran* (Revolutionary Guards) want you, and Agha Pirooz, too."

My heart suddenly races and dark thoughts whip my mind. What is wrong? I have had little contact with anyone. "Why?" I protest aloud.

"I don't know, Agha," the maid replies.

Sitareh slips on a robe, picks up a document, and heads downstairs grumbling, "I know the problem. It will be all right."

"Your chador, Sitareh!" I warn her, chasing after her in my sweat suit.

"I am in my own house, and it is none of their business," she declares defiantly.

"But everything is. Even God is theirs," the maid mumbles sarcastically.

We rush across the walled courtyard.

"Open the door, infidels!" the Guards yell.

"Damn the fanatics!" I grumble as I catch up with Sitareh and unlatch the door. Five young men burst in, the eldest in command. All are in fatigues, bearded, brandishing pistols, looking determined and menacing.

"You are under arrest," the commander declares.

"On what charge?" Sitareh demands calmly.

"Not specified," one Guard asserts indifferently.

"Not specified!" I protest.

"The charge is moral corruption," the commander specifies.

My temper flares, furious and uncontrolled. I shout, "Nonsense! Get out of this house immediately! All of you!"

Instantly two of the Guards thrust me against the wall and pin me tightly. A pistol hits my nose, slides down, and stops against my pounding heart. Its icy persuasion stills me. "You are a trigger away from hell, big mouth!" the Guard growls and shoves the muzzle into my chest. Suddenly torn from bed, I now face death. A cold sweat pours over me. My nose begins to bleed. Sitareh struggles to escape from a Guard's restraint. "No 'West-toxicated' imbecile can challenge us," the commander says. "America's ways are forbidden here."

I feel an excruciating rage, an urge to kill or be killed, but stand coldly like a grenade on ice.

"What is your defense?" he demands.

"This is not a court. What do you want?" Then I fall silent, defiant, thinking. Sitareh begins, "Wait . . ."

"Shut up, *jendeh* [prostitute]," a Guard stops her.

"Why are you here?" Sitareh ignores the insult as she fumbles for the document in her pocket. The Guard grabs Sitareh and covers her mouth. "I told you to shut up."

"Shoot him!" the commander orders to the Guard next to me.

Sitareh's muted scream rises: "No! No!"

I try to jerk myself free, but the trigger clicks and a bullet thunders. An absolute numbness invades me. Dizziness. No pain. My legs weaken, but the wall holds me up. I wait to die, but death comes slowly, distractingly. Suddenly hellish laughter assails me. Laughter in hell? Am I in hell? Torture by laughter? But I see, hear, bleed, breathe, think; therefore I am not dead. This is not death. This is not hell. Just the land of *pasdaran*.

I am the subject of their ridicule; a Guard mimics someone wounded writhing on the ground. Smoke rises in the air. I understand. A blank bullet; execution without killing; a deadly joke. The atrocity violates the safe-conduct guarantees of Iran's representatives in Washington to me. I am a victim of psychological torture. Suddenly, I am more concerned about my rights than about my health.

Then the grinning commander decides, "He is a prize catch, more useful alive than dead. Take him away!"

"Yes, brother *pasdar* (Guard)."

Sitareh yanks herself free from the Guard's grip and steps forward. "You are making a mistake! He is my husband! Here is the proof!" She hands over a certificate. "This is our home, our sanctuary, forbidden to uninvited strangers. Islam respects sanctuaries. You have violated the faith," she snaps, her voice rising, her face red with rage.

The older Guard appears surprised. He frowns while carefully examining the document. "That damn hotel clerk has bungled it," he whispers to a Guard, but I manage to overhear. He turns to us. "We were misinformed. Sorry for the inconvenience. Let us leave, brothers."

"Wait," Sitareh commands. "Who are you?"

"Why?" the oldest asks, on his way out the door.

"This must be reported."

They laugh. A heavyset Guard jumps on the flowerbed, kicks and tramples some pansies. "Is this reportable, too?" he harries us while ruining more plants.

We watch with our hearts in our throats as they depart singing revolutionary songs. I stand speechless against the wall, still feeling the gun on my chest, the mock execution, the numbness, the hellish laughter. Sitareh calmly takes my hand and, studying my ashen face, softly says, "They are gone, dear. Let us go to bed."

She helps me upstairs. Like a terminally ill patient released from the hospital, I walk on weak, shaky legs, dazed, despairing, and hopeless. I feel I am being taken home to die. Yet the pride of survival helps move my legs. So, I struggled against the monarchy for this! More burning thoughts cross my mind like lightning striking the ground. The nation revolted for democracy, for justice, for freedom and national independence, but instead it got a theocratic counter-revolution.

Firoozeh, shaken and with tears on her face, rushes to us and says, "Nothing is safe anymore, even poor little pansies are crushed. What was their crime? Are they subversive or adulterous?" A bitter smile flares in Sitareh's eyes, for she loves Firoozeh like a younger sister.

I sit dejectedly on the edge of the bed with my head down, angry and saddened at my inability to keep cool or to fight back and disappointed in everything. Sitareh holds my hand tenderly. Her eyes are calm and calming. "At least you have not been drafted to walk through minefields. The government has admitted to mistaken real executions. This is a regime of mistakes. This is history drunk with power. I wish their joke had been on me, not you, Pirooz. You are a guest. What a homecoming for you. My God, what has become of the home of Rumi, of Persian civilization?" After a pause, she changes her tone,

"Pirooz, you must become more tolerant to survive here; academia may have softened you a bit too much."

"No, on the contrary. It has hardened me, but not for this savagery. There, in the U.S., the media drill into my head, 'Rejoice, rejoice, that you are free in America, and you will succeed in the land of opportunity!' But I know very well that I must watch what I say at work, in crowds, even at parties. No one will arrest me, but they may reject me. Indoctrinated folks, emotionally charged, reject foreigners who fail to mimic them who mimic TV. So I bewail and bewail secretly instead of rejoice and rejoice publicly. I dissimulate my thoughts, frustrations and even anger to avoid being isolated. Now at home just as I open my mouth justly I find a gun pressing at my heart. To where must I vanish to be myself? Is it God's will that I must pretend to be someone else no matter where I go? Is being myself my guilt? Must I be ashamed to be what I am, and I'm what I think. Must I sew my lips to be safe?"

Sitareh squeezes my hand, knowing I need to talk. She hands me a glass of ice water Firoozeh has brought. I drink it and feel calmer. A teardrop rolls down her cheek, and I smile as though I have just swallowed a cyanide capsule. "Sitareh-*jon*, I am sorry I didn't keep cool or resist the Guards more strongly. A gruesome lump sticks in my throat; it is frozen rage. The clerics control the state, the individual, Islam, even God, and use them for their own intentions. There is no respect for citizens, for guests, or for Islamic law. I am ridiculed, degraded, executed, laughed at. I despise my own feelings because I feel hateful. I wish I could kill the executioners!"

"You could not kill a fly, Pirooz!" She smiles at me. "You resisted and survived. The best possible outcome." She continues in a conciliatory voice, "That was our nightmare, but it is over now. We are safe and awake—"

"The nation's agony is not over," I insist.

"Perhaps not, Pirooz, but tomorrow we will visit Alvand, climb its heights, view the vastness of things, and swim in a lovely pond that I know will be exclusively for us. You will learn to accept tonight's darkness, the darkest of your life, perhaps. But the night is not over yet!" she promises, kissing my lips softly, which always cheers me up. "It's not over yet! Meanwhile, I will present your birthday gift—a well-kept secret—a bit earlier than June twenty-seventh, your birthday."

She knows how to arouse my curiosity and extract my agony, like an aching rotten tooth, from my soul. She leaves the room and returns with a *tar* in her arms, my favorite Persian musical instrument, six-stringed like a guitar but with a long neck and two round resonating chambers, one small and one big. She places it on the floor and smiles her transcendent, radiant smile, looking like Sitareh Poonia with her sitar. I shudder at the astonishing similarities. She leaves again to return with a bottle of white wine and glasses.

We sit facing each other on the rug and toast our survival and togetherness. "Bottoms up!" she commands. Then she takes the *tar* and her fingers create the most heavenly sounds. The *tar* speaks to me such wondrous words of wisdom, tranquility, humility, tolerance, and love; such despairing phrases, such inspiring tones, such long stories in single notes, stories of spiritual dilemmas, of journeys wished for but never undertaken, of man's loneliness in the universe. Her fingers evoke vivid notes, diamonds shining boldly. I hear the great tragedy of life: that happiness is inseparable from suffering, the two covers of the book of creation. She repeats, "The night is not over yet," as she takes me to a magnificent pavilion of sounds. She nods and I pour us another glass. I put my arms around her and kiss her the kiss of my life.

Sitareh plays and sings lyric *ghazals* of Hafiz, including "Love seems easy at first, then come the difficulties." They soothe my soul. I listen and stroll in an imagined garden of rhapsodic poems with fragrances for meanings. I find a pond kissing a canoe with its ripples. The canoe quivers away, but returns asking for more kisses—how charming! Soon I imagine paddling with Sitareh at my side, with so much love riding along the canoe becomes giddy and swings around. Jumping fish glitter in gold, birds sing love songs, a worm dances into the water and offers itself to a duck. I breathe deeply the smell of liberty rising from the shores' soil—such beautiful shores. All shores! O God, how wondrous hope is! If only You had given us more hope, suffering would be more bearable. We drink some more. We drink hope mixed with uncertainty. And we drink even our love.

The music of the *tar* accompanies my mind from place to place, from time to time, from hope to hope, love to love, and resignation to resignation. I find in my dream that hope, love, and resignation are compatible in my heart.

Sitareh's words from the real world break through, "Dream for me, too, my love."

"I do! You are in my dreams. You are my dream, Sitareh-*jon*. I love you life after life."

She sets down the *tar* and quietly disrobes us, and gently our bodies and spirits merge. In oneness with Sitareh, I accept the world as it is, I join it in unity.

Just before sunrise, with my throat finally free of the lump, I fall asleep to the sound of her last words, "Though difficulties rifle the heart, they bring something better in return."

Chapter Eighteen: The Prisoner

The next morning Sitareh, dreading the Guards' return, throws away her makeup, pours the wine down the drain and shatters the bottles, breaks the records, and shreds the playing cards—all considered instruments of *Shaitan* (Satan). She takes an old Koran from the bookcase and displays it in the living room. I hate this sham. Most Persians can only parrot the Holy Book, which is in Arabic.

I try to rescue an antique ivory chess set. "It is our lives, not chessmen, that I intend to safeguard," she reasons.

"But the chessmen knew our ancestors!" I object. My face is aflame, my heart clenches like a fist, and rage at my mock execution explodes. "Chess is illegal here, but flogging or stoning is not. The rest of the world is sinful or wrong, they say. History will spit out those thugs and their superiors like rotten seeds."

Sitareh glides toward me and holds me gently. "Promise me you will not let that nightmare make your beautiful heart the house of hate. Promise, Pirooz-*jon*."

"I promise." I scarcely hear my murmured vow, as if to repudiate it.

When Firoozeh suggests hiding the chess set in the stable, Sitareh relents. That afternoon, I notice I am passing blood. My ulcer has returned with a vengeance. I am reluctant to bother Sitareh, but when I do she must call several pharmacies to find the wonder drug, Tagamet. She again begs me to come to terms with my mock execution and concentrate on our journey to truth and hopefully to happiness together.

In the next few days, my physical and emotional healing continues. One morning as I stroll through the bazaar, I chance upon a small shop with the twin of my tree-of-life carpet and its silk butterfly. Each such pair is unique. They must have been split up a long time ago, and it brings me great joy to reunite them. After bargaining briefly, I buy it. The old merchant grasps that the carpet is very dear to me "I wish you a hundred and twenty years of happiness with it," he says. I carry it home in a plastic bag, pretending to bring new clothes.

After a few days of discussing Ibn Sina and our predicament, Sitareh asks, "Do you wish to undergo another hypnosis?"

"Yes, I do. I realize this is not a game, just as life is not a game."

"I agree. I hope you talk as clearly as last time," she says.

Seated next to me in the living room, Sitareh gently puts me under. As my eyelids become heavier and heavier, I hear her words: "You, Pirooz, know all that Gorgani knew. Tell me what happened on the road to Hamadan."

. . . I, Gorgani, feel so weary that I wonder if I can continue. I am bearded now and grown to a man. Ibn Sina and I stayed in Qazvin longer than we anticipated, but it was just a stop-over between Ray and Hamadan. Yesterday he said, "Home and the psyche are interwoven like plant and soil. Departure is an agonizing rupture, especially when one can never return, no more than to the womb. Only death will end my exile, as it will my life. Life itself is an exile from where our souls belong, in heaven." After a difficult month of traveling, we have at last passed through Hamadan's gate.

"What is his situation there?" I hear a voice say.

He arrived mildly depressed, but his reputation has preceded him. He became physician and advisor to a wealthy woman. Word of her admiration for Ibn Sina reached her kinsman, the Amir, who suffers from illness, dishonest officials, and incursions on his territories. He has summoned Ibn Sina today to treat his colic. Ibn Sina tells me he must stay at court until the Amir is cured. I am alone and miss him at morning prayers. When he effects a cure, the news spreads throughout Hamadan.

Soon Ibn Sina becomes vizier, hoping to cure the afflictions of state, as well. I am surprised when Ibn Sina accepts the appointment, for he is enchanted with justice, not politics; with truth, not power; and with love, not wealth. He explains to me, "I must be vizier to understand power and the functions and structure of the state. How better to learn statecraft, except by practicing it?"

"Why do you wish to learn about the state?"

"Because it hovers overhead, like a dark rain cloud that can nourish the fields or destroy them in a flood."

"And what of your other research?" I ask.

"This will be research into politics and finance. The Amir's offer was as inevitable and unavoidable as winter."

"Is his administration a success?" I hear a voice inquire.

Ibn Sina has wonderful ideas, but implementing them is a struggle. I warn him that wielding power is not his forte; he is too just, too logical, and too faithful to the truth to survive as a politician. Is politics for smoothing out inbred crudities in man, like ironing out wrinkles in the cloth of time? He agrees that it is at best the wise use of coercion, not a philosophical debate or medical treatment. "The dominion of politics requires compromises of evidence and ideals, and has no room for love, unless it be the lust for power. But this is my chance to shape a portion of the world according to just ideals," he says with a sparkle in his eye.

"How do you and Ibn Sina get along?" The voice returns.

I no longer imagine a life apart from Ibn Sina, even as I endure his sufferings. Since the early death of my father, I have sought him in others, and Ibn Sina is a kindred spirit. However, his overwhelming intellectual and moral stature makes me feel unworthy. I enjoy the unity of our minds and spirits, but I sometimes long for a separate identity. "Your doubts are healthy," he diagnoses me, "and should impel you to become more skeptical, more creative, and more independent. Growth will not kill you." His compelling arguments leave me no choice but to agree, even about my problem of agreeing too much with him.

"What is Ibn Sina's life like?" interrupts a soft voice.

Ibn Sina rises every day before dawn, says his prayers, and writes several pages of the *Shifa*, *The Book of Healing*, a title seemingly inadequate for his vast philosophical and scientific encyclopedia. He has a simple breakfast of yoghurt, bread and fruit, and then students and scholars join us to discuss his work. When, he rides his horse to court, crowds gather along the way to catch a glimpse of the Leading Wise Man. He holds a public audience that is always open to whoever feels aggrieved. After lunch with associates and a midday rest, he presents himself to the Amir to report and discuss affairs of state. He remembers every face, name, problem and discussion. He sees the roots of conflicts, no matter how deep, and effortlessly crafts creative solutions to resolve them. The Amir declares that no vizier has ever demonstrated such memory and vision.

Ibn Sina enjoys political challenges and believes no obstacle insurmountable, for his mind has unparalleled suppleness and optimism. No emotion, no thought, no person, no field of inquiry is beyond his grasp nor beneath his concern. He wholeheartedly agrees when I say, "Only the dead have indisputable reason to be pessimistic." He must often choose between justice and expediency, and this wears him down. He knows his political future is short. Just rulers, no matter how wise, age quickly in these turbulent times.

"What about his evenings?" A question breaks the pause.

More readings and discussion of his work follow a supper at home. Finally, late at night, Ibn Sina declares to his guests, "Now body and mind and spirit must join to celebrate one more day of living, learning, and coming one step closer to the Beloved." Flagons of wine appear, music plays, and poems are recited. Sometimes Ibn Sina sings the verses, and this soothes his tension. We sometimes dance and chant as a group. Ibn Sina always asks me to play my *ney*. He loves its sound, telling me, "When you play, Gorgani, God fixes one of His numberless ears in sublunary space. He loves your music. Did He not bestow on you the talent to compose and perform such heavenly and therapeutic melodies for the soul?"

"And what does God do when you sing, Master?"

"God must think, 'Oh, no, not him again! Ibn Sina deserves a better voice for his enthusiasm.'" He flashes his disarming smile.

A voice interjects, "Does Ibn Sina's private life bring trouble?"

Sometimes he worries that his love of music, wine, or the pleasures of the flesh, all scandalous in a puritanical society, will cause him grief. But he doesn't succumb to fear. I reassured him once, "You are a true Sufi, since you have conquered fear."

"I have fears, too." he replied. "Whenever fear conquers me, I doubt if its cause is worth it. So I fight back tooth and nail, with hope, and push it back. I am not yet a Sufi, although I wish to become one. Sufism is a path, not a destination—the journey is long and life is short."

"You are very hard on yourself, Ibn Sina."

"Ever since I can remember, I have wanted to be my own harshest critic. Without self-criticism, the carriage of self-realization will lose a wheel and founder in the mud of self-deception."

"What about his research?" the voice urges me on.

Ibn Sina still performs autopsies in a secret location beyond the city gates. He wants to know everything about human anatomy, so he makes detailed drawings no one has even attempted before. He once jested, "I prefer the living to the dead and the beautiful to the ugly, but for science I treat all corpses equally." It is a perilous secret, whose revelation would be fatal. "I wish that politics and religion did not interfere in good-intentioned research," he says. "But to attain truth one must accept risks. Ignorance is the greatest risk, the most hazardous of all possible human conditions. The lover must strive, even if forbidden, to reach the beloved. I love truth, though the clerics draw borders around it. How do they know that God disapproves of the search for truth wherever it leads?"

"What do you mean? Would you risk your life for truth?" I ask him.

"If survival requires it, one may withhold the discovered truth temporarily, but never stop searching."

"What is happening in the kingdom?" the voice prompts.

The Amir has suffered military setbacks, state revenues have dried up and his rule totters. Just when Ibn Sina has unraveled the financial wrongdoing of some officials, he is ousted as vizier. A mob surrounds our house and ransacks it. We hide at the home of a trusted friend, Abu-Saeed Dakhook. The Amir saves his throne and his own life only after consenting to Ibn Sina's banishment. But when the Amir's colic returns, he sends again for Ibn Sina, who reluctantly appears at court. Having regained control of his kingdom, the Amir, with great pomp, appoints Ibn Sina vizier a second time. I watch these reversals of fortune in amazement. How day and night manage to bring darkness and light to the fortunes of men!

"What happened next?" I hear the voice again.

History takes a new turn when God recalls the Amir with little forewarning. His son is crowned, and, supported by most tribal chiefs and prominent citizens, he asks Ibn Sina to stay on as vizier. But Ibn Sina, worn out and dissatisfied, declines.

Fearing the consequences of rejecting the Amir's offer, we hide at a friend's house. Relieved of governing, Ibn Sina works untiringly on his great book, the *Shifa*, writing, over twenty-five pages a day, on logic, natural sciences, psychology, mathematics, astronomy, music and metaphysics. He works without notes or research sources, for he seems to hold a big library inside his head. Yesterday I told him, "Only God has a better memory than you."

He winked and replied, "What is your evidence that His is better, Gorgani?"

I answered, "Your memory can be only a part of His."

"Only if God wishes to remember every detail of human affairs, as I do!"

Because he wants to continue his research and healing exclusively, he writes to the ruler of Isfahan. Ibn Sina needs a new city, a new lover, new peers, new challenges. For the time being he is done with Hamadan, as if it were a book he had read. He tells me, "Boredom is like fasting: you can only take so much."

"Our imaginations journey far beyond what is necessary or even possible, so boredom from the mundane covers most lives most of the time," I answer. With a sparkle in his eyes, Ibn Sina agrees.

Our productive days in hiding soon come to an end. Someone betrays Ibn Sina, and the Amir imprisons the two of us in an old fortress outside Hamadan. Staring deep into the gray wall, he announces, "I am amazed at life's irony: imprisonment for refusing to become vizier. But there is some good in this, for the certainty of being a prisoner is a relief from the uncertainty of being a refugee. Life reminds me again and again that I am just a refugee until the hereafter."

"Is not mankind a refugee in history, as we are on Earth?"

"Yes, but people are not conscious of it, or else they would be kinder to each other and our progeny, bequeathing more knowledge and wisdom than was left to us."

A voice demands, "Tell me about your time in prison."

The cell is large but bare and drafty. Light enters through a small window beyond our reach. We are provided with pen, paper and a candle. Painful weeks of adjustment go by. Our guard routinely escorts us outside to a pool for our ablutions. In the morning it is quite chilly, and the pool seems to wish to be left alone. The large yard is empty except for a silent fog that stares at our misery and a frozen frog that stares at our uncertainty. I look at Mount Alvand, but it wears a thin veil, and the stars are too far away and too many to count. Kings cannot imprison those stars, fortunately, as they do the sublunary stars like Ibn Sina.

One day I ask, "Master, why is it that what ought to be is not what is?"

He points to the walls.

> "My going in was sure, as you have seen,
> My going out is what many will doubt.

"So what exists not, our freedom, is what we wish. The two sum up human fate." The moonlight reaches in to shine on Ibn Sina's face where the candlelight performs its shadow dance.

"Your poem is true of prison, but not of life. Coming into this world is improbable, but exiting it is certain."

"Right, Gorgani! Go on."

"Everything has come to a halt. Mortally wounded, time is numb in prison, and though we try to nurse it back to health, the cure lies beyond these walls. Look, Ibn Sina, space has grown fixed and rectangular and gray; the cell is dead. The candle has reached its end—its last flame is about to drown in a pool of its own tears. The moon has moved from the window, already bored at my complaints, so I can no longer see your face. It is late and dark but I cannot even take refuge in sleep, for I am not yet tired. Our enclosure bars any rhythm of life; it is a tomb for the dead who yet live."

"We are not dead, Gorgani. We can think and imagine and be lively."

"Yes, inside our skin we are not dead. You taught me that the body is a prison cage for the soul, so now my soul twice a prisoner."

"But observe, Gorgani, time still flows. It will never die, nor even catch a cold."

He extracts a smile from me, as he can even in the worst of times. Inspired and always welcome to challenge him, I object, "But what of life have we here? The walls shut off fresh experiences from our senses. Once time took us to new fields, mountains, cities, people, books, seasons, wines, melodies, views of canaries, words of parrots, and scents of opium and rosewater and lovers, and the voice of the Muezzin's exhilarating call to prayer before dawn. We saw the sun's greetings and farewells. We saw the moon seeing us. We saw the clouds cry and the emerging turquoise dome of the sky cheer. We heard our jokes laugh at us and we laughed at them. We made up stories and saw them come to life and tell us their stories. We saw children laugh and their mothers laugh with them. We saw our women naked, and we kissed their skins that burned with desire and we kissed them up and down the lips of their bodies."

"Yes, but all is not lost, for our imaginations can find no walls," Ibn Sina says.

I reply, "My dread is entrenched now. We saw and we saw and we heard and we heard and we tasted and we tasted, and we took them all for granted. I always thought they were there because I was there, but now I am here while they are there still. Oh, my God, why do men deprive me of Your blessings?"

Ibn Sina responds, "With self-imposed restrictions, man suffocates his own intellectual and spiritual life. But whoever seeks to break the constrictions risks becoming a log on history's fire, consumed for the comfort of future generations, my dear colleague."

I am elated, for he has called me his colleague for the first time.

Ibn Sina falls into one of his thoughtful silences. His words are usually my words; today mine are his, too.

One day I say, "We should thank God we are still alive."

"More important, praise be to Him, you have your flute," Ibn Sina replies.

"True. Without you and my flute, I would cease to be what I am," I add.

"Only you can make yourself you, Gorgani, since the world tries relentlessly to make you what is not you. Now, Gorgani, your flute! Play by night and play by day. Play the heavenly melodies that speak of love in primeval gaiety. Play, Gorgani. Play the music of my soul, play the *ney*, and then I will pray."

I play and see the music bring joy to my beloved teacher, but I stop suddenly, overcome by sadness, and he respects my silence.

"Then what happened?" Sitareh's voice prompts me.

One day when the guard brings us bread and yoghurt, he complains of a backache, and Ibn Sina prescribes a simple exercise and an ointment. In a couple of days the guard is joyful and free of pain. When Ibn Sina cures his wife of stomach problems, the guard's heart falls into his palms. He offers us whatever we wish.

"Wine!" Ibn Sina answers, and there is wine. The guard asks, what else? "The Koran," and one appears.

"But you know the Koran by heart!" I protest.

"It is the Holy Book's display that matters, not understanding it or loving it."

The next day the guard asks, "What else does the Master wish?"

Ibn Sina says, "Open minds, open doors."

The guard replies like a shy girl asked for a kiss, "God must make it possible."

"Thank you for your kindness," Ibn Sina answers.

"Every gift is below your greatness, Master."

The guard prays with us now. "God is with the innocent even in prison," he says. The Koran lies open beside Ibn Sina; a candle flickers over the holy words we recite while a moth flutters around the candlelight. Ibn Sina recites by heart a verse slightly changed to fit our misfortune. "And the undesired imprisonment may be beneficial, while the cherished freedom may prove harmful."

The revealed words seem to bring him peace and inspire the Leading Wise Man. "As you say, Gorgani, since time can no longer take us where we wish, then let us resurrect time and take it on a journey to the vast field left fallow within us, to find what we failed to see when we thought we were free to see. Let us embark on our inner journey, and show time something it has failed to show us."

Sitareh interjects, "What did he mean by that?"

I do not know, but this thought changes his mood profoundly. From then on he meditates for long hours and writes furiously. He begins and completes *The Book of Guidance* and *The Book of Cardiac Remedies* and several other works. His experience as vizier and our imprisonment provoke him to write on political economy. He exercises to maintain his vitality. I play the flute, Ibn Sina sings verses, and we drink wine in moderation. We meditate together, taking long, long journeys into ourselves. He opens my eyes to the flower garden within me, whose beauty and fragrances intoxicate me. My journey leads me to an inner heaven of peace and tranquility. Ibn Sina guides me to Him, so that at times I feel that I touch the Beloved. It is like touching light, wisdom, happiness, strength, the source of love, the essence of truth, and the purity of justice. Now I see what Ibn Sina meant by journeying in a prison. I could never imagine so much freedom, so much learning and meaning, and so much self-fulfillment while I sat in confinement. One day I offer to kiss his hand, but Ibn Sina gives me a bear hug and we touch cheeks and hearts.

We lose track of time. When the army of Isfahan appears before Hamadan, our guard seizes the opportunity and releases us. He tells Ibn Sina, "The Amir imprisoned you, but his servant has set you free." Ibn Sina will now be able to finish the *Shifa*.

Dressed as Sufis, Ibn Sina and I, with his brother and two slaves, depart for Isfahan. At Isfahan's gates representatives of the Amir Ala el-Dowleh greet us and shower us with everything we need, my wish in prison coming true. Suddenly I wake from the dream, exhausted. Sitareh holds my hands. "Incredible! You are walking history, Pirooz. You even sound old-fashioned."

"I miss the prison, Sitareh. I miss my cell-mate." I almost cry.

"We must be patient, search and gather information until we find him. No one will do it for us. And, as you said, we may find ourselves, too. Before I forget, what do you know of Ibn Sina's political economy, Pirooz?"

"It is rather modern. He explored the advantages of the division of labor and specialization and their link to specialized training. He considered a person's skills a form of wealth more secure than material possessions. He described the household and state economy and administration, recognized exploitation by subtle appropriation as well as forceful expropriation, and opposed both. It is as if he read Adam Smith and Marx. He also distinguished the question of what is from that of what ought to be, a long time before it was formalized in the West."

Firoozeh enters the room to show a newspaper report that yesterday's bombing has killed a prominent Hamadan citizen Sitareh knows. We also read that some well-known writers, poets and journalists who have not exiled themselves have been arrested, and scores of prisoners were executed in Teheran. My stomach churns and I become bitter and enraged. Has our progress since ancient times been only more people, more waste, more efficient instruments of torture and murder by mustard gas? How can the clergy bear so much shame under their turbans? I always thought shame was a powerful emotion among Muslims.

"Islam's supposed revitalization hurts the faith worse than Satan would if he could," I say. "Muslims are losing their trust in a politicized Islam and feuding Ayatollahs. Women can tell you that; the workers, the thinkers, the artists and refugees can tell you that, even the new graves can tell you that."

Sitareh, noticing my distress, declares, "For the sake of your ulcer, I hereby ban newspapers, radio, and television from this house. The government censors their content, so I censor their presence."

I bask in her protectiveness, but suddenly an air-raid alert sends us scurrying for the basement. The siren and the Iraqi jets' thunder mix. Sitareh, Firoozeh and I huddle against the wall under a sturdy table.

An explosion shakes the ground, shattering a small window above us. Terror gallops across the faces of the two women, while my hands tremble. Animals scream; then a deadly silence falls. No more explosions. Time struggles in agony like a defeated army. I look out the window—blue-gray smoke rises from the adjacent yard. An unearthly chorus of dying animals emerges from the eerie silence. We rush to the stable, which looks like the scene of a plane crash, except that horses and donkeys are strewn about instead of passengers. A horrible stink, meant for the dead only, strikes me. Spilled blood mixes and spreads, as though still in veins. Steam rises from the ground. Sitareh's white horse lies scattered in pieces; a leg bent at the knee dangles from a tilted railing and drips dark, thickening blood.

My guts churn. I turn away just as Sitareh and Firoozeh catch up with me. The view of an ear twitching on a severed head jerks Sitareh's face to one side, where a single eye sits atop a smoking tree stump, turning it into a face. The eye stares right at her. Sitareh screams and covers her face, but the one-eyed stump is deaf. Firoozeh stands frozen in shock before she breaks into a sob. People in uniform and neighbors pour into the stable as I guide the two women back to the house.

The sirens are deafening. In the stable shots ring out to hasten death for the dying. Each shot shatters the brain of an animal that would not have understood human conduct, even if it were as intelligent as we.

In the living room, I hold a weeping Sitareh folded in my arms and try to console her. "I am so sorry, but we are still alive and will rebuild, Sitareh-*jon*. This will pass. I promise." Helping her to the couch, I try to hide my own shock and dismay. Observing a war is so different from reading the history of one, I realize. I wish there had been no casualties, no damaged monuments, and instead the war would turn inward to kill itself.

"Pirooz?" she says softly. "I think insanity is contagious, and we have been exposed to so much of it that I am really frightened for us."

"Yes, Sitareh-*jon*, these are strange times when both winning sides assert that insanity is God's will. We must protect our sanity from God's abducted will."

"How?" she responds. "Cities are crumbling, civility is vanishing, and only the graveyards and yards of mendacity prosper. Tell me how we resist this."

"I don't know," I answer. "But this is a temporary insanity, I hope."

"Temporary? Remember, it was the same in Ibn Sina's times. We need more wisdom urgently, but our civilization can only produce more weapons urgently. The world arms itself as if it expects an invasion of aliens from outer space."

"Damn it, we are the aliens ourselves!" I hold her, trembling like a seedling, in my arms to keep her safe. For once I feel stronger than her. Firoozeh stands on the balcony holding her face, weeping, so I bring her in with us. She casts her innocent eyes at me in appreciation, as if they had never seen foulness. Sitareh holds her hands and they weep together. I, too, feel my own tears. "Crying is good for both men and women," my mother said to me. I am glad she is safe in New York.

Sitareh gently hugs Firoozeh and says, "The mother of my white horse and I were the closest of friends. I brushed her often; it was my way of loving her. We roamed over fields and hills, exploring the world together, when I could trust my hair to the wind without fear of arrest. We were free, and Alvand could look at me, and that was no sin. Now the white horse's death has killed the lineage and our dear kinship, and the wind will sin if it touches my hair. The chess pieces that knew our grandfathers are dead and buried like themselves. We cannot save anything anymore."

Firoozeh replies, "That white horse was my favorite, too. He would look into my eyes as if he understood my heartaches or knew my dreams. He was a loving friend who always understood but never complained."

As they share their mourning I withdraw to the kitchen, to return bearing tea. Their tenderness to each other comforts me, as well. I feel good serving them.

The next morning Sitareh's pillow is wet with her tears. As the sun rises her first word to me is, "Why?" Hurt and saddened, I place my hand on her forehead.

"It is now your turn to come to terms with a tragedy." Hearing her own advice from me, she examines me with an appreciative glance.

I bring the tree-of-life carpet, spread it open before her bewildered eyes and say, "This tree of life is yours. It is one of a pair, and I have the other at home, handed down to me from my grandfather. They are reunited at last."

Sitareh comes to me and holds me tight. "Thank you," she says, kissing my lips. "Beauty nourishes my sight, and this is a lovely work, alive like my white horse."

Later when I am alone and remember Ibn Sina's request that we must wait to learn his mysteries, the echoes haunt me, "My mother, my son." My mood turns sour, for I don't fit into the family. An eerie quiet surrounds me. Momentarily I find neither the past nor present nor future defined, clear, desirous, or even comforting. Maybe I am not fit for this world. I wish to be and imagined being in a world where healing is in the ascendance and wounding is in the descendance. But my mind swoops and finds the globe twisting in agony everywhere. I feel starved for time and seclusion to heal, but keep my thoughts to myself.

For a while Sitareh and I avoid discussing Ibn Sina, perhaps apprehensive of what we know or what we may come to know. We have opened a gateway to the past, but I am not sure why I am allowed to enter and leave it. It seems impossible to connect the fossilized past to an uncertain future, but I must try. Oh, how I wish I could glimpse the future that I suspect will frustrate my hopes. The future lies and we believe it, since the boundary blurs between hope and wishful thinking.

Chapter Nineteen: Joining the Beloved

The next evening, with the urgency of an impending deadline, Sitareh appeals for me to go under hypnosis again. Even though it will be excruciating, I cannot say no to her. To know thyself may require walking over fire, I reflect.

"Ibn Sina spent fourteen good years in Isfahan with Amir Ala el-Dowleh," she declares. "Let us discover how they ended."

She takes me back to that time in a trance. For a while I see nothing, as if I were watching a blank film rolling. Gradually a grisly chaos takes shape to surround Ibn Sina and me. We stand on a hilltop as a battle swirls across the plain below with choruses of screams, moans, and braying. Life intertwines with death. The dust of battle obscures the combatants, some crushed under fallen horses. A dark cloud sweeps over intermingled swords, spears, motions, tears, fears, and commands, threatening to drown everything in a flood. The desert waxes and wanes in agony, as war swallows the warriors. Once again a crisis in history overwhelms me. My thumbs are over my ears, and the rest of my hands hide the carnage from my eyes. Ibn Sina speaks. "Our minds cannot bear to contemplate their own creation, war."

"Yes," I answer, "we devour our own souls when the beast in us overcomes the angel. If God is not in conflict with Himself, then why do God's creatures harm God's creatures?"

Ibn Sina glances skyward. "Day by day I understand less and less. Why did God grant us the possibility of blasphemy? Life is a web of questions, and we are trapped in it." He shakes his head.

Sultan Mahmood is dead, but his empire still grows. All peace gestures have failed and the invading army stands victorious near Isfahan. The Amir Ala el-Dowleh, who loved learning and supported scholarship, has lost his army, his garden, his palace, his city, his kingdom, and now flees south toward the Persian Gulf. Whatever warfare wins, warfare can also lose. Ibn Sina dedicated a great book in Persian to Ala el-Dowleh, fulfilling his promise to Ferdowsi.

Amputating soldiers' limbs day and night has drained him. He falls ill, lacking the strength to repel an attack of colic. In the confusion of battle he mistakenly took an overdose of medicine, and his health worsened. Still he worries more about his patients. Having run out of alcohol to use as an antiseptic, he knows that infection will finish off those that the enemy could not.

Separated from the Amir, Ibn Sina must escape westward to Hamadan to save his life, trudging alongside the fleeing and dying. We reach Hamadan with great difficulty, and take refuge in the house of a Christian friend who reminds Ibn Sina of the physician Masihi, his beloved colleague, buried years ago in a sandstorm. A magnificent garden surrounds the house, but Ibn Sina cannot enjoy it. His condition has grown worse, and he must take to his bed. He looks shrunken and older than his fifty-seven years, but even on his deathbed, the truth-seeker is radiant, like the sun at dusk before sinking into the sea. In anticipation of passing away, he recites the entire Holy Koran by heart in three days. His thoughts and faith still glisten, and he smiles on his deathbed as if it were his wedding day.

"I have returned to Hamadan, but only as a last stop before leaving for Him." He glances at me, "Say something, Gorgani!"

"Life is the journey of exiles; it ends where it begins, in the unknown." I pause to gather courage. "God may be in exile, too, for where would he be if not everywhere? Perhaps we are exiles made in His image. One is in exile even upon returning home, since home is a false notion; it does not exist. We are in good company, though, Even the truth is in exile, even the world is in exile, ever since God let it out of His hands. So man must create a real home, happy and free from invasion, since no one will do it for him."

"How wise, Gorgani, my dearest friend," he says. "Now that ruin is upon me, I understand your point more clearly."

I hear Sitareh's voice. "Who is with you, Pirooz?"

His beloved Esther and his brother have escaped to Hamadan with us, and now they stand by his bedside with our host and Baba Tahir, Sufi poet, sage and good friend. The Leading Wise Man's incredible stamina, strength, and willpower have succumbed to years of exhausting activity. The struggles and the sudden flights, the women, the sleepless nights, and the opium in recent years have destroyed his health. He has arranged his affairs, given away his possessions, and provided for Esther. He asks for a puff of opium. I shake my head no, protecting him from excess even when it is no longer necessary.

"Give me some opium, please, Gorgani. What governed my body governs no more. The physician who took care of me is dying. Don't deny me relief. I am finished beyond repair. My pain distorts my concentration, and I wish to die without pain. Nothing matters now but a decent good-bye and a painless journey from those I love to the One I love most. I want to witness my soul's farewell to my body. They have been intimates since I was born."

Refusing to yield to his charming persuasion, I turn to Esther. Without her veil, she is beautiful and sad, as she fights back her tears. She would do anything for Ibn Sina. "Give him what he wants," she says. Baba Tahir shrugs resignedly.

A servant fetches some opium. The pipe ends in a round ceramic bowl a bit larger than a green walnut with a tiny opening at the top. Tongs hold a lump of hot charcoal to light the opium on the bowl near the hole. Ibn Sina draws and inhales as I hold the pipe and tongs for him. Opium—God's thought—is the greatest painkiller and pleasure-giver known, Ibn Sina always said. His brother returns with a bottle of his favorite vintage, and Ibn Sina sighs and closes his eyes to speak. "I am neither happy nor unhappy that I am dying, only curious. Oh, my God, is curiosity my curse or my luck? I am even curious about curiosity. It dragged me hither and thither like an irresistible lover, and took the place of family and so many other things for me. Curiosity and my wish to ascend beyond what I was at times overwhelmed even my love of healing.

"I have seen human fetuses with fins—when is man a fish? I wanted to investigate this matter further, but I was loath to violate the Holy Book's revelation of creation. Often have I crushed my curiosity for fear of my life. Like breathing, dissimulation is second nature to me. God forbid! Science must be free of dogma and politics and must never consort with evil." He nearly screams, "Damn those stone-headed clergy with false dogma engraved upon their heads. Damn them for hounding me to and fro." I am shocked, for he has never spoken so harshly.

"My friend," Baba Tahir remarks, "your life has proved that human potential overflows any presumed boundary."

Seeing his brother weep, Ibn Sina calmly says, "Please shed no tears for me, now or when I am gone. Cheer for me, everyone! I know my fate. With death so near, speculation about this life ends. How wonderful! Soon I will crystallize in an immutable past, no longer becoming, but forever gone. I am now what I will be in the next world. My glowing curiosity about the next existence has been melting me down from within, like a candle shrinking into a little pool of its own tears. Now my last flame is about to submerge in a liquid that will flow away flamelessly. I shall enjoy this new adventure."

"Just as you enjoyed life fully," Esther adds.

"Yes, yes. Death brings new possibilities, just as it ends existing ones. I grow weary of life's necessities twisting me.

I have seen men arm in arm and horses shoulder to shoulder in endless battle lines, marching to kill in swamps, in mountains, or in deserts. The kings and men died because the victors wanted to annex their territories or the clergy wished to annex their souls. Nevertheless, conquerors leave this life empty-handed. Time empties memories, even poems from their meaning. And what it does not empty, it wastes.

"Consider Sultan Mahmood. With a huge brush he tried to paint the globe in the one color he likes most—the color of his dominion and righteousness. I have been on the run from his brush, his armies, clerics, viziers, his poets, his gold and silver. He even commandeered our sacred Islam as a pretext to invade India and pillage Hindu temples of their riches. My colleague, Biruni, must have loved truth more than justice, since he accompanied the Sultan's invasion of India. There Biruni mastered Sanskrit and the discoveries of the East, so that his knowledge of Greek sciences could be enriched with those of the Orient. Perhaps in the next world I will have to please only one patron—truth. I have found that wealth and poverty, wars over territories or beliefs, the suppression of creativity, slavery, the subjugation of women, and the rigidity of matrimony exact a great toll on us. We must never forget that our integrity is inbred in our potential to be perfect."

"Do you oppose the subordination of women?" asks his brother.

Ibn Sina painfully lifts himself on his side. "I, know women's equality is unorthodox, but Esther's wisdom has awakened me to its truth. No one should be kept ignorant and in servitude. Let me confess. I regret having once declared that I do not like women who talk back to me. What I detest is ignorance, only that. Men and women must have the same opportunity for self-realization. If women are educated like men, as Islam commands, then they may talk back to men as much as they like. Just as stones alter their shape over time, we must change our views when we find better ones. Even God replaces holy verses with superior ones when appropriate.

"At one time I wondered about the magical force that draws me to women. I hoped to find some answers in the mysteries of their bodies, their enigmatic organs of sex. But Esther guided me to search in their minds and spirit, too. She laughed at me once. 'You are a sensualist near a woman's body and a spiritualist elsewhere. Very inconsistent, but convenient, indeed!' she said."

Esther smiles broadly, "Your memory is still perfect."

Baba Tahir gently intervenes, "Let us not waste precious moments on what is wrong. If you must tire yourself, tell us what ought to be done, Ibn Sina."

"My dear friend, I cannot do that," Ibn Sina says. "What must be will be. Review my life! I have left what I could, my best effort in hardship, but I wonder if what I have left . . ." He falls silent, deep in thought it seems, his eyes closed. I realize that he never owned property or had a family, yet he would leave so much to so many.

"God, why are you taking him from us?" I murmur so that only God can hear.

"Please pour me some wine," Ibn Sina says. "Though I am still thirsty for everything on earth, I want to plunge naked into the river of death, where I shall bathe stripped of all possessions and ambition."

Esther cradles his head as I pour his favorite red wine. He sips it appreciatively before speaking. "Each soul—God's creature—is unique, but rulers like Sultan Mahmood force us to choose between integrity and safety in uniformity. Nevertheless, so many are brought up to follow a Sultan or become like him. Those who pretend adherence to the will of God ruin our potential for self-transcendence and force us to live in violation of God's will. Coercion is ugly and fleeting; only unity in love and truth is beautiful and permanent."

Our host states solemnly, "Well said, Leading Wise Man. As one family, we share one home, this good Earth, and must share one great idea, our oneness."

"Yes, yes, my Christian brother," Ibn Sina answers. He looks up at me.

"Love must be universal," I say, "but it is not, because we perceive God differently, we love Him differently. Only truth is both unique and universal."

"True, true, Gorgani. Tell us more."

"I have been searching for who I am, where I come from, where I am going. You opened my eyes to a new world, but not to what I want to find in it."

"I could not even do that for myself, Gorgani," he replies, "though I have searched everywhere for an answer, even in mirrors, even at mountains, at clouds, stars and waterfalls, even into my heart."

"Do we seek something that does not exist?" I wonder aloud. "Hope is our prize possession. From hope we gain the willpower to ascend. We can overcome setbacks and tragedies through its power, which rejuvenates our heartbeat that wishes to stop dead. And if a goal is impossible, hope directs us to fresh goals."

"How true, Gorgani. Your discussion of hope is enlightening, and so hopeful. Hope is a devoted friend, a healing medicine. God created hope to combat despair and prompt us to strive toward perfection—toward Himself. Ibn Sina inhales the opium smoke and raises his voice. "Oh, my good God! What is this life all about? What is in Your mind, God? Is it too late for me to understand Your wisdom? From where do ugly deeds spring? Did the devil create them or find them? Will they ever end? My body may die, but my hopes will live." His body shaking, Ibn Sina cries, "God, God, God! I call unto You, please call unto me! Take me now!"

"Calm yourself, my beloved," Esther says softly. Baba Tahir presses a cold towel to his forehead.

But Ibn Sina resumes, while his hand trembles. "I can see the atrocities of the Sultan's army against the aged, women, children, even against animals, plants, and monuments, even against gravestones, even stones! I see Masihi's eyes filled with hot sand, his tears dried up. God save us, Your people!"

Esther strokes his hand. "Be calm, my dear. Be calm, my love, Ibn Sina."

Ibn Sina, always attentive to her, relaxes and stares at her fondly, his voice softening. "I love you, Esther, as much as I love truth. And you are one beautiful truth I have touched. Oh, I still feel the truth flowing from your heart to mine, from your skin to my skin. When I touch you, it is God I touch. Did you not come from God, Esther?"

She recites a quatrain of Baba Tahir for him as she wipes away an unruly tear:

> Ah, for my eyes and heart in agony
> That heart should crave for all that eyes can see.
> I'll rise and forge a sword with edge of steel
> And strike at eyes and set my lone heart free.

Ibn Sina, still alert, with an almost magical lilt in his voice, replies with another verse of Baba Tahir's:

> But now, alone, my heart is filled with pain
> My longings search for happiness in vain
> At eve of death I breathe your breath of love,
> At dawn of hope I dream and rise again.

I add a third verse from Baba Tahir:

> Your glorious face is like a trace of light
> That strikes and shines amidst the gloom of night.
> I saw a mole in black upon your cheek
> As if the sun had kissed you in its flight.

And Baba Tahir himself, the mystic poet, a tender, profound man and a more famous citizen of Hamadan than its kings, recites his own:

> If you can break my heart—fear not
> If you can tear my soul apart—fear not
> In me one heart has found its home of bliss
> You are the home of every heart—fear not.

Ibn Sina, hearing some of his favorite verses, smiles and exclaims, "Oh God, how I wished to know all the answers! When I was young I wanted to know the beginning of everything, but now I would prefer to know the end of everything. What use is mathematics, physics, chemistry, biology, astronomy, philosophy, art, wine, or faith, if we find no connection among them, if they do not enable us to detect falsehood, to distinguish between good and evil, and to discover the true essence of love? I am satisfied with my striving to be God's instrument of healing on Earth. I have also worked to create ideas, but we are doomed if we think ideas alone will save us."

Ibn Sina coughs violently. When he regains his voice, it is weak and tremulous. "I know my soul, good or bad, will survive my death, but my work will survive only if it is good. I wanted to spiritualize physics or else materialize the spirit and unify subject and object. I have accomplished neither. Besides you, my dear friends, what have I to lose by dying? Nothing but my decaying body, my pains and wonderings." His eyes sweep the sides of his bed from where our eyes focus on him.

"I spoke to myself thoughtfully," he continues, "and I listened carefully for an answer. What is mind, just a clump of matter that can understand words and become wise? What is matter? Is mind matter or is what matters in the mind? Are ideas before or after matter? Tell me, Wise Matter! Are you the only thing that matters, Matter? Tell me, God, that matter is not first and last. I still wonder what is man, who is man, when is man humane, and where does he journey with blinders on." Ibn Sina coughs until his face is purple. "Esther, ask the next breeze to come inside and tell me who we are. The wind is old and wise, yet alert and vigorous. It has been everywhere; it has seen and heard everything. The terrible, total truth is that I know not one answer to my questions. Maybe man, me, all of us are just eggplants that talk. We eat animals that emerge from seeds and eggs, and we eat plants; so, we become . . . eggplants! Our skin is soft, is it not? We have seeds in us, do we not? We turn purple from fear. And life cooks us well, even broils us to charcoal, does it not?"

We cannot help but grin—even on his deathbed Ibn Sina dazzles with delightful wit. Basking in our amusement, he turns to Esther and smiles, "But your skin is softer than an eggplant's! I wanted to understand the deepest secrets of the flesh, especially Esther's tempting flesh, but one touch of her skin would so intoxicate me that I forgot what I learned from it, or that my intent was knowledge, not pleasure."

Esther blushes, her eyes glisten, and a teardrop incited by her love of the wisest man rolls down her pink cheek.

"Yes, Ibn Sina-*jon*. Yes, *nooreh cheshmam*, the light of my sight. I am most pleased to be as you wish me to be, because we wish the same—we are one."

Ibn Sina smokes more opium and washes it down with wine before continuing. "One must be or not be. Nothing can both exist and not exist. I cannot be with you and with Him, too. The choice is no longer mine. My last project is death, and it will be accomplished for me and by me alone. And on time! I am not angry. I will not deny or resist death, nor shall I bargain with fate. I welcome death which has stalked me since birth and I will embrace whatever comes after death, but damn it, I am still curious. Curious to the hilt. Curious, that is what I am, that is what I have been, that is what I will be, if I will be again. I wonder why God gave me all this curiosity but not enough time to quench it." He takes a deep breath and recites his own poem:

> In the vast desert of life
> My mind searched for truth, and
> Found no pointers, even within the split hair.
> A thousand suns shone in my mind,
> But the mystery of an atom remains undisclosed.

We all keep silent before the sage. "If I did in fact choose this life, it must have been so long ago that I don't remember. I always thought when my time ended I would crawl away and die someplace alone, not surrounded by those whom I love. Death will wash away my residual righteousness, and I am not frightened of the cleansing. Those who fear death also fear change, even happiness. They also fear ascendance, truth, love, and God. Oh, my God! I see wild birds flutter from my mind carrying colorful flowers, and Tahir's poems to You whom I must greet next.

> I seldom rove in fields where roses bloom,
> Where nightingales rehearse their songs of gloom.
> I seldom rove in fields where fate has trapped
> Some soul like mine behind the bars of doom."

He squeezes Esther's hand and with his other hand he closes his own eyelids as though already dead. She kisses his forehead, her tear dropping on his pillow. Our host prays under his breath in an alien tongue.

Gradually his voice diminishes to a whisper reaching us from the furthest places. "God, oh God. I hear colorful sounds, see melodic lights, touch cool flames. I see flowers sprouting from snow and diamonds scattered as gravel. Shining! Each one with a little sun within. I taste wine squeezed from my poems and inhale wonderful fragrances from Sufi songs. Giant bells ring inside spheres of light, the sounds of celestial love. Death is beautiful, death is the most beautiful event in creation. It is liberty at last."

His words journey into me like light through water, turning my mind aglow but also disclosing the darkness of sublunary existence. Once, full of joy, he said, "If I am leading 'me,' then why am 'I' going to places I ought not?" Where is Ibn Sina going now? Who leads the Leading Wise Man now—God? Ibn Sina lies dead but looks so magnificent. He seems deep in thought, resting before his next adventure.

A string of pearls like teardrops roll down Esther's face. Baba Tahir says softly, "God bless his gentle soul," then whispers a Muslim prayer. I hear Esther's Hebrew words and see our host make the sign of the cross. So befitting that the man for all times receive such diverse blessings. He is gone. What next? I ask myself, and feel free to weep. I weep like a punctured cactus.

Religious ceremonies are rushed in wartime, and Hamadan may be sacked any day, any hour. The next day we gather in a mosque, its blue dome merging with the blue sky. Men line one side, women, their faces covered, the other. Baba Tahir and his mystic brotherhood are present. Esther hides beneath a scarf. I can distinguish her green eyes from a thousand others, though, for their magnetism attracts all the rest. They are as much as one can see of a woman in public. A pair of eyes, searching for something, for some light, for some rights, understanding, respect, searching to be a whole person, not a man's woman, I think, inspired by Ibn Sina, in sympathy with women and in antipathy of rigid rules.

After the memorial, Esther stops me in a narrow street and whispers, "I am done with the love of men. Now I glow in the love of the one who waits for me, He who shines upon me from Alvand's peak and beyond. Peace may come between people of different faiths and interests, but not in our time, I fear. Sometime, somewhere, people will realize their oneness and stop hurting each other. Oh, my God, I talk like Ibn Sina. He helped the cause as much as he could."

"Yes, Esther," I say. "Peace is one of the most difficult goals of man, so we must work all the harder for it, and in a thousand different ways." Leaving me, she disappears down the street in a swirl of black.

I make my way alone to the outskirts of the city, where the Master will come to rest near the grave of the wonderful Queen Esther of the Hebrew Bible—the most beautiful and understanding queen of ancient Persia. I wonder about Esther the Queen and the Esther who chose Ibn Sina for her lover. Is it just a name that they share?

Nature rages around us, demanding human submission. Thunder pounds our wailing to silence, wind whips away our tears, rain threatens to absorb us all into eternity. Ibn Sina's body wears no coffin; he is simply wrapped in a large, white cotton sheet. The humble grave is ready to receive the great man. The ceremony is short, with only Esther, a few friends, and his brother standing by. He is buried in silence. The heart of the grave trembles with his presence, and I shudder, too, as the earth covers him from my sight. A tremendous flash and a deafening clap of thunder split the clouds wide apart for his soul's unimpeded flight. The faces around me show panic as a new downpour threatens. Careless of appearances, Esther, in need of consolation, approaches me and takes my hand. A thunderbolt shatters the world and sunders a tree from its roots. A shower tries to wash away our sorrows, but we stand silently in the rain. Then the clouds take flight behind Alvand to cry in solitude. The sun thrusts into view, like Ibn Sina's ideas, to enlighten the world with the sound of trumpets that are felt but not heard.

The awful otherness of the world frowns at me. Without Ibn Sina, nothing looks familiar. I must henceforth live someone else's life, because, with him gone, I am not me and know not who I am. I leave the cemetery alone and wander toward the mountain's base. I feel the crispness of autumn; I see nature in a rage and colorful leaves shed glistening tears in big drops, mourning Ibn Sina's death. He often went into the mountains to meditate and think and worship alone. The mountain taught him stability and forbearance, the trees resilience and growth, the sun the path to truth, and the clouds transcendence beyond the self. He loved nature for its richness, generosity, resoluteness, and loyalty. Seasons come, provide, and pass on steadily, more dependably than the most trusted friend. Nature is our mother and we love our mother.

It would be a wonder if history would open one of its many eyes and understand itself, and abandon its unconscious goal of self-destruction and adopt the conscious goal of self-perfection. But what is history but us?

I hear a flute but see no shepherd to give it voice. It sounds as though someone plays while walking in the skies. It is soothing, nourishing—nursing, healing beyond healing. I am alone but not lonely. Our twenty-five years together have ended. Ibn Sina was father, teacher, physician, brother, friend, and colleague to me, as he was to the world. Our relationship grew, as I myself did. I came to feel at ease with the great man. During the last few years he sought my counsel more and more, and appreciated my learning. I became truly his colleague.

He is gone but he is everywhere—in the sunlight, in the wind, in the shadow dance of wildflowers. He is the herbs and seeds he used for medicine that heals multitudes. He is in my mind, in Esther's heart, in the poems of Tahir, Hafiz, and Rumi, in the songs of nature, in the dust rising in sunbeams that streak through flapping leaves. He is in the atom whose mystery he wished to crack open. He is where history and geography meet, where time, the dimension of becoming, and space, the dimension of motion, merge and the boundary between them disappears. The melody I hear seems far-traveled, telling its story of a long journey.

I know his life force does not end here in death. People of all faiths will love him as he loved them and healed them without discrimination. His ideas will become inseparable from the collective mind; and his name, his story, will never be lost to rain, thunder, snow, envy, dogmatism, war or time. I know I loved him every day of twenty-five years, even when I was angry with him, and I will love him more as I walk out of his glow and disappear into my own obscurity. Our flight together, our journey of spirits, now becomes my solo flight. Oh God, how lonely I am without him, and how empty the world appears without his presence. I shall finish the biography of the Leading Wise

Man, my beloved colleague, Ibn Sina. It will be my gift to history in his memory.

I wake from hypnosis to see my sadness reflected in Sitareh's melancholy eyes. It is as if Ibn Sina just died. I want to cry, but is it for a man who died a thousand years ago or for me? How old am I myself? We are all very old, a residue of untold lives, of evolution in nature and culture. It is time for us to become wise before it is too late.

Sitareh senses my sorrow and my urge to cry. "I heard everything you said, Pirooz. If you must cry, cry. Don't let my presence inhibit you."

"Sitareh, Sitareh, what is the matter with this world? He longed for truth and justice to the bitter end." I beg for an answer as I feel my tears. "I have a great weeping in me, but I don't know for whom or for what. Maybe it is for some peace and for some respect for truth, the two victims of the human race."

She puts her arm around my shoulder as our heads bow together in sorrow. "Truth can be arrested only temporarily. Falsehood cannot roam free forever. You know that," she says.

"I wish I knew for certain," I whisper to myself.

That night I nuzzle in her arms like a child and feel my tears again, keeping me from sleep. I repeat my words of a difficult era, "I have been searching for something but cannot say what. Something different from what is and someone different from who I am. I want a transcendence, and nothing short of that."

"Speaking of transcendence," she says, "why does God meditate?"

"If God is perfect, then He can never improve Himself, but if He made us in His image then He needs meditation like us." I reply.

"And what about Ibn Sina?" The lovely psychiatrist asks, to cleanse me of my unspoken words.

"Him? His wisdom, compassion, love and curiosity were a wave of understanding taking the world to new shores. Ibn Sina ran and ran and ran, yet he ran from evil, not good. He ran headlong until he crashed into the walls of his own curiosity or the walls of his time's constrictions. He was self-taught, and, if anyone ever was, self-invented. The greatest invention of Ibn Sina, who is the inventor of modernity, is Ibn Sina. He was a prophet too modest to claim its mantle. From the jewels of history, he made a brilliant crown for the king of minds, for Ibn Sina, for our king, the true king of Persia! We must not only learn his wisdom, but why and how he acquired it, and what he did with it and wanted to do had he lived longer. We must know his shortcomings, too. The possibility of ascendance is within us like an unborn baby in its mother's womb. I feel ascendance in my womb!"

"Your womb?" Sitareh smiles.

"Yes. mine! I have conceived ascendance. We all have."

Sitareh falls silent, while I feel a nagging hunger in my gut that will not go away, a hunger for ideas, liberty, happiness and transcendence. Then I think of all the hunger for food, shelter, love, and security in this world. We are born hungry and die still hungry. History is a history of hunger. The hunger for self-esteem, integrity, and truth, too. "Hear me, my love," I exclaim. "I am starving for human ascendance beyond violence. I am starving for peace on earth, Sitareh-*jon*. I'm starving for the sight of the *tar* in your arms, for your music."

"Don't worry so, Pirooz. Try to get some rest." I hear her caring voice. "I will play you a lullaby." Soon the sounds of the *tar*, and Tahir's poem put me to sleep.

> I'll wander further than I've ever gone,
> Through land and sea, then on beyond the dawn.
> I'll reach the pilgrim's home and ask its saints,
> "Is this my goal, or shall I wander on?"

Chapter Twenty: Being and Nothingness

I open my eyes to see Sitareh lying on her elbow, smiling at me.

"Good morning to you, Pirooz-*jon*."

Sunshine floods the bed. "Good morning, Sitareh. Is it that late?"

"No, the light just arrived," she replies. "And I must leave for my room. It is just for appearance' sake. Firoozeh's parents are visiting, and they don' t know I am a *seegheh*," Sitareh says.

I am disappointed. "I once heard Ibn Sina say, 'Clerics teach that wine is a sin, but they behave as if hypocrisy is not.' Hypocrisy is always for the sake of others."

She sits upright in amazement. "What do you mean, you once heard? When did you hear it?"

"I heard it then, just as I see it happening now. Oh, I see! I heard it so long ago that I don't remember."

"Why did this memory come to you now, Pirooz?"

"Because your running away seems pretentious," I reply sharply.

"So you wish me to remain in bed?"

"Yes. Stay with me and let my ecstasy last longer than this morning," I plead.

"All right, Pirooz-*jon*, I'd love to share your ecstasy."

"How do you feel about our waking together, Sitareh?"

"My feelings are mixed, all mixed. Tradition clashes with modernity within me. I am embarrassed renouncing my upbringing to be a *seegheh*. One is both married and divorced, and emotionally both involved and uninvolved. It is offensive being a rented woman, but I have only myself to blame. How irrational to rent myself so I can keep my options open. Of course, my fear of arrest for living with you must have influenced my decision, too."

I kiss her eyes softly. "My love for you is beyond vows and laws; it is yours however you desire it."

She smiles majestically, but bit by bit the smile turns into an enigmatic frown as she gazes at the bed sheets full of wildflowers. I watch and speculate and wait.

"Pirooz," she says, "you know that the first thought in the first moments of wakefulness may be significant, since the mind is not yet cluttered with the daily routine. Is your awakening today still fresh?"

"A couple of minutes and a few words couldn't have spoiled it very much."

"Out of curiosity, tell me, if someone like Ibn Sina were born today, which culture would better nurture his genius, East or West?"

"Definitely not Iran under the Islamic Republic," I respond without hesitation.

She stares into my eyes as if measuring my resolve. I see her fears fall like teardrops on the sheets, watering the lifeless flowers. A long silence grips us, and she seems to hold something back. I dismiss my curiosity, trying to fulfill her expectations not to be too inquisitive. I am not sure how I manage this act, for questions stick painfully in my throat.

As if running away from my thoughts, Sitareh changes the subject. "Last night I dreamt of two huge scorpions in a dance of love and death. They were locked together at the mouth and front legs in a long, violent waltz. The male kept stinging the female as the female thrashed about. And then, after mating, the female ate the male with the horrible, magnified sound of tearing flesh."

"What does your dream mean?" I ask.

"Nothing," she replies. "I have watched scorpions mate."

Despite her reassurance, I get a chilling premonition. Will she eat my hopes? I try to change our moods. "Do you want to hear a story about Ibn Sina?"

"I'd love to!" she exclaims.

"Ibn Sina and I were drinking wine and talking of truth, fate, God and other baffling mysteries. The colorful autumn, the sun, Mount Alvand, and our feelings seemed in perfect harmony. Suddenly, an earth tremor upset the jug of wine. The spilled liquid ran through his food and onto my robes. Once our shock subsided, Ibn Sina stamped on the ground and said, 'I wonder who is drinking and who is drunk.'

"I replied, 'Maybe the Lady Earth is asking for some wine. But this lady has no will of her own, does she?' Ibn Sina covered his uncertainty with a mysterious grin."

She interjects, "So Ibn Sina was unsure if God gave free will to the universe?"

"Yes, he was. He loved God, but he couldn't always understand Him. He said, 'Because the world is imperfect and my curiosity intense and my intelligence limited, I question and complain often. God will not listen to the fainthearted.'"

"One day I told Ibn Sina, 'If you were to claim to be a prophet, people would follow you.' He smiled mysteriously—just like your smile, Sitareh, with a dimple on the chin—and said, 'We will see what we will see.' So one cold, dark, windy winter morning, right here, a thousand years ago, he asked me from his bed for a drink of water. I replied, 'I have placed the jug beside your bed, Master. You can help yourself.' At that moment came the call to prayer. Ibn Sina told me while performing his ablutions, 'You see, Gorgani, the real Prophet, His Excellency Mohammed, hundreds of years after he has gone, can inspire the muezzin to withstand the freezing winds from the height of the minaret, but I am alive and here, and yet you hesitated to leave your warm bed to hand me the jug of water. Do you still want me to claim the gift of prophecy?'"

Sitareh quietly reflects before speaking. "Remember that Ibn Sina was a Sufi. Can you tell me more about Sufism beyond what we have already discussed, Pirooz?"

"Why not? Anything to keep you in bed beside me." We both smile. "I begin with Attar, whose *Parliament of the Birds* is an allegory of the Sufi path. In it a flock of birds set out to join the King of the Birds, the *Simurgh*, whose eggs were the ultimate wisdom. Before they began, the birds voiced their fears about the seven onerous obstacles, like men about to embark on the Sufi way."

"Or women on the way to free themselves—and men—from false notions about their relationships. Is it not tragic that men have barred women from the Sufi way?"

"Absolutely, Sitareh-*jon*. I am for unlocking all gates and letting everybody in."

"Good!" She flashes her winning smile that I love to watch.

Enjoying her attention, even her interruptions, I clear my throat. "Well, the birds elected the hoopoe their leader, and he dealt wisely with their questions and concerns as they went in search of the mystical *Simurgh*. At last, after a long, arduous journey filled with physical, mental and spiritual difficulties, only thirty birds survived, and the pilgrims arrived at the mountain peak of truth—the *Simurgh*'s throne. Only thirty birds survived. When they drew back the mystic curtain—the last obstacle that separated them from the *Simurgh*—the birds found their own reflection in a giant mirror, for *Simurgh* is a Persian homonym for 'thirty birds.' They realized in amazement that what they had sought was none other than their own ascended and united souls."

"A very pleasant tale," she says. "Tell me the Sufi story of the soul. Remember again, we are in pursuit of the soul of Ibn Sina, and ours, as well."

"Do you want all of this in bed?" I ask.

"How about at breakfast?"

"Fine," I agree.

"But before that . . ." She moves toward me.

As I reply, "I cannot resist you," her full lips surround mine, our skins become one, our limbs mesh and our hands clench tightly, trying to become inseparable from each other. Our passions melt together and we make love.

It is a perfect morning, and my happiness finds no ceiling, exceeding even the sky's blue dome. Sitareh smiles at me over a light breakfast, when, as I sip my tea, she says, "Now, Pirooz-*jon*, you must tell me about the soul's journey."

I put down the teacup. "The Sufis believe that the human soul, demoted from its heavenly home, is trapped on its descent to earth by the human body and spoiled by the passions and vices of the flesh in this imperfect but tempting world. To ascend to its lost home, the soul must regain its purity by cleansing itself with two divine emanations: the outer light, truth, which awakens and illumines lives, and the inner one, love, which inspires all creatures to aspire to self-perfection. *Mehr* is the unity of truth and love springing from God to unify all existence."

"Do you believe this supernatural tale, Pirooz?"

"I do symbolically, but I am just reporting, not answering the unanswerable."

"This morning is magnificent," Sitareh declares, "because you will tell me all about Sufism."

"I will summarize what I know, but remember, I'm no expert." I hold my forehead in one hand. "Sufism begins with *Erfan*, the knowledge of the self, the most revered knowledge, according to the Sufis."

"Why is that the most revered form of knowledge?" she questions.

"Because it is vital, it is the hardest to come by, and it colors all other types of knowledge. The true self lies buried within a false self through faulty upbringing and pressures to conform. We unwittingly pursue paths that divide us and sacrifice truth and love, which would unite us. A Sufi tries to cast out falsehoods and understand the true self and the oneness of the Creator and the created. As the Prophet Mohammed proclaims, 'He who knows himself, knows God.'"

Sitareh interrupts me with a mischievous smile. "Perhaps she—not necessarily he—who knows herself, knows God."

"I agree, but I can't help it if God revealed Himself in chauvinist language!"

"Get on with it, Pirooz." She takes my hand in hers and smiles brilliantly.

"The Sufi embarks on both an inner journey and an outer journey," I continue. "The inner journey is termed *Sayer*, the Sufi's voyage to purify one's inner being, with a heightened consciousness of reality and God. The outer journey is *Suluk*, to perfect his—or her—social conduct with the absolute inability to think, utter or do what is evil. The two entwined paths, *Sayer* and *Suluk*, will lift the Sufi like a pair of wings to transcend mundane existence and give him the attributes of God—understanding, generosity and compassion. But obstacles riddle the Sufi's passage from hatred to love, from falsehood to truth, and from fiction to fact, so it demands discipline and sacrifice. It is not easy."

"Very well, how do Sufis embark on this journey?"

"Sufism has no codified doctrine, and even the term Sufi is not precisely defined. So, to reach a common destination, each Sufi may journey differently, but in two general ways. The first is to conquer the ego and purify the soul through rigorous ascetic discipline, worship and repentance of sins, while the second is to search for truth and to love the self and other beings and God through humility, charity and sincerity. Humility stems from understanding that everything is subordinate to God's will, and that others can teach us what we have ignored learning ourselves. By offering one's soul to God, the individual offers it to his fellow men, too, so humility leads to charity, which unifies humanity, and the two lead to sincerity, which is the apogee of the path. Searching for truth ends with reaching the ultimate truth. Love, like fire, cleanses the soul by expunging the whims of the ego. The first way may be called the path of denial, and the second the path of acceptance."

"Are the two practices mutually exclusive?"

"No. Rumi practiced both. The Sufi path of love has Persian origins, and evolved over thousands of years from the doctrine that light and love bring eternal illumination. In sum," I say, "the Sufi way—the catharsis of the soul and the perfection of social conduct—transforms earthly existence into Divine Being, and singularity into unity. The discovery of the true self and its oneness with all beings is the rending of the veil. The cleansed soul, joined in love to all other souls, ascends to its eternal home, from where it originally emanated—the Divine Being."

"I wonder if this implies what I think it does?" Sitareh muses.

"The journey dissolves the apparent divisions that conceal the oneness of man and God. In Attar's allegory, the cleansed and joined souls become one being, one and the same as God. Ibn Sina also considered the ascendance of a single soul, a solo flight to divinity, so to speak. In either case, transcendence through the Sufi way is the supreme good. Another interpretation of transcendence is evolution, namely, the transcendence of inert matter into primitive life, animals, man, mind and the flight of the spirit, as Rumi elaborated it."

"Thank you. Now tell me all about the Sufi's transcendental path."

"I shall," I reply, "but I must tell you this before we embark on our Sufi discourse again." I pause and, inexplicably Sitareh Poonia emerges in my mind before I can start, her words becoming mine. "The *Avesta* mentions a wise and healing phoenix, the *Sina*—a Sanskrit name. The wisdom and power to heal of Sina, the man, and *Sina*, the king of birds like the *Simurgh* in the *Shahnameh* and Attar's story, is a mystical confluence. In my dream in New York, Ibn Sina alluded to a wish for reincarnation. The revivifier may try to resurrect himself. Ibn Sina may cure death!"

"That is a very intriguing observation, Pirooz." After reflection she demands, "Go on, please. What are the stages of the Sufi path?"

"The first step of the Sufi path is the search. It is a search for the true self, for divine wisdom, and the recognition that souls have an affinity for God. Uncorrupted, they gravitate in love to God, like a child to its mother, which is natural, since the created emanates from the Creator. After all, you and I must have existed as a potentiality in the mind of God before we came to be. That is why some Sufis have dared to claim, 'I am the truth,' or even, 'I am God.'"

"So the ultimate destination is reunion with God or actually becoming God?"

"Yes. One reunites with God by purifying one's soul from instinctual desires. Surely you know all this, Sitareh."

"True, but I want to know Sufism according to Pirooz-*jon*, if that is admissible."

I throw up my hands. "I give up, Sitareh!"

"I accept your unconditional surrender, Pirooz." Smiling all-knowingly, she gazes into my eyes and I into hers with love. "Now, what is union?" she asks.

"It is both losing and gaining something. Union can be physical, chemical, biological, social or spiritual. With mankind, it is losing false sovereignty and gaining the sovereignty of oneness, which precludes conflict and tragedy."

As I take a deep breath, Sitareh asks, "What is the next step on the Sufi way?"

"The second step is to experience and accept love in all its manifestations—the love of God, truth, nature and one's fellow man. The third step is the mystic's comprehension of his own insignificance, and the fourth is his break from worldly desires and freedom from earthly pitfalls like greed or dread. The fifth step is a fearless ascent towards understanding and pure love for God, which leads the Sufi to an uninterrupted vision of the Almighty. In the sixth step, the magnificence, beauty and greatness of God bewilders and transmutes the Sufi, like a caterpillar into a butterfly that can soar to the seventh heaven. This prepares him for the final step of annihilation, when the self, the Sufi's soul, dissolves in the Divine Being, like a grain of salt in the ocean."

"Why is the Sufi's goal annihilation, Pirooz?"

"For one to abandon the singular and selfish self and let it disappear into Him brings ultimate fulfillment, the Creator and created becoming one again."

I stop and wonder aloud, "Why must we make the effort to reach God, when it was Him or Her who separated from us?"

Sitareh gazes at me for a long moment. "Would you like more tea, Pirooz?"

"No, thank you. For once you allow us a break?"

"Yes. Are you still complaining after your surrender?" She grins. After pouring some tea for herself, she says, "So that is the Sufi path to love and truth. Still, I would like you to tell me, Pirooz, what is love?"

"My version?" I am puzzled by her ceaseless probing into my understanding.

"Yes, of course."

"I think love is a mysterious experience that begins with an attraction of one for another, and ends with 'one-another,' a word I have invented to reflect the unity of two souls, neither the one nor the other, but both. Love is more than just attraction and affinity. For instance, a magnet and iron have a physical affinity, the hydrogen and oxygen of water have a chemical affinity, and sperm and egg have a biological affinity, but in each case one feels no loss if the other is pried apart, since they are not united mentally or spiritually. Nature has a hand in love, culture has a hand in it, and mystery has a hand in it, as it does in everything else. Status and beauty, defined culturally, may also induce false attraction. Loving requires a conscious effort to abandon the self for the other—the end of selfishness and the beginning of voluntary vulnerability. "

Glancing at me more lovingly, her irresistible smile flashing, Sitareh says, "My love for you is biological and everything else, Pirooz-*jon*. Now, what is truth?"

"It is knowing the world as it is. But truth is a mystery, since, even if we did know it, we would never be certain of it, except for trivial cases like arithmetic. In my version, truth, the outer light, is a genuine component of light."

"It is? How? You sound more puzzling as you go on."

"Green plants, which form the basis of everything edible, use photosynthesis to capture the energy of sunlight. Digestion generates the electro-chemical energy that our brains use to search for the truth. So rhythm, meter and meaning in poetry; melody and harmony in music; intuition and logic in science; and all human thoughts and deeds—even my passion for you, Sitareh-*jon*—are energized by sunlight. Our minds are just the instruments by which light investigates its own nature and attempts to know itself as if it were a Sufi."

"A Sufi is light and light is a Sufi. This is new to me."

"It is new to me, too. I am inspired by the sunlight that brings me your smile and nourishes my attraction for you. Look at this loving sun, Sitareh, hugging us both and bringing us warmth with its gentle beams and nourishment for the canary's song."

Sitareh puts her lips to mine for a long, innocent kiss. "The day is better yet," she replies, "knowing how much you love me. But don't let a kiss stop you, Pirooz."

"OK. Sufism is the light in which one can see things as they really are."

"Are you attracted to Sufism, Pirooz?"

"I am attracted to self-criticism, self-understanding, self-realization, unity with my fellow man, and spiritual ascendance. I only know it imperfectly, from readings, mostly, but I wish to know the Sufi way by experience. I wish Attar were my guide."

"What about Sufis?"

"Well," I reply, "Sufism is a transcendental experience, the rejection of what is ugly and the absorption of what is beautiful. It may come into conflict with authorities, and Sufis have suffered from kings, clerics and fanatics, the ugly people, Hafiz called them. So Hafiz' home was ransacked and he had to burn some of his poetry before it was confiscated. Can you imagine? The man Nietzsche admired and everyone loved was treated like that."

"Sufis are supposed to be fearless, no?" Her glance glistens in the sunlight.

"Yes, a Sufi could risk death, as Attar did, but other Sufis retreated into ambiguities, paradoxes and dissimulation."

"I doubt you could be a passive or submissive Sufi."

"Never! Sufism is a medicine with side-effects. Some Sufis ignore the real world, but I prefer those who strive to better it, like Ibn Sina. I like the ascendance of one and all together, as much as possible. This is an immortal vision and act. Even an atheist could believe this."

"What a dream," Sitareh exclaims.

"We are a dream. If it weren't for dreams, we would still live in the trees. So we must act immortally to become immortal like God. Or else we will do no better than the dinosaurs. The Zoroastrians' good thoughts, good words and good deeds, or the Christians' love of neighbor are only good for the here and now, but immortal thoughts, words and deeds are boundless; they will fill the universe and eternity with humanity ascended."

Sitareh stares at me as though at a car that stopped unexpectedly. Her eyes urge me on. Suddenly a small fear threads through me. Why is she so intent to know my understanding of Sufism? I know she has studied Sufism, too. I conceal my concern and suggest, "Let us stop here and do something else."

"We will. We will, Pirooz-*jon*. But don't you think we ought to explore all sides of this issue? What do you think of God?"

"God made everything imperfectly, if he made anything, but we made Him perfectly in the image of what we wish to be."

"Is anything perfect to you, Pirooz?"

"I'm not sure. Even if something were perfect, no one would know that it was."

"What do you mean?" she asks. You talk like a modern-day Gorgani."

"What do you expect?" I reply. "Anyhow, our senses don't tell us most of what happens around us. We hear only a small fraction of sound frequencies, we see even less of the light spectrum, and we smell only a minute fraction of odors around. Our perceptions let us muddle through but can't quench our curiosity. But, amazingly, we still know far more than we need to know to survive in contrast to other mammals. Man is God's puzzle. We invent instruments to observe more of the bottomless reality, but we have no way of knowing what we are missing still."

"We can mistake a perfect being as imperfect, too?"

"Yes, and that proves our collective imperfection," I reply and fall silent.

"Wake up, Pirooz! Continue," she demands, smiling.

"How about a compromise? I will read a few lines of Attar that will tell it all."

"Fine, Pirooz, but I am still curious about your version of Sufism."

"My version is Attar's version, supplemented with my immortality provision. I consider God to be the human ascendance to its ultimate and collective possibilities." I take a deep breath and retrieve some of his couplets from memory.

> "The self has swallowed you for its delight;
> How long will you endure its mindless spite?
> Consider carefully before you start;
> The journey asks of you a lion's heart.
> First wash your hands of life if you would say:
> I am a pilgrim on our Almighty's way.
>
> Next comes the valley of detachment, here
> All claims, all lust for meaning disappear.
> Whoever can evade the self transcends
> This world, and as lover he ascends.
> Be nothing first! and then you will exist;
> You cannot live whilst life and Self persist.
>
> No sage could understand His perfect grace,
> Nor seer discern the beauty of His face.
> There soul and mind bewildered miss the mark
> And, faced by Him, like dazzled eyes, are dark—
> The substance of [your] being is undone
> And [you] are lost like shade before the sun."
>
> "That after nothingness they have attained
> Eternal life, and self-hood is regained.
> At last, made perfect in Reality
> You will be gone, and only God will be.
> This is the oneness of diversity,
> Not oneness locked in singularity."

I stop and notice two sparrows mating on a clothesline and then darting away in a chase. A thirst for an uncomplicated love wells up in me. Sitareh breaks my reverie. "It is the sun's energy in their feed that keeps them afloat and love that directs their flight. I see God's *mehr*, light and love, as you said, in all creatures." She then puts her hands over mine. "Thank you for awakening me to such wonderful words. Let us not be singular ourselves, Pirooz-*jon*. Now let's go to Alvand, my wise mountain."

"As Ibn Sina said, 'My Sufi mount.'"

"Did you read that somewhere?"

"No, but I know he said it. Alvand is patient, stable, fearless and humble, a witness to history with enormous forbearance. It never cries for help; it knows the louder you cry, the less the world hears."

"A certain deafness pervades the universe," she says. It reminds me of what Poonia said: "I must return to where people listen to one another with care."

We go to Mount Alvand to eat and drink and sing and, after a nap, swim naked in a lovely pond on her family's property. The memorable celebration sweeps away the last of my reservations. I feel an intense desire for life, and life with Sitareh.

Back home in the evening she says, "I want to tell you something. It is not easy for me to say and not easy for you to hear."

"I am a big boy," I respond, but I feel bound up in an emotional turmoil.

She tells me she is on her way to Teheran for a few weeks to attend to her patients and her aging parents. She wants me to stay in Hamadan, preferring to miss me rather than feel guilty for not going. "Discipline is the Sufi way; indulgence is not," she assures me. "Love and guilt can coexist."

She is very determined. I could no more change her mind than change a planet's orbit. "You are excused from any excuses, Sitareh," I respond.

She stares, then smiles in wonder. "I have no choice but to do what I must, Pirooz-*jon*. And you have your own choices to make." Her reasonable reply penetrates like a cold wind.

The next morning we kiss farewell. I tell her, "I love you."

She replies, "I will let love guide me, Pirooz. I love you, too."

She will go by bus, leaving me her car. She presents me with an international driver's license, explaining, "Money speaks louder than prayer here."

Without Sitareh, the house is quiet, and I feel as if my home is a foreign country. I visit places, but mostly in my imagination. Her sudden departure baffles me, and strange noises echo in my bones, with the marrow sucked out. What am I doing in Hamadan? I am in one of the world's oldest cities, yet there is no one here for me, as if the place had been devastated in a nuclear blast. Hamadan has not uplifted me to my future nor lowered me to my past; it seems to have set me aside in oblivion. In trying to answer these questions and conquer my despair, a tiny light within me, flickers like a distant star, as I remember my imprisonment in Hamadan a millennium ago, and how good it was for me. Maybe this solitude is good for me, too.

I try to cope by going to Ibn Sina's tomb and drowning myself in reading. I long for Ibn Sina's return, as though he, too, were only away on a trip. But I no longer want to know everything—my names or where I come from or what my intentions are or ought to be. I wish to abandon the past, not remember the two Sitarehs. But instead, the past grows more vivid as my memory focuses clearly, and I cannot tell myself from Gorgani. Whatever I do, I wonder who wills it—me, Gorgani, Ibn Sina, Sitareh, culture, or an unknown force like the evolution of the universe?

Who am I? Who am I in love with? Who am I missing or misleading? Who will answer my questions? As before, no one answers. A thought besieges me: Why do I long to belong to someone, to something, even to a memory?

I read Arabic texts to see if I can understand them as well as Gorgani did. I cannot. I try to recall verses of the Holy Book by heart, some of the verses I had learned to recite as the young Pirooz. But I remember only a few. I rush to a music shop and try to play a flute. The shopkeeper winces at my awful sounds. I may lack Gorgani's skills and talent, but I also know things Gorgani couldn't have known. We are not the same person, even if we were at birth, yet we are linked as if we were one, Siamese twins befriended by the cosmos. A couplet from Attar comes to mind.

> Be nothing first! and then you will exist;
> You cannot live whilst life and self persist.

After three weeks without word from Sitareh or her returning my calls, the foreboding surfaces that I may never see her again. The pangs of emptiness and isolation are unceasing. I lose my appetite, eat little and lose weight. I think and rethink, read newspapers, listen to the radio and watch TV, now that Sitareh is gone. The war enters my mind viciously. I cannot believe my senses; these lies and this killing are not real.

The phone stands mute for one more week as I struggle with time. In her simple but subtle ways, Firoozeh tries to make my loneliness bearable. I appreciate her caring and tell her so. She smiles stoically, but then she must leave to visit her sick mother for a few days. Ibn Sina makes no appearance. Nothing seems sensitive to my plight. "I am lonely, God," I scream in the ancient, deserted house. "Come and hold me."

Why doesn't Sitareh call? Why does God remain aloof? Unfortunately, the world can't teach me deafness towards myself. My options are clear, and I hear them in my head. A deaf world and a capricious lover are terrors when one is alone. I try to concentrate on how wonderful it would be if everything could turn out well in the end, but I succumb to depression, despair, even helplessness. My old thoughts of suicide, severed from me, reappear in the distance. Until death, one always has the option of death, which de-solves life's problems and ends the dread of being. Nevertheless I hold on to my flickering hopes and nurse my patience. Without hope and patience, I scold myself, life is a slow torture, the road to doom.

I phone Sitareh again. Her mother tells me she is away on a retreat. I recall how I missed everything while in prison with Ibn Sina and survived it.

I must think things over; maybe she is doing the same. Sitareh's swift resolve and abrupt departure puzzle me, but I must accept them. It feels as if I must wait helplessly for a cancer diagnosis. Was I in her dream of the scorpions, locked in a dance of love and death with her? Is mine the lonely love Tahir complains about?

> How fair is love with two hearts so blest.
> One-sided love is the ache of soul at best.

In the fifth week, when passing thoughts of returning to New York cross my mind, I receive a postcard announcing she is in Teheran, safe and well. She isn't clear about when she will be back, nor is she clear why she is not being clear.

Iraqi aircraft are now bombing civilians regularly in Teheran, and chemical weapons proliferate at the front. Muslims are killing Muslims, all for God's sake, the same as when Ibn Sina and I found our times wanting. Suddenly I imagine the horse's eye on a smoldering stump fixed on me, asking me why. I bang my head hard against an oak to get an answer, some answer. I only get a bump on my forehead and the young, thin tree sheds a couple of acorns. Fortunately, Firoozeh returns. Her presence is soothing; she is lovely.

I take long walks to the countryside and into my soul. I wonder about our discussion of Sufism, Sitareh's questions, my revelations. I remember her saying she wanted to know my versions and opinions. Why?

As I stroll by the fish pool thinking of her, I hear the phone ring. It is Sitareh. I don't complain and she doesn't explain.

"Well, Pirooz . . ."

"Well what, dear Sitareh?"

"I am pregnant. It must have occurred on our first night together. Ibn Sina must have known! God knows he has been in charge of our lives. He is using us to . . ."

"To do what?"

"I am not really sure."

She will come to Hamadan tomorrow. We will think and rethink, we will talk, retalk, and we will decide together, she assures me. That is all, cut and dry. We offer no congratulations, and have no laughter and no tears. I receive a report, I freeze, and she leaves me frozen. Others appear to program my life. I was wound up to mate with Sitareh and now wound up to report to Ibn Sina in one week. I am passive like a mirror, and everything passes through me beyond my control. I despise my powerlessness, and experience deep sympathy with womankind.

Finally Sitareh's aloof voice leaves me, easing the night for me. I will be a father, a Baba! The word, the ideas pour pride and happiness into me, like beautiful music into the imagination of a composer. My joy is deeper than life itself. I will solve all my problems, I assure myself. This sudden surge of hope surprises me. I put my hand to my forehead and ask myself, are you all right, Pirooz? Still sane? Why did you act like a statue when you heard the news?

Sitareh arrives late the next day. Under the moonlight, we hold hands and just watch each other in bewilderment, like strangers striving to be kind to each other. Even as strangers, we seem to search in one another for what we cannot find in ourselves, something that would complete us. How can one talk about two lives that throb with impossibilities and a fetus hidden more in an enigma than a womb.

"How are you, Sitareh?" I break the silence.

"I am fine. And you?"

"All right, but mercilessly attacked by loneliness and uncertainty."

"We are inside events unlike any we could imagine," she explains. "Nothing is normal, not even your loneliness."

"True," I answer as I pull her toward me. I feel her trembling and then her tears. "All will be well, Sitareh-jon," I console her as I run my hand through her hair.

"I am sorry, Pirooz. It sounds weird, but I deprived myself of you. I needed the time, the distance, the retreat, the complete separation."

"Without warning, Sitareh-jon."

"Yes. I wished not to have to explain—you have the same rights."

I stare into her eyes with mixed emotions. "I may have the right, but not the will. What was your intent? Can you tell me now?"

"I wanted to see things through, to find out if I can live alone again."

I dare not ask why she wishes to know that and what she found out. I welcome ignorance to silence my curiosity. Is she weaning herself from me?

Sitareh softens her voice. "Hafiz said, 'Love seemed easy at first; then came the difficulties.' Love exhilarated me at first, but now I feel a foreboding in my bones."

"I feel it, too, even in my remote future, Sitareh."

"You do? Then will you try to understand me, Pirooz?"

"The more I try, the less I understand, but I promise to try harder. But what about your trying to understand me?"

"I want to understand you, and I think I do. How can I love you without understanding? But our difficulties are not because we lack understanding."

"We are avoiding the fact that we are parents, Sitareh."

"I am not, I am just trying to overcome the shock."

"I want to know how you feel about becoming a mother."

"I feel wonderful, but beyond that, it depends."

"It depends on what, Sitareh?"

"Pirooz, can we discuss this later? Can't we just enjoy the moment?"

"Yes. But may I say something about ending this talk? One wonderful or terrible thing about this world is that everything comes to a stop. The stops! One must stop pretending, stop making excuses, stop dreaming, hating, loving, forgetting, forgiving and struggling. My control over my life has stopped, too. The ultimate end, perhaps a gift, is the red light that stays red—death, the stop of being. And I seem to be reaching . . ." Then I stop, as if I have dropped something.

Before she has a chance to respond, a furious knock comes at the door. My heart pounds as Sitareh's face pales and her hands begin to tremble. We have feared arrest and expect it now, as if they have already proved us guilty. I protest, "What is it now?" Sitareh throws up her hands. My fears reach my ears, where I feel my lobes burning. The wolves are at the door again, I worry, but I keep my silence.

"A telegram has arrived for Agha Pirooz," Firoozeh announces.

We sigh and bask in a fearless moment of relief. The tumor is not malignant. The telegram comes from my mother. "Leave the war zone and come home without delay," she implores me.

I tell Sitareh, "Note her words, 'Come home.' What times! I must travel continents away from home to be safe at home. Anyhow, ever since I can remember, my mother has been rescuing me from one thing or another."

"Home or not, the war and the Guards are making us paranoid," she answers.

"Not just us, but the nation, even the world."

Chapter Twenty-One: Reincarnation

In the evening Sitareh gently announces that she wishes to sleep in a separate bedroom. "Everything must be proper before we meet Ibn Sina tomorrow. I am sorry, but I cannot help it. A *seegheh* is not a wife, and I'm not ready to be a wife. It is mind before heart, duty before love, and logic before passion. This is our point to stop, as you are fond of saying. We will move on later." I wonder what this could mean.

This time I don't let the question stick in my throat for fear of offending her. "What brought this on? We vowed to keep no secrets."

"I am not keeping secrets from you."

"Then open your soul to my soul, Sitareh."

"You have already come into my home, into my heart, into me. The secret is not in me, but between us."

"It is because I was once Gorgani. It is beneath you to sleep with him, with me, who is not me, but Gorgani. Isn't that it, Sitareh?"

She shuts her eyes as if in pain, before opening them to look reassuringly into mine. "Pirooz-*jon*, please let's not argue now. All will end well." I surrender to her like a prisoner of war, keeping my misgivings to myself, wanting to understand my own deepest feelings before I explain them to the mother of our child. Until midnight we discuss many things, as if to make up for what she will not talk about. Sitareh, warm but unyielding, listens to my grief and holds me in her arms, but we sleep apart.

The next day before sunrise, Sitareh prays on the verandah, enunciating the magnificent holy words, just like my mother. I have not seen her pray before. Is it a change of heart after experiencing the other world?

Distant explosions distract and sadden me even more. The war is a demon that demands its daily sacrifices. Where is Mehr, the god of love and truth? Would She visit Iran—Her place of birth—to comfort it?

Late in the evening, feeling anxious, I drive us to the mausoleum to meet Ibn Sina. Sitareh seems unruffled, and I admire her strength. We are both impatient and uncertain. Will Ibn Sina keep his promise to visit us and reveal his secrets?

"This is the night of discovery," she says. "Will the mausoleum guard leave the gate open, Pirooz?"

"As open as the night we met," I assure her.

"Are you carrying our *seegheh* document with you?"

"Of course. I carry it everywhere," I reply.

She swiftly shifts to another concern. "We must find out if you have been anyone else and why we are together."

I stare at her in disbelief. Even now, despite everything, she talks as if we were just marionettes and our love had not sprung from our own hearts. "Keep your eyes on the road, Pirooz. Please," she says, sensing my sudden change of mood.

"I am who I am now. It is not my identity—over a thousand years ago—which ought to be the question, but whether God heard your morning prayer, Sitareh. I do exist, but does God?" I say sarcastically.

"This is not the time for such comments, Pirooz. I loved you before and I love you now that we sleep apart. God is awake, even in meditation. He hears! He sees! He knows! God exists. I no longer need to understand God's ways to believe in Her or Him. Love is one of His emanations. My love for you is my love for Him, too, and I do not wish to bury it in passion before I learn where we stand. I did what I did because Ibn Sina persuaded me."

"What about our *seegheh* affair?"

"That was for the government, for our safety from the Guards," she says.

"And everything else?"

"All true. My love is for you, then and now. But this journey of spirits is the essence of my life, Pirooz, or else I would not risk so much. I must complete this mission I'm entrusted with as best I can."

Turning a corner sharply, I reply, "I just want to remind you that It was I who made love to you at your request, Sitareh, not a historical figure, and it is I who loves you dearly now, no matter what happens tonight. And it isn't sex I demand, but the intimacy of lovers or parents. I know that an invisible wall separates us right now. I can even touch it. I despise walls, especially hidden ones."

She stares out the window. While I may think of the three of us first, she thinks first of Ibn Sina, so I say no more. Gradually my rage dissolves into resignation, as sorrow melts in the last teardrops of mourners. Maybe I should be more forbearing.

Sitareh and I arrive at the mausoleum early, to be ready to see in the darkness with clear minds. We will let Ibn Sina tell us whatever he wishes, but also ask him what we want to know, especially: Why did he call Sitareh his mother, who am I, why did he bring us together, and what are his intentions?

I bring the car to a screeching halt in the parking lot. "Calm down, Pirooz-*jon*," her concerned voice says.

My heartbeat picks up as we reach the wooden door. A foreboding stillness prevails. We search the darkness like thieves. I push at the door, but it won't move.

"It—is—locked!" Sitareh exclaims, breathless, her pupils widening.

The lock will not yield. We stare at each other hopelessly as though we have missed the last train to eternal bliss. I try to jiggle the latch, but, adamantly, the lock remains locked. Banging on the gate, I declare, "There must be a way."

"This is not the way," she responds coolly. "You will alert the Guards."

My heart pounds. We are both frustrated and apprehensive. What can we do? Our future is locked behind a cold, lifeless contraption. Strange ideas intrude: Hope is hope, reality is reality, and light and darkness do keep apart. The bursts of bombshells in the background signal more deaths. The Guards' demonic laughter echoes in my head. I see a horse's eye shed tears on a smoldering stump.

"Pirooz, where are you?" Sitareh demands. Glancing at her watch with forced calmness, she warns, "We only have one hour to midnight."

We drive to the Ibn Sina Hotel to phone the mausoleum guard. We wait anxiously as irretrievable seconds fly away. A boy answers, and I hear a commotion in the background. "What do you want?" he demands.

"I need to talk to your father."

A long, muted moment ends with a woman moaning and declaring, "My husband is dead. Finished. Gone! A martyr killed by the winged savages who bomb the poor!" She falls silent until at length she screams," We will starve to death."

Speechless, I drop the receiver, unable to untangle our misfortunes.

Sitareh pulls at my sleeve. "Where is he?"

"God bless his soul," I say into the phone and hang up, feeling the heavy weight of time. I turn to Sitareh. "The guard is dead."

She glances at her watch, betraying her anxiety. I want to calm her, but I am not calm myself. "Let's go," she commands. "Our best chance is to be nearby."

At the mausoleum, we examine the lock again before abandoning it like the crew of a sinking ship. Sitareh looks crestfallen. Frustration, disappointment and deep anger sculpt minute ripples across her beautiful face.

Without warning an otherworldly breeze springs up, and we hear the lock click. My heart pounds wildly as I try the latch. "It is unlocked!" I exclaim.

She trembles before finding her tongue. "The dead guard's ghost must have opened it." He did promise you, didn't he, Pirooz?" She meets my doubt head on and firmly twists the point into me.

I hear a hush behind us. When I turn to look, the eyes of a stray cat blaze behind a rosebush, focused on me like those of a wolf or of the Guards watching our illegal entry.

"Let's get going," Sitareh says. I push the door open and we walk into the foyer and thus break the law. Sitareh shuts the door behind us and takes my hand. Only the moon refracted in he skylight disturbs the darkness. "Behold,

Pirooz!" she whispers. "The convergence of two worlds is upon us. We are the chosen ones, so let's prove that we are trustworthy."

Random forebodings gush through my veins as Sitareh calmly guides us to the library. The moon no longer lights our way. We walk cautiously, apprehensively and expectantly. My footsteps question me: Which do you prefer, knowing that you are no more than Gorgani, whom Sitareh would abandon, or living with doubts?

As we enter the library, Sitareh lights the candle she has brought, for we cannot risk the electric light. Fear of being caught stays with me and eats into me like cancer. We sit side by side, stiff under the heavy burden of so much hope and so much dread packed in one crucial moment molding our expectations. The room is as quiet as a Paleolithic cave, with its memories and paintings waiting forever to be discovered and appreciated. I try to get hold of myself. How can Sitareh be so calm?

My watch points to midnight. I pick up Ibn Sina's *Canon* and try to read from a page, hoping to recall something. At a perturbing sound, I stop reading, breathing or thinking, to try to see into the darkness. Suddenly the candle flame becomes distraught, flickering and dipping like a pigeon evading an approaching eagle's claw. Did someone open the door and let a draft in? Soon I perceive a light in motion, an afterglow emerging in the dark. Our hands clench each other's tightly. Anxiety, curiosity and exaltation flutter inside me. My heart pounds in my ears. Abruptly, the shade of Ibn Sina enters the room and approaches us calmly, thoughtfully, it seems. He has arrived! A grave stillness pervades everything, as though the universe were emptied of its contents. We wait and wait. Sitareh's hand has grown icy as centuries whisk backwards. The spirit's words glow in the dark.

"We all do exist, dead or alive!" It is the unmistakable voice of the Philosopher of Existence. In the deep silence, the magic sound of a flute comes softly from afar, soothing our taut nerves. We listen; we need to listen. Sitareh and I glance at each other in amazement. Our beings seem in harmony again, and my fear vanishes.

I sense Ibn Sina's presence at the far end of the table. His words flow easily. "Salaam, my most beloved. Greetings from another world. It is love that bridges times and spaces, the living and the dead. Love, the wisest and most potent force God created. God endowed love with goodness, with the power to create, to heal, and to enhance life. We are all one by virtue of love. God revealed that, when He loves you, He becomes the ear with which you hear, the eye with which you see, the tongue with which you speak, the mind with which you think, and the hand with which you work." Ibn Sina pauses. "I love you both, and I love your togetherness."

"Where are you, Ibn Sina?" Sitareh asks.

"Right opposite you, face to face."

"What are you made of?" I ask.

"Of invisible light with the gift of speech."

"You said you loved us. Why?" Sitareh inquires.

"Because you have the soul of my mother, and because you are lovable."

"And me?" I cannot stay quiet.

"You are the reincarnation of my friend, Gorgani."

"That is all, just another Gorgani? Then why did you maneuver me into this bizarre and dangerous affair with your mother?"

"One question at a time, my dearest. I don't want to shock you prematurely."

Sitareh scowls at my impatience, as if I were at fault for being only Gorgani. Even the candlelight seems confused. Ibn Sina's books that line the shelves appear and disappear in the flame's shadow dance. I burn to know why Ibn Sina wanted me to father Sitareh's child. The candlelight elongates into one motionless flame, waiting.

Very agitated, I let Sitareh direct the inquiry. No need to rush. She is a psychiatrist, who knows how to wait for a crucial revelation. She looks deadly serious, uncompromising. "And—" she begins.

Ibn Sina interrupts, "Oh, Mother, I regret . . . I regret so many things! I feel immensely guilty for abandoning you in Bukhara. I never saw you again after I fled and left you with relatives. But it was you who urged me to flee for my life. I never knew how you lived or when you died. I only heard much later. I agonized why fate split us apart. All my life I remained attached to your memory, to your love, to your mysterious smile, to your teaching me arithmetic before I could run to your lap, where I would place my head to nap in the deepest security and fulfillment possible."

"Why did you wander so much?" Sitareh asks.

"The Prophet took flight, *hijrah*. when in danger, and so did I."

"But *hijrah* includes the return home."

"True. But home was never safe and I had a craving to visit new places, meet new people, even though happiness often ends with the sadness of departure. I would feel a strange boredom, like a statue eternally burdened by bird droppings, if I were to stay in one spot."

"What about stability?" she inquires.

"If it means immobility, then a paraplegic person is very stable, the dead even more so, and Alvand the most stable of all."

"I see," Sitareh says, sounding like an understanding mother.

"I did remain stable in pursuit of the truth that you lullabied as I suckled at your breast, Mother." He stops. Leaden wrinkles tumble to the edge of her face. I hear a sound and imagine the Guards. We wait. He waits, but no one intrudes.

Will someone ask why Gorgani has become Sitareh's lover? I scream soundlessly. I know she wants to know, too. The psychiatrist's patience amazes me and makes me more impatient. We wait forever, it seems, each second getting heavier, slower and older, dragging itself to nowhere.

"Tell me all you know about Gorgani. Please!" she finally asks.

"I hope you will not be alarmed. I have brought you the facts gradually, but now I see you are impatient."

"Please tell us what we want to know. I'm alarmed already!" Sitareh pleads.

"All right, then. Pirooz, you are Gorgani, but Gorgani was the reincarnation of my father." Sitareh gasps loudly, not so much from surprise but from her expectations being fulfilled—a monumental relief, like being reprieved from a death sentence. I drop the *Canon*, and its impact echoes through the deserted mausoleum and upsets the candlelight. For an instant some dark spots in space light up, and some lit spots grow dark. Now I have three identities in one person. The spirit waits for his revelation to sink in. The Earth stops spinning for me, so that I may catch up to events. Everything turns blank, and Sitareh glows in that blankness. Me? That's all I can think. My tongue cleaves to my palate. I feel an excruciating thirst, but also triumph, like having crossed the Sahara in the heat of summer. Sitareh flashes her approving smile, as if I have passed the test of my life.

"After his death, my father took care of me in rebirth as Gorgani. He wanted to help me achieve all I could. He was an enlightened man who strove to see mankind enlightened, too. That is why, no matter how much Gorgani shared my suffering, he never left me. Oh, how grateful I am to you, father dear, Pirooz. I know your sufferings. The fanatics persecuted you for being an Ismaili, whose guilt was his search for the deepest truths of the Holy Book, while the clergy wanted only interpretations that suited them. And now, and now . . ."

He stops and a huge silence grows in the grave and penetrates the dark cavities surrounding us. Why is he silent? Did he leave without letting us know what he wished to reveal? His voice returns. "And now, my most beloved parents, you can bring me to life again through your love for each other, and for me. So—"

"Please, great spirit, complete your story and end our torment!" My anxieties boil over as if everything hung on his next word. Tightening her grip on my hand, Sitareh softly commands me, "Let him speak, dear."

As if listening to her, Ibn Sina continues, "Mother, you have a life in your womb ready to accept a soul. It can be me. I wish to be your son again, so that I may serve you, my mother, in a new life, and make you happy."

I am lost in my own blinding thoughts. Sitareh is as calm as the books looking at us from their shelves, thoughtful as owls, seeing the world as it is. I feel trapped in a fiery spacecraft entering the atmosphere. "It can be me, it can be me," echoes in the candlelight. So Sitareh's pregnancy was no accident.

"Are we somehow your creation?" I say, barely managing to find my tongue.

"I arranged for the angels to copy your souls. Don't you see, I am the first spirit ever to choose his parents, and I selected the ones I had before. A child's greatest compliment is to prefer his own parents to all real and imagined ones before birth or after death. I have chosen you."

"You mean we were the cause of your birth, and you were the cause of ours, and now the cycle repeats itself?"

"Yes, yes. Cause and effect are one, since the effect must already exist in the cause before being actualized. And every effect becomes a cause in its turn."

"But how did you make us fall in love, my son?" I ask.

"I didn't have to, father dear, you were already in love. I just brought you together. Your love has lasted for life after life."

I glance at Sitareh. Her eyes are full of love for me, for the future, for the life within her. I am the man she loves, the one she loved a millennium ago, the one she ought to love, and the man who would father Ibn Sina into bigger times and achievements, perhaps. I have been his father and I will be his father again. I am the one, the only one. Sitareh chose me in ancient times, and Ibn Sina chose me now. I feel pride bubbling inside me for being the object of love of such magnificent souls. I exhort myself: Be humble. Pirooz. Don't let pride consume you.

"How did you manage to recreate us?" I ask. "Please be specific."

"I influenced heavenly events as an intermediary between rival archangels, Michael, Gabriel and Uriel. Maybe God wishes to know what would happen to His creation during His meditation and not to know the future in advance purposefully." Ibn Sina responds and falls silent.

"Unknowns are plentiful in both worlds, then. We have only our curiosity to counter them. Nothing would be known or remain unknown if nothing existed. But in the world that we find ourselves in, we must struggle between knowns and unknowns. Help us to know, Ibn Sina!" I demand.

Sitareh appears pleased but still bent on getting to the bottom of everything. I marvel at the impossible: I am his father, he is my cause. My son has brought me to life. The paradox leaves me dazed, but then I see. We recreate the past by history as the past recreates us biologically and culturally.

"Why did you ask us about modern scientific progress?" I demand.

"Curiosity! To learn as much as possible before my rebirth in this century."

"Why do you want to be reborn?" she asks softly.

"Yes," I add. "Why would you exchange heaven for this hell?"

"I have several reasons," the spirit says. "I have saved many lives, but I have never been the cause of one. I desire the ecstasy of parenthood and want to take care of my own parents in their old age. Also, I long to heal again, for the dead need no healing. I yearn to resume my research free of dissimulation. I could never do that then. Damn the clergy. They kept Ferdowsi from being buried in a Muslim cemetery. They insulted him in death, so he was buried in his own garden, contrary to custom. At any rate, I have been in one place for too long. Growth dies with death, and I long for the great joys of growth again. What joy could surpass continuing one's ascendance? I want a new life."

"So no growth is death," I reply. "Some dissimulation persists. Academic editors or grant officials, decide what is science and what is not or if an inquiry is worthy or not, or what aspect of reality should be included or excluded in the assumptions or the theory itself. To challenge their biases or expertise is professional suicide. And an ancient mentality rules Iran now, so it is no better, if not worse, than in your time."

Ibn Sina remains silent and Sitareh frowns, perhaps objecting to my long comment at this time. But something impelled me to inform Ibn Sina of the reality of my life. At last the spirit replies, "My father also had to dissimulate a thousand years ago. Evidently progress since then has been mostly illusory."

Sitareh finally asks, "How can you become my child again?"

"The human soul enters the embryo once it has acquired human anatomy. But some angels disagree, saying that the human soul enters at conception, because now and then beasts are incarnated in human bodies."

"Fundamentalists on Earth also believe life begins at conception," I add.

"Is that true? Some sublunary conflicts are reflections of heavenly confusion."

"But how can you become my child?" Sitareh insists.

"I know how to fuse myself into your fetus. Your child can be me." His words numb us like tranquilizer shots. A long silence prevails, until the spirit speaks again. "I am not the only frustrated soul. Socrates waited forever for reincarnation. He welcomed death, thinking he would meet Homer, whom he loved more than anything except truth. But alas, Homer was already reincarnated, and Socrates became trapped in the angelocracy, like me. I helped him become reincarnated as a brilliant American professor with radical views, but he still thinks of poison and poisoning. His name is Chomsky, I believe. He finds hemlock superfluous now that there is television to poison people's minds while leaving their bodies alive."

I remember an old puzzle and interrupt Ibn Sina. "Who were the male and female cockroaches in New York?" Sitareh scowls.

"I investigated that for you, Father. They were Sultan Mahmood and Queen Saeedia. Sultan Mahmood will return a thousand times as a cockroach and be crushed a thousand times for being an unjust ruler." Suddenly Ibn Sina's voice becomes alarmed. "Oh, my God! I have only a few minutes left. Since I have chosen you to be my parents again, will you choose me as your child? This is the right moment."

"What if we don't?" Sitareh speaks with a tongue of steel it seems.

"Then either the fetus will not come to term, or it will receive another soul. Please let me know now, do you accept me as your progeny? Do you?"

"Yes, yes, I do," Sitareh says. "Yes, I do, too. We do," I add hurriedly.

The flame of the candle bends toward Sitareh. I feel a huge pulse in her wrist and she sighs as if something like a soul had filled her. She shudders and I shudder with her as she leans on me, placing her head on my shoulder, smiling a happy and weary smile. We know we are the parents of Ibn Sina once more.

"I love you, Baba Pirooz, for yourself," she whispers, reassuring me.

"And history? And humanity? And medicine?"

"I want the best for them, but I don't love them like I love you."

At last the mystery has disclosed itself, freeing me of anxiety. An exhilaration engulfs my several identities.

Suddenly menacing noises shock my eardrums. "We must get out of here," I urge Sitareh. We find our way home in an intoxicated daze. Feeling safe, I fall into a chair, exhausted. "Oh dear, I forgot to ask him what was death," I tell Sitareh.

"It is time to think of life, not death, Pirooz-*jon*." she smiles brilliantly.

Later, I wonder aloud if, in ancient times, Ibn Sina would have considered our story intellectually intelligible.

"What made you bring that up now?" Sitareh inquires.

"It just occurred to me that one of the most important ideas of the great twentieth century philosopher, Wittgenstein, restates Ibn Sina's concept."

"What is that?" The proud mother becomes very curious.

"Wittgenstein wrote that the task of philosophy was 'to set limits on what can be thought, and, in doing so, on what cannot be thought. . . . It will signify what cannot be said, by presenting clearly what can be said.'"

She stares at me, "So what is unthinkable and inexpressible to Wittgenstein is intellectually unintelligible to Ibn Sina." I nod in agreement and hear her whisper, "My genius son!"

Chapter Twenty-Two: Upbringing

After Firoozeh leaves for a summer visit to her family, Sitareh and I spend a few days of unqualified happiness. Sitareh's tranquility and subtle beauty are irresistible. We stroll in the countryside oblivious to everything around us. We feast on the vegetarian dishes Sitareh concocts, we swim, bike, dance, fly kites as high as our joy, and watch the moon nursing the stars. It is all unreal to me. I put my ear to her abdomen and listen to the miracle. When I kiss it, she giggles and pushes me away.

"I love you, Pirooz, and wish to share life after life with you. How glorious that you and I will raise the Leading Wise Man again. I will sacrifice anything for it."

"But loving you would be enough for me, Sitareh-*jon*," I respond. Her voice is as melodic as the sound of the *tar* she plays every evening. I think that one way to know about the mind is to learn how music affects our changes of mood and brings ecstasy or peace to the brain's neurons. Why have I fallen in love with the sounds of her voice and the *tar* chasing each other like sparrows in love?

Days turn like pages in book of poems. No memory haunts me and no foreboding disturbs me, since the present has distilled all my past happiness and all my future dreams. Each moment is complete and absolute; the present holds all the answers. Ibn Sina's reincarnation is a miracle, but so is Creation. We are miracles who know that we are miracles. All we need to do is act like miracles!

"How wonderful! I am a miracle in love, according to Pirooz-*jon*," she exclaims.

Sitareh and I visit the widow of the mausoleum guard and comfort her, but she weeps for her daughter, crippled in the bombing raid. Sitareh promises to seek help in repairing her humble home.

One day a harbinger of autumn appears: a few leaves, like girls in their first make-up, are tempted to fall from the height of their innocence. As the leaves begin to fall, I know that we need to plan for our new life together. Our temporary marriage is due to end soon and I must leave this war-torn and suppressed country to return to New York. Will she come with me? Somehow I hesitate to ask.

I am a snowshoe hare, anxious that my pelt won't change from russet to solemn white for the first snowfall, while hungry wolves howl on the horizon. My life since I met Poonia seems like a fiction that I have co-authored with history. But a chapter is missing; a gust of wind flings the lost pages across a meadow at the foot of Mount Alvand, and I mourn the scattered ideas, their meanings lost. What is wrong with me? I feel like a soul alone but I don't know why. Who but me governs my feelings, but who is me? Maybe I am not used to happiness and distrust its loyalty, as if it were a lover. Something is ruffling Sitareh, too. What is wrong with her? I dread her single-mindedness and independence, I must admit, but how could my happiness blow away with one frown? What should we do, with two countries but one life together?

After dinner, Sitareh sits beside me on the living room sofa. I put my hand on her belly, and she puts her hand on mine and smiles affectionately. "Do you like our togetherness?" I ask as I stroke her hand.

"More than anything. You beside me are as comforting as the life within me, yet it is all so confounding. No happiness can top that of lovers reunited after a long voyage between two worlds."

"Our love, who is both you and me, is inside you," I whisper.

"Yes," She pauses. "He is most precious for us and for everyone."

She sounds strangely formal. Am I a victim of a false sense of danger? I think, but continue, "I have been thinking about Ibn Sina's upbringing, Sitareh."

"So have I, Pirooz. What is on your mind?"

"We were married in ancient times—should we not marry again for his re-birth?"

"You sound aggrieved."

"Well, we should settle everything before leaving," I remark softly.

"Leaving for where?" She sounds alarmed.

"Leaving Iran together, I hope. If that is impossible, you can join me later."

She stares through me. "I asked you once where you wanted us to live, and you said, 'Not in Iran.' Is that still your answer, despite Ibn Sina's resurrection?"

"Is that a problem, Sitareh-*jon*?" I ask as warmly as I can.

"Of course it is!" she says, her tone becoming impersonal. "First of all, you assume I will follow wherever you go, period. Well, this woman will not be defined by or follow any man, even for love. I defy the chains fastened on my gender, Pirooz."

"But love is not a chain."

"Exactly! Love should be blind to gender. You can follow me just as I can follow you. Women can no longer afford to behave sweetly and obediently, as expected of them. They must become as tough and devious as men, to defend their own identity, even to defend men from men by stopping wars."

Surprised, I decide simply to listen to her. "Ibn Sina was born and raised in Iran. He ate Persian food, spoke Persian, read Persian history, and heard Persian music. He studied medicine, the Koran, science and philosophy and Sufism. He dreamed in Persian! How could he recover his true identity in America, with its standardized tests, televised rubbish and junk food? An

American school will teach him: 'Pay attention and do as you are told!'—the opposite of Ibn Sina's self-education and creative thinking. No leading wise man could be raised in the U.S. today."

"Indoctrination and insecurity here are also harmful to creativity," I reply.

"I've never met an American who wasn't insecure. There, insecurity triumphs over sympathy. You admitted that you've been cowed to dissimulate for so long that now you feel more real when you are acting than when you are yourself. You also said that the U.S. pursues irrational goals with ever more rational means and that Americans need the media to tell them what they see, or what to do as if they had no eyes, or will, of their own." Her hypnotic eyes fall on mine like a prosecutor about to hammer her point through me.

"Listen, Sitareh-*jon*."

"I am listening, Pirooz-*jon*!" She sounds impetuous, even angry.

I struggle to be calm realizing that she is pregnant, and testy. "Arts and sciences and artifacts like beautiful mosques, are valuable sediments of the past, but ought not be duplicated. Ibn Sina wants to ask new questions, discover new answers, and create new ideas and follow new paths of understanding towards perfection, not to regress to the imperfections of the past. Persia is no longer the intellectual center of the world. He deserves the best, but instead mullahs will hang him by his tongue." I try to wear a smile as I finish.

"As a start he will find enough science here and he will teach himself as before. Ibn Sina knows how to survive the clergy, and to create. But do you think the best place for him is where God is dead, Pirooz?" She asks querulously with a flash of irritation reddening her face.

"I never knew you were so religious. Once you said you didn't know what religion really was." My voice weakens, as I gaze almost hopelessly at her defiance.

"I am religious now. What else can I possibly be? He spoke to us from another world, didn't he? Ibn Sina believes in God, doesn't he?"

"But Ibn Sina has not seen God, either—just like us." I finish and realize that the undeniable miracle is causing conflict between us.

"Face it, Pirooz, you do enjoy the U.S. version of comfort, and safety."

"What is wrong with comfort and safety? Bombs do kill children here, and everyday living is a high wire act." I assert.

She swallows a gulp of air as if it were vinegar "I was mugged and nearly raped when I was at Johns Hopkins; my apartment was burglarized; and I had to fend off the sexual advances of the chief of residents—all in one year! There are no bomb shelters for such attacks." She runs her hand through her hair nervously. "These are ugly times in the U.S., times of cash and trash accumulation. Job insecurity, ethical erosion, and crime leave no one safe. It is dreadful to live in a country where tycoons get rich on the backs of the poor, where food is plentiful but hunger persists, and where the indifference and rage are tragic twins, and yet the Presidents do behest the rest of the world to imitate U.S. I will not allow my son to grow up among people who are losing faith in themselves, in their leaders and their past, and are frightened of their future."

Her revelation nails my tongue still. A painful silence befalls us. I'm shocked. Finally I mange to say, "I abhor the horrible acts perpetrated against you, as all decent Americans do, but could we not live in a serene, and safe college town?"

"A charming veneer is not enough for me. Children are abused privately while adored publicly, women are battered but the family values praised, even in those serene little towns. Would he become a sage in a society where image is everything—even democracy, even compassion, even religion?"

"Sitareh, there is no heaven on earth. Ibn Sina knows that! Compare countries, please! Life is a torture in Iran. We can avoid the worst in the U.S., and take advantage of the best. No?"

With a twitch in her face, she replies, "I am comparing! Life is a subtle torture for most Americans. Many citizens are insane or are losing their minds. Even the old shrinks need shrinks." Sitareh circles around disturbingly. She is not the one I knew. I step to her and gently take her by the arms. "Calm down please, Sitareh-jon."

She withdraws her arms. "Impossible! We cannot block now-ism, me-ism, sexism, racism, and chauvinism from polluting his innocent mind. From TV—the archangel Gabriel, as you called it—kids learn to demand, 'I want it now!' as if nothing else mattered."

"But Persian TV is nothing but manipulation," I counter.

"At least there is no sex, violence or alcohol—"

"Maybe not, but it promotes intolerance and glorifies war."

"American television belittles or demonizes other countries, while portraying the U.S. as righteous. War is the great American art. Santa Claus brings children toy guns and video games that extol mass destruction. Natural sciences are used to produce gruesome weapons for profit, and social sciences are used to fool the unwary—by justifying the status quo. So scientists are turned into gutless, shameless apologizing eunuchs." She pauses then raises her voice: "Pirooz, wake up! The U.S. pilot who incinerated Nagasaki with an atom bomb announced, 'It was the thrill of my life,' and everybody applauded him. They have a million lawyers and even more prisoners and still their leaders scream for more police, judges and prisons, but not proper upbringing. It is their system, not genes, that produces the highest crime rate in the world. But they would never admit it. No flesh and blood of mine will become a careerist eunuch if I can help it." She stares straight into my eyes.

Agitated, I remind myself: Pirooz, the object is to convince her, not to defeat her. Be calm, be tender to dear Sitareh, the mother of your son. I let her empty her rage, even on me if necessary, for I remember the night of the mock execution and how tenderly she revived my spirit. But I also note that she withheld her terrible ordeal in Baltimore from me until today. What else is she keeping from me?

Sitareh sighs an angry sigh: "And their laws in medicine! They fight terminal diseases with gadgets. This is torture for profit—a new industry! Meanwhile the curable poor are abandoned to pain and death. U.S. medicine is too much drugs, too much surgery, too much fear of lawsuits, defensive therapy, and attention to who pays, but too little prevention, and too little concern for the patient as a person. Ibn Sina would be crushed if he tries to fight the system."

"That is hell you describe, not the U.S., where immigrants clamor to get in."

"Western Europeans prefer where they are. The U.S. is a haven only for the poor and persecuted," she replies. "A drowning man will latch on even to a crocodile."

"Our home was invaded; I was injured. Remember?" I respond desperately.

"It was savage, but all we had to do was show them a certificate."

I gasp. "You are raising your voice," I say, my fingers clenching tightly.

Her lips crease and she hisses, "Do the decibels really matter?"

I breathe deeply and take a sip of water, slowly. "No, not really." I stare back feeling torn and distant from her. She seems enraged, as though reliving a horror, maybe the ones in Baltimore.

"What is your main objection, Pirooz?" she demands, her voice lowered.

"Can Ibn Sina research freely and publish his discoveries here?" I ask.

"He won't have to until he is older." She hesitates. Nervously I chuckle internally, but she resumes shooting arrows. "But if he is raised to be a salaried eunuch, he will never challenge boards of trustees, deans or indoctrinated students for fear of being sent into academic oblivion. Truth is perilous in the U.S., isn't it?"

I hear the howling of a tempest in my brain. "Not everyone is a eunuch. He won't be one. Some U.S. scholars are as critical as you are, Sitareh."

"Most of them are powerless, voiceless, lost, good souls all wasted."

"This regime sentences even the foreign writers to death, remember that."

"They will turn Ibn Sina into a weapons expert or a corporate magnate in the U.S. This is worse than the death sentence, Pirooz! I want him to grow up where people love nature, not rape it, where even the illiterate can quote Hafiz, where elders are respected, not junked like old refrigerators; where life is more than business. And God is in the hearts of people, not just printed on money, sung in anthems, used by greedy evangelists or pronounced dead. The U.S. poisons nature and corrupts the human soul—God's most wonderful creations. America is at war with God."

"God is a victim here, too," I interrupt. "Firoozeh said that."

She grimaces in surprise before resuming. "Remember, Ibn Sina preferred Iran to anywhere else and Sufism to materialism."

"Why not let him decide, then?"

"How? Tell me how, Pirooz. Maybe if he speaks from my womb."

"I hope he just does that; he has done everything else!" I pause for a long moment and speak as calmly as I can, "I don't want him raised here; you don't want him raised there. Sitareh-*jon*, how about somewhere else?"

"Iran is the only practical answer. Despite all its pitfalls, it is the culture from which Ibn Sina emerged. As his nest, Iran is the risk I will take." Her eyes sparkle like those of a lioness defending her cub.

Firoozeh comes in with a bowl of fruit. Her beautiful eyes shed fear like teardrops. I am shocked when Sitareh frowns and waves her away unkindly.

Ignoring my point, Sitareh continues. "Ibn Sina is a great gift to humanity, and he will not go anywhere without me."

"What do you mean?" my voice wavers.

"I mean, he is inside me, attached to me cell by cell! You can be with us too."

"But he couldn't possibly be inside me," I respond, as I look at Ibn Sina's poster reflected in the mirror, watching us. My mind smolders, and I sense the smoke.

"It is God's will that you are a man and I am a woman."

"God is unfair, Sitareh."

"That is just your American righteousness!"

"This debate is outrageous."

"You mean that my position is outrageous, don't you, Pirooz?" She drills her stare straight through me, looking as angry as I feel.

"Am I a compromising eunuch?" I ask.

"You dissimulate too much, Pirooz."

"Don't you dissimulate, too? Wearing the chador and all?"

"Yes, I dissimulate when there is absolutely no choice," she replies.

"But you judge me."

"Not unless you ask."

"I love you, Sitareh, don't you see?"

"Yes, but only on your terms," she softens her voice.

"Do I have any say about my son?"

"Not the final say!"

"But that's all that matters."

"That's how it will be. You will get used to it!" Each word is a hammer blow. You. Will. Get. Used. to it. My heart chills from the coldness in her green tiger eyes.

How could I share my life with her, I ask myself, but only say, "That's my fate, then. I must choose to live in a world according to you."

"I am what I am. Remember, the world isn't flat like a map."

I wince at the blows of her childish defiance, and blood gushes inside me, filling my stomach. A fire sweeps through my mind as I explode with rage, screaming, "How the hell can you be so cocksure? Even God's revelations are not so assertive. No wonder no one can agree on interpreting the Koran. God damn your clever debate and stubbornness! Damn your sudden piety, your brand of dissimulation and feminist righteousness! Damn your words of love for me! Damn the invisible wall between us! Damn my helplessness! Damn this world as I find it." Then I stop, at the edge of a cliff, and my vertigo is unbearable.

"Say what you really want to say, Pirooz! Be specific Say it! 'Damn Iran, damn Ibn Sina, damn his upbringing, damn women's liberation, and damn you, Sitareh!' Get it off your chest! Damn everything!"

Her bleak anger wrings my guts. Rage blinds me. I yank off my shoe and hurl it at the mirror that reflects me, her, Ibn Sina's poster and the world. The glass shatters, but its antique frame holds our fractured faces.

"Throw the other shoe at me. I am the obstacle. Me, Pirooz. Let Ibn Sina know everything!" She hisses. Our gazes lock like bulls' horns in the ensuing silence.

"Let him. Let him hear you, too, Sitareh." I point at the poster.

She examines the cracked mirror on the ledge, as if to see if she is herself. Her profile shines copper red under the chandelier; while the other side of her face reflected in the mirror is slashed, making her appear two-faced. The image of Ibn Sina's forehead is fractured across his eyebrow. He looks hurt. My face in the mirror's corner is from a Chagall landscape, green and black, a cross between man and beast.

Sitareh plucks a cigarette from a drawer and stuffs it in her mouth, chewing it unlit between her teeth. Is she grinding the words she wants to censor? A mystic thread between us has snapped, and I feel as if I'm falling through the ice. I struggle to grab something but shiver in shock, as uncertainty creeps up the back of my neck like an ice cube with sharp claws.

I wait in stifling silence as we avoid eye contact. The chasm that yawns between us is unbridgeable, so I step to the window, trembling and suffocating as I did at Poonia's funeral, when I could not finish the eulogy. Is this another death in my life?

My sorrows that I thought had disappeared return with a vengeance to assault me as I try to cast away my anger. The sky sparkles and the view calms me, reminding me how transitory the cares of this life are. It is a cool, clear night, and I wish I were also cool and clear. But the stars twinkling on the blue apron of the moon seem to mock my despair. Trying to gauge her, I wonder if

I am being fair. How far is Sitareh from her true self, or is she closest to it now? How far am I from my true self? Am I a reincarnation of Chagall's bull-man?

The cracks in the mirror are fault lines that pull Sitareh, Ibn Sina and me apart. Is this the end of our togetherness that survived death? A sudden pang in my abdomen reminds me that my father died of a bleeding ulcer. His last letter reached me after he was already dead. I loved him so much—it is odd that I would think of him at this moment. But Sitareh may resent leaving her aging parents, and her trauma in Baltimore could account for her harsh judgment of the U.S. But is she letting these things cloud her vision? Am I not attached to my work and family?

Standing with my back to Sitareh, I see the futility of trying to convince her by comparing values, cultures, possibilities or futures. It is easier to subdue than to convert, but even if I had the power to subdue her, I wouldn't. I would not violate her strong resolve. Thoughts of living away from them choking me, I turn around. She is watching me, now waiting for my words like the psychiatrist that she is.

"Sitareh, I am very sorry."

"I understand."

"No good comes from hurting one another."

"I agree," she answers with a subtle chill in her voice.

I walk to her and she takes a step toward me and lets me embrace her. I look into her eyes and feel her tears. She shivers in my shivering.

I cradle her head on my shoulder. "But I am his only father, Sitareh-*jon*."

"Iran is his only home, too, where the love of his grandparents awaits his arrival." She smiles warmly and continues, "Dear Pirooz, be what you were, be what you ought to be, renounce your desires, and help me raise him here. I would give up everything for him, and I ask you to do the same."

I whisper, "My God, must I renounce everything? What is the matter?"

Softly but firmly she responds, "The matter is settled!"

"We only talked about where to bring him up, not how."

"Where and how are nearly the same, Pirooz."

I let go of her, looking at her at arm's length. Sitareh looks at me with sympathy, knowing the storm has spent itself.

It seems so simple for her. In the U.S. greed implants false ideas, and in Iran power censors good ideas. Which is worse? My options seem to be self-confinement here at home or alienation abroad, and probably a bleeding ulcer either way. The unknown became known, and sorrow became happiness for a moment, and then it all vanished, like fireflies mating in the dark, the male dying right away and the female after she lays her eggs. I fear losing too easily what was nearly impossible to find—Ibn Sina. "Why, Sitareh?" I ask her. "Why does each word distance us further? How wrong can either of us be?

Must we let our differences, or our indifference, dissolve our love and commitments? Why does the invisible wall between us grow thicker? Our words, ideas, even skins flow through it like light through glass, but it stops something vital between us, perhaps our totalities. Maybe our isolation is inevitable; even within us, our heart and mind often stand apart."

She answers calmly, "Dear Pirooz! We two are who we are, and the two societies are what they are. Nothing fits. No one is wrong. The West cares about things and the East the essence of things—a simplification, admittedly, but broadly true. And when the West tries spiritualism and the East materialism, they seem out of place—pretentious or lost. Ibn Sina, if we raised him in the West, would grow up barren, neither Westerner nor Easterner, like a poem of Hafiz in translation."

"But ignorance is the cost of purity. Cultures can learn from each other," I suggest gently. She remains silent, but since she is the one who carries the baby, I give in, at least for now. "Sitareh, let me think about this tonight."

"All right, Pirooz-*jon*." Her voice sounds charming, as though nothing has happened. I am baffled by her changeability. Her lovely face holds no answers. I kiss her goodnight. I kiss Ibn Sina good-night, too, in my mind. Then I give her one big hug. I walk to my bedroom struggling with melancholia, alienation, despair, a burning anguish. I fight in vain to push them away, but sleep will not come. Her goodnight kiss tastes bitter, like an unwanted good-bye. I know her mind is set.

I remember that in ancient times in Bukhara she stood up to her father—a most unusual deed for a woman then—to marry me. A girl of sixteen, she had seen me, a guest in her house, through the crack in a doorway and dared to court me in secret. I was in love with her then as I am now. But we are not the same persons, even though we have the same souls, because our upbringing is different. I must fight my own upbringing to learn to seal my thoughts tightly to survive in Iran. Upbringing; the word is alive, and I picture a movie of prehistoric life, with mankind acquiring language and consciousness, and brought up by a self-created history. The whole species needs a new upbringing. Sitareh saw only greed and decadence in the U.S., and I saw rigidity and repression in Persia. We ignored how much good remains in both countries.

A silence grows in my throat like a rose. At the window I see all the things that speak to me in their tongues. The flowerbed below, wrapped sweetly in the moonlight, reminds me that temporariness is permanent for everything, and I, too, am temporary. A bird perched on a willow suggests patience. A huge oak gives me a lesson in serenity, tenacity, and the constant search for light. It tells me, I constantly battle three thousand enemies—insects and bacteria and elements—and I have survived for three hundred years! You can do it, too. The pond shimmering in the moonlight tells me to look clearly at myself and the world reflected in it and to find who I am, what I am, and where I am and must go. The breeze sweetly whispers a calming lullaby: This pond is smart, but her advice is impractical. Some things will never be known. That is why I will change my mind, if I must, to find the easiest path. Ancient Alvand presides over everything, counseling forbearance, and the sky is a sparkling tent over the shadows laid by walls and trees. A couple of doves soar on high, trying to catch stars in their beaks. All things seem pegged to something else. The stars sing: "This too will pass. Afire, we witness and silently expire. Follow us, understand, burn and expire."

The whole universe is within reach. I touch the land, the sky, life, happiness, sadness, even the unbelievable God. I breathe the night air deeply and I water the rose of silence in my throat. Strengthened by a new sense of union with all things, I listen; I listen to the inspiring voice of love. Nature senses it, too, for light, photosynthesis, life, mind, society, beauty, and love are all her inventions. In flowers, butterflies, birds, even in Sitareh's eyes, beauty attracts mates or pollinators. Only the beautiful survive the contest, like the best poems, melodies or paintings, which live to inspire souls forever. Nature holds an inner life, a mystery, and when man kills anything, he kills a part of that mystery, which is a part of himself, without knowing what it was that he killed. If God is in our minds, then He is in nature's mind, too, since our mind is nature's. I am you and you are me. I look to my right and I look to my left, and I find neither Hell nor Heaven. I look within and find them both.

The moon winks at me. Nagging doubts and the pain of separation will hound you if you leave Sitareh and Ibn Sina, it says. Stay in Iran, Pirooz! The stars advise me, Shine with Sitareh and Ibn Sina. Seek liberty within yourself. Become an instructor at home and teach what is possible. Love will ease your difficulties.

I swallow some starlight like a starved man and feel its sparkle within me. I will live tongue-less in Iran, and yet I will triumph by helping to raise Ibn Sina and leaving the country when Sitareh sees the light. Meanwhile I will enjoy nature with my wife and son. No regime can censor their beauty from me. Finally at peace, I gaze through the window and hear the chorus of all things around me: "In God's mind we were once mere ideas. In existence we speak His mind." I squeeze my resolve in my heart and finally fall into a deep sleep.

Early in the morning, I wake to see the moon shadow of Sitareh praying on the balcony. I go back to sleep with the joy of having seen her shadow and faintly heard her prayer beginning, "In the name of God the merciful and compassionate." I wish all Muslims would practice these heavenly attributes of God.

Later a knock at the door wakes me, and Firoozeh hands me a note.

Dear Pirooz,

Circumstances dictate this hurried note. I am afraid that you cannot survive in Iran, not the way you are. I have no time to explain, but I fear you will try to change my mind if I stay beyond this morning. I shall contact you when it is appropriate. Please don't come seeking us. I am taking your gift, the tree of life, with me. The butterfly is still in flight and will stay close to me wherever I go.

With all my love,
Sitareh

Her words slice through me with the force of a dagger's thrust. Fear spreads inside me like a brushfire, burning everything in its path. I cry until I am burned out. Why? No ultimatum, no waiting for my decision. She knew I would agree to stay with her, but she didn't think I could. She rejected me, severed me from her and Ibn Sina, cut me out like a malignant tumor. "My life is malignant! Everything I touch dies!" I scream over and over. Why did Ibn Sina suggest I come to Iran? Did he mean to sacrifice me so he could enjoy life again? Just that! I am just a tool—a damn fool. Shocked, enraged, helpless, isolated, despairing, I weep like one who after an arduous journey home finds that home is not where he left it.

I take a long walk, with nowhere else to turn, realizing that the ambiguity of daybreak has snatched away my hope. I ask my shadow to stop following me. Drop dead, it replies. I would prefer to disappear, too. I do not want to be your shadow!

Just when I had accepted my fate, my fate rejected me, just like my shadow.

I wander the streets aimlessly, as I did in New York on the day of Sitareh's funeral. In a poor neighborhood. I pass dispossessed people scattered like weeds, but I am blind, no less than the authorities. My mind is not where my eyes are. From nowhere sick and poorly-clad children surround me, begging fiercely for some change. I give them what I have mechanically but cannot hear their thanks, or their demands for more. A young veteran, his leg amputated, drives them away with his crutch. I give him some paper money. At that, a pocket of veterans, some missing legs or faces, pushes toward me. I dig into my wallet for more bills. They are not beggars, they have been forced to beg. In their eyes I can see the dead and dying—the battle casualties choking the Karoon River that flows along this narrow alley.

A gruesome moaning swiftly hauls me back to reality. Beside a mud wall to my right, a knot of people huddle. Together they form a single fearsome being. They look like lepers, seeming to hug each other from the dread of disease. But this is no leper colony, and they wear their horror masks for no holiday. My

God, they are victims of mustard gas, the yellow poison that eats away flesh like speeded-up leprosy. I put the rest of my cash into the pile of hands and tormented souls and run away from the nightmare. But it follows me home and into my dreams that night. I am in a madhouse, with the mad getting madder, and my sanity slipping away from my sight.

The next day, I pace nervously in the garden, tormented by guilt that all I could do for my desperate countrymen was to throw some money at them and run away. Shame on me! My loss and guilt cut me to pieces like a pair of scissors. Firoozeh watches me and knows what has happened. I must understand what has happened myself. Who is Sitareh? What do I know about her, the woman I thought I knew a thousand years ago? Where did she come from, and where has she gone? Our invisible wall stood firm, no matter what I did. The few things I know about her are vague, like distant lights shimmering through a thick fog. I know little about her brother who died in a car accident or her parents in Teheran. Perhaps her mystery attracted me. I know she was tender, considerate, patient, reasonable, yet unpredictable. She was charming, resolute, bright a brilliant cook and debater. She was a truly strong-willed Persian feminist who wore the chador only out of necessity. She lifted me from the gravestone in the mausoleum, she fed me, shared secrets with me, and made love to me unexpectedly with spontaneous passion. She held aloof when she thought I was merely Gorgani, but, once she learned I was Ibn Sina's father, she returned with an armful of love. She proposed marriage, withdrew the proposal, became my *seegheh*, but deserted me. Ibn Sina was everything to her. She even turned to God, devoted enough to pray like my mother. Then we argued and she fled, even knowing I would consent to her plans.

She surprised me at every turn, from beginning to end, dictating the terms of our relationship all along. She never lied, but she never told me everything, either. I must still decipher those blank spaces between her words, where what was unsaid said the most, though not for my ears.

Perhaps she asked about Ibn Sina's life and Sufism so persistently to decide if I was capable of living in Iran with her, but I admired rebellious Sufis, implying that I'm oblivious to my own safety. So I failed the interview and the final test. Her cold words haunt me: "You will get used to it."

I thought our love led us, but to where I wonder now? Why couldn't I discover it before it was too late? I was possessed from the beginning, thinking, whenever I had doubts, that she was a resurrection of Sitareh Poonia, when the two were worlds apart. How could you be so naive, Pirooz? I kept my eyes shut, and my mind, too, and saw only my wishful thinking, and neglected to pursue the truth. I admired her dedication to Ibn Sina, heard her reasons, understood her curiosity, but I failed to understand her intentions. I didn't resist her assertion that women should become tough and devious like men.

She brilliantly explained away everything she did, and I never pushed her to the end, because I feared the end. Was I blind, or was I afraid to know the truth? I have a terror that one day every vagueness will become cruelly clear to me. The loss of all comforting illusions would be a bitter end. I feel pain and uncertainty mixed with anger, but no insight to help me see through my insistent mental fog. If only to soothe my torment, I blame myself for everything.

A bitter smile comes to my dried-up face. When I was with Sitareh, time entered into my body and my body entered into time, while I missed the importance of what was passing by. I was so lost in our pursuit of the future and the ancient past that I forgot the present, the person, or the thought I loved.

I hardly asked Sitareh about this life of hers, and she hardly asked about mine. We pledged our love, searched for a spirit, and neglected to know each other. Who was she, anyhow? Who is she now? I ask myself, repeatedly.

Hearing morbid answers from nowhere, and seeing the faces of the mustard gas victims, I cover my eyes. These are your answers, Pirooz, answers for a man who wore a blindfold. The answers are maddening, they are made of foul noises, stink, smoke, and repetitions, like a chainsaw thrashing back and forth in a blue smoke inside my head.

At last a temporary peace befalls me as what she told me, "You will get used to it," begin to sound less brutal. To ward off dark thoughts, I compose an imaginary letter to Sitareh.

Sitareh-*jon*, I write. I will journey to you through a pack of wolves in a wood and swim a shark-infested sea if you tell me where you are. I know that with you I will be in the freest place I can be. I will ask you who made you what you are, why you decided for us that we must part. This time you will tell me everything. Everything! You will let me know you, even the slow me! This is not the final page. Not yet! I will let nothing come between us but love. Love is our journey and our destination.

I write letter after letter in my mind and send them to an imaginary address. But Sitareh answers none of them.

Depression is a vampire latched onto my insides, as I look at my shoe, pretending to reprimand it for its high-flying escapade. "I threw you at myself for letting you take me to this sadness here." You threw me at your own fate, it replies. But give me a chance, and I will take you to happiness there. "We will see," I reply.

Then the futility of my efforts hits me. She is saving me from what? The shoe will take me where? Shoes only go where we take them. Am I a shoe worn by someone invisible who takes me where I don't want to go?

My birth cast me into the web of life. But liberty is possible—suicide would free me into an infinity of death—my choice, not my shoe's, not Sitareh's, not Ibn Sina's, not even God's. No one consulted me if I wished to start my life, and I will consult no one when I want it to stop. I will turn on the red light myself.

So this is a farewell, the end of my magic journey. Who cares that I was young once, am in love now, my story is untold, God's creations are so imperfect, or if I live or die? I wish to phone the Divine Being, but I must dial infinity, the impossible, so I give up. Nevertheless I scream in the direction of the stars: "This is all senseless. The universe, Your creation, is senseless to me. What must I do, Almighty God?"

My inner voice overcomes the indifferent, isotropic cosmic background hum. "By now you ought to know! Cross the man-made boundaries. Life and death are two stages of being, and no one knows which is more beautiful, or ugly. You know that now. It is all up to you, Pirooz."

Chapter Twenty-Three: Death Is Beautiful

The solemnity of autumn surrounds Mount Alvand as I sit in the garden under a weeping willow, with no bottom to my sadness. Like me, the branches reach for their roots despairingly. What am I going to do, now that Sitareh and Ibn Sina have vanished behind a curtain of time, years in thickness? All seasons past and future have shriveled to a moment that I must cross now, the only moment that is truly mine. I cannot resume my professional life in New York, nor can I stay here in Iran. I feel homeless. I am immortal only in my imagination. All souls are! I find a resolve inside me stronger than me. What is it?

I consider Iran and find her twisting in agony. Where are the friendships, the smiles and laughter, the men of letters and good will? What happened to the great attribute of God, compassion, which Muslims ought to emulate? Is there one good Muslim in authority? They silence, exile and execute critics and call it holy. Is it right to kill for Islam, even if all believers could agree on interpreting God's will, although they have not since the Prophet's times? If dogma is so clear, why do interpretations and interpretations of interpretations proliferate? Wherever I turn, I must close my eyes and cover my ears and shut down my mind, since reality torments me.

Inexplicably, the new street names in Hamadan zoom from my mind like bees disturbed in their hive. An official who renames a thing does not make himself its builder, only a thief of history. The unfamiliar names and estrangements add to my uprootedness.

My transcendental journey hasn't gotten me anywhere. I tried to direct my deeds towards the immortality of mankind. What are beauty, justice, love, truth, even God, if not ideas residing in the human mind? How can they prosper and become universal, in a far distant future unless the mind becomes immortal and unveils the ultimate truth?

I have resisted all the attempts of authorities—even teachers, even my parents—to mold me against my will into someone I was not meant to be but they thought I ought to be, for their own mundane interests. I held on to my own consciousness rather than absorb theirs. I scream. I have been screaming all along: I won't harm a soul. Let me be—let me be myself. But the world is hard of hearing, lost in its own concerns, and I am just a noisy nobody, spent, nearly wasted, shouting at nothing specific. Everyone is a censor by not listening or by appearing to disapprove of what is not yet said.

To survive professionally with dignity, I have walked a tightrope, while deluding myself that I could strip the Establishment of its pretensions. What foolish ambition, doomed from the start. Doomed! The system subtly ambushed me, subverted me and swallowed me whole. I longed for acceptance, even praise, from colleagues and from a world I disapproved of. How vain and contradictory! I wanted to tear all pretensions to shreds, but instead, I stitched them into a cloak to wear like everyone else. I complained about ancestor worshipping, but I'm guilty of it myself. I failed to de-program myself from my upbringing. The great Hafiz would not have wished to kill young poets by shadowing them out of limelight; why should we? If I have to pretend in death, then I know I am in Hell. I find a resolve inside me more powerful than my will to live.

True, I had noble ideals, but my reaction to Sitareh proved that my feminism is shallow. My allegiance to human rights is alloyed with elitism. I am not sure if I could live and die among the wretched for whom I have struggled without end. A failure not only in appearance, only to the world, I have failed my own soul.

So, what went wrong? I walk into the house and look in the broken mirror. How many doomed loves can my heart hold without tearing apart, I ask my shattered reflection? How many knots can my mind hold without becoming insane? I have fought off suicidal despair before, but can I do it once again? How can I live in this world without Sitareh and my son? Wishes, fulfilled or not, evolve into memories, and memories inspire new wishes and dreams, but the cycle is over for me.

Staring into the past I find undesired surprises and time taking me to destinations unmarked even on an imaginary map. My alienation, insecurity and, more so, dissimulation, have cut my soul to pieces like expert butchers, like this mirror. Happiness is a disloyal lover who will sleep with anyone but stays with no one. We have led happiness astray, turned her into a whore, by not ornamenting it with immortal values. I can accept life's ambiguity, and death's inevitability, but only on my own terms. They are facts, but I can and will espouse them as if they were my own choices. My last self-delusion brings an inner freedom even some peace.

Again I ask myself: If I am not where Sitareh and Ibn Sina are, then where am I? And if I cannot change anything, then what am I? Alas, another lost opportunity, like my life, like mankind winged to ascend to infinity—spiritually, intellectually and physically and master everything from beginnings to the ends—but tied fast to its bestial roots on earth. Yes we have the wings but not the will—not yet. Who can we blame for these lost opportunities but ourselves? Who can I blame for the murders of Sitareh Poonia, my uncle, the mausoleum guard, Firoozeh's sister, the unknown citizens, Sitareh's white horse, or for the aching in my eyes from what I have seen, and the soreness in my ears from what I have heard? I wish the bombs had hit me. What is the ultimate cause of these losses? Of my losses? Damn it, my being is sordid! A resolve grips me from inside. It is death.

I no longer rationalize by placing blame, which makes right from wrong in one's mind. Blame enlightens nothing, heals nothing. Sitareh is blameless, whether she possesses the best or the worst instincts. She did what she thought best. I cannot blame the world, or my fate, because I do not know what they are.

No voice emboldens me to go on living. I must fight my suicidal mood, but with what? This world is not for me, not any more, not this time around. Nothing in me desires life, not my mind, not my heart. Even my white blood cells declare in unison, "We are tired of fighting for your life. Give up, Pirooz." And I reply, "I am tired of feeding and defending you, too." My soul is eager to leave my body, like a wild bird struggling with beak and claw against a trap. I want to be free from my own memories and dreams, which torment me now. I stare at Alvand and scream: "Be my witness, old mountain! My God is truth; my happiness is love; and my soul is mine. No authority will tear us apart." Alvand concurs with its eternal silence.

The maid rushes into the room. "Is anything wrong, Agha?" she pleads with her magical eyes that seem to see everything.

"No, Firoozeh Khanoom (lady), but I wish to be alone."

When she leaves, I see her tears through the window.

I suffer an unbearable aloneness, like a sticky dusk. Perhaps death is less harrowing than life, where being myself is safe. Now facing two gates—life or death—I wonder which one to enter. What is beyond each of them? I missed my chance to ask the spirit what death was. Is it relief? Reward for a difficult life? Anything? Something? Everything? Nothing? What is nothingness? What could my nothingness be: perhaps a void lost in eternity? A void in eternity may be just a name lost in an obscure corner of the Milky Way. My name. I want some answers before I do what I must do, but I'm not going to get them, like everything else I never got.

Suicide is the pinnacle of pessimism and the end of blame. That may be the gate I must enter. I remember Attar's couplet:

> Be nothing first! And then you will exist;
> You cannot live whilst life and self persist.

I am afraid of nothingness, but life is a battle with fear. The threats of change and of death arising from uncertainty and ambivalence conjure up most of our fears. Even my birth, my expulsion from the womb, the first change, was a practice for death, my expulsion from the womb of life.

I remember Sitareh's thoughts: "To prolong dying is savagery, even if the law calls it life support." To I live in times when men isolate themselves by fiercely competing among themselves and by subjugating women—their other-selves—is torture, too. Death may be less lonely. To want to die is made out to be shameful, and shame is the most gnawing emotion. But to be emotional is shameful, too. I have had to censor my emotions all my life. To disguise my passions, I pretend to be someone else. So my true being never really existed, and that is the case for so many souls. Now I know that I am never going to be what I have never been—myself! I will die an stranger to myself.

Is suicide a kindness or the savagery of self preying on self? Authorities, who fear death, forbid suicide, but yet they order mass killing out of their sight in wars. I shall rebel against their shackles on death. I will not allow death to be chained! I screamed at birth; I will laugh at death. Suicide is the only real choice I will ever make. Maybe in the next life my consciousness will transcend its delusions. Maybe I am too hard on myself, but isn't that how it should be, before one takes his own life? Remember, saints are always dead, because, once dead, one can do no wrong, and I want to do no wrong anymore. Listen, Pirooz, you were born in these times, but you need not dwell in them. You have had enough. You must become dead.

I am not obliged to live longer, or to think death is forever. I know better now. Having seen, said, thought, done, suffered, and changed all I wanted to or was able to, now I am ready for death, and death is ready for me. So I install my stop light for this world, a red light that will stay red.

I write a letter to my mother pleading for forgiveness: I am selfish, and this is the best I can do for myself.

Next I write a letter to myself. Dear Pirooz, You must not return to America. You must not stay in Iran. You must not go any place where the times are foul, and unfortunately, nowhere today are they pure. Poison lurks in a drink of water, in a breath of air, in the colorful skins of fruit, in a blossom, in a humane idea the rulers dislike. Our insides absorb the outside we have fouled with toxic waste, through winds, streams and food. There is no outside on earth, everywhere is inside. You look worn out from absorbing that bitter medicine, reality, just to exist from dusk to dusk. Haven't you been tortured by a life-support system called civilization long enough, Pirooz? Don't you see that your immortal thoughts are very mortal?

I stop writing. I stop! My train of thought is about to pull out of Sanity Station, chugging towards the regions of madness. An imaginary clock on the imaginary station platform waves its loose arms good-bye to me. "Your time is up," the clock growls. "Your time is up." And a parrot perched on a column of steam screeches, "Your time is up." A farewell to life—even the clock, even the parrot, know that my time is up. I know it, too. I know my time is up. The train huffs and puffs and vents its steam, for it is impatient to depart. The conductor announces that the destination is beyond everything: unfulfilled hopes, dreams, all constrictions, insecurity and anxiety. It is called Death.

Death represents hope, not hopelessness, because it will take me where I have never been before from where I wish not be anymore. When what is known holds no value, then the unknown becomes valuable, and so death becomes preferable to life. I talk as if I know what death is. Maybe I do, without knowing how I know. But I know what life ought not to be. I know, I know. I wish someone would ask me, "What is it that life ought not to be, Pirooz?" and I would say, "Ask my eyes, ask my ears! They will tell you."

I trust death more than life. Fearful? That is what I am. Saint? No. Wicked? No. Dead? Yes, that is what I will be soon. I must go. I have died before, so I know there is nothing to it. Life is magic that is trapped in the mysteries of birth and death, but the magic has lost its allure for me. I will spring the trap with my will.

At the juncture of life and death, all things turn into the footprint of dusk. Inspect your imaginary luggage once more. Discard your wishes, neatly pack away your memories, and leave nothing unattended to. What you take with you, like your name, is really what you leave behind. You must pass a dark, stormy sea to reach a sanctuary where war and conflict are eternally dead. There, blossoms are everlasting, fragrances carry your wishes, melon vines run out of snowdrifts, roses grow out of singing rocks, colorful leaves dance in flight long after autumn has gone, shadows play the flute, ice crystals carry love letters on streams of wine, honesty flows on a breeze, and truth spreads over the ground like the light of a sun that never sets.

Stop! Stop fooling yourself, Pirooz, I scream. The voice's urgency, even compulsion, rises within me. "Is your mind set to go? Is your suitcase ready? Have you packed whatever knowledge and wisdom you may have picked up along the way? Have you dispelled what must be dispelled and amassed what must be amassed, sorted out what you have done from what you have left undone? Have you collected your reasons for living this long, and for dying now, for Him who may judge your judgments? Can you muster the courage to ask Him why He didn't create even one perfect being, why He put such big souls and imaginations in limited, mortal bodies? You need not be hasty, but you must be steady and determined for this journey. Yes, Pirooz, you must go. Take a pair of scissors and cut constrictions and life apart. Your birthplace rejects you; even your shadow rejects you. Pack. Leave. Be gone!"

My mind made up, I head downstairs to look for Firoozeh.

"Is there any opium in this house?" I ask her, hopeful that in old houses tradition is more powerful than the new laws.

"Yes, Agha." I ignore her bewildered look as she guides me to a secret cabinet. I ask her for some tea, and she goes to make it.

The opium is brown like caramel, malleable, imperishable, cylindrical like a pencil and expensive. Opium relieves pain and induces pleasure. Some opium derivatives are inside every family medicine cabinet, and some are criminal possessions. "Business holds the monopoly on opium distribution," I used to tell my students. Opium has been used as currency, and it caused the Opium Wars because the British wanted to market it to China. Imagining the past, a bittersweet smile wraps my thoughts. Strangely, I allow myself the luxury of reminiscing before death, while waiting for the tea to wash the opium down. My father once said, "Gold treats the maladies of greed and conceit but sets aflame conflict and war. Opium treats almost every illness temporarily, but its widespread use can put a nation into hibernation. And an overdose ends all life's constrictions. It kills."

My father and his friends used to smoke opium on Friday afternoons, drinking vodka, exchanging stories and wisdom, listening to music, occasionally reciting poetry, and often laughing at themselves, at history, at the cosmos, at the silliness of life with so many puzzles, even at the puzzles.

On one occasion one of my father's friends announced, "I feel that the Grand Puzzle Maker is among us now, laughing with us at His own puzzles and at each of us, who try so hard to solve them."

"The compassionate God is beyond frivolous laughter," someone objected.

"No, no," said the first man, laughing. "Laughter is God's invention, just as the atom bomb is ours. Come to think of it, the Creation itself is a comedy. Who said that God frowns all the time?"

"Quite right, "said another. "His prophets made Him a wrathful God to throw fear into the hearts of unruly subjects."

I remember the scent of the opium smoke intoxicating me, a little boy, even the fish, even the plants, it seemed. A physician said, "Evolution is in a slow take-off of life, like a crane, into crystalline space. Opium accomplishes this with one puff, lifting our lives into the imagined skies without anxiety or a rocket's noise."

"What is life up there, or even down here?" A smoker wondered out loud.

My father responded: "I Life is a journey full of repetitions, of scents, sights, tastes, touches and sounds, but with the destination fixed. Life is another hunger, meal and cleaning up, another cry, laugh, headache, aspirin, another book, dream or nightmare, another growth and decline, and another bending to authorities and to aging, the worst despots in creation. Life is just a chore, a response to irritations. It is life which is to be feared, not death. In death there is no irritations or tragedies!" He paused to take a deep breath.

"You forgot the most important 'another,' a necessity," a friend declared with a grin almost lost in the opium smoke.

"Oh, so true. Life is another orgasm."

He mentioned orgasm right in front of me, when I was only seven and giddy from the opium smoke that hovered in the air. In Persia, fathers are like oak trees when it comes to discussing sex with their children: one hears nothing but silence from them. My father was different, though—very different.

He resumed after a mischievous smile, "Orgasm must have happened first in the mind of God. He conceived it, examined it, and liked it, before bestowing it on us."

"Orgasm in the mind of God! This is blasphemy!" a guest protested.

"A rooster is no Edison; it didn't invent orgasm itself, my friend."

The smokers giggled and one said, "Pirooz, you are inconsistent, a believer one moment and a non-believer the next."

"He can also be nonsensical."

"Gentlemen," my father asserted, "let us be realistic. Consistency is for the dead, nonsense is for the living, and truth is blasphemous for the clergy."

In the crossfire, an intoxicated professor raised his slumped-over head and said, "The Big Bang was a cosmic orgasm into the womb of space."

"A heavenly conception of everything," someone interjected.

"We are God's sperm and eggs lost in space," said another amid laughter.

A young man said, "Heaven is heaven because orgasms can last there forever."

"Or you wish it did, young man! Anyhow, orgasm must stop for a smoke of opium, even in heaven don't you agree?" my father rejoined. All hell broke loose.

"Heaven, or hell is a story confirmable only by the angels or by the dead, who are not confirmable themselves. All these after life hocus pocus are rooted on the un-confirmables!"

"Science is a story, too, always in fear of failing." Someone rebutted.

"Except that science either works or is falsified, unlike faith. Planes defy gravity, and vaccines make up for God's error, also, or His unkindness to man."

"Faith works, too. Look at the holy wars that strew corpses all over geography and history. On occasion praying has been a prelude to murder."

"Science kills, too. Let's not forget the atom bomb. Life is one pain after another. Ask my prostate, ask my joints! And I want someone to tell me what death is." The icy words of an old man froze the joy.

"Death is an unconditional surrender to the worms," my father replied and continued. "If suicide is possible, then freedom is possible. If freedom is not possible, then suicide is not possible, either." The smoke hung in a bittersweet silence for an uncertain moment.

"What is orgasm, Baba?" My question broke the ice, and thunderlaughs kicked clouds of opium smoke higher.

My father waited until quiet prevailed. "It cannot be described. It must be experienced, my son."

"Why?"

"It is like describing a rainbow to a blind man."

"I am not blind," I objected.

"True, but orgasm is in your future and no one can see into the future."

"How will I know it when it happens, Baba?" Another huge laugh filled my ears. The man who held the pipe almost choked.

"That is not funny!" I protested to the intoxicated adults.

My father waved his hand for quiet. "You will experience it when you are older, my dear son. You will know! You must wait, just as you had to wait to walk, to talk, to read, and to differentiate between good and bad. You must wait until time carries you to the experience. We must wait for experiences, just as experiences must wait for us."

My uncle said, "What about women, the other enigma?"

"I don't know," said another man, "but I do know that buttocks are God's most voluptuous creation. When He created them, God rubbed His holy hands together and spoke to Himself: 'Oh your holiness, you did it!'"

"What more, Pirooz?" my uncle insisted.

"Well, there is scarcity. God created only a few great buttocks and—"

"Stop kidding. Say what is on your mind, Pirooz."

"All right, gentlemen. A woman possesses many delicate parts, inside and out, like lips, breasts, clitoris, vagina, and a soul. We brutes pay no attention to the most delicate part—her soul. We impregnate our wives without ever knowing them. No wonder women are mysteries to us." My father winked amid sobering approval.

"God reveals in the Holy Koran that women, our mothers, are irrational, but we men, the warmongers, are rational. Why did God create an irrational gender to mother a rational one? And why does the stuff hanging between our legs certify our rationality? It boggles my mind." I heard the great laughter, but I was not sure what it all meant. No one uttered a word for a while.

"Finish telling us about life, Pirooz."

"Oh, yes, the point. Life is a repetition of one thing after another until it freezes at what it was. That is, that which is, becomes that which is not."

"Pirooz, slow down. Don't answer us with a puzzle."

"You mean death is not another something, a routine?" someone else said.

"No! I mean yes," my father replied.

"Why?"

"Because death is never repeated. It happens once and it lasts."

"You don't believe in reincarnation, then?"

"No. Every journey, like history, is irreversible. Since everything depends on everything else, if only one thing is not repeated, then nothing can be repeated. The smoke freed by a volcano will never return to the womb of Earth."

"The universe may contract and collapse to the primeval atom it once was. A new Big Bang, and all things could be repeated again," the physicist interjected.

"Then you tell us, what is life?" someone asked him.

"Life is a love-feast of atoms, and death is their return to nature."

"That is life? Atoms copulating. Atoms thinking. Atoms saying bye bye?"

"What else is there?"

"Wait a second," someone raised his voice above the others. "Maybe I will never know who I am, but I know now what I am. According to you, I am the feces and piss of dead people and animals, and they will be made of my piss and feces and disintegrated body? So, I am a recycled shit who knows that he is recycled shit! God have mercy on us misbehaving shits!"

"You are not the only one. Even His Majesty the Shah is no exception, although he traded his conscience for the crown," my father interjected.

"From shit to shit, what is the purpose of life, then?"

"Purpose stems from consciousness—a product of life itself to enrich life. Nature is purposeful, and God agrees with nature," my father calmly said.

"Does God have a choice? Can He declare gravitation a sin, and stop the heavenly bodies from gravitating to each other, like my mistress and me?" The scientist wiggled in mock sensuality to illustrate.

"Not God, but an Ayatollah may declare it a sin." A garbled voice said.

"The dead leap over galaxies while we are stuck in the mud down here without asking ourselves why we are purposeless. I want to get rid of generals! Their souls have sharp teeth on them," my young uncle declared.

"Let us wash down this nonsense with smoke and vodka."

"No, let us drink to Agha Pirooz, who frees us of mental boundaries."

"Bottoms up! To Pirooz!" They shouted with joy.

"Thank you. I drink to our unknown purposes," my father replied.

A musician raised his head. "All I know is that, life is a screechy note the listeners will never forget!"

Suddenly a mathematician screams, "I see, I see. The opium bares everything, even infinity! I never saw it like this. Zero and infinity creating by what hangs between them like lovers. If a number mounts zero, as in a fraction, infinity will explode, and if the same number mounts infinity, zero will implode with a whimper. Each and every number between them is full of eggs it seems." The crowd burst into laughter.

"Opium just opened my mind wider, too," my father declared. "So to get rid of Satan, once the prince of angels, and to create the world in one stroke, the lonely God commanded Satan to mount the Zero, the Nothingness. Since angels have mass at rest, this caused the Big Bang, and the universe exploded and sped towards infinity. So Satan's debris contaminated everything with evil and imperfection. I believe this manner of creation was the first error in the history of the universe and, of course, the most costly one. Then God fashioned man from matter already tainted with evil. Thus evil got into every soul and was declared the original sin. So Adam and Eve were already bad apples before they touched any apple! In the *Avesta*, the holy book of the Zoroaster, God, who is Ahura-Mazda, asked us to fight Ahriman or Satan, inside and outside of ourselves, in order to cleanse evil from everything. Jews, Christians and Muslims appropriated dualism, along with the ideas of resurrection, the day of the judgment, Heaven and Hell, even names of the angels, and other pious tidbits from the Zoroastrians. God damn Persian imagination for inventing these stories. We should be incarcerated for the guilt of our ancestors! Come to think of it we are. And..."

"How plausible! Even dogma declares that at first there was only God and Nothingness, and then came the creation and the original sin. Satan sitting on the nothingness—igniting the biggest bang there ever was—is a big story, worthy of revelation in a holy-science text. Unwittingly Pirooz has united science and faith—something which even Ibn Sina could not do. The clergy and the scientists are finally one in one big brotherhood. Too bad that like other luminaries, you, Pirooz must die before you are recognized. Your thoughts will be interpreted and the interpretations reinterpreted as worms feast on you turning you into pure worm shit!" The scientist interjected.

"How true." My father acknowledged amid laughter. "And so man proceeded to fill himself and the world with stories—from the formulas of physics to the verses of the holy books. But, God should have consulted a psychiatrist before creation. Look how sadistic every creature in nature is. The cat tortures the songbird before killing it. Man hunts down harmless animals just for fun, and kills his own kind, too. Who gave every being the potential of what it could become, but God? I am certain that God, the compassionate and benevolent, suffers when He watches His own creatures do what they do. Since God willed His own suffering, then He may have been touched by a holy masochism at the time of Creation. So the universe needs a universal shrink."

"Shrink, shrink—Holy Shrink," the crowd of intoxicated smokers chanted.

"Now I understand my wife and children better," a man interrupted. "If they torture me, it isn't their fault, it is the bit of Satan embedded in them."

"Let Pirooz finish," an old man lying on the floor suggested.

"When God is bored," my father said, "He will command a dead general to mount by then the infinitely expanded universe, restoring Nothingness with one big implosion just as zero would emerge if a number mounts infinity."

"What happens to God?"

"He holds the nothingness in His holy palms, and laughs forever."

"So Heaven and Hell will be inside nothingness," said another man.

"Yes. And behold, maybe it is nothingness who will laugh forever."

"Why can't I mount zero now? I am better than Satan," a general complained.

"Hardly, General. You are probably worse! And there exist no nothingness anywhere for you to mount, God bless." Thunderlaughs broke loose.

"It is intoxication that makes you damn fools claim God is sick! It is blasphemous to think that God's loneliness brought about the birth of the universe, and his boredom its demise. The fires of Hell will teach you!" A non-drinking guest protested seriously.

"Come now, my friend, use your gray matter and keep the party joyous," the physicist said. "Why would the Almighty keep charcoaling somebody in Hell forever? Is this not a little, just a little sick?" More laughter broke through.

"Blasphemy. Damn you Pirooz, for saying that, and damn me for hearing it!"

"Don't worry, my clean-shaven Ayatollah! Your God will punish me if I deserve it. I am who I am. I was not even asked if I wanted to be born, and had I been born dumb, my tongue couldn't say what I just said, and had I been born retarded, my mind couldn't think it." A moment of silence engulfed my father's response.

The professor interrupted, "Such a couple, Zero and Infinity. One is the beginning, the other the end. So close, yet so far apart."

"Like me and my wife!"

"Which wife?" The laughter made the smoke sway like a drunk.

"Listen to this! Opium undresses everything, even the mind, my crazy friends."

"Opium is better than sex. It makes you feel that the earth swings in space for you, making life a cosmic joyride," my father said, entering the fray amid a fresh roar of laughter.

"All this is nonsense!" A napping smoker opened his mouth and eyes at the same time.

"The truth has been called nonsense before," my father responded, "and it will be called nonsense again. What is new?"

A man spread on the carpet raised his glass. "A toast to God, our only friend!"

"No," someone disagreed. "To God, our only enemy."

Their words flooded the air, so that it no longer mattered who said what. "God is not an enemy." "God is not a friend." "God is most beautiful." "God created ugly things." "God is generous." "God is stingy." "God is most powerful." "God has lost control." "God is the wisest of all." "God is the maddest of all." "God will punish the blasphemers."

"God is everything."

"God is nothing."

Nothing. The word nothing sticks in my mind. The opium smoke and the sound of the men's laughter fused into an alloy that clung to the air for a long moment, like a ballerina, and then disappeared, except in my memory. My father is dead and the smokers are all gone now, like their smoke. I seem to know more dead than living people. How odd that the sight of the opium should trigger such memories. My bittersweet smile turns into a heartache as I contemplate my own death. My eyes squeeze shut. As I open them, big, hot tears spurt out. I want to exit with no fears. How did my mind decide to become a self-annihilator?

Omar Khayyam's Rubaiyat springs to mind as if to help my last journey along.

> There was a Door to which I found no Key,
> There was a Veil past which I might not see;
> Some little Talk awhile of Me and Thee
> There seem'd—and then no more of Thee and Me.

> One Moment in Annihilation's Waste,
> One Moment, of the Well of Life to taste—
> The Stars are setting and the Caravan
> Starts for the Dawn of Nothing—Oh, make haste!

Now, about to bring my own death myself, I smile. How much I loved my father. I wonder if he knew it. He certainly could not know from my words spoken to him, but perhaps he knew from my glances. He seemed to know everything fathers know. Unlike my mother, he accepted me as I was. It is worth dying to hold his soul in my arms just once. Oh God, Holder of all possibilities, send one possibility to me! Just one. Make it possible for me to tell him how much I loved him.

I miss Sitareh. I miss Ibn Sina, his curiosity as big as the universe and still expanding. Missing one more sight of them, one more hug, I imagine little Ibn Sina sucking her milk, doing arithmetic at three, writing poems at four, composing the music of love and peace at five, and addressing the world at the UN at ten.

I remember the day Sitareh and I swam naked in a naked pond in a naked valley below a naked Alvand under naked skies. We saw the world as it was because it was naked, and we saw our happiness because it was naked, too. We made promises with our heads above the water, but it no longer matters who promised what. Life, even history, is an unfulfilled promise. Sitareh left me, never knowing that I would have agreed to stay in Iran, or perhaps it was because she knew I would stay and saw beyond it that she left me.

That glorious day Sitareh stood in the pond and the clear water came up to her beautiful breasts. Like exotic fish with pink nipples, her breasts floated on the glistening waves as though needing to breathe. Her lower parts seemed divided from her upper parts by the light's refraction. The water was warm, but we were hot, fired by the love and longing of a millennium. The pond heard what we said and felt what we felt. Emotionally nude, too, we became transparent in the pond's embrace, caressed by its intoxicating fingers. The lips of its waves slipped over our bodies and set us quivering. The pond made love to our togetherness. A pair of canaries serenaded us and a puff of wind showered us with colorful petals and divine fragrances. Sitareh closed her eyes, held me tightly, and whispered, "We are in paradise, my love!" Soon there was no water between us, no time between us, no skin between us. No sin could enter our paradise. *Paradeese*, garden, the word and idea Persians invented, perhaps here in Hamadan. I felt as though our togetherness covered us like a tent, with a diamond lighting the inside.

I put my memories aside and take a piece of the opium roll and walk back to my room. I kick off my shoes. One falls upside down, the other stands like an empty grave, black and desolate. Imagining my corpse rotting in it, I shudder. "I know what I am doing, Father," I say. "I am beaten but not brought to my knees. I have lost everything, but I have not been stripped of my dignity. Life is difficult, but death will be as easy as a puff of opium. Remember it was you who said that father."

I note Firoozeh's fearful eyes when she brings my tea up to my room. They tell me everything she can't tell me in words; they speak of sympathy, even of love. She seems to feel so much, yet allows herself so few words. The poor in Iran are reared to behave like a sea broken by islands of silent yeses. Firoozeh is a great soul caged in a deprived upbringing.

On the one hand the opium winks at me, even invites me; on the other hand, armies of despair and anguish hold spears aimed at my brain. The brain must be killed. "Death, Pirooz?" I ask myself, wishing I knew less but understood more. Where can I exchange knowledge for understanding at this late hour?

I hear an answer from within, "Death is not a philosophical question, it is an experience, an entering through a gate where absolute bodily submission to a blind earthworm is the beginning. Come on, Pirooz, you have traveled to a name, not to your country, to a memory, not to your home. I'm telling you, your real home is death."

I trim my moustache, shower in cold water, shave, dress, put on a red tie, run a comb through my hair and feel my chilled skull, soon to be the home of nothing.

I choose to die cleanly, by not being injected with toxic chemicals or radioactive cancer medication in old age. I have no mercury fillings and carry no dangerous germs; my burial or cremation will not contaminate the environment. I will not be hazardous waste and threaten life when I am dead. I will be beneficial at last, fall like a raindrop, and be absorbed by the earth and became a link in the food chain. How wonderful: a clean death! I feel a strange elation like a light within a light. Oh, my mind! I myself shall be recycled, as everything else should be. How pleasing!

Just taste the opium, I implore myself, surprised at my lack of fear. I cut and swallow some opium the size of a lentil grain. The taste is very bitter. I wash it down with tea. I wait for a while, before taking another pill, and then another. The opium begins to taste less bitter. It seems as though death will taste less and less bitter as I get used to the idea. Life ends when a crystal ball holding one's hopes smashes against the wall of death, the broken pieces still glistening with shattered hopes.

I am a damn intellectual to the end. So I let one more idea rush to my mind. Bounded by possibilities, I must constantly choose, and exclude, among alternative actions. My limited freedom expresses my finitude. By suicide, I negate all my possibilities in this world. Death is an implosion of finitude. By leaving the question, Do I have a duty to live? unanswered, I treat myself, for once, as life has treated me always, with unanswered questions. A bitter thought crosses my mind. Are we nothing but germs who infest and kill Mother Nature like unconscious bacteria killing their host in a mass suicide? Nothing matters now, not the answer, not all my questions or curiosity, not my doubts or hopes or insights or memories.

Lightly I walk away from doubts toward horizons of curiosity and look around me. The furniture looks exhausted, the nightingale is asleep, dusk has arrived early, and my wishes and memories intermingle. Ibn Sina's poster stares at me disapprovingly. But the flowers in the vase smile, welcoming me to where they have journeyed uprooted. There is no Hell! Hell is only a scarecrow. If God is just, then we all will be in heaven, since life itself is our ultimate punishment.

Fears and doubts rush to me one last time and I respectfully welcome them one last time. Fear is a good antidote to foolishness, but doubt is an uncut diamond, curiosity the cut gem, and truth the brilliant crown. My mood changes capriciously. A tempest howls in my brain. Deeply weary of life, I cannot wait for death.

The snow-faced Alvand looks grim. It speaks to me silently and disapprovingly, "Man is a rebellious offspring of nature." But I no longer believe in Mount Alvand, or the pond or the Sun and stars, or the butterfly I once imagined breaking free of its carpet to speak to me. I reject the world, either real or fanciful. I don't need my shadow to reject me; I reject my own naked self from everything.

I stare into the mirror at an empty face. My life was an illusion. Stripped of the ideals of ascendance and immortality, nothing is left but a man utterly alone with nowhere to go. Should I take more opium? Something tells me, "That is enough for your journey." Everything I valued is pointless now. I raise the glass of maroon-colored tea. "Long live Death!" My shoes repeat after me, "Long live Death, Pirooz."

My eyes close on their own. A bat flutters in the dark rays of my imagination and shouts, "My darkened cave is the happiest place. My bed is the rough ceiling from which I hang upside down for the most comforting rest. I love the darkness of my cave! You will love your death, Pirooz. Immortality is none of your business, even if it is the supreme good." "Yes, yes," I whisper, "I will love my death at first sight!"

A rainbow rises over a darkening panorama. I hear my mother sing a lullaby to me, her firstborn, now to keep me from falling asleep, from dying. But my eyes close. I cannot help it and I do not wish to. My eyes and ears and heart and mind split apart and wander in space to observe one another with some curiosity.

An empty train waits at the station for me, its lone passenger. I see intelligence and warmth in everything—a new experience. An overdose of opium over-intoxicates me before it kills me. The moon, clouds, the wind, trees, the clock, the huge station gate, the rails, even the parrot, are all wise. They wish me well; even the ballast thrown indifferently between the rails that rise into the clouds says to me, "Happy transcendence!" Full of exuberance, a horse with crystal wings pulls the train up and away into the sky. Glittering fish swim in the dark like fireflies that are never extinguished. The Persian who invented the harp plays it for the cosmos. He is accompanied by a dancing angel who plays the *nay*. Stars that were nailed hard to the sky shake themselves loose and celebrate the end of their cosmic bondage. "Oh, God, the stars are dancing!" I exclaim. A strange moon steps onto the stage like a ballerina, joining our moon. Two moons, side by side! They kiss furiously like lost lovers. One says, "My love, I would have waited for you forever." The sun just above the horizon attempts to jump into the fray but the angels of light grab its tail and hold it back. "Wait!" they proclaim. The sun kicks with its beams to free itself, but the angels are stern disciplinarians.

I am riding a carriage made of honeysuckle blossoms and powered by their fragrance. It rises gently like a loosed balloon. I feel buoyant. Everything around me is beautiful and all in the most wonderful proportions and moods. I inhale the most exotic scents and see giddy flowers and fruits running after intoxicated birds. Beasts of all hues glow in the dark, and ideas of all colors hold hands, feelings for all wonderful moments smile, poems drink wine gulp after gulp, dolls made of curiosity play hide-and-seek, happiness strings across the heavens like a garland and twinkles with joy. Everything is loving and sweet, and the early autumn leaves wave their greetings to me like the ripe persimmons on my favorite tree at home. Angels carry a gilded espresso machine the size of a cathedral behind my carriage. The wonderful aroma of freshly brewed coffee fills the skies as I hear my own sigh of relief: how wonderful is voluntary death. No hospital. No pain. I glance below at the Earth, which wears a heavy mist of silence like a holy tomb, but my mood transforms from somber to luminous and from tremulous to exuberant as my distance from life increases.

Now a little goldfish swims up to me. "Welcome home. Plunge into happiness, be yourself, abandon dissimulation. Happy transcendence to you, Pirooz!"

The Earth and what roams over it sing to me, "Happy transcendence!"

Massive colorful clouds like abstract paintings float by. The Earth grows smaller and smaller, becoming a dot before it vanishes altogether. A most satisfied smile spreads from my face to my whole body and then to everything around me and beyond. To infinity. Everything becomes a part of my smile. I pass through a throbbing dark tunnel just like the birth canal. At the end of the tunnel I see lights and crystals and hear a celebration: "You are free at last. Congratulations, Pirooz. Happy Death Day! Happy death day to you, dear Pirooz."

Chapter Twenty-Four: Another Flight

The Big Bang, consumed by infinity and eternity, has lost its thunder. A lonely sun, pale and shrunken to the size of a light bulb, hangs from a diminished sky. Time is absent, space frozen, sounds silenced, motions stilled. What is left of the universe is colorless, odorless, tasteless, painless—bordering on nothingness. Ghosts with frigid smiles and white robes stand transfixed. Death rules on all sides. Like deadwood I sense no feelings, no thoughts, no consciousness, but I am not nothing. I am a piece of driftwood washed up on the shores of nowhere, planted by the ghosts, who can revive the dead. The driftwood—me—begins to breathe and turn green again. Instantly space congeals, its bones cracking, and time reappears, its heart ticking. A clock's hand—long, black and slender—pounces on the next second like a dragonfly on a gnat. The new tree—my reincarnation, perhaps—strives to capture some light, a wisp of life, selfhood, something—anything. Finally it—me—focuses. Traces of sensation arrive haltingly. Inexplicably the tree becomes a crane that soars toward a thin awakening. As though pursued by a phalanx of hunters, it ascends still higher to the zone of curiosity and asks: "Is this the province of a bygone era? Am I a bird at last, as I have always wanted to be? But can birds ask questions?" The choked silence proves that perhaps this is it—my fate after death.

Finally I ask the ghosts surrounding me, "Who or what am I?" But I cannot hear my own voice. Language exists, but sound is dead. I am not inanimate. I am me—a mere bird-soul, perhaps, tongueless in punishment for talking too much in a previous life. Mustering what strength I have, I try to shout, "Where am I?"

"A place with no name." I hear and realize I'm not deaf.

"Names are dead, too; a world without names," I try to voice the thought.

A ghost shrugs.

I lack the nerve and the verve to ask directly: Which side am I on, life or death? Maybe I fear looking straight in the eye of impossibility. But the ghost's eyes focused on me are speechless.

"Am I alive?" I finally hear my own trembling voice clearly.

"Just barely. You barely survived." comes a reply.

"Where am I? Please!"

"This used to be the American Hospital," a ghost says in a normal pitch.

"In where?"

"Where it used to be, in Hamadan."

"Are you physicians and nurses in uniforms, not ghosts?" I ask to make sure.

"Yes." A heavy silence swells into an expanding white room.

Suddenly more lights, sounds, thoughts and feelings, augmented by fear as a red tributary, flow into my consciousness. My abrupt understanding demonstrates that not mystery but abilities, disabilities, inclinations and activities define one's mind. My consciousness arises and expands, just as it must have for Stone Age man. But petrified, I conclude that life and anxiety coexist. It is puzzling: I thought I would wake with Ibn Sina in the next world, but instead, I have experienced at firsthand his philosophy: the transformation from physical to vegetative to animal to human organism—a sweeping evolution with the potential for spiritual transcendence. The ghosts are doctors and nurses, but everything else remains hazy, so I ask, "What did you mean, this used to be the American hospital?"

"Dr. Pirooz, history, places and names are ripped apart like worn books and maps. The Guards tore down this hospital's sign. Now, nameless and lost, the old place awaits a new name from Teheran. If we protest we will be punished. Even the dead mourn for what has happened, since graves are dug up, the dead exhumed and put on trial as if it were the Day of Judgment."

"Whose graves are dug up?"

"The graves of past leaders."

"That isn't Islamic," I say, pointing out the obvious.

"No, but it is the Islamic Republic."

Graves are dug up, the dead mourn . . . . I wish to be dead again.

The doctor breaks the silence. "May I be frank with you, Professor Pirooz?" I nod. "You must have died or come perilously close to it—perhaps moments away from irretrievability. The relatively small dose of opium you took, the maid's alertness, and the availability of a cab favored your survival. The cabdriver carried you on his back into this compound. He knew your name and seemed to care very specially for you." The doctor pauses and I remember the big, white teeth of Heyroun Gholi, the cabdriver puzzled by the mysteries of life.

"But, Professor Pirooz, the address of death is known," the doctor resumes. "It is just around the corner. And no matter what road one takes in life, one eventually ends up there. Meanwhile, it is fun to get lost in detours, to enjoy the ride, so to speak, and to let death find you. Death wins all the games of hide-and-seek. Suicide is a fool's shortcut. Dying is easy, but living is a great art."

"Only if there is something worth living for," I add bitterly.

"With namelessness or new names, new martyrs, and new ruins, we need scholars and builders to report and reconstruct. The other day I couldn't recall the new name of a street, and I was afraid to give a taxi driver the old one.

Much of our past has become taboo. We are citizens of nowhere, Professor Pirooz."

"Why?" I ask, even though I have an idea.

Mischievously he replies, "I think they are enforcing a national state of amnesia. To remember that everything was not pitch black in Iran before Islam and did not become light after Islam is hazardous. For instance, they are silent about how much Zoroastrianism influenced Islam through the Old and New Testaments. So we must forget who we are, and where we come from, and not question where we are being dragged to. It is blasphemous to indicate where you stand, if it is not with them. This is feigning amnesia. The theocracy interprets and reinterprets dogma to justify its interests; it is not interested in facts. A multitude of the faithful have suffered for not submitting to the official line ."

An agitated nurse protests: "You do agree, Doctor, that Islam is the most beautiful creation of God, don't you?"

The doctor's lip twitches. "Well, yes. Yes, of course Islam is beautiful, but its beauty could become disfigured by garish make-up."

As I am discharged the next day, a smiling old nurse whispers to me, "You are lucky, Dr. Pirooz. You were able to die and yet live, to leave this world and yet return."

"Thank you, but death is just another mode of being," I assert.

As I step out of the building, the doctor catches up and opens his arms to me, whispering in my ears, "Remain a free spirit. Please!"

In his embrace, I whisper back, "It will be tough, Doctor. God in heaven is indifferent, and the gods on earth are threatening. Where do free spirits belong?" He kisses my cheeks before letting go.

The nurse turns a strange gaze on me. I grin and think to myself: "What next, Pirooz? What must you do after suicide?"

The next day at the house, Firoozeh brings me tea in the bedroom. I squeeze her hand and say, "Thank you for saving my life, even though it was against my will."

She casts a long and loving eye on me. "It was my duty and . . ." Her voice trails off. "Anyhow, your fate was to live on. The cab was passing here at midnight, a miracle. And the driver refused his fare, as if he had been sent by God."

"I'd rather be a dead body than a dead soul," I confess to her as a friend.

"I understand, Agha. But I pray you will be neither."

We stare at one another affectionately. I notice joy in her face and a healthy sparkle in her eyes. She looks so wholesome in her baggy black slacks, white cotton shirt, and bright saffron-colored scarf. She wears no makeup and no bra. Her simplicity, large dusky eyes, pure full lips, and ebony brows and hair are humble, beautiful and sensuous.

"I have something to ask you, may I?" Her voice is the music of tradition.

"Of course, Firoozeh."

"I enjoy the blossoms in the spring, the fruits in the summer, beauty in the fall, and gathering twigs for fire in the winter. I wonder why God's gifts or what you and Lady Sitareh can do for each other are not enough."

"Dear Firoozeh, I wish I knew the answer. As soon as I do, I will let you know."

Blushing solid red, she confides to me, "I would never have left you, Agha!"

My astonishment melts into silence; there is nothing to say. The woman who saved my life walks away. Feelings heaped upon feelings accumulate in me. I realize that in every person there is an undamaged spirit, a marvelous world to discover.

Later that afternoon Firoozeh sends a telegram for me to my mother, to inform her that I will be on my way back to New York and asking her not to open my letter.

The next day, feeling my strength returning, I leave the house to purchase a turquoise necklace and earrings for Firoozeh as a going-away gift. They match her turquoise ring, the sky, her name, which means 'turquoise,' and my mood, bluish but positive. She brings the jewelry to her lips and thanks me with her eyes fixed on mine. I have also bought her a few books. I hug her good-bye and thank her once more for saving my life. Her eyes light up in appreciation. She spends her few words carefully: "Dr. Pirooz, I hope Hamadan will draw you back under happier circumstances."

"Who knows?" I reply. "I may come back to visit an angel in Hamadan."

She blushes, her story-filled, melancholy eyes growing moist.

"I will write to you." I try to be tearless, unemotional, someone else.

"Thank you. I have never received a letter from America."

Before I leave, Firoozeh checks the mail and, with a bittersweet smile, hands me a letter from Sitareh. Instantly, I am one of the stars in the Pleiades. I grab her and hug her again, jubilant. Firoozeh, on her toes, holds me without reservation. I sense a tiny shiver in her slim, delicate body. She squeezes me gently, as though trying to both cover and bare her feelings. She whispers, and casts her mystical eyes on me.

Overwhelmed and lost where sadness and happiness and strangeness mingle, I close my eyes. Firoozeh's lips touch mine for a fleeting moment. Our tears join drop by drop. Stillness prevails. When I open my eyes, her hand slides off my neck, and her glance at me, burdened with an impossible love, flees. She bursts into stifled sobs with her face against my chest. After a long time, she pulls herself away.

I miss her warmth. An emptiness engulfs me, watching her in tears as she waves to me while my taxi starts for the airport. How could fate keep such jewels hidden? I should have paid more attention to understanding her, I admonish myself, instead of dwelling on my own happiness and misery.

Instead of watching Hamadan one last time, I let the all-knowing city take a good look at me as the taxi passes through. Anxious, I turn to Sitareh's letter.

> Dear Pirooz,
> My greetings and best wishes to you. I want you to know what I couldn't tell you in my hurried and painful departure from Hamadan. Let me say this. I love God and His creation first, Ibn Sina and you second, and myself last. I have left because, even if you agree to stay in Iran, you would not be safe or happy here. Let me tell you, my suffering is great knowing I have hurt you. My husband, Ibn Sina's father, the Ismaili, braved a hostile environment to bring up Ibn Sina. I know you would do the same by jeopardizing your life, but I can never accept that. Never, no matter how I suffer missing you, even missing our disagreements that opened my eyes. I shall protect you from yourself, my beloved!
>
> Ibn Sina can only become Ibn Sina in Iran. This is my judgment as a mother and a physician of the mind. We must leave you until human rights are restored here or until Ibn Sina decides to go elsewhere. He will know about you, of course, and he will know I love you. He will also know you love him and how much you love liberty, even a little bit of it, even the appearance of it even in exile. Soon he will seek you. I am sure he will! I will seek you myself.
>
> As you know, women have little say in the debate about their status in this Islamic resurgence. It is not easy to resign myself to this, realizing that in public or private a woman without a plan is a bird with her wings clipped; she can chirp but not fly. A woman must have a design for her future or must resign herself to the will of men—the usual case. I have a plan and hope it is good.
>
> Forgive me for not being what you wish me to be. I could not, I cannot be what I wish to be myself, or else I would be in your arms now. I am trying to save Ibn Sina for humanity and you for him and me. Please try to understand this. We will be gone only temporarily, temporarily even in our temporary lives. You waited a thousand years before, but this time perhaps you will

not wait a thousand days. I hope the reasons for our separation will disappear soon. Remember the Sufi journey, remember the great joy of reunion with the Beloved. You are a beloved, too. We will savor the image of our reunion, we will live with it and for it, my dear Pirooz. I will nourish and touch this image often as I wait for you.

We love you with all our hearts,
Sitareh and Ibn Sina

I murmur to Sitareh, "Don't mind my departure. Don't doubt my loyalty. Don't forget me. Don't stay away too long, Sitareh. Death has rejected me; I will live for you."

Just as I put the letter away, a voice reminds me I am not alone. "I didn't want to interrupt you, Agha. Thank God I was there to take you to the hospital."

The rear-view mirror reflects the cabdriver's drooping mustache and big, white teeth, a familiar face, though drawn in sadness. Still shocked, I try to listen, to focus.

"Remember me, Agha? The mystery talk!"

"Of course," I answer, happy for the chance to talk to him. Good to see you again, Heyroun Gholi. And thank you for saving my life."

"It was nothing. I know better than to become attached to my passengers."

"But everyone is a passenger," I say sadly, with everyone close to me in mind.

"Tell me, Agha, a passenger from where to where?"

"From mystery to mystery. The genesis. The journey. The destiny."

"In times of a famine of understanding, you are a treat, Agha."

There is a pause, like waiting for an eclipse to end. In darkness, I feel starved for sympathy myself, so I search for a more cheerful topic, "And Zahra, the girl with the tempestuous walk, how is she?"

Heyroun's head plunges to the steering wheel as though hammered from behind. The taxi veers off the road and comes to a halt, throwing me forward.

Sobbing, he manages, "Damn it. Damn all mysteries. Damn my luck, Agha."

Regretting my question, I remain silent.

"The bombing raid, the one that killed my wife and oldest son, crippled Zahra and killed her father, the mausoleum guard. I pray for a miracle every day."

His words wring my heart. "I am sorry to hear that." And then, thinking of the guard, I add, "Bless the dead who enrich the living with fond memories. But the truth is that there are more and more humans, but less and less humanity."

Heyroun talks to himself. "Those were such glorious moments when Zahra walked and I watched. I wanted more, but glimpses of her were all I would allow myself. Her fiery walk is gone, Agha. All gone. Now the impossible has become possible, and I love her no less."

Remaining still, I listen like Alvand, letting him pour his heart out. He turns the ignition key; the cab gets back on the road. "God leaves no clues as to what He is up to," he says. "We are not mankind but perplexed-kind. I wish I were stone-kind, deaf, blind and without passion. I am running out of patience with . . . Oh! Almighty God forgive me! I need more patience. I would steal it if I could, Agha!"

"You are right." I comfort him as sorrow weighs on my own shoulders.

At the airport he unloads the cab. Reaching for my wallet, I hear his emphatic words, "No, no, Agha. Please, I will accept no fare."

"It is lunch time. Could you join me for a bite, Heyroun Gholi?"

"Thank you, Agha, but Zahra is having lunch at our house."

"I understand."

"One last question, Agha. Would mysteries ever be solved?"

"No, Heyroun. For instance, nature is an impossible mystery, because we are a part of it. It is like a story telling the story of all other stories, yet still remaining just a story itself. All we see is a framed picture of reality. Just a picture."

He shakes his head. Out of the cab, we hug and depart without a word. His teardrop rolling from his cheek to mine is for both of us. Entering the departure building, I turn and wave to the man who pointed out the mystery rainbow to me.

Waving back, he breaks his silence. "*Khoda Hafiz. Khoda Hafiz*, Agha."

And in my heart I respond, "*Khoda Hafiz*, Heyroun Gholi. *Khoda Hafiz* to the unknown philosopher of mystery."

The plane grumbles as I gaze out the window taking a last look at the soil, remembering the silk butterfly who once flew out of my old tapestry in New York to tell me: "You may find freedom even in a prison. Free yourself from yourself, and all will be free." A small hope flickers in my heart, promising an illumination, perhaps. The plane, airborne, climbs out of the unfinished stories. In a thin mist, and on a thinner road, Heyroun's silver cab begins to disappear in a blue-tinged mystery.

Above the clouds, and into a restless wind, I come face to face with Alvand. The mountain smiles and billows snow in circles, like my grandfather's pipe smoke. Then Alvand flings a last puff in which flashes the magnificent wink of my grandfather.

Perhaps Sitareh was right. Under the circumstances, I prefer self-exile to life at home in Iran. Home is not where one lives in terror and dies early. I am flying away from where prayer is presumed to be the answer, toward where money is thought to be the answer, from Iran, where painful facts dominate appearances, to the U.S., where appearances cover painful facts. I wish history would bite them both awake, but both are home for me. My argument with Sitareh comes to mind, and for just one gloomy instant I would still prefer to be dead rather than alive. I think of the tens of thousands of citizens who commit suicide yearly, choosing death over the "pursuit of happiness" in America, where I shall live. It is not easy to be in a pack of money wolves.

With infinite sorrow stuck in my throat, I want to crawl into the midst of barren Persian mountains and cry in a voice that would shatter the stones: "Is there an end to the unwanted arrivals and departures? An end to tragic endings?" Instead, I close my eyes and pretend to float in the shadow of the eternal silence, imagining a saffron-color scarf flapping in the wind. How fortunate I am that Firoozeh loves me, and how unfortunate that I cannot return her love the way that would please her. But remembering her courageous kiss, her unforgettable going-away gift, will fill me with joy or boldness whenever I need them.

From Teheran's Mehrabad Airport, I phone my cousin to say good-bye. He complains that I came and left like a ghost. Little does he know how close he is to the truth. I extend my best to each and every member of our extended family through him, and I beg their forgiveness for my neglect.

The crowded plane takes off, shaking like a rotten tooth under a tough bite. It accelerates to overcome gravity, and struggles up like an old man climbing a hill. It must now cross the vast geography and history between Teheran and New York in a few hours.

Sitting in the next seat, a man with the thickest mustache I have ever seen, silver-white hair and blue eyes says to me, "Why are you so sad, young man? I feel triumphant at leaving my birthplace, Shiraz. There is a chance for happiness in unknown places, even for an old man.." He sighs. "I will return home someday to die."

He speaks his mind, and I like him. "Where are you heading?" I ask.

"To my son in Tucson. Is it true that Tucson is like Shiraz?"

"Tucson is a bit hotter," I tell him, "but Tucson is young and Shiraz is old. Tucson has wise cacti, Shiraz has wise poets."

Then I notice his barely detectable frown. "What is wrong?" I ask.

"Well, I won't be able to speak to my grandchildren in English. I will just have to hug and kiss them over and over again. Fortunately, even infants understand touch and love. Come to think of it, I can also pantomime ancient stories for them. Persians have become experts at that. Iran is a grand school of pantomime today."

I nod my head and smile. Soon the old man falls asleep, and I am left to feel my loneliness. I imagine myself in the branches of a white mulberry tree I used to climb as a child to gorge myself on its fruit. I savor the sweetness to counter my bitterness now.

Glancing down at boulder-like cloud patches and up at the turquoise sky, I notice a kind of devolution—my body high in the sky, my spirit struggling to ascend from the ground, science turning creation upside down. I find a ladder of understanding and climb it without hesitation. I know it can collapse like a seedling cut from its roots, yet I feel lighter and more enlightened mounting each rung. I want to reach higher, in my imagination, than where the plane can fly.

I feel like an old bridge trying to connect solitude to love, East to West, past to present. Suspended between heaven and earth, I feel history, even evolution, threaded together through me. Since the human creations or artifacts reflect the structure of the brain, then the brain—a creation of the universe—must reflect the structure of the cosmos. My thoughts whirl through the skies. My brain is a galaxy, the neurons are stars and electrochemical signals the light linking the stars, and love holds all minds together, just as gravity holds the universe. The void and non-void, eternity and infinity, reason and love, all congeal and become one in me. Seeing the darkness and feeling attuned to it, I walk with a lantern to the darkest corners of life and acknowledge that, with light, I can find truth.

After swallowing the deadly opium, I imagined my mother's lullaby keeping me awake. Whose lullaby will keep us all from putting ourselves to sleep? Who can keep us awake but us? Listening to the cosmos, I hear nothing but its constant hum, a boring lullaby. I shall refuse to let it put me to sleep. But I am alone, and emptiness retains its residence within me. Is life an illusory tent with real holes in it?

But suddenly, out of nowhere, a spark fills that void, that tent, and it gives birth to a resolve. That's it! I will try to live as long as springs arrive on time, as long as lilies greet grasshoppers, as long as I can wait for my beloved. I think of Alvand, who understands patience and loneliness; it loves the wind, but its capricious lover can turn hot or cold, it slips away and returns unannounced, wounding the steady mountain as its tears water endless fields. Why is understanding so scarce? Is man blinded to human possibilities, or is he deluded by the impossible that disguises itself as a mirage glimmering on the horizon? Is human unity possible or impossible?

The old man sighs in his sleep. My mood swings to despair once more. Again the vast emptiness squeezes into my being. The void will disappear, I reason, when Sitareh and I reunite, so I accept it for now. Others have suffered worse.

The old man opens his eyes and stares into mine. The vitality in his gleam ignites a spark within me. I touch the light within myself. It is hope, stranger than before, solid and sweet like an apple, glistening like a ruby. Hope is in flight with me; I see its shadow on the clouds in pursuit. Hope is beautiful! It weaves the universe into a magnificent tapestry. The ground thaws, the sap flows, the leaves grow, the birds smile, and life blossoms with hope. I feel this where I felt emptiness before.

I talk to myself: I will do this and that until Sitareh and Ibn Sina seek me. Then my thoughts focus on myself again. I will try to know the multiself and the multifaceted society and find which makes which and how. I will try to know me, I and my selves better, and unite them into the self I can become, what I want to be. I will not give up on humanity or accept any mold someone casts me in, be intimidated by pain or fear of change or remain stuck in a psychological and conceptual pigeonhole. I will burst out of constrictions like Ibn Sina. I am still putty, not hardened clay—even in death one is not clay. Time molds and remolds even stones; I am more malleable than stone. And will be more patient than stone. These ideas anneal in me, harder than a diamond.

I will cease trying to define existence, since definitions—the results of formal thinking—are rigid and artificial. The quality of things cannot be defined or measured. I know some of the faces of quality without knowing how I know, and know that quality pleases my unhampered nature.

I will share in the joy of others as if they were mine, and I will welcome others to enjoy my happiness, for there is so little happiness allotted to any of us. My newly felt equanimity will let me dispossess myself of constricting attachments to things and beliefs and even virtues. The compassion simmering within me since my resurrection will stop me from falling into cold indifference. I will ascend with the three wings of sympathetic joy, equanimity, and compassion. I will try to tie what must be tied: lover to lover, goodness to goodness, and untie what must be untied, like my injuries, from my soul. I will listen to the heartfelt message of hope. Oh! How one letter, one wondrous letter, her letter, has changed my mood. Oh, my mind! Oh, my God, how love makes the narrow heart as wide as the world and as deep as history. Oh, let me feel that love that is as unbounded as imagination.

My remembrance of difficult loves, of Firoozeh for me and Heyroun Gholi for Zahra, unsettles me. My feelings for Firoozeh are not just affection and gratitude, but a love that will be unborn. I imagine the braid of woe and bliss uniting humanity, weeping like an evergreen thawing under the sun after an ice storm.

Hope pours into me like a vibrant spring into a drying pond. I feel Firoozeh's wholesome hug, and I miss her without shame. She shivered in my arms without the shame of impropriety. Love leaps over social barriers. Who is Firoozeh, I wonder? Could it be she cares for me specially . . .? No! It cannot be! But why not? I bask in an imponderable moment of being loved by Firoozeh. What could I do?

Feeling so lonely, I reach for the old man's hand.

He smiles, "Love begets love."

"But doubt and hope are symbiotic," I respond aloud to my own inner turmoil.

He senses my struggle and replies, "So true, young man."

"But I am not young. Look at my gray hair," I protest, smiling, and see in his eyes his appreciation that I am enchanted with him.

"Everyone is young compared to me, even I am young compared to myself," he says. "Flying disrupts sunrise and sunset, and the prayer schedule."

"I don't pray. Maybe I should, but I must find what to say and to whom . . ."

"I pray now and then."

"But you don't pray regularly? My friend, I am shocked," I say with a wink.

"This is my natural reaction to the upheavals around us," he tells me. "I think faith must be inspired and felt, not mandated and monitored as it is by the theocracy. If the state enforces faith and proper conduct, then God must judge the state and not the individual. If one acts religiously simply out of fear of the mullahs, does that count as good or bad? Excuse me, my friend, for the unpleasant thought. I shall speak no more of it." His frown turns back to a smile. "What are you taking to America with you?"

"Virtually nothing."

"Surely you bring something with you."

"Only a story that no one would believe."

The old man sighs, "Oh, my God, that is exactly what I am taking away, too. It seems everyone takes away stories no one would believe."

After a while the old man stretches his hand to me. "I am Pirooz Parveen."

"Feraydoon Pirooz," I grin.

He unseals an innocent smile. "Pirooz, the Victor," he addresses me. "I have conquered nothing, so why should my first name be Pirooz? Knowing how bestial all conquerors have been, I would personally prefer to be called one of the conquered. Being vanquished brings less dishonor. But if I can quell the evil within me, then I am Pirooz, The Conqueror, with glory. Yes, we must earn our names by our deeds. Just as the Prince of Physicians, the Leading Wise Man, Ibn Sina, earned his titles."

"I have given him the title, Grandfather of Modernity. What do you think?"

"Yes, that, too. His era spearheaded the Renaissance. It is true and fitting, but let his descendant be only what is good in modernity." He reflects for a moment before asking, "Now, my friend, what have you conquered, that your last name is Pirooz?"

"I have conquered death," I reply instantly. "A given name is not the wish of the newborn anyhow, except at least in one case."

His blue eyes lighting up, he inquires, "What do you mean, Pirooz? We have a long trip, the clouds have no ears, and I can keep a secret," he reassures me.

So I tell him my tale. By the time I am finished we have crossed Asia Minor and Greece, changed planes in Frankfurt, and covered the width of the Atlantic. We are close to New York when I recount Sitareh's disappearance. A single teardrop rolls down my face and I see it fall on the back of his hand, which now holds mine. My voice fails me, but I become aware of a new awareness in me. He senses it, his eyes full of curious interest, unlike a mirror that absorbs without absorbing.

The sun hovers on the eastern horizon. Its rays flutter in space, grazing the scattered clouds and our plane, like the delicate multicolored feathers of a parakeet against the bronze bars of its cage. The sun sings a song of solitude, and I realize that even the sun feels its loneliness like a candle left in a vast desert to burn alone.

The old man lets me think my thoughts, lets me feel my feelings, lets me climb the higher peaks of my imagination into regions of knowing. I imagine a downpour, with each drop of rain holding a new light for humanity, a new understanding, a new lesson in resignation and forbearance, a new appreciation for the lonely journey from temporariness to permanence. Soaked in the vital rain and tasting an insight full of hope, I notice the sharp swings of my emotions. I understand it and don't deny it. Finally, when Pirooz finds me ready and needing his words, he says, "Accept the Sitarehs as they are: different and yet the same. The steady Poonia had no grand plan for humanity, only for you and her together. In contrast, Bastan determined to create Ibn Sina for us all, at any cost to herself or to you. Bastan told you everything, but you refused to hear it, as most men do. Poonia compelled you to find Ibn Sina, and Bastan induced you to find yourself. And then . . ." He stops.

"Then what, Pirooz?" I ask.

"And then, if you tell this story, it will help people to understand Ibn Sina's way; the unceasing striving for self-realization and truth and love."

"Yes, I agree. Love is a struggle."

"True love demands work—deep understanding, caring, sacrifice. Love is a gift; sometimes it comes easily but is difficult to keep."

"What do you mean? How can I nourish love?"

"Tell your story. Describe the world as you find it and don't avoid taking sides. Any artwork is persuasion in disguise, however subtle, beautiful or profound, just as God's Creation embodies His intentions. But let your intention be love and truth, like Ibn Sina's. The writing will make your tale believable, even to yourself."

"What are you getting at?" I ask.

"Let me give you an example. Everything that man produces, like a poem, is an extension of himself, good or evil. A poem is the poet's skin, as Eve is Adam's rib. It reaches like hands for things, listens like ears to sounds, tries like eyes to find beauty, and searches like the mind for spirits. It reaches for essences. It is an amalgam of intentions, imagination, skill and labor, the attributers of man."

"But what was God's intention in His Creation?" I ask in childlike eagerness.

A sparkling smile that vanishes to a deep thoughtfulness is my answer.

"How about your work—your intentions, my friend?" he asks. "Stay with that!"

"My scholarly writing has been a compromise between my real intention and what my profession demands. Questioning dogmas or authorities is self-flagellation. Most of what I want to say remains unsaid, and some of what I have said need not or should not have been said. I have felt free only to pretend. U.S.-inspected freedom is largely the freedom to pretend, not the freedom to be oneself. I have dissimulated in every classroom lecture of mine. My life has been a cover-up, a burdensome one."

"Find a way to say what must be said," the old man counsels. "Be creative like Attar, Hafiz, and Rumi, reach for light and courage within you. Truth unifies and falsehood divides humanity, since, with truth, belief comes from understanding, not from deception or coercion. Be Gorgani again and tell the story of the Leading Wise Man, the Grandfather of Modernity. Introduce Iran standing high geographically and culturally on a plateau between the Tigris and Indus Rivers, forever flowing at the edge of the Milky Way. Explain how Zoroaster was a major source of Western ethics. This may further an interest in our past. Enrich America with the millennial civilization of Persia, its achievements and its shortcomings." He reflects for a moment. "Every nation must tell its story for mankind to know itself. Cultures are unique, but we must not insulate them. Awaken the West to its seemingly self-serving, but really self-wounding, illusion of superiority. Inform Westerners that without us, they could not have become them. Tell them that we all spring from the same source. Open the gates of mutual enrichment. Let Ibn Sina teach them humility: 'My knowledge soared so high only to know that I don't know.'"

"Such impossible tasks, Pirooz."

"Try it, Pirooz, try. Confront the difficulties. Don't let them conquer you. Remember your name! Be optimistic, but know that optimism is as mortal as everything else. Writing resurrects the writer from loneliness, even oblivion. Embrace contradictions within yourself, for they are you, too. Remember that the world evolves through resolving its contradictions. Look at it and learn from it with your own eyes, not with those of strangers. Examine reality, science, the holy books. All are packed with contradictions. Your inner conflicts are one aspect of existence. Believe and disbelieve simultaneously, if you must. This keeps one alert, curious and searching. Promote transcendence and be a part of it. And if I'm talking too much, let me know."

"No. No. Not at all. Please speak to me some more. I need to hear it more than you need to say it. Now tell me, what is transcendence?"

"It is a journey to the kernel of existence. Constrictions fill the outer layers, but at the core you will find only unity majestically residing. There you will meet God within you and you will embrace Him. Or if not God you will find yourself—your true self—holding hands with love and truth, God's attributes."

"What is so special about unity?"

"Unity dissolves all contradictions by seizing the innermost truth." He takes a deep breath. "Seize that one true inner voice. Trust it! It will save you if you bring it forth, and it will ruin you if you don't."

I listen, enthralled by his wisdom.

"You know, Pirooz . . ." He stops to search for a thought. "One may lust for the lives one does not live, but one cannot live more than one life. We are fated to live within the realm of our possibilities, but we must discover what they are. You seem to know now the right thing for you to do and how to do it. Only a few accomplish this in one life." I wait for more. However, he abruptly changes the subject. "Do you believe in God, Pirooz?"

"There are numerous gods," I answer without hesitation. "I am one, you are one. Together we are God. We have no other choice but to proceed as if we were God. Who is the master of or lives but us? Tell me, Pirooz. Who? And who is your God?" I ask the old man.

"If God exists, and what or who He is, are the most unknown of all unknowns. But, nevertheless, man makes up in his own mind God's attributes of infinity, immutability, eternity, omniscience, and omnipotence. But, these imagined qualities are just human dreams for itself, since God is a mystery." He smiles an enigmatic smile. "Pirooz, you claim man the creator can become his own dream—God. Fine. But what is your faith, Pirooz?"

"My faith is immortality," I respond instantly.

"What do you mean?" he asks.

"To become omniscient, and omnipotent, and to acquire other attributes of God man must search and tread the path of immortality. This faith must guide our choices, from those of one person to all of mankind. For instance, we must seek qualities instead of quantities even in ourselves, and look into infinite horizons for universal goals. The science of spiritual growth, the science of nature, and the science of conflict dissolution are the means to achieve immortality. But means and goals interact. Faith in immortality guides us to identify what means are necessary, and the means bring faith closer to reality. Thus immortality becomes clearer, and the means become more effective with each progressive step. In the Abrahamic religions', goals and means are fixed, but those of immortality, will be evolving. Our progeny would ultimately turn the universe to its own heaven according to its own taste. Despite setbacks, mankind has unconsciously marched along that path. Now we must make it conscious and avoid costly setbacks or catastrophe. In effect, immortality is the fulfillment of human full potential which is also the ultimate self-realization of the universe, to know itself and become master of its own destiny. After all existence created human mind as the supreme quality of existence! This is the immortal vision."

"You are persuasive. Do you seek converts?" he says, smiling brilliantly.

"No, not yet." I smile back. Some details are yet to be revealed! But, there would be no need for missionaries, crusaders, or holy wars. The evolving ideas will march into minds and hearts on their own." I let my grin spread beyond my face realizing what I have just said.

"Thank you, Pirooz. I wish you a happy transcendence," he says.

"I wish you one too, my dear friend. Oh, one more thing," I add.

"You have heard my story. Any suggestions for a name?"

He twists his huge mustache. "All right, how about *A Patient Bridge*, or *Beyond Healing*, or *The Prince of Love*, which were Poonia's ideas, or *Grand Meditation*, which was Ibn Sina's report, or *Ruin and Creation*, which was Bastan's theory? Even your words, *Arrivals and Departures*."

"But my story is a quest for love, and ascendance with Ibn Sina as a guide."

He muses. "Mysterious, love is also an unceasing investigation of differences between souls. Tell me, what would you call your story?"

"*The Journey of Spirits*," I say.

"Wonderful! That is the Sufi's voyage. The title will reflect the actual story—your tribulations. I think all the souls you have touched would like it, too." His eyes gleam with approval. Thoughtfully and softly he adds, "Consider also *Ibn Sina and I*, the 'I' standing for you and me and everyone whose soul and body Ibn Sina would heal."

"There is still one thing about this story that puzzles me most," I wonder aloud.

"What is that?"

"Why would God want to meditate?"

"He may not be perfect in His own eyes. As a physician he would have been tried for malpractice—for contaminating the environment with diseases. Maybe He strives for transcendence, too. Maybe perfection has more than one peak. I wish I knew why He meditates, or why He does anything else, for that matter."

"Nothing is constant. Change is changing and God is changing and perfection is not a unique or crystallized notion," I add.

"How true, Pirooz. To be perfectly compassionate, God must forgive without qualification, which contradicts His role as perfect judge, requiring dispassionate justice," the old man replies. "It is impossible to be absolutely compassionate and absolutely dispassionate simultaneously. May be God meditates to de-solve the conflict between these principals."

We fall silent. I can see the continental coastline coming into view, the skyscrapers appearing like little boxes thrown around by a child. Pirooz looks down and says, "What gravestones!" I shudder as the plane, losing altitude, shudders and lands at Kennedy Airport.

I think that I must order my life in the West around a hope glimmering from the East. A prayer comes to my lips: "Awaken from your Grand Meditation, my Divine Wisdom. Awaken, the Source of All Sources. The universe needs your full attention."

Pirooz and I promise to keep in touch. Embracing each other as old friends, he tells me, "Share your story and let your loss be a gain for all." I give him my word on it, while I recall Sitareh's remark that creative work transforms a loss into a gain.

Departing from Pirooz, I feel the sadness of those brought together by circumstances into unexpected, illuminating, and sudden intimacy, as in a hospital ward. His wave is a memory of the future; it tells me he will be with me even when he is gone. Yes, I have a new friend. And a new will. And a new life in a New World.

Chapter Twenty-Five: Happy Transcendence

As I speed through Manhattan in a taxicab, I already miss Pirooz Parveen's eyes, two tranquil seas of wisdom and stories untold. I look out the window, ignoring the bustle, and wonder. Is my hope of understanding the meaning of all the starts and stops in my life a mere fantasy? What kind of life am I starting now? Will these questions ever go away? Is a science of soul possible, and should I become its student? Perhaps the answer is that there is no answer, the only answer now and forever. Is there something wrong with everything, or is there nothing wrong with anything, or is it just me? Does humanity swing between extremes, incapable of determining where to stop? Stop! A favorite word of mine. I must learn when to stop questioning. Stopping and beginning are complementary aspects of transcendence. Man stopped instinct as his sole master to let consciousness emerge as his guide. He must stop self-deception now, to know everything as it is. I feel a fire in my mind, and only I can extinguish it.

I must become practical, but how should I deal with the conflicting demands of my own desires and chores, science, politics and immortal behavior? How would I know which actions are immortal and which are not? For instance, why do we let our interests ruin he habitat of our progeny? Maybe there is something wrong with what we consider to be our interests today, since man needs a healthy Earth, just as an infant needs a healthy breast. How did we come to know what is good and what is bad? Immortal vision would dissolve such conflicts. A path strewn with the multiplication of things and people without regard to quality is a path to extinction, not to immortality. As I look at New York, it seems that the plows of technology and greed have recklessly overturned our lives. Is this progress? Does the bustle signify people's confidence in their own intentions, or just purposeless movement? Is the American decline due to diminished curiosity, inventiveness and productivity, or diminished communality and spirituality?

The steel-and-glass skyscrapers and the flow of paper money and checks through them remind me that some of the oldest glassware and steel and paper money was found in Iran. Letters of credit (checks) appeared in ancient Persia just after the birth of Christ. Persia's indirect contribution to the steel and glass and finance, and thus the bustle, of Manhattan makes me marvel at history's twists and turns. I wonder if the seeds sown here by modern business are fertile, or will they just yield more glitter, deprivation and poison? Can anyone learn from the past when swift change swallows it up? Does history guide or misguide? If clarity is not at hand, why don't we all have more doubt? What has robbed us of our ability to doubt, to be curious, and to question authorities, anything and everything—even ourselves? I wish we had more doubt and curiosity and a greater desire to search beyond convention, beyond immediate gratification and self-interest. Daily problems and chores suppress our curiosity like despots. We must struggle against their subjugation.

"OK, pal, here we are." I pay the cabdriver and disappear into my apartment building tightly clutching my luggage. What else is mine, except my luggage? In these familiar surroundings I remember Poonia in her blue sari with yellow hem, as I pressed my face against her chest and heard her heartbeat with my eyes. Love of the dead and love of the living are my most precious possessions, and I shall carry them in my heart wherever I journey.

In the elevator I think of Ibn Sina's words, "How I wish I could know who I am, what it is in this world that I seek." Passing Sitareh's apartment, she swings into my vision, and I feel my lips over hers, as in our first goodnight kiss.

At home everything appears the same. Before I can unpack, the fatigue of the long journey puts me to sleep, though I sleep fitfully. In a nightmare two scorpions dance in love and death, their mouth-parts and pincers locked in the intricate mating ritual. Then, after copulation, the female consumes the male in a cannibalistic feast, giving him no chance to ever see his children.

I wake up in horror and confusion. A bitter thought crosses my mind: Sitareh Bastan also abandoned me for the child, Ibn Sina. Perplexed, I remember that she had the same nightmare. It is not a nightmare after all. Being eaten is loving, too. The father scorpion enhances the survival chances of the mother and her fertilized eggs by becoming their meal. Maybe the father is absorbed in his progeny. I think of the wafer and wine consumed as the body and blood of Christ in a similar act of love. I imagine the food chain crisscrossing all life, me included, in a worldwide Holy Communion: mineral, plant, animal and man continuously becoming one another, a universal love affair of absorption and re-absorption and resurrection. A fear runs through me: I am performing a love and death dance with time, and time's pincers are already at my throat. I fear time may swallow me whole before I see my son and Sitareh. No, I must try to cast out all negative thoughts.

A few days after my return, with a cup of espresso warming my hand and thoughts, I visualize old Pirooz Parveen in Tucson, miming Persian stories for his grandchildren, with a bittersweet smile on his face—the emblem of an incredible life I can only guess at. I have been a mime, too, even though I know English since no language can really bridge diverse cultures, times and emotions.

I hear again old Pirooz' ominous assertion: "The mullahs use Imam Hussain to promote war. That ancient saint, grandson of the Prophet Mohammed, all praise be unto him, is portrayed as the living uncle of the young, demanding their martyrdom. How dare anyone refuse the Imam's summons?" I shudder at the thought of my son being raised there. Lounging around my apartment, watching myself fall apart memory by memory is not the wise path to self-realization. Stop worrying so much, Pirooz. This is not Ibn Sina's way I remind myself. Work! Work will heal you! So I halt rage and frustration from creeping into me again, and try to end pessimism, and begin optimism. I glance at my friend, the Monarch butterfly in the carpet on the wall. Seeing that I need her counsel, she flutters to me again.

"How was your journey, Pirooz?"

"Circular. I am back where I began, except for memories."

"Not quite so, Pirooz. You have returned to the same place, but you have not returned the same person."

"How can you tell, Monarch?"

"Well, I watched you enjoy every drop of your espresso. Now you savor life to its fullest. You experience even your sadness fully, without dread. The past or future no longer spoils your present, you cherish the moment which is yours. You are often meditative and sometimes lost in Sufi poetry. You practice yoga: in the mornings you salute the sun, which empowers you indirectly through the miracle of photosynthesis. You have accepted the inevitability of imperfect circumstances and enjoy your efforts to change them. You don't fight the impossible and you don't follow the easiest path just because it's easy. You melt your agony in your writing, and you find peace in every color in every leaf. You are the friend of your hope and your hope is loyal to you. I heard you say to a friend, 'God is waiting to become the immortal man. We must ascend to become God.'" The Monarch hesitates before continuing. "When the sky is turquoise blue, you remember Firoozeh, sweet and wondrous, wrapped in a saffron scarf flaming in the wind. You thank Firoozeh in your dreams. You are not guilty to love her, too. You delight in the joys of others, and your equanimity and compassion inspire you to immortal deeds, however minute or unappreciated. Yesterday, you laughed heartily at your image in the mirror and said, 'Like old Pirooz Parveen, I will one day take my wrinkles and fly hither and thither searching for happiness.' You never laughed at yourself and your fate before—never. You mostly complained, but now I heard you declare: 'if I am not my own god who is? Who is the master of our fate, who shall inherit the universe but us—the beloved immortals.'"

"You read my life," I say to the butterfly.

"Yes, with a brain the size of a pinhead, but I use it fully."

"How does your tiny brain manage to navigate the vast terrain between Canada and a mountain enclave in Mexico a place you have never seen?"

"Ask not how one Monarch finds anyplace, but how we all do it together."

"What do you mean?" I ask.

"We put our minds together, choose what is best for everyone and flutter together. We hold to our solidarity knowing that a solo flight can't lift us to the desired destination."

"But how do you find a never-before-seen destination on your first and only journey?" I insist, longing to do it myself, as Ibn Sina tried it a thousand years ago.

"We are one with our ancestors and descendants, who have made the journey or will make it. Our knowledge comes by birth and rebirth. That is all I know. How else could cocooned caterpillars become instant gliders, Monarchs and explorers who catch rides on eccentric winds to reach an unseen destination far, far away, unerringly, without map or experience? How could we go where we have never been before?"

"Nature's program in the Monarchs' brains, perhaps?"

"It works, whatever it is," the butterfly replies.

So nature made computers, and put them in the Monarchs' head eons before man arrived on the stage of existence. The universe is a computer, and nature's laws are its program. Mankind is a second-generation computer capable of programming itself and nature, too. Our machines are third-generation computers. "But who programmed the ultimate programmer?" I ask aloud.

"Will you stop asking unanswerable questions, Pirooz?" says the butterfly. "You know all about stopping. Practice it."

"Questions invade me; I need an army to stop them. Stop asking the impossible from me monarch!" I respond. We are programmed with different languages, national prides, religions, biases, a sense of beauty, ugliness, and also emotions like shame. Seldom are we aware that we are the carriers of prejudice or intolerance. I want to tell the world that these programs confine us in invisible cocoons. We know others are in cocoons, but we are not conscious that we are, too. Like the Monarchs, each of us must rip open his cocoons and take flight together to places we have never been. I visualize the shimmering masses of brilliantly colored Monarchs sweeping along the California coast on their long journey. The caterpillar retains the bitter poison of the milkweed because the toxin inhibits predators. Clearly I must also ingest the poison of some dissimulation to survive, as Ibn Sina did in his time. I must acknowledge what is beyond my control.

"Pirooz!" The butterfly interrupts my reverie. "The map of your journey also lies within you. Find it and use it. Then you will glide on time, as we glide on the wind, all the way to your destination."

"But where will my journey take me?" I ask.

"To goodness. You are new to yourself now, light as a sailboat, unloaded and unanchored, free to ride the waves to any port, to where you have never been before."

The Monarch and I exchange one last glance, then she flies back to her place on the wall. I shudder, for her voice was Poonia's, saying, "When your mind is wandering, or wondering unsteadily, it is your duty to impel it to a deeper understanding of itself." I open my eyes to a new world, neither real nor a dream, but imagined, a world in which nationality, religion, and ideology are each a flower in a garden, and not barbed wire meant to separate and injure. To become immortal we must transcend our upbringing that is meant to isolate us, without abandoning our uniqueness. My imagined world is feasible if we let our good will, skills and creativity converge.

A caterpillar cocooned by my upbringing, I have ingested the necessary poisons and now have pierced my wrapping, ready to take flight to a destination I have never seen. I have already conquered the fear of loss, rejection, love, God, pain, death and nothingness, and am liberated to search without qualification. Anger and hatred can motivate man more than even hunger and sex, but ideas could supersede instinct, and psychology could outrank biology. I feel the truth of this in my bones.

No barbed wire wraps around my heart any longer. Looking at myself objectively, self-criticism comes easily to me. I am a dust mote. No, not even that. Before the vastness of time and space, I am nothing—but a nothing that can see, hear, feel, think, understand, and even create. I am a nothing who sees and knows galaxies, though they know nothing of my existence. I can bring a galaxy to life in my imagination and order it around, left, right and center, even make it serve me freshly brewed tea with its luminous spiral arms. What a mote of dust I am! What a mote of dust all humanity is before everything else that exists. I must go on and will go on, while listening to myself and to what is not me, to the Other. I feel no shame asking unanswerable questions. I must speak to myselves, but must also listen in order to be spoken to. I shall find myself before anyone else does and identify with the future, since it sides with freedom. My journey will take me to the unimaginable. The destination need not be specific or located in advance.

In my cubicle I talk to myself. Aloneness is self-inflicted. We are not born alone, we need not live alone or die alone. We have been, are, and can be a whole. I have no room in my heart but for love, no room in my mind but for truth, and no room in my body but for immortal deeds. By seeing things as they are, as they were, even as they will be, I am inseparable from the creator and the created, because I am both. I will conquer my aloneness. Everything is within reach and reaches out to me. Gazing into the future optimistically, I smile at my resolve, at all of existence beyond the window. The world flashes back at me a colorful smile. I will not just try to dodge what America was turning me into, but I will try to enrich it with my culture.

Sitting on a bench in Central Park, I notice a robin munching on an earthworm. The bird is beautiful, the earthworm is useful. Both are good, but, as the earthworm screams from the robin's beak, "This relationship is not so good."

Watching the sunset in a fountain, I see the water vapor diffusing sunlight into all its visible colors. I think of Ibn Sina, who recognized before anyone else that within each color were species of shades differing in intensity, its lightness or darkness, and that there was a sequence from white through gray to black. Will I ever see Ibn Sina, the man who knew light, the man who saw through it? I want to tell him and whoever will listen that we are each a light frequency, and, banding together, we can go far and fast and enlighten ourselves and the world. In the womb of my star, Sitareh, Ibn Sina is now thinking. I remember that the day before I was born I wondered if I had a choice to leave a secure darkness and enter a difficult light. My question was answered the next day in my own birth cry that there was no choice. From then on I leaned that I—mankind—must find my own answers and solve my own problems on this Earth, and no matter where else we may journey. No one will help us but us. Prayers do nothing. Mankind creates many good things that God didn't, and destroys bad things God did create. We shall perfect God's work!

My life becomes brighter in the light of my new resolve. My brother declares, "How happy I am that you are back safe in the bosom of New York. I will never pick another argument with you again. Unless it is absolutely necessary, of course." He surprises me with a canary, which soon learns to hop across my shoulders, as if it were the reincarnation of my old one.

My mother promises not to harass me any more about the hazards of city life. She returns my suicide letter unopened, as I requested. My friends, some nearly forgotten, visit me again. What I liked about them grows in brightness, and what I disliked dims to insignificance. Pleasure returns as I focus on what is good, not just on what should be better. I write intensely for myself and you.

I also write to Firoozeh and confess that I miss her, and ask what she needs. In her lovely reply, she requests some medicine for her mother that is unavailable in the war and embargo. I ask her to find Heyroun Gholi, so I can write to him that, maybe, Zahra's walk can be restored in America. Maybe he is praying for a miracle that is a prosthesis. I know in my heart that Heyroun Gholi will marry the legless Zahra even now that she has lost that tormenting walk to the war.

Optimism flares within me and brings warmth to everything around me. Back at the university, teaching no longer seems just a chore for which I must cover my true feelings. Students confide to me more and my colleagues are friendlier to me, even when I dissimulate less and state my politically incorrect views. Alienation still lurks in the shadows, but when it appears I pet it like a pussycat until it purrs and walks away. It is not the world, but me, who has changed. Life is not, or need not be, a cover-up, I conclude, though one must take cover even from too much sun.

Pirooz Parveen is much on my mind. Somehow he reminds me of the great Sufi, Abu Said Ali al-Khayr, whom I can recall meeting in ancient times, as Gorgani. Upon emerging from a prolonged discussion with Ibn Sina, Abu Said announced their differences to me, "Ibn Sina knows what I see, and I see what he knows." I wonder to myself now, do I know what I understand, and do I understand what I know?

I continue to write my story, while resigned to the persistence of unanswered questions. I still wonder why Persians treat dead thinkers as if they were alive and living thinkers as if they were dead. I do not let the thought discourage me. I search for a way of achieving seemingly contradictory goals: spontaneity and discipline, responsibility and lightheartedness, the emotional and the rational, pride and humility, courage and foresight, criticism and tolerance. I know this will be a life-long journey. The secret is to learn the supreme values, the most humane means, and what is possible. Trying to become a wisdom-maker and wisdom-keeper and commanding myself to bend every deed towards the greatest happiness for the greatest number, I meditate, live to know, live to love, and live to transcend to immortal deeds. About Sitareh and the baby Ibn Sina, I resolve that waiting is all I can do, and it's not a whole lot. I urge myself to have faith in her wisdom, wait, wait, and wait for our reunion.

The Persian New Year, *Now-Ruz* (new day), the first day of spring, returns. Even indifferent New York notices its majestic arrival. It is time for Ibn Sina's birth. Sitareh will let me know when; I trust her meticulous sense of timing.

Late one morning I hear a knock at the door. A friend of Sitareh's, just arrived from Iran, hands me a letter, not mailed to avoid the Iranian censor. Before leaving, she whispers to me, "Last fall, a bomb killed Sitareh's parents, but she has overcome her grief. You will know why."

I open the letter with the bittersweet expectation of an innocent defendant about to hear the jury's verdict. Thirsty for news, I gulp the words like water— a man reaching an oasis after trudging past mirages.

> My Dear Pirooz,
> Happy New Year! Our hearts surge for you. Rejoice! Rejoice, my love, you are a father! And rejoice even more, you are the father of a girl! In rebirth, Ibn Sina is a female. Her first name is Akhtar (the star Sirius), and her middle name is Sina. She was

> born on Now-Ruz. She has brown eyes like you and light skin like me. She smiled early and smiles more often than we did. I will send you a picture soon. I hope that, like the star of Bethlehem, she will guide seekers to divine wisdom. I composed my first lullaby for her: "Dream of lights, my beloved; the lights for us and for them." It is not much of a lullaby for the daughter of modernity, but what do you expect from a psychiatrist, Pirooz?

A shock wave surges through me. A girl! A girl! Akhtar Sina, my daughter! My heart racing, I absorb the jolt, try to understand and to finish reading. My hands tremble and I collapse into the nearest chair. Finally, on their own, my eyes focus on the letter again.

> What a delightful surprise, and how problematic! I never thought of a female Ibn Sina when I argued with you in Hamadan. Your genuine, wise and luminous thoughts haunt me. If she has a great judicial mind, Islam will never permit her to become a judge. If she has the talent to be a spiritual leader, Islam won't accept it. If she is capable of becoming a great president, tradition won't allow it. In medicine and science she will have slightly better chances because there is no law against her progress there. But the whole social structure, brick by brick, mullah by mullah, discourages women's leadership in every field except motherhood. Women are not allowed to make important decisions because it is written in the Holy Koran: "Men have authority over women because Allah has made one superior to the other." For her self-realization, Akhtar Sina will have to stand against God and the state, the poor child.

The telephone rings. A salesman wants me to subscribe to the *Times*. I protest "One a day is more than enough," and hang up. With my eyes still glued to the letter, I return to the chair.

> But what is unseen and unsaid is worse yet. Forgive me if I engage in psychobabble. It is necessary because Akhtar's future is at stake. Condemned by my profession to listening, I am treated like a pair of ears here. I have no one to listen to me, except you. I kiss your sympathetic heart and share its rhythm of hope.
> The clergy here manipulate dogma and the myths of martyrs to silence dissent and veil women. Islam—submission to the

will of Allah—has been turned into submission to the will of the mullah. Many people talk to themselves as though demented; they reject reality. Emotionally castrated men, sunk low in self-esteem, turn into despots at home and take out their frustrations on women—the lowly creatures of Islam. Females then develop an acute empathy sickness, knowing and sensing the feelings of the men better than their own, while the politically impotent men plunge deep into an empathy deficiency—an inability to understand how women feel. Though masters of women's lives, most men have little control over their own. So ideology and psychology interact to create miseries. Such empathy crises or maladies exist in the U.S., too, but not so intense or so widespread. Oh, Pirooz, we need more self-esteem, not less. How would Akhtar contend with this dreadful milieu and sexist pedagogy at school, the fear and poison forged into a weapon against her self-realization, which Ibn Sina considered paramount in education? How can anyone—even Ibn Sina—achieve self-realization if they are bounded by the holy voice of the State subduing all other voices?

Under these circumstances, Akhtar's main role in life here would be to become a good mother. Ibn Sina didn't even have time to be a father as a man. Motherhood is crucial, but it is not for everyone and should not be coerced, however subtly. Here our baby could become just another mother among untold multitudes, mostly unfulfilled and treated like faithful dogs. Dogs—that is just how we are treated here, despite high praise for the sanctity of motherhood. Mothers must work hard, raise their children, be loyal and obedient, and never talk back. The Holy Book's precepts, turned into biased laws and practices, limit opportunities and choices for women and create gender inequality, which then becomes a pretext to subjugate and exploit women—at home, in the market, and in government. The dread of losing custody of their children, due to biased matrimonial laws favoring fathers, often reduces mothers to hostages in tragic marriages. There is a saying in our culture: 'Heaven lies under the feet of mothers.' But I say, under the feet of the Guards lie the mothers. The holy verse on female inferiority should have been replaced by a superior one. You said it is impossible to be perfect in everything, and ibn Sina said what is impossible is impossible even for God.

And summer is torture under the veil—a violation of human rights. Female hair is sexy, so it must be covered. But how can anyone prove that women's is sexier than men's? I find yours sexier than mine! Women have to dissimulate even more than men, who find their dissimulation unbearable. We must cover up our inner self with a thicker veil than our outer self. Women are inmates in a prison within a prison within a prison. I wish God would put Himself in a Black Hole to feel how it is to have a woman's imagination trapped in a woman's body and be called inferior because of it. The Islamic Republic has brought me back to my senses.

Iranian women have a difficult and protracted struggle ahead of them. This patriarchal and phallocentric revolution worries me more now, since I never imagined our Ibn Sina as a girl. It was our need to sacrifice for his upbringing that I argued for. This is different now. I regret not having considered this possibility. Due to mental obstacles, even I, a liberated person, could not envision the possibility of a female Ibn Sina. How tragic the perceptions, how tragic that history has wasted so many brilliant women. I want to raise Akhtar Sina where women are not just honored commodities who produce and reproduce their own owners—men.

Let me get everything off my chest, Pirooz, even about America. Unfortunately, the law in the U.S. treats women the way men perceive and treat them. In numerous cases, women have to live and compromise with the enemy, since domestic violence is common there. Female sexuality is also exploited in the U.S., like labor power in the marketplace; as you explained to me. Men claim that women open their legs voluntarily for the world to see in pornographic pictures. But for some women, this is the best, or the only choice to earn a living or advancement. There appears to be a universal conspiracy to deny women creativity, empowerment and choice over their own bodies and lives. Since men are raised by unliberated women, they can never become truly free unless women liberate themselves. So women who suffer most must take the lead to free both sexes. I intend to do so, and I hope that you and Akhtar will join me.

Taking my eyes off the letter, I wonder if her first letter to me should contain such stuff, and answer myself, Why not, if she wants to? After all, that is what is on her mind.

Is there a sanctuary for us in this life, Pirooz? Oh, Pirooz-*jon*, shall I cry for joy or from sadness? Shall I stay here or fly to you? My God, guide me to the right decision. The other day I asked God: "Have You ended Your Grand Meditation? And are You listening again? Will You listen to me? God, you are the only one who can compel a deaf world to hear, or a world without a tongue to speak. Will You send one more prophet, a woman this time, for all people and all times? Perhaps she could teach us how mankind can become immortal—your favorite idea. You know that a few miracles here and there—even if true—have accomplished nothing enduring, except to fill the pockets of the clergy with the bread money of the poor. Let the new prophet explain why so many creatures, as Pirooz says, are made imperfect. Let her bring not miracles for individuals, but just one big miracle for humanity. Let her teach us to become perfect and immortal," And then I said: "Please, God. Ship me to Pirooz! Ibn Sina needs his father who is a heretic now, as he was before." I see you smiling your half mischievous, half all-knowing smile, Pirooz! I know that you know that it is a passport, a visa and a ticket I need. But come to think of it, one needs God or money to obtain them here nowadays. A bribe can make the gun-toting clergy purr.

>The birth of Akhtar has forced me to think deeply about many things I took for granted. If Ibn Sina could be a woman, then why can't many other things differ from what I presumed. And then—still in my womb—Akhtar Sina made her wish known to me, "I want to be with my Baba."
>
>I miss you, Pirooz. I miss your wise disagreements and tender love. I miss playing the *tar* for you and feeling your intoxication from it. Will you ever forgive me for protecting you by abandoning you—the most difficult decision I have ever had to make, Pirooz? I am sorry, very sorry to have hurt you, my beloved. I shall be steady, not just for my own goals, but for yours, too, since we no longer differ on what now separates us.
>
>Akhtar just woke up. She needs my attention now. I will write again soon. I love you now as I did in the past and as I will in the future, life after life.
>
>Sitareh

Oh, my mind! Dazed, I take a deep breath. Even though the letter is both gloomy and heartening, it fails to unsettle me. Sitareh sees through appearances—the sexuality and socio-politics of gender exploitation. She still shields me, not wanting to sadden me with the death of the grandparents of our

Akhtar. She wants to be in control of happiness and sadness like a goddess. I see Sitareh and Akhtar, the stars of my life, twinkling through the dark clouds of my imagination, and my happiness begs me to forsake the past and trust the future. Sitareh's ill-boding words miraculously make me feel stronger for the challenges ahead. I must teach Akhtar what my grandfather taught me: "Whatever imponderable obstacles stand in the way of perfection, creativity will overcome them."

A blasphemous thought crosses my mind. I hear the voice of Him or Her. "Thou shalt do as I command, not as I do. Only I, the Almighty, am allowed to create lemons, since I will recall them all in the Day of Judgment. Man's creations are complements to Mine, but they had better be less imperfect. And beyond that, as My extensions, thou shalt perfect thine own imperfections and those of My other creations. And never mind your imagination being too big for your body, or your limited possibilities. This will teach you discipline!" Such a paradox that God reveals to me something He withheld from the prophets. So it is true we are made in God's image—imperfect! No wonder He has taken to meditation.

My swing—from attempted suicide to a lust for self-realization—astounds me. Maybe death is also a path to self-realization. A possible happiness in this life could always be traded for the liberty attainable by death. Happiness and freedom are complements in life and substitutes in death, since for the dead earthly restrictions are also dead. I choose to live now and strive to become that which is beyond imagination. And I shall die while I soar like the butterfly, not worrying about what kind of being, or non-being, death may be. All I know is how to get there, even though I have never been there before. I cannot wait to hear Sitareh's insights about her journey.

Overjoyed that my family is well, I daydream of Sitareh bathing, feeding, and loving our baby girl, the daughter of modernity, the liberator of women and men in our time, I hope. Bearing good and bad like a patient bridge, I look out at the sky and find Akhtar, the brightest star. I find her between my two Sitarehs and other stars, all women, and I wonder why men don't see these stars among us. We must find what is blinding us from our ultimate interest and stop it. My lingering woes spontaneously explode into happiness, knowing our family will be together soon—after a thousand years of wandering. What a reunion! What a daughter! The mirror reflects a beaming Baba, me! Me! A father at last, the father of a star, the father of Akhtar Sina! The mirror trembles and twinkles with the image that rejoices in it. My reflection! I share my joy with my image in the mirror. All at once I see people in colorful costumes of all nationalities joining me and rejoicing with me in the mirror. After all, Ibn Sina belongs to us all. Does Akhtar in the sky have a nationality? No! I know this answer! Akhtar will be the citizen of all times and places and create immortal thoughts and wisdom to make us all immortal. We will discover the beginnings and endings of everything and be guided by love. Suddenly the people in the mirror and I join in a chant: "We are one, we are God."

I live in times of transcendence. Oh, my mind! I am in the city of spring! Here beauty and wisdom flow in streams.

That evening, enjoying a rare visit of the moon to New York, I put on a cassette of Sitareh playing the *tar*. The music seeping through my roots obliges me to dance—a solo dance of ascendance. I move slowly to touch space, time, the moonlight, life, the beauty in all things, even forgiveness, even images of the future. Even God! Exhilarated, I dance with my soul in my arms, a soul that never lost faith in me. Light as a butterfly, yet strong as a bridge, I am on my way to immortality, to where there are no boundaries, to where I have never been before. My heart sings songs in different tongues, languages that I never knew I knew. My mind opens its wings and embraces all ideals and all people, and ascends into a union with all of creation, until the world is me, and I am the world. I close my eyes, close my arms around me in a loving hug, and wish me, and you, "Happy transcendence!"

Appreciation

I thank the architect H. Seyhoun, who helped me patiently to understand the soul of Avicenna's mausoleum, which he designed. These kindred spirits have shared the novel with me before print: Professor Charles Butterworth, Professor Faridoun Farrokh, Professor M. R. Ghanoonparvar, Professor Robert Haynes, Professor Peter Heath, Professor Ahmad Karimi-Hakkak, Dr. Laurence O. Michalak, Professor Nasrin Rahimieh, and Professor Mohamad Tavakoli-Targhi. I thank Richard Fioravanti, Lisa Lemke, and Becky Tompkins for the final preparation.

Acknowledgments

Some of the poems in this volume are taken from references listed below. The rest are author's own poems or renditions.

Poems on pages 10, 11 and 32 are from the Rig Veda, translated by A.L. Basham, "The Wonder that was India," in *Indira Gandhi, Eternal India,* translated by Mavis Guinard, B.I. Publications, New Delhi. Copyright, 1978 by Edita SA, Lausanne.

Poem on page 35 and continued on top of page 36 is from Rabindranath Tagore, *Selected Poems,* translated by William Radice, Penguin Books, Ltd., 1993.

Poems on pages 40 (top) and 44 are from Rumi, *Mathnawi,* adapted from Eva de Vitray-Meyerovich, *Rumi and Sufism,* translated from the French by Simone Fattal, Post-Apollo Press, Saualito, CA 1987. Poem on page 40 (bottom) is taken from Sayyed Hossein Nasr, *An Introduction to Islamic Cosmological Doctrines, Conceptions of Nature and Methods Used for Its Study by the Ikhwan al-Safa, al-Biruni, and Ibn Sina,* SUNY Press, Albany, New York 1993.

Poem on page 63 is from R.A. Nicholson, *Rumi, Poet and Mystic,* Oneworld Press, Oxford, 1995.

Poem on page 75 is from Soheil M. Afnan, *Avicenna, His Life and Works,* George Allen & Unwin, London, 1954.

Poems on pages 88 and 206 are from Farid ud-Din Attar, *The Conference of the Birds,* translated by Afkham Darbandi and Dick Davis, Penguin Books, Harmondsworth, England, 1984.

Poem on pages 110 is from A.J. Arberry, "Avicenna, His Life and Times," in George M. Wickens, Ed., *Avicenna: Scientist and Philosopher,* Luzac, London, 1952.

Poems on pages 111 and 191 are from. George Fry and Jon Paul Fry, *Avicenna's Philosophy of Education: An Introduction,* Routledge and Kegan Paul, London, 1950.

Poem on page 115 is from Annemarie Schimmel, *As Through a Veil: Mystical Poetry in Islam,* Columbia University Press, 1982.

Poems on pages 122, 189 and 190 are from Mehdi Nakhosteen, *The Rubaiyyat of Baba Tahir Oryan of Hamadan,* University of Colorado Press, Boulder, 1967.

Poem on page 131 is from E.G. Browne, *A Literary History of Persia,* Volume 1, Ibex Publishers, 1997.

Translations of the Rubaiyyat of Omar Khayyam are those of Edward Fitzgerald.

Printed in the United States
66334LVS00002B/214-240